MW01230952

Lumina

Shawn Mihalik

Asymmetrical Press

Published by Asymmetrical Press.

Library of Congress Cataloging-In-Publication Data
Lumina / Shawn Mihalik — 1st ed.
ISBN: 978-1-68287-028-0
eISBN: 978-1-68287-029-7
WC: 168,315
1. Silicon Valley. 2. San Francisco. 3. Artificial Intelligence. 4. Montana. 5. Speculative Fiction.

Cover design by Shawn Mihalik
Typeset in Garamond
Formatted in Portland, Oregon
Printed in the U.S.A.

Author info:
Website: www.ShawnMihalik.com

ASYM
METR
ICAL

For Paige

"Let me sing to you now, about how people turn into other things."

— Ovid, *The Metamorphosis*

"When Steve introduced the world to iPhone, he closed with a quote from Wayne Gretzky. It said: 'I skate to where the puck is going to be, not where it has been.'"

— Phil Schiller, iPhone X launch event

Lumina

The Avon Café

THERE'S A SIGN ABOVE THE service counter of a diner in Avon, Montana. It says: *We reserve the right to refuse service to anyone, no matter who you are, who you think you are, or who your daddy is.*

When Eric Hauser pulled his car (which had until this point been doing most of the driving itself) off U.S. Route 12 and into the diner's gravel parking lot, he parked it in an undefined space, turned off the ignition, and pulled his red down vest tighter around his torso. Under the vest he wore a flannel shirt, because that's what people wore here. This was not a place he'd been before. It was hard to believe it was a place anyone had ever been before—Montana, the Northwest, sometimes even America—but they had: lots of people had been here. Even now, there were people here. There were other cars in this parking lot, parked in other unmarked spaces.

These days, the Avon Café, abandoned and empty and decaying, is the only building in the lot there off Interstate 12, but it wasn't when Eric pulled in. When Eric pulled in and tightened his vest and stepped out of his car into the icy sub-zero assault, there were a couple houses, just to his right when he faced the diner, and a few hundred feet away an antique shop with a sign that bore the name Beautiful Finds but was unlit, unwelcoming, cold. The question that evening: How were you supposed to find beautiful things if the places where they existed weren't open to your searching?

According to an official government census, way back in the year 2000 there were 124 people living in Avon, Montana. Forty-eight households and sixty-two houses. Thirteen-point-four square miles, most of them farmland. For each man, woman, and child: almost but not quite an eleventh of a mile. In 2010, there were 111 people; what happened to the other thirteen in ten years, who knows, but at some point they lived there, and at some point they left or stopped living.

In the year of the evening Eric pulled into the parking lot, no census was taken, so it can't be said how many people lived in Avon then, but in the Avon Café when he walked through the door, there were twelve people.

Behind the bar counter stood a tall young Black man, fiddling with a small stack of menus. In one booth there was a smiling white man with thick black glasses, his hair swept back, sitting across from a tan woman with bright eyes who cooed at the infant's carseat she had planted next to her. Presumably in the infant's carseat there was an infant, but a small pull-down shroud attached to the seat blocked it from Eric's view. In the booth a middle-aged woman was reading an honest-to-God paperback novel, and in the booth next to hers a bearded man was staring at a tablet screen. When Eric walked in he'd seen a sign on the door that said "free wifi for our customers." Two old men shared a cheeseburger—a single plate, the burger cut in half with a steak knife—and a side of fries; the old men were speaking few words, but they seemed happy. There were tables, too, not just booths. Tables, square, one with a family sitting at it, two adults and two children, and the youngest scribbled scribbled scribbled with a purple crayon on the table cloth. The table cloths here were brown paper of the sort you used to see a grocery sack made of. To Eric it looked like the purple scribbles were of a dog, although barely so. Beneath the wifi sign Eric had seen another sign that said "service animals welcome," but there were no service animals there that evening. The diner was almost full. The tables were full. The booths were full.

Eric sat at the counter, where the diner's only empty seats were. He saw the sign about who your daddy is and smirked. Below the sign, behind the counter: a chalkboard with a hand-written list of specials boasting fresh pies, twelve teas, and nine varieties of milkshake (this chalkboard is still there today, and if you look closely you'll see that it's smattered with flecks of dried blood, but the specials have long since faded). A soda fountain. Three coffee pots—two regular, one orange-handled decaf.

"Howdy," said the young man behind the counter.

"Howdy," Eric replied, slowly. He did not usually speak slowly, but the word was unfamiliar to him.

"Coffee for you this evening?" the man said. "Tea? Something warm?" The young man had very large arms. Very solid arms and shoulders. No tattoos on them, though, no scars or blemishes or other signs of a life lived—which didn't seem right. Eric didn't look at his face and didn't intend to, afraid that if he bore witness to the youthfulness in the man's eyes something inside himself would break.

"Coffee would be great, please. Thanks," Eric said.

He unzipped the front of his down vest, because if he didn't unzip it it had a way of choking him when he was sitting—the collar pushed against the space where the top of the throat met the underside of the chin, putting a pressure there that was uncomfortable and frightening and made his beard itch. He probably should have had over the vest another coat of some kind, but he didn't, not tonight, not for the whole drive. He'd just been keeping the heat on high and zipping the vest and holding himself close whenever he had to exit the car. These vests were all the rage in the Bay Area these days, Eric had learned before he'd hit the road —you could wear them over suit jackets even, said some of the fashion magazines, if you matched the colors right, or even better if your suit was a shade of grey and your down vest was something wild and neon and unpredictable like the way Eric's was such a bright red. The flannel shirt underneath the vest had cost fifty dollars at a mall outside Palo Alto. Eric's watch was gold, and its bluish-silver faceplate shined as the diner's lights hit it just right. The faceplate was not sapphire but tanzanite. This was Eric's personal HoloWatch. A special model Hector had designed just for him. Your average consumer couldn't buy a HoloWatch like this one, built with these materials. It did so many things, so many magical things, but the only capability that mattered to Eric right now was that it told the time —and he couldn't shake the feeling that time was running out.

The coffee was in front of him on the countertop, just like that.

"Thanks," he said.

Staring into the cup, Eric deliberated. And when the young man walked from behind the counter and went to check on other customers, Eric made a decision. He pulled a titanium flask from a small pocket. He poured from the flask into the coffee cup. It was a waste to put Scotch like this inside coffee, some would say, a damned waste, but Eric could afford it—at least he thought he still could. But affording it was meaningless anyway and all that mattered in that moment was the pouring. He'd already had too much. A little more wouldn't matter.

"You can't do that," the young man said. The young man was back behind the counter, or maybe he'd never left it.

Eric looked at the young man's chest. "Why not?"

"This is a family place. We don't do alcohol in here. And besides, even if we did I couldn't let you bring your own in here like that."

"Yeah, okay," Eric said. He twisted the cap back on the flask and left it on the counter. "I guess I'll order a fresh cup of coffee then," he said.

The young man sighed. "You can keep that cup. Just don't tell anyone I let you do it."

Eric raised his mug. "Thanks," he said.

"Here's a menu."

There was art in the Avon Café. Paintings on the walls of buffalo and landscapes and old pickup trucks. Crafts and t-shirts for sale. On the sill of the window were handmade pegboard games and cribbage sets.

Eric drank the coffee. It was weak but not bad.

On all the tables and in front of each bar seat were both Tabasco and Smoked Tabasco. Maybe Eric would order eggs and he could put Smoked Tabasco on them.

He was getting close now. His vehicle's GPS told him he was just 12.3 miles from McDonald Pass, and just over that pass was his destination. He wasn't sure what he'd find when he got there, or whether he'd be wanted, but he knew he had to cross those mountains. He should have crossed them a long time ago.

"This is not science fiction," Eric said to the man behind the counter.

The man put a fork on a plate next to a piece of pie. "What's that?" he said.

"I'm thinking I'm going to order some food."

"Great. Just let me take this out there and I'll be right back to take your order."

Eric felt a phantom buzzing in his pocket. He made no move for it. After all, there was nothing there. He sat and breathed, his eyes unfocused like that monk in Nepal had shown him.

"What was it you wanted to order?"

"Did you ever stop to think about the way all of this happened?" Eric said.

"Sorry. What?"

"About the way it all worked out? About that you're here in this place, for example, serving pie and coffee."

"Are you saying you'd like pie, because I can get you some pie, but I don't have time for—"

"For what?"

"For . . . for stories or whatever this is."

"I'm just talking about you being here, instead of somewhere else. About me being here, too, you know?"

"If you stick around a while, this place will die down soon, and I always have time to chat with customers then."

"So you're happy here?"

"Um, yes—I guess. I'm going back to school next semester. Like right now I'm just here saving money. My G-Pops owns the café."

"I'm going to order some eggs. Three eggs. And some bacon. Three strips of bacon."

"Got it," the young man said, writing the order on a slip of paper. He turned around and slid it through a small window. The paper disappeared, taken by an unseen entity.

Eric said, "I'm going to go to the bathroom."

After using the restroom and washing his hands and face with freezing water, Eric stopped to stare at a bulletin board by the door. It was overrun with outdated fliers, waiting for decomposition or an ice age, for the world to crumble away. Which will crumble first, it asked, you or the world?

Between the bathroom and the bulletin board stood a sturdy jukebox, a relic in a world where so many things were labeled relics, things that still existed, that *were used*. The jukebox didn't spin vinyls—it wasn't *that* old (although devices that did spin vinyls, *new* devices, could be found in certain places even still, because retro chic would never go out of style)— but a mechanical arm did pluck from a menagerie of compact discs the disc with the song you chose, and that made the machine a relic. You used buttons to flip the pages of a book visible through the window of the machine to find your artist and your song and the corresponding number. Eric found one. He did not have quarters but a sign on the machine said OUT OF ORDER FOR DECORATIVE PURPOSES ONLY. Eric stared at the song he wanted to play. He thought maybe it would play anyway, if he keyed in the numbers. So he keyed them in. "Oh, Muse," he mumbled after nothing happened and as he returned to his seat at the bar, where his coffee had been refilled. He snuck another pour from his flask —nobody said a thing this time.

"Recount to me," Eric whispered.

Before him appeared a plate with eggs and bacon and sliced tomatoes that he didn't remember having ordered and a parsley garnish. "Thanks," he said.

"Listen," said the young man. "I can tell you're having a day, and you need to talk about it, and I'm all for helping out. We get people like you in here a lot. Travelers. Asking questions, telling stories, wanting conversation. Dinner rush'll die down soon. Shouldn't be long before I can chat with you, listen to you talk if you want."

Eric said nothing.

"Can I get you anything else with your food?"

Eric looked up and did now catch the young man's eyes. Just a kid, but not the kid he was looking for. "No. Thank you," Eric said. "It looks great."

And then the young man's body was still, and he squinted. "Wait— you're Eric Hauser, aren't you? You founded Lumina."

"I am," Eric admitted. There was no point denying it.

"Dude—Where the hell have you been?"

Encounters at Farpoint

1

LIKE MANY GREAT CHIEF EXECUTIVE officers, Eric Hauser was adopted.

The legend goes that one day one of the technology gods, sitting on his Olympic throne, became bored. He was bored with the lack of female companionship offered by his existence on the mountain—for in those days, in the Pantheon of tech moguls and oil barons and Wall Street titans and Fortune 500 CEOs there were few women—and he was bored with what he saw when he gazed upon the world of mortals: stagnation, desperation, an inability to innovate beyond the things already built and released unto the world by the Pantheon. Decades ago the mortal world, which has been dying since the day of its creation, had begun to accelerate its own extinction. And decades are to the deities of progress, theoretically, an eternity in which multiplicities can occur.

So, on that day of his supreme boredom, this particular technology god took the form of a golden silicone deep penetration g-spot vibrator with fifteen vibration modes, and in this form he impregnated a young woman, and nine months later that young woman, who was alone in the world and had neither family nor money nor a support system of any kind, gave birth to a healthy baby boy in the stall of a mall's department store bathroom. The woman, having nothing to offer the child except her love, wrapped him in the only blanket she owned (a gray, almost silver, blanket that she'd knitted with her own two hands over the course of many months spent working the graveyard shift at that same department store) and deposited him in the middle of the night on the steps of the emergency room of Cleveland University Hospitals Case Medical Center, where the infant was found by a nurse, examined by a pediatric specialist, and found to be in excellent health save for a congenital heart defect that, after a short surgery was performed, would likely require no further treatment. The hospital staff called the police, who began an investigation, and the news of the abandoned infant was reported by two of the three local news stations, but no one with information about the child's parents' whereabouts ever came forward, and the police had no leads, no fingerprints, no reason, really, to care, and their investigation remained open but untouched in a sheet-metal filing cabinet next to a desk, somewhere.

That is the legend. It's the tale Eric Hauser liked to tell himself. Because he did not know who his biological parents were, he was free to invent for them whatever sad tale he liked. For if this legend was true, it absolved both biological parents of any responsibility. His biological mother: surely she could not be expected to raise a child under those circumstances. His biological father: a god! And once a god births a demigod, the demigod is always on his own. That's just how such legends go. It's not the god's fault—not at all!

Of course, the true story of Eric Hauser's birth parents is fare more mundane than the legend. There was no department store bathroom. No hospital steps. No news coverage. Just a young, single mother named Marissa Blake—and a normal adoption process (records now sealed), with Blake's only stipulation being that her child be placed in the care of college graduates, which Wallace and Amanda Hauser, who could have no children of there own, were.

2

THEY'RE ONE OF THE FIRST things biographers talk about: the parents. It's always something about the parents. They're important. They shape things from the start, from in most cases birth to in most cases somewhere around the subject's eighteenth year. And of course in some cases the years the parents shape equal fewer than eighteen, and in rare cases a few more, and in cases rarer still, if the parents are good parents, they shape the subject forever, because the subject cares about and respects them, and what they would do or advise the subject to do or have to say to the subject about his or her decisions is always on the subject's mind. This is why the biographers start with the parents.

There were no authorized biographies of Eric Hauser during his life, just a Wikipedia page and a handful of profiles in *Forbes* and *Business Week* and, early in his career, when he was still only a "CEO to keep an eye on," *Inc. Magazine.* He would not participate in biographies, and even the magazine profiles received input from him sparsely, begrudgingly; he was always eager to offer comments on Lumina and on its products, but almost never on the details of his own life. After Eric's death, the first authorized biography (authorized, that is, by Lumina's board of directors, since Eric Hauser left no estate) would characterize him as the most paradoxically private and ego-driven man in all of business. This was a public image he'd put much effort into cultivating.

The first authorized biography would also deem it, in the spirit of the genre, appropriate to start with Eric's parents. What it should have done differently, however, was start further back from where most biographies start, not with how the parents raised the subject, but with how the parents came to possess the wherewithal to warrant the custody of a child in the first place. But there were many details the first authorized biography of Eric Hauser, not to mention all future biographies, would miss out on.

In summary: Eric Hauser's parents probably didn't possess it, the wherewithal—but do any parents, really? Aren't they all just faking it? Especially the first time around, and probably the second and the third and, in the case of certain reality television stars, the sixteenth? Aren't they all just playing pretend?

It was spring when Amanda Hauser became pregnant. Seven months before, she had, with her husband's consent—because this was something they'd been talking about for a while and something they both wanted and were ready for now that Wallace's career was finally stable and they had some cash stashed away and had just purchased, with an admittedly small down payment, their first house, a cute two-bedroom one-story with light-blue vinyl siding and new rain gutters and a small green yard in the front and back—stopped refilling the prescription for her daily birth control pill. Within weeks, two interesting things happened to Amanda: she became both more interested in sex and less interested in her husband. She was thirty-four years old.

Amanda was twenty-two when she met Wallace on the campus of Cleveland State University during her senior year. She was an enlightened, sex-positive woman. A feminist with the maiden name Parkinian who was convinced that her body was her own and she could do with it as she saw fit, which meant that, if she wanted to (and she did) she could have sex with whomever she desired, whenever she desired, so long as she was safe and responsible and took care of her mental and spiritual well-being. And despite feeling this way since her early teens, when her parents long-waning church habit had ceased being a habit at all, it wasn't like she'd started then and there having casual sex with anyone who asked. In fact, she was seventeen when she lost her virginity to a fellow high school junior, Brady Johnson, her boyfriend since freshman year, with whom she'd until that time only made out and let finger her a few times under a blanket and once given a blowjob to in his car to celebrate the fact that he had been given by his father a car, finally, finally, baby, I have a car and we can go places. When she was ready, she let Brady fuck her in his bedroom while his father, who worked nights, was out of the house. It was an acceptable experience: minimal pain, minimal blood, *some* pleasure but no real orgasm for her—the whole event lasting somewhere longer than seven minutes but fewer than fifteen. To be honest, she enjoyed masturbating, which she did at least few times a week, more than she enjoyed that inaugural session with Brady, but while her first time didn't succeed in providing the gratification her own fingers had been able to bring her for most of her teenage years, it did give her hope that the things she'd been reading about in pilfered erotica and watching on cable television were possible—men *would* have sex with her. Sex could be a part of her life.

She decided to break up with Brady three days later, but when she found him in the hallway by his locker that morning, he beat her to it. "I just think there's more out there for us, y'know?" Brady said. "I wouldn't want you to be stuck with just me for the rest of your life. You need freedom, that sort of thing."

And even though she knew it was bullshit coming from him, it was also exactly what Amanda had been planning to say to Brady—that she was young and needed freedom and variety and possibility—so, yeah, she replied, whatever—and they hugged.

She slept with two other boys from her high school during the next year, both multiple times, but both without attachment or the pressure of anything more than having sex and going to the movies together every once in a while. She'd hardly call the two guys she slept with her boyfriends, but she managed to avoid acquiring what she'd seen described in teen dramas as a *reputation*; men didn't proposition her, and women didn't hate her or call her a slut or spread rumors about her being easy. Sex was just a thing she was doing. A part of her life, just as she'd imagined it would be. And that probably meant it was part of lots of other people's lives too, she realized. It wasn't a *thing*, it was just, you know, a thing.

In college, she became a little more adventurous. Her partner count grew by a factor of ten. She tried things she'd never tried before. She asked to try these new things. "Teach me," she'd whisper breathily into the ear of the young scholar she was pulling onto the thin, lumpy mattress of a dorm-room bed. "Show me what you know that I don't. *Educate* me." (When she thought back on this words some years later, she would cringe.) And sometimes they would: sometimes they'd show her mind-blowing things, do incredible things to her body or have her do incredible things to them, and sometimes they'd do things to her that, while interesting on an intellectual level, didn't excite her as much as other things. Other times, they had nothing to teach her, because their experience was less than hers—sometimes even they were virgins, young men grateful to her for initiating what they'd been too afraid to initiate ever since they'd started sneaking peeks at their fathers' porn magazines and jerking off—in which instances *she* educated *them*.

The day after one mildly embarrassing drunken encounter, at the end of which she'd had to fish from deep inside herself a slimy, incorrectly donned condom, she visited the CSU Health & Wellness Center.

"Hi," she said to the administrative volunteer at the counter. "I think I might be pregnant. He didn't put the condom on right. And—well."

"Um . . . right," said the volunteer. The volunteer was short, with hair the color of Amanda's strawberry blonde but frizzier, bigger. Amanda was pretty sure this girl was in her Tuesday/Thursday calculus class. The girl was playing with her glasses with one hand and searching the admin desk for a clipboard with the other. "There's no one here at the moment. I mean, besides me. But the nurse will be back in a few minutes. She can help you. Can you fill this out?"

Amanda took the clipboard. "Do you have a pen?"

"Oh—uh—yeah. Of course. Yeah, here."

"Thanks."

Amanda sat in one of the three stiff chairs against the wall, near a water cooler and an end table stacked with pop culture magazines and months-old copies of the *Plain Dealer* and the student newspaper. She examined the papers on the clipboard thoroughly before filling in any part of them; she'd learned long ago to read things, always read things, before you put your name on them. The information the forms asked for was straightforward: name, phone number, address (with an option to check off the name of a campus dorm and insert the room number), student ID number, nature of your visit, insurance information.

Hmmm. Insurance information was a tough one, maybe. As a student, Amanda was still covered under her parents' insurance, and it was good coverage—with her father working at General Motors her family had always had quick and easy access to dentists, general practitioners, and gynecologists, all with very little, if any, copay. And nothing terribly grim had ever happened to she or them, but if it had—if one of them, say, was in a bad car accident or had an appendix burst or was diagnosed with cancer—her father's insurance would cover most any treatment: such were the benefits of being upper middle class with no preexisting conditions in the 1980s. So it wasn't like any treatment she might need today wouldn't be covered—*would* she need treatment today?—but she wasn't sure she wanted her parents to see the insurance records. Even a trip to the campus medical center on their statement would cause them to ask questions. If she *was* pregnant, now that she thought about it, could the nurse even do anything?

She brought the clipboard back to the volunteer. "I'm finished," she said. "I left the insurance part blank. I'll probably just pay for this out of pocket."

"Okay," the girl said. "Thanks."

Amanda stood, waiting.

"The nurse will be here soon. Like ten minutes. You should probably just wait over there."

"Right." Amanda returned to her seat.

The hum of the water cooler permeated the room's dense silence. The volunteer was reading a thick paperback textbook: *19th-Century Britain.*

"So, hey," Amanda said. "How about that stuff on fractals the other day?"

"Excuse me?"

"In Calc 102. Like didn't it seem like that was more like geometry stuff? What was it doing in Calc 102?"

"I'm not in Calc 102. I'm a grad student. English Lit and European History."

"Oh."

"Yeah."

"My bad, I guess."

"It's okay."

The next few minutes passed in awkward silence. The volunteer continued her reading. Amanda hadn't brought a book—she didn't read books often, mostly because she didn't have the time, working hard as she was to maintain a high GPA while also making sure she attended most parties and on-campus events where she might meet new people—and besides her wallet, in her purse were only a couple of tampons, some lipstick, a small mirror, and a copy of *Afterimage* that she'd flipped through twice now. She picked up the *Plain Dealer* from the table and scanned the front-page headlines. NASA was launching another shuttle later this year, two years after the Challenger explosion. The water cooler gurgled.

"Miss Parkinian?"

Amanda looked up. A middle-aged woman wearing a blue smock and horned-rimmed glasses in front of her dull eyes stood in a doorway behind the administrative counter, holding the very clipboard Amanda had filled out. "That's me," Amanda said, as if she weren't the only patient in the room.

"This way, please."

As Amanda walked past the counter and through the doorway to the clinic, she could feel the grad student's eyes somewhere on her back.

The nurse led Amanda down a short hallway and into a room saturated with a sterility that felt out of place in an academic facility. There were two hard-backed chairs and an examination table and a linoleum countertop with jars of cotton balls and cotton swabs and tongue depressors. What a job: depressing tongues. The nurse took one of the seats and gestured for Amanda to take the other.

"What can I *do* for you?" the nurse said, gesturing to the clipboard she still held.

On the form under REASON FOR VISIT, Amanda had written: Birth control?

"I think I might be pregnant," Amanda said.

The nurse nodded, but her lifeless expression remained. "Of course. Of course," she said. "Have you taken a pregnancy test, then?"

"Well, no. But yesterday I had sex with a guy and—"

"Your boyfriend?"

"What? No. Just a guy."

"Did you *know* this guy?"

"No. I mean, yes, I met him a couple hours—wait, that doesn't even matter. That part isn't any of your business."

The nurse didn't move, didn't make any marks on the paper, but she seemed to be making notes on a clipboard inside her head. "Okay. So?"

"So we had sex and the condom slipped off, is what happened, and now I just want to make sure I'm not pregnant. And maybe get some birth control, like The Pill. I probably should have gotten on it a while ago, I guess."

The nurse reached up to her glasses and pulled them forward, as if to ensure she would have to look down her nose to say what she wanted to say next. "Young lady, if you just experienced this . . . incident . . . yesterday, there's no way to tell right now whether you're pregnant. You're going to have to wait several weeks. Come back in if you miss your cycle; then we test you."

Of course. Duh. Amanda should have realized this, and she was a little embarrassed she hadn't. Embarrassed because she could now be assumed to be naive, and she was *not* a naive person, just a little hungover. "Okay," she said. "But so what about The Pill? Can I at least get that while I'm here."

"Not if you're pregnant you can't, Miss." The nurse saying *Miss* did not sound as polite as one would think it should. "That could lead to complications, including termination of the pregnancy."

"But that's okay. If I *am* pregnant I would want to have an abortion anyway."

The nurse was making more notes on her mental clipboard. "Good for you,""she said. "But it doesn't matter. Come back once you've missed your cycle—or haven't—and we'll take things from there."

Amanda had expected more to happen here, but now she was realizing how futile it was that she'd come to the clinic today at all. Of course she should have waited. She probably wasn't event pregnant.

"Is there anything else?" the nurse said.

"No, I guess not. Not at all."

"Dismissed," the nurse said, as if she had called Amanda here in the first place, as if it was her right to tell Amanda when to leave.

Amanda felt the need to say something, to respond to the dismissal or to defend herself against any perception the nurse had of her, which was ridiculous—she'd never felt ashamed of her behavior before, and she certainly wasn't ashamed now. (She *wasn't*. She *was not*.) The nurse was a stuffy conservative bitch, was the thing, obviously, and Amanda didn't like conservative bitches, especially not ones that couldn't even become doctors. "Thanks," was all she said. She escorted herself back to the waiting room. On her way out she stopped at the counter where the grad student sat, still reading her book on 19th-century Britain. "How much is this?"

The grad student put down her book. "What?"

"How much for this visit?"

"Oh, um, I don't know. I don't do that part. They'll send you a bill, I think. They have your address."

Amanda was grateful she'd been able to list a dorm room as her address, that even though she went to school in the same city who's suburbs she'd grown up in, she'd opted to live on campus rather than with her parents, and that the bill would find her there. "Okay then."

"Bye."

"Bye."

But as Amanda opened the clinic's door and stepped out into the early-spring campus chill, she heard the grad student say behind her. "Wait."

Amanda turned. The grad student was there, right there behind her, her textbook tucked under her arm. "Yeah?"

"Um, well, um—I was just—I couldn't help but overhear your conversation with the nurse and I was just wondering . . . how do you do it?"

Amanda frowned. "Do what?"

"Get guys to like you."

"How do I get guys to like me? You mean like hook up with me."

"Well, yeah."

"Have you ever—"

"I mean I had a boyfriend in high school, but he was lame—it was lame—and I haven't really had much success on campus the last few years."

"I see."

"So," the grad student said, "and I realize this is a really weird thing to ask a stranger, but,"—the textbook slipped and she caught it gracelessly —"will you help me?"

Two weeks later at 10 p.m., Amanda arrived at a fraternity party indistinguishable from the dozens of other parties she'd been to during the first three years of her higher education experience. By the look of things, the festivities had already been raging for at least an hour. Amongst a beer-perfumed crowd of at least a hundred dancing people— likely students as well as people who didn't attend CSU but knew people who did—shirtless frat boys with various amounts and colors (dark green, dark blue, purple, gold) of paint on their torsos marched, locked together, each with at least one hand on the waist of the guy in front of him, bouncing to the beat of Duran Duran, the vague homoeroticism of the pose probably lost on all of them. The edges of the celebrating throng (celebrating what, though?, Amanda assigned a small portion of her mental faculties to wondering) cheered and cawed as the train of boys parted them. Some of the boys held their heads tilted back and their mouths open, and members of the crowd poured cans of beer onto them, in most cases missing their mouths and even their faces, instead letting the beer run down their chests, smudging but not washing free the pigments with which they were colored.

"So," Amanda said, "are you ready?"

The grad student squinted at her. "You mean one of *them*?"

"Oh, dear God, no," Amanda said. "No no no no no. Never frat boys. *Never* frat boys. If you try to fuck a frat boy it's either going to end up being terrible or obnoxious or lazy or some combination of all three. Plus the smell . . ."

"Okay. So, who, then?"

Amanda spread an arm majestically in front of her. "Anyone else," she said. "It's your choice. There is a world of possibility before you."

Amanda had spent the last two weeks preparing the grad student for this moment. She'd thought it would take far longer for her to make her debut, but the grad student was eager, motivated. She believed that if she could do it just once, it would open floodgates—her inhibitions would part and the libido she'd always known she had would gush forth. Amanda told her that, yes, if she was lucky, there would be gushing.

They went that first afternoon to a coffee shop just off campus, where the drinks were good but the patronage tended to skew toward people who worked downtown rather than students, meaning the grad student would feel more comfortable discussing her situation, knowing she had little chance of being overheard by her peers. After ordering lattes and dumping into them several packets of sugar each, they sat at a corner table and Amanda asked the grad student to describe her sexual history, in detail, please, and when the grad student veered into the realm of small talk Amanda told her she wasn't there to be her friend, just to help her make a conquest, to become the sort of person who conquers. The grad student's name was Stephanie Folsom, and her history with men (telling, in retrospect, that she worded it that way), she told Amanda, was effectively nonexistent, except for her disappointing high school boyfriend. She'd been hit on, catcalled like every woman, but catcalls don't translate to dates, don't translate (and how long, dear God, would it take the male species to realize this?) to intercourse. Stephanie *had* been asked on dates, of course, she told Amanda, but the sort of men who'd asked her on dates (frumpy, nerdish, insecure) had never appealed to her, so she always declined.

They had a conversation like this one three days in a row, and on the third day Stephanie told Amanda that she had an important test in two days, which she needed to study for, but could they continue talking after the test was over, maybe the evening after the test? Amanda could come over to the house Stephanie shared with several other grad students. The place was often very busy, she said, but Stephanie of course had her own room, and they could talk there, have some drinks.

Amanda at first hesitated to say yes. Drinks in someone's room could lead to friendship, and as Amanda had told Stephanie, she wasn't interested in making friends. She'd gone almost three years without making a single university friendship—she'd hardly made acquaintances, and of this she was proud. Friends would mean people who expected her to give some, if not most, of her time to them. Friends meant people who felt owed a part of you. But without them, you could do what you wanted, who you wanted, on the nights you wanted; you could go to parties because you wanted to, campus events because you wanted to, movies or concerts because you wanted to—not because someone you were supposed to care about was throwing them or had purchased you a ticket as *gift*. Even Amanda's roommate interacted with her on a strictly professional basis.

"You'll have me from 6 p.m. to 9 p.m.," Amanda told Stephanie after some consideration. "And you're providing the beer, something good, nothing shitty."

But they didn't stay in Stephanie's room. They ventured downstairs, into the kitchen, to make margaritas, and then in a lateral move they found themselves in the living room, talking about Stephanie's explorations of literature and history, even Amanda's faint interest in art, and watching *Late Night with David Letterman*—and it wasn't until 1:30 the following morning that a mildly drunk Amanda inserted the key into her dorm room door, entered, careful not to wake her roommate, and fell asleep in her own bed. Stephanie had told her she could crash on the couch—"Or, if y'want, I have a sleeping bag, and you can sleep on the floor, up in my room, or I could sleep on the floor, and . . ."—but even as her drunkenness progressed Amanda could see that she and Stephanie were way too close to becoming friends, and she had to stop it now by taking leave of the other woman.

"Let's do coffee again, on Monday. We need to get back to the real issue here: your guy problems."

"Right, m' guy problems," Stephanie said.

Finally, after another week or so of morning coffees, Amanda had decided that really the only way anything was going to happen for the grad student (Amanda called her Stephanie out loud but in her mental narration had decided "the grad student" was appropriately distant) was if she just went for it. So Amanda told her as much. "I'm realize now that this isn't really a thing you can be taught, " she told her, "You're going to have to just go for it." And then she brought her to tonight's party.

Amanda watched now as the grad student, emboldened (by what Amanda would later find out was a bump of cocaine), ventured into the throng of drunken, stupid, horny men and women. Amanda had planned on keeping an eye on the grad student, but her watchful gaze shifted with her thoughts and she went to find herself a beer.

Her period should have started three days ago, but it hadn't. She was concerned. She hadn't gone back to the clinic yet—and she was afraid to. It was the first time she'd really been afraid of anything in her life. What if she *was* pregnant? What if that nurse was there again, judged her, examined the state of her morality and found it lacking? Amanda knew definitively that her lifestyle wasn't wrong, and she'd always been able to enjoy exploring her sexuality, but when she thought of the way the nurse had looked at her, talked to her, she felt bad about herself. She hadn't slept with anyone since that visit. Two weeks, for her, was a long time.

She pulled the tab on a Coors Light and settled against a wall. She watched the people move before her. She'd lost track of the grad student already, but she was sure she was out there, trying to get her game on. Probably failing to get her game on. Amanda didn't have high expectations for the girl, or for herself as a teacher. The best she could do was motivate and let the girl do the rest.

Halfway through her second beer (she'd moved from the wall only for the purpose of finding that second one and then had returned to it) the grad student appeared before her. "It's not working," the grad student said.

"What?" Amanda said. The music had gotten louder.

"It's not working. I don't want any of them."

"How can you not want any of them? Every kind of guy possible is here—that's always how it is at these parties. Even the really good guys, the sort of guys who don't go to frat parties, are at frat parties. You're just nervous. You're just scared."

Duran Duran was still blaring throughout the room. As far as Amanda could tell, whoever was in charge of the music had decided to play only Duran Duran.

"I'm not scared," the grad student called over the noise. "I think I'm actually into women. I mean, I know I am. I've always known."

Amanda stared at her. "Well then what the hell did you need me for? Why bother asking me to help you get with *men*?"

The grad student leaned in, and Amanda could tell by her breath that she'd found the beer, too, but hadn't drank much of it. "Because I'm kind of into *you*."

"Oh . . ." Amanda said. "Okay—I guess. Why didn't you just ask me out?"

"Because I really am actually not so good at that part."

"Right . . ." Amanda said. She paused for a moment. Despite her highly sexual nature, she'd never been with a woman before, hadn't even thought about it, except for when she'd seen the movies *Personal Best* and *Desert Hearts,* but the idea now intrigued her. And sleeping with the Stephanie—the *grad student*—would do away with any risk of friendship. Because once you fucked someone you couldn't be friends with them. Amanda felt the concerns of possible pregnancy and the moral merits of her promiscuity fade; they didn't disappear, but they receded to a place in the back of her mind where she could retrieve them later for further musing.

The grad student stood there, waiting.

"Just a second," Amanda said. She downed the rest of her beer in a long gulp and set the can on a nearby table. She pulled a hair tie from her pocket and fastened her hair into a haphazard bun. "Okay," she said. "I guess let's do it."

The next morning, Amanda woke in the grad student's bed. She rolled over, careful not to cause too much noise by disturbing the cheap mattress. The grad student lay there next to her, her glasses off her face and on the night stand. Amanda groggily remembered pulling them off and saying "I want to better see your eyes." (Not "I want to see your eyes better" but "I want to better see your eyes"—like some sort of nerve-wracked asshole.) The grad student was sleeping deeply, her little nostrils flaring. Amanda slid out of the bed, stepping into a pile of hers and hers clothing: undergarments, washed-out jean shorts, t-shirts converted to tank tops by the cutting off of the sleeves with kitchen scissors. The night before had been fine, and Amanda was glad she'd done it—for the experience, and for the grad student—but now in the space of the morning she was able to decide it wasn't her thing. During the acts of the night before she thought maybe she wasn't enjoying it so much, but she'd pushed that thought aside and kept going with it, because she couldn't do something for the experience of the thing if she didn't follow that experience through to its completion. But the point now was it turned out she didn't enjoy women the same as she enjoyed men . . . although she had allowed the grad student to make her come.

She dressed in front of the window, the early-morning sun on her shoulders. She thought about saying goodbye, leaving a note, but decided not to. Maybe she would see the grad student around. She found her shoes in two separate places in the bedroom—one next to the bed, part of the pile of clothes, and the other leaning against a stack of books, most of which appeared to be specimens of Western European literature —slipped them on, and tiptoed out the bedroom door. She walked to her dorm as the cool air began to warm. She had an art history class at 10 a.m.

At 10:05, as she sat in that class, listening to the professor's recap of last week's lecture, her period started, and she excused herself to the bathroom, where she sighed with relief.

3

SOME TWELVE YEARS LATER, WHEN Amanda went off birth control so that she and her husband—who she met only six months after sleeping with the grad student, in October, at an on-campus party celebrating the launch of Space Shuttle *Discovery*—could try to have a baby, she put her marriage in jeopardy.

It turns out one of the not-uncommon side effects of hormonal birth control is a diminished sex drive; it *does* work by fucking with your hormones after all. It also turns out that, when your hormones are being fucked with, certain of your perceptions change. You can become interested in different foods or desire to participate in different activities, and you can even, it turns out, become attracted to people you might otherwise not have been attracted to. Amanda started taking hormonal birth control five and a half months before she met Wallace Hauser. In those five and a half months, she had sex with only three different men, only three different times. In an ironic twist, the chance of the thing she was trying to prevent by going on the pill decreased significantly, not because of the pill's primary effect, but because of its secondary. And while she and Wallace did have sex several times a week once they started, they didn't first sleep together until nearly two months into their courtship.

So—the mid-2000s. Amanda Hauser stops taking her birth control so she and Wallace Hauser can have a child. But suddenly, Wallace Hauser, her husband, is not so attractive to her anymore. Also suddenly, she wants sex. A lot of sex. Sex like she did when she was in college. She wants sex, but not with her husband. The problem here is obvious.

Amanda cheated on Wallace an unknown number of times over a period of three months. He should have discovered his wife's infidelity sooner than he did; at the very least he should have known *something* was going on with her, and for years afterward, long after they'd adopted Eric, he would feel a certain kind of guilt deep in his gut at least once a day, and with that guilt he would wonder if she still felt any herself, or ever had at all.

One would think it would be easier to find work with a pharmaceutical degree. After all, once you've completed your prerequisites, which in the United States when Walter was going to school included at least two years of some sort of degree- or non-degree-related laboratory science experience, and then have completed the grueling four years required to receive your PharmD, the last year of which pretty much always involves extensive hands-on experience and several twenty-four-hour clinical rotations, you're technically a Doctor of Pharmacy. That's what *PharmD* stands for: *Doctor of Pharmacy*. And when has it ever been difficult for a doctor to find work? Don't doctors just have work automatically, by virtue of being doctors? Wallace Hauser had never met someone who introduced themself by saying "I'm a doctor" who wasn't employed in some capacity, let alone in a capacity that wasn't glamorous and well-paying, which was why Wallace had decided he wanted to be a doctor in the first place. But he hadn't wanted to complete the potentially sixteen years of medical school he'd heard was involved in becoming a surgeon, and even becoming a pediatrician took at least seven. But the six years required to acquire a PharmD had seemed reasonable to him, had seemed like the right amount of work that would lead to the most lucrative career options, to a steady job, normal hours, a large salary, etc. So he'd gone for two years to a little off-campus vocational school in Cleveland (he was born and raised about a hundred miles south, in Steubenville), where he got his laboratory experience while working at a Wendy's, saving the bulk of his hourly wage to pay for the four years he would then spend at CSU acquiring his PharmD.

Wallace worked hard in college. He'd always been a hard worker—a trait instilled in him by his father, who worked in the Youngstown steel mills until the last one shut down in '79, driving Wallace's father into a deep depression followed by his suicide just before Wallace graduated high school—and it was a trait he'd later pass on to Eric Hauser. That said, even though Wallace was a good student, he'd made a mistake by acquiring his lab experience at a vocational school: if he'd acquired it at an accredited university, like CSU, before moving on to his PharmD, he would have received a bachelor's degree and would have been that far ahead no matter what happened later.

So, anyway, he worked hard at CSU, spent long hours studying, reading, learning about pharmacy law and pharmacy ethics and how to use dosage forms. He tried to keep his fast food job at first, but after his first year, when it become clear that the next three years were going to require a lot from him, including shifts with doctors and in clinics, he quit and took out loans to pay for the portion of his tuition he hadn't been able to save for. He made few friends his first year at CSU, or his second, but at the beginning of the third he joined the Campus Space Club, which referred to itself, for brevity's sake, and because it sounded cooler, as the CSC.

The CSC wasn't what what one might expect from a space-admiring organization at an accredited university with a large and diverse sciences program. It wasn't an official university-sanctioned group, and among its members there were no students for whom space would be part of an actual, logical career path—there were no astronomers, no engineers, no physicists or environmentalists. In fact, Wallace, with his pursuit of a degree in pharmacy, was the only member of the CSC who was involved in science at an academic level, and even then just barely. Rather, the CSC comprised hobbyists, science fiction lovers and comic book nerds, and the sort of geeks who are just really into a thing but lack the will and/or belief in themselves necessary to pursue that thing to any world-changing conclusion. Wallace was one of these people. A Trekkie since he first saw reruns of *The Original Series* (at the time the *only* series) on NBC and then made it a priority to finish his homework every day after school so that he could catch them at 6 p.m., he had an intense interest in sci-fi television.

He watched *Star Trek* and *Battlestar Galactica* and *Galactica 1980* and *V*; but he was interested only in shows with spaceships and ray guns, didn't really watch *The Twilight Zone* or *The Six Million Dollar Man* or even, as a kid, *Land of the Lost*. His father, before he killed himself, would ridicule Wallace's obsession with the good ship Enterprise:

"Fuckin' bullshit. Fucking kid thinks he's going to go to space someday, meet the space aliens, save the galaxy. Fuckin' build something, goddamn loser. Why can't you be like your brother? Frank wants to be an electrician, don't you Frank? Frank wants to do something fuckin' useful."

Wallace's mother, to her credit, would tell his father to knock it off, to leave the kid alone, albeit weakly, as if her duty as a mother to protect her son from harsh words conflicted with her duty as a wife to support her husband's harshness. "Fuckin' waste of time," his father would say.

The only person in the CSC who had any chance of space involving itself in any way in the career path he'd chosen was a fellow junior named Fred Dyer. Fred was the founder of the CSC, and he was a liberal arts major, and he wanted to write for television, wanted to write sci-fi, and he even had a television in his dorm room. Which was really what the CSC was: a group of students, mostly male, who gathered once a week in Fred Dyer's dorm room to watch *Star Trek: The Next Generation*, which premiered during Wallace's junior year.

Wallace saw the hand-made fliers start appearing around campus in early September:

DO YOU WANT TO EXPLORE STRANGE NEW WORLDS, TO SEEK OUT NEW LIFE AND NEW CIVILIZATIONS? DO YOU HAVE WHAT IT TAKES TO BOLDY GO WHERE NO MAN HAS GONE BEFORE? IF SO, COME TO THE FIRST MEETING OF THE CAMPUS SPACE CLUB.

WHEN: SEPTEMBER 28, 1987, 7 P.M.

WHERE: EUCLID COMMONS, ROOM 2B.

WHAT (IN CASE YOU COULDN'T TELL): THE SERIES PREMIER OF STAR TREK: THE NEXT GENERATION, THE NEXT CHAPTER IN GENE RODDENBERRY'S BRILLIANT SAGA OF THE FUTURE.

And underneath the words was a hand drawing of the Enterprise-D, based, presumably, on promotional material that had been released for the show.

To Wallace, who had begun to feel the slow encroach of academic loneliness, the CSC sounded like an opportunity to finally make friends. He arrived at the Euclid Commons dorms, room 2B, at 6:45, thinking the show aired at 7 o'clock. It turned out, however, that the time on the flier indicated pre-show meeting and greeting, and the episode aired at 8 p.m., so when Wallace arrived the only other person there was Fred Dyer, sitting on a brown Barcalounger eating from a bag of salt-and-vinegar potato chips.

"Um, hey," Wallace said. "I'm here for the . . . the space club thing."

"Oh, yeah. Cool. Cool cool cool. Sweet. Hey, I'm Fred."

"Wallace," Wallace said, shaking Fred's proffered greasy hand.

"So, hey, yeah. Lets get you something to drink. Do you like beer?"

"Sure," Wallace said.

"Cool. Here." Fred opened a mini fridge next to the Barcalounger and retrieved a silver can. He tossed it to Wallace, who caught it gracefully.

"Thanks," Wallace said, fingering the tab on the can.

"Shit, no. Wait." Fred retrieved another can from mini fridge and, before Wallace could open his, swapped the cans, without tossing this time. "Last time I threw a beer to someone like that, the whole thing kind of just exploded when they opened it. I need to remember to not be so enthusiastic about things."

"Ah," Wallace said. He held the new can protectively, not opening it just quite yet in case there was going to be another unexpected swapping.

"I do that a lot. Get too enthusiastic about things."

"Ah. Well, so do a lot of people, I suppose. It's no big deal."

"I don't like beer myself, but I thought it would be a good idea to have some in the ol' fridgaroonie here, because most guys like beer, and I'm hoping a lot of people show up to this thing."

"Yeah," Wallace said, deciding it was safe to open the can. "This sounds like fun. I like *Star Trek*, and I can't wait to see what they do with this new series."

"Right? I mean, I'm skeptical, of course—it's gonna be so hard to outdo the original—but I'm excited. I hear DeForest Kelly is gonna be in the first episode, like a handoff sort of thing, like a passing of the torch."

"Very cool," Wallace said.

"And I read that the new Enterprise is like *four times* the size of the original. *Galaxy Class*, they're calling it."

"Yeah, I read that too. *TV Guide*, right? Very cool."

The conversation morphed into a semi-comfortable silence then, for several minutes. Wallace slurped at his beer, which wasn't a brand he was especially fond of (he didn't drink regularly), but he wasn't focused on the taste, anyway, but rather on the social act of drinking in the presence of another person. Fred sipped Yoo-hoo through a straw. He emptied the bag of salt-and-vinegar chips into a large bowl and offered some to Wallace. There were more snacks, too, Fred told him. He indicated a square card table against the wall, rife with bowls and bags and packages of snack food.

"So—I haven't seen you around campus, I don't think," Fred finally said. "Freshman?"

Wallace was sitting on a plastic folding chair, one of three that Fred had set up for the viewing party. There were also (in the surprisingly large dorm room) two bean bag chairs, two double beds (each with nightstands, their own reading lamps, and refinished wooden trunks at their feet), a sink, a second mini fridge, and the television, which was impressively large at maybe twenty-five inches. One of the beds, as well as its accompanying furniture, seemed spectacularly lived in; the other showed no signs of occupation. "Junior," Wallace replied. He felt the urge to shake Fred's hand again, as if this were a second introduction. "I just don't get around much, I guess."

"Hey, that's cool. I guess I don't get around much either, to be honest. That's why I'm doing this thing"—he made a gesture that encompassed the snack table, the chairs, the television—"hoping I can do my part to bring some people together. How's the semester treating you?"

The semester was treating Wallace not unwell. He was just slightly less than a month in, true, but already he had more focus, more drive, than last year. He told Fred as much.

"That's really good to hear," Fred said. He was a junior as well. "Pharmacology, eh? Myself, I'm going to be a writer."

"That's neat," Wallace said.

And again the conversation morphed into selfsame silence. The TV was on but the sound was muted, and a cathodic hum filled the room.

"This is a really big dorm room," Wallace finally observed.

"Yeah, right? So I actually got kinda lucky and they let me keep this room two years in a row. I had a roommate last year, but I guess this year he got off-campus housing or dropped out or whatever, and for some reason they didn't assign anyone else. I mentioned it to the CHA once—because like I've got to do my due diligence, right?—but they kind of ignored me, and I'm not going to mention it again, no way. If they don't want to do the administrative work of finding me a roommate, that's fine with me. I mean, I like having one, but I think I'd rather be alone than with a stranger."

The time was 7:15, and it was seeming likely that Wallace and Fred might be the only two people in the CSC, but at around 7:25 two more guys arrived, and ten minutes after that, another. By the time the show started, at 8 o'clock, seven young men, all freshmen or sophomores except for Fred and Wallace, were huddled around the TV, eating snacks, drinking beer, and laughing at each other's jokes.

The CSC met again to watch the next episode, and the next. As the weeks went on and *The Next Generation* became more popular and word spread that there was a place on campus you could watch it with other people, the club grew. By the time the show's second season started, in the fall of '88, the Campus Space Club boasted a rotating roster of thirty-three members, at least fifteen of whom showed up for "meetings" on any given Monday night.

Not long after that first meeting, Wallace and Fred started running the club together. Wallace's own roommate at the beginning of junior year was an asshole, a mediocre football player who hadn't been able to get onto an Ivy League team and resented it deeply, and in his resentment he stayed up late playing hip hop on cassette, brought girls back to the dorm room, failing every time but once that Wallace saw to get the girls to do anything but make out with him, and took steroids, which turned him into what the roommate liked to call a "raging 'roid monster" (this raging 'roid monster, by the way, pretty much just sat on his dorm room bed and brooded, too grumpy to do much in the way of actual raging). By early November, Wallace had had enough of his roommate's deportment, and after a CSC meeting (Episode 7, "Lonely Among Us"), when the rest of the club members had left and Wallace and Fred sat, talking, as they'd taken to doing, Wallace drinking a third and usually final beer and Fred a sixth and probably not final Yoo-hoo, when Wallace said as much, Fred said, "So why don't you move in here?"

"Really?"

"Sure! I've got space. I've got an unused bed. I've got a TV, eh? A TV! And the fridge. And I'm thinking of getting a Nintendo. Plus we get along so well. I don't like hip hop, girls hate me, and the only thing I'm ever up late doing is watching *Star Trek*, which you like. The whole idea seems obvious to me."

Wallace smiled. "A Nintendo?"

So Wallace moved in. By some miracle of administrative oversight—which Wallace later learned was that Fred came from a wealthy family of frequent and plentiful university donors who had pull with the administration and, thus, the campus housing authority—they lived in that dorm room through the end of senior year in a partnership that was comradic if not superpowered. They gave each other space; they kept each other company. Fred went to visit his parents during holidays and summer and often on weekends, while Wallace had the room to himself. On the two occasions Wallace thought he might succeed in bringing a girl over, he let Fred know in advance and Fred said "No problem, brother" and slept next door, on the floor of one of the CSC's most loyal members.

In the spring of the CSC's first year, Wallace suggested they start taking voluntary donations at each meeting—"You know, to cover things like food, like we could start doing better snacks, better beer"—and Fred, who was becoming more and more uncomfortable taking as much of his parents' money as he did, said it sounded like a good idea. When they proposed it at the next meeting nearly everyone present threw a few bucks into the shoebox Wallace had appropriated for the purpose, and Wallace and Fred were able to purchase liquor and liqueurs and all manner of mixers for the next meeting, and they made *Star Trek*-themed drinks: Romulan Ale and Saurian Brandy and Warp Core Breaches. The Warp Core Breaches were particularly potent, and several club members spent that night on Wallace and Fred's floor rather than return to their own dorms, and the next day word was spreading among a certain community about the crazy parties at the CSC.

Now Wallace was enjoying college. *Now* he had a purpose, an *immediate* purpose, something beyond the pharmacy counter, which seemed far away and unattainable. Even as he entered his fourth year, which was going to be full of *practical experience*, pharmacy didn't quite seem like a real thing he was going to spend his time participating in. Would he really be behind a counter the rest of his life? What made a pharmacy counter different from that one at Wendy's except for the bigger paycheck and lack of greasy smell? Wallace wasn't going to be *making* the drugs, the medications, only giving them to people—it was a service, sure, but couldn't anyone do it? Couldn't anyone read a script and say *Give me about ten minutes, please* and fill a bottle? He was on the verge of spending his life as an instrument of cures, but himself curing nothing. And the dilemma was that he'd known this before, when he'd made the decision to become a *Doctor of Pharmacy*. And the *real* dilemma was that he wasn't actually sure he was going to have a problem with it. Because certainly not everyone could save the world, but everyone was at least obligated to do something practical, useful, with their lives.

On September 29, 1988, the Campus Space Club would have its first and only non-*The Next Generation*-related party, because on September 29, 1988, almost three years after the destruction of the the Space Shuttle *Challenger*, NASA was going to inspire America again.

"There's nothing *inspiring* about it," said a pockmarked junior named, unfortunately, Fitzwilliam ("My mother is a Jane Austin fan") Farnham. "The U.S. space program's been a joke for almost two decades now."

It was September 25, four days days before the launch of *Discovery*, during one of the CSC's regular meetings. They were watching reruns of *The Next Generation* this month, because the show's second season wouldn't premier until November. There were twenty-one people—seventeen young men, including Fred and Wallace, and four women—stuffed into the dorm room, some on beanbag chairs, a few in folding chairs, most on the floor, sitting cross-legged or self-arranged on their backs side-by-side, facing the television, which showed blue end credits against a moving starscape. One of the young women had just expressed her extreme excitement at the upcoming launch, because, she'd said, NASA was going to inspire America again.

"So we had a setback a few years ago," Fred said in reply to Fitzwilliam. "A tragic one, even, but that doesn't make the program a *joke*. We'd be a joke if we weren't getting back in the saddle, maybe, but the fact that we're trying again surely makes us the opposite of a joke. And we're doing more than any other country right now, or ever."

"Every country's space program is a joke," Fitzwilliam said.

One of the other students, whose name Wallace couldn't remember, chimed in. "How the hell is going to space—to *space*—a joke?"

"Because it's only going to space is what we're doing. And it's only low-Earth orbit."

"So what does that matter? It's space, man. I don't see you going to space."

"*No*, of course I'm not going to space, stupid, I'm not equipped to go to space. But you know who *is* fucking equipped to go to fucking space? NASA."

"Right. Exactly. So that's what they're doing. They're going to space."

"They're going into low-Earth orbit."

"Which is *space*."

Fitzwilliam sighed in a way that indicated, for anyone who'd been doubting, that he was clearly smarter than everyone else in the room. Couldn't you see it, how smart he was? "Look. Let me put it to you like this," he said. "I'm not equipped to go into space, meaning I don't exactly have the means or the skill to leave this planet. Okay, I get that. But what I do have is the ability to leave my dorm, right? Like I can go anywhere I want to go *on* this planet—"

"Really?" the other student said. "So you could go, say, to Antarctica, then?"

"Shut up, fuckwad. It's rude to interrupt people when they're talking."

The other student shrugged.

"Does that mean you're not gonna interrupt me again? Can I trust you to not interrupt me when I'm talking?"

The other student said, "Whatever, man."

"Good. *Thank* you. I *appreciate* it," Fitzwilliam said.

Fred had gotten up from his chair, was maneuvering his way through the bodies toward the liquor table. He often made cocktails for club members once the night's episode was over, *cocktails* meaning things like Jägerbombs and Irish Car Bombs—various bombs; when the show was over was when the real drinking always began.

Fitzwilliam, the chunk of his honor that the interruption had taken now sufficiently restored, continued. "So I can go anywhere on this planet, is what I'm saying. I leave my dorm room, and I can go to class, or the cafeteria, or my parents' house, or Pittsburgh, or fuckin' wherever. So how stupid would it be if the farthest I ever decided to go was the hallway outside the dorm room? Would I ever see anything, learn anything? Fuck no."

Fred started handing drinks to Wallace, who passed them to attendees, starting with the girl who'd prompted the conversation in the first place.

"So, then," Fitzwilliam said, "that's what NASA—and every other space agency on the fuckin' planet—is doing. Get it? They can go anywhere in the solar system—and they *have* gone to the moon before—but for the last twenty years they stick to Earth's front sidewalk! Get it? It's a joke!" He seemed to sit back down, even though he'd never been standing up. Wallace handed him a Jack and Coke.

"Well," said the young lady who'd started the conversation, her face and voice showing signs of spiritual deflation, "I still think it's exciting."

"Whatever," Fitzwilliam said, shaking his head.

"Anyway," Fred said. "I would like to remind everyone that the party-slash-club meeting in which we watch the *Discovery* launch will *not*, for once, be held here. We've secured a room at the campus rec center, and we'll have like a dozen TVs in there, and everyone on campus is invited. You're all welcome, encouraged, really, to bring whatever food or drink you like; however, no alcohol—"

The dorm room filled with the hum of more than a dozen groans.

"Hey, what are you gonna do? Campus policy. It's either finally put on a large, campus-wide event celebrating a great achievement in science and exploration, putting the CSC on the map of this university's collective consciousness, or alcohol."

"Alcohol!" yelled one of the attendees from his supine position on the floor. Everyone laughed.

"Anyway, what there *will* be is lots of coffee, lots of donuts, and lots of people. And hopefully no launch failures." Nobody laughed at that. *Challenger* still gaped as a significant wound on the body of America, and the wound wouldn't begin to heal until after *Discovery* had made it to orbit. Fred seemed to realize that the last bit, whether he'd meant it as a joke or not, was in poor taste. "So then, the launch is at 11:30 on Thursday; we'll start gathering in the rec center at eleven. Be there or be square."

Nobody laughed at that last sentence either: calling someone square hadn't been funny for decades.

Wallace brought a Jägerbomb to the girl who'd triggered Fitzwilliam's rant. "I've never seen you here before," he said after she'd taken it and downed only half.

"Really?" she said. "I've been to like six of these, at least."

"Oh."

"Yeah."

"Fred and I—this is our room. We're kinda the guys who put this together. I'm Wallace."

"Yeah, I know."

"Oh."

"Yeah."

Wallace realized he hadn't gotten a drink for himself, and he desperately wished he had. "So, hey, I thought that stuff you said about the Space Shuttle, about it being inspiring and stuff, I totally agree with you. Maybe we could get together some time and talk about it more, get to know each other better."

"I'm gay," she said.

"What?"

"I'm a dyke," she said. "A lesbian. I like women."

"Oh," Wallace said. "Oh, hey, that's cool. Hey, I'm gonna go get myself a drink."

For his part, Wallace didn't care much about the space program. He liked science fiction, sure—*loved* science fiction, even—but for him it was an escape, not some sort of inspiration. It was about stories and alien characters and massive spaceships with massive weapons and teleporters and bombastic special effects. But in the real world space travel wasn't like that. Where was the fun in shuttles that fit five people in bulky space suits who did science experiments for a few days? Besides, there were far more important things happening here on earth: there were wars in the Middle East, and there were the Soviets probably planning to nuke the entire planet, and there was a national debt of almost three trillion dollars. *Trillion.* How the hell did you spend even *one* trillion dollars? The government had way more to do here than spend further billions on space. And Wallace just wanted to get a good job, pay his student loans, not have to work too hard.

He spent the next three days alternating shifts at the Cleveland Clinic. He followed physicians as they met with patients, recorded symptoms, made diagnoses, met patients again for follow-ups. *Is he a doctor too?* patients always asked, pointing to Wallace, and the doctors would laugh. *No, he's just a student, going to school for pharmacy.* The doctors would quiz Wallace, ask him what medications he would recommend. He was right about seventy percent of the time.

Thursday came and Wallace woke late to an empty dorm room. He didn't sleep well during the day, had never even been a napper, but since much of his training this year consisted of late-night or even over-night stints at the hospital, sleeping during the day had become a necessity, and he'd prepared for this by installing black-out curtains in the room, which Fred hadn't complained about. Wallace pulled a curtain back now and blinked at the light. He checked the clock on his nightstand: 11:23. *Shit.* He was supposed to have helped Fred with the set up; hell, he was supposed to have showered before pulling on jeans and a large red t-shirt and sneakers and running out the door, but it was too late for either.

The campus rec center was on Chester Avenue, not far, not if you biked or ran very very fast. Wallace didn't own a bike, never had, and he despised running with a passion stronger than any other feeling he had for anything, but he ran anyway. He tripped once when he attempted a daring jump over a cement bench in front of Fenn Hall, tearing skin off the palm of his right hand, but he rolled, almost gracefully, very much concerned with but refusing to acknowledge the stares of any nearby students or faculty, and kept running. He slowed as he approached the many glass doors of the rec center's front entrance. He winced as pulled a handle with his right hand, switched to his left. He realized then that he'd forgotten—or had never asked; he couldn't remember—which room Fed had reserved. The rec center was a big place. There was a food court and computer labs and a pub-like establishment that didn't serve alcohol but had pool tables and dart boards; there were also small lecture halls and conference rooms and a large auditorium where things like author readings and orientations were held; and there were at least ten multipurpose rooms, available to clubs and other campus organizations for meetings and events. Wallace knew the group wouldn't be in the food court, but the food court was right there on the right when you entered the building, so he checked it anyway. He checked the conference rooms on the ground floor. He checked one of the lecture halls. Then he saw a sign at the base of the stairs, a diagonal red arrow and the words THE CAMPUS SPACE CLUB INVITES YOU TO CELEBRATE THE LAUNCH OF *DISCOVERY* WITH US (FREE FOOD AND COFFEE). Wallace ran up the stairs and heard cheers and applause, and when he found the room there were maybe fifty people, and on the televisions was a blue sky and a trail of smoke that went upward, fading high into the atmosphere.

4

JUST THREE DAYS AFTER HER experimental night with Stephanie, Amanda was forced to visit the campus clinic again. She tried to avoid it, but this stomach thing she had going on was unbearable; diarrhea was quickly accompanied by vomiting, and the vomit tasted not dissimilar to how the diarrhea smelled. When after eight hours of involuntary evacuations from both of ends of her digestive tract Amanda broke out in a 102-degree fever, she decided to hedge her bets and hope someone else would be staffing the clinic that day. But sure enough, Stephanie was there, sitting behind the desk, with her glasses and her big hair, the bookmark in *19th Century Britain* now located only a few pages from the back cover. She didn't have to look up—for she was already staring at the door when Amanda walked in. "Hey," she said.

"Hey," Amanda said, wishing she had something with which to fidget besides her sweat-soaked hair.

"Let me guess: Your stomach's bothering you?"

Amanda nodded. "More than a little."

"You drink orange juice from the Viking dining hall?"

Amanda nodded again. "Yesterday."

"Apparently it was tainted. May have been a prank, they think. But also it could have been manufacturer error—might lead to a whole recall, like a national thing. I'd send you right through, but there's a line."

Amanda turned. The four waiting-area chairs were occupied by silently moaning students, some with hands on bellies; several more stood against the walls. Somehow, Amanda hadn't been aware of the presence of anyone but Stephanie when she'd come in. "I think . . . I also have a fever . . . I took my temperature."

"I could give you preferential treatment, of course," Stephanie said. "On account of our . . . 'special relationship.'"

Amanda forced a laugh. "I don't think that would be appropriate," she said.

"No. No, I don't suppose it would."

Amanda smiled a tight smile. She turned to join the students along the wall. But then she turned back. "Listen," she said, her voice low but not a whisper. "I had fun the other night . . ."

"But not *a lot* of fun, right? Not the *right kind* of fun."

"I mean, well, first off, it *felt* really good. You made me feel really good."

"Right, but I didn't make you *feel* really good. I don't make you feel that way."

"Not exactly, no."

Stephanie nodded.

"But . . . but in a way you do. Like I like spending time with you."

"I like spending time with you, too."

Two more students came in then, in need of Stephanie's administrative attention, and the nurse, the same nurse from before, came out and called a patient into the exam room. Amanda waited against a wall for her turn, and when it came the nurse gave no indication she remembered Amanda. When, an hour after arriving, Amanda left, Stephanie stopped her and said they needed to continue this conversation.

So the next week, they did.

"The thing is, though," Amanda was saying over coffee, "is I think I'm done with *all* of that now. The sex, I mean. The promiscuous stuff. Like of course I still don't think there's anything *wrong* with it—I'm still an enlightened, feminist woman—but it's not for me anymore."

"You've sowed your wild oats," Stephanie said, lifting her mug to her mouth with both hands.

"Yes—that's it! I've sowed my wild oats."

Stephanie laughed. She set her mug down and there was whipped cream on her nose and Amanda hadn't realized before just how cute that nose was—for just a moment she wanted to lick the whipped cream off of it. But instead she continued: "And so I think I'm going to focus on just *being* for a while, you know? Like just being me. And just being places, like here, and around people, and *with* people, but not with them in a sexual way."

"I think that's a good idea. 'Life is all memory, except for the one present moment that goes by you so quickly you hardly catch it going.'"

"Was that a quote?"

Stephanie nodded. "Tennessee Williams."

"I like it."

"You know," Stephanie said, reaching both hands across the table, palms up, an invitation. "I wouldn't mind spending some of those present moments together."

Amanda smiled then, and not a tight smile but a big one, relaxed and in her eyes. She put her palms on top of Stephanie's. "I wouldn't mind that either," she said.

Their friendship blossomed after that. They drank coffee together most mornings, except for when one of them had an early class. They talked; they sat. Stephanie was full of quotes and aphorisms, and she shared them indiscriminately; often when Amanda said something, expressed a thought or a feeling or an opinion, Stephanie replied with something someone else had said. When Amanda observed this out loud, Stephanie told her that humans had been thinking and feeling for hundreds of thousands of years, and they'd been writing those thoughts and feelings down for maybe six thousand, and how could anything she had to say be wiser than any of that? "Oh, but you're very wise," Amanda told her.

As spring drew to a close they studied together for their respective finals, which Stephanie passed with flying colors and which Amanda, who in her decision to *just be* had stopped caring so much about a thing as ephemeral as grades, passed too, but only with marks just above average.

Sometimes—and this surprised her whenever it happened—Amanda remembered the whipped cream on Stephanie's nose.

Amanda spent the summer at home, with her parents, while Stephanie went for six weeks to San Francisco to intern with a new literary magazine publisher that was beginning to gain national attention.

While Amanda's previous summers had been spent at home, they hadn't really been spent *at home*—she'd gone out most nights, with boys and old friends from high school, slept during the day and left again as soon as she woke up, but this summer she had little interest in any of that, little interest in what her old friends were doing, little belief that the people you meet in high school are really your friends at all, just other young people born, with no choice, in the same town as you were, placed, with no choice, in the same public education institution by virtue of geography. This summer she spent her days helping around the house and watching a lot of television. Her parents commented on these changes in her social life, asked her whether she was feeling okay, whether maybe she was down or depressed. "No," she told them, "I think I just grew up. I don't know when it happened, but it did."

The end of the six weeks came and Stephanie called to tell Amanda about all the exciting things happening in San Francisco. The city was a big deal: the publishers, the businesses, the people, the drugs, the food. The gays and lesbians. She was extending her trip for another two weeks, she said, so she could take a real vacation, without the internship, which, by the way, had gone splendidly, she might come back and join the publisher for good after next year, after she had her MFA.

And then, two weeks later, she was back, and she and Amanda were drinking coffee in the mornings again, discussing the idea of getting an apartment somewhere just off campus. And two weeks after that, they had one, Stephanie paying rent with money earned from articles she was writing, Amanda paying rent with money her parents gave her when she asked them if they would give her money, and they were moving their things in, and then they were staying up late the first few nights, drinking margaritas and laughing, and then it was September and they were awake early but at slightly different times, their schedules not quite in sync. Amanda might wake to the sound of the front door shutting. In the evening often she'd return home to find that Stephanie had already gone to bed, her bedroom door closed. Sometimes they'd both be home at midday, between classes, but Amanda had taken to napping, and when she woke, Stephanie would again be gone. Funny how you could have coffee with a person you hardly knew every day for months, but when you started living together you barely saw them.

"Hey, do you have any classes Thursday morning?" Stephanie asked one night as they sat miraculously in the living room together, Stephanie focused on a textbook, Amanda on a spiraled sketchpad.

"Yeah," Amanda said, "this stupid weather elective. I found out I needed one more elective credit this year—somehow I'd missed that— and I heard weather was easy, so I took it, but it turns out it's just stupid."

"Oh, well maybe you could skip it then."

"It's still a credit."

"Right," Stephanie said. "Well, anyway, there was just this thing I thought you might want to go to with me."

"Really?" Amanda said, a tinge of colored excitement rising within her. "What is it?"

"Well, I guess it's just this stupid thing—gotta love those stupid things, right—but I think it's going to be fun. It's just a . . . remember I told you about that *Star Trek* thing I go to sometimes."

"Yes . . ." Amanda said cautiously.

"Well, they're having a thing"—she saw the look on Amanda's face— "No no no. It's not that. I mean, yeah, it's the stupid *Star Trek* club, but the thing, it's like a party, for the space shuttle."

"The space shuttle?"

"Yeah, the space shuttle is launching on Thursday, after the last one blew up. It's like a big national thing, and they're having a live viewing, with food and stuff."

"Hmm," Amanda said.

"And so, well, the real reason I want you to go is there's this guy you might like . . ."

"A guy?"

"Yeah. He's one of the guys who runs the thing. But he's really not too nerdy. And he's kinda cute. Going to be some kind of doctor."

Doctor was good. At this, the beginning of her likely final year of higher education (grad school held little appeal for her—she'd been studying hard for three years now, had one year left, and didn't think she wanted to, like Stephanie, keep going), Amanda was thinking a lot about where her degree would take her, where she wanted it to take her. A Bachelor of Fine Arts is useful for so many things, they always said, which probably was just a way of saying it's useful for nothing. Amanda had only gone to college for the *adventure*, and she didn't have that anymore, didn't *want* that so much anymore. But if she dated a doctor . . . if she married a doctor . . . .

And so then here was this young man, Wallace Hauser, late for the shuttle launch, so late he'd missed it, bruised and sweaty, with scraped and bloody palms, but sincere in his bruisedness and his sweatiness. He was attractive in a normal way, which is not to say a conventional way—attractive because of his normality; his body was trim but not hard, not harsh in the way of most of the men she'd slept with; the body fit well the light-washed jeans and tucked-in t-shirts he wore, no belt; his hair was dry, a little brittle, but that meant when she touch it she wouldn't be afraid to then touch something else because of the grease on her hands; his glasses were like Stephanie's, and when he took them off you could tell his eyes weren't gray, but gray-blue. On the afternoon of their first date, at the Viking Market (from which Amanda would never purchase orange juice again), he showed up stubbled, tired; but on the evening of their second, dinner and a viewing of the new film *The Kiss*, he was fresh, aware, clean-shaven and even witty, and Amanda decided there, that night, while she ate a cheeseburger and he ate a double cheeseburger and they shared a basket of fries, that someday she might love him.

The next decade happened fast in the way all decades happen fast: the days go by one by one and then the next thing you know you're ten years closer to your last one.

Wallace and Amanda dated through the rest of 1988 and deep into the spring of '89. It wasn't until three months into their courtship that Amanda realized he was two years older than she was—she'd assumed, since they were both seniors, that they were the same age, not realizing he'd done two years of lab prep pre-university. It was in their relationship's sixth month she realized he was going to be a pharmacist, not a surgeon or a general practitioner or anything else about which she could tell her parents and rest assured they'd think it prestigious. Wallace laughed when he realized she was just now realizing. "Well surely you didn't think I was going to be some other kind of doctor," he said. "I mean I'm graduating with you in a month. If I was going to be a surgeon or something, it would take many more years of schooling, at least four. Surely you put two and two together. Surely you're smart enough for that."

Was she smart enough for that? She *hadn't* put the pieces together, was the thing. But did it actually matter whether she was that smart? Because, the way he had addressed her just then, it didn't seem like he thought she was, and at that she should take offense, she decided.

So they had their first fight, sixth months in, which, the fact that it had taken them that long to hurt each other's feelings probably meant they were doing pretty well, and they could make up quickly, resume their normal interaction. But Amanda had never been in a real fight before, and she was sure she was supposed to draw out situations like this, make him feel guilt or sorrow or disappointment with himself for having hurt her with his words. He bought her flowers and brought them to her apartment. She had Stephanie open the door, accept them wordlessly but glarefully on her behalf. He bought her more flowers, two days later, a bigger bouquet, and chocolates too—again these were accepted without comment, but by Stephanie herself this time, and she even let him try to apologize but made sure to close the door before he could complete his second sentence. One more time he tried: flowers, chocolates, tickets to see The Who in July. It was the tickets that did it, she told him after she, feigning hesitation, let him into the apartment. Really, she'd planned the whole time on accepting whatever third apology she knew he'd offer, satisfied that he'd been sufficiently chastised for his *insensitive remarks* about her intelligence, but what she told him was that the fact that he'd bought tickets for a concert in July, three months from now, gave her confidence that he truly believed they had a future together. "I do think we have a future together," he said. "I really really do. And I *am* going to be a doctor, you know, pharmacists have a doctorate degree." Stephanie wasn't home that night, so Wallace and Amanda made out on the couch for a while and then had sex for the first time.

They settled, then (*then* comprising the next twelve years of their lives, which happened vaguely and in explicit detail and slowly and all at once). They graduated, received their degrees, Wallace with a passable GPA, Amanda with a more passable one, They moved away from the university, into the suburbs, to Chagrin Falls where Amanda's parents lived, to an apartment just a few blocks from Amanda's parents. They got jobs. Amanda started working as a secretary for a small-claims law firm, which had assumed that her BFA made her qualified for writing legal documents, filing papers creatively, learning to use one of those personal computers that everyone was saying they really should start using soon, things like that. Wallace started working at a Sears distribution center: he needed a job like this, at first, so he could pay rent with Amanda and come up with the $500 he needed to take the North American Pharmacist Licensure Examination, which would give him license to practice. "Life's all about degrees and licenses," he said one early Sunday afternoon to Amanda's parents, who had just returned from church (having recently recommitted to their weekly habit; they would go every Sunday for the rest of their lives). "Ain't that the truth," Amanda said. "*Ain't* ain't a word," her father said, taking a pull from a pilsner.

There was the distinct possibility that Amanda's parents didn't like Wallace Hauser, didn't approve of something or some things about him, although they never vocalized any negative opinions. They bought or made the young couple a late lunch (after church) every Sunday, wrote them checks every few months, every time Amanda sheepishly told them they were having *just a little money trouble* and Wallace said, "Oh, it's nothing, really. We weren't even sure we should bring it up." They never said a negative word about the young couple's living situation, which for a time was certainly sinful, and when they did marry, Amanda's parents footed the bill.

(Amanda's parents would never meet their grandson, Eric Hauser. Amanda's father died from a stroke in 1997, her mother the following year from a cancer that started on her cervix and spread rapidly. Wallace held

Amanda in the hospital room on both occasions, experienced as he was with parental deaths.)

Wallace took the NAPLEX in '91, failed it the first time, struggled for more years to come up again with the $500 he'd need to retake it. Amanda moved on from the secretary position, said she needed to do something more creative with her life, you know? More *real*. And of course she had Wallace's full support, my dear, my love. So she converted a corner of their apartment to a painting nook, bought an easel and put a polyethylene drop cloth over the carpet, started doing what she was pretty sure now she was always meant to do—that is, to be an *artist*.

Each day Wallace woke at 5 a.m., showered and brushed his teeth, dressed and then ate breakfast. Some days he considered waiting until after breakfast to brush his teeth, but it was the way he'd been raised, to brush his teeth first thing in the morning, to clean them each night before bed and to clean them again each morning, damned be your tastebuds if you were going to drink coffee or orange juice with breakfast. After breakfast he poked his head into the bedroom, watched for a few moments Amanda still sleeping there, beautiful, her faux-satin-nightgowned chest rising and falling. As the years went on Amanda slept worse and worse at night, something to do with the drinking she did more and more in the evenings, the wines and, more often, the beers. Her waistline began to reflect this lack of sleep and abundance of drink, but only in a small, soft way, and Wallace didn't mind. They made love two or three times a week and he loved her, loved caring for her and being a man who cared for her, who worked hard even if he didn't like the work he was doing—because even if he didn't like the work, he loved what the existence of the work meant, what it said of him, as a person and a husband.

He moved boxes from warehouse to loading dock, from loading dock to truck. Sometimes from truck to truck, a mediator in the journey of appliances—lawnmowers, electric ranges, side-by-side refrigerators, leaf blowers and weed whackers, dishwashers and convection ovens—from manufacturer to consumers' American Dream–inspired homes. He returned to the apartment at 5 p.m. each day, found Amanda making dinner, a blank or (when she'd had a *good* day) sparsely painted easel in the corner. Some days being an artist was hard for her, Wallace knew. Some days the paints never made it out of their tubes. But one day he came home and she presented him with a lavender-colored flower; another day with something resembling a detailless sparrow; and another day the image of a woman, naked maybe, smeared in red and surrounded by pillows and detailless sparrows. "It's beautiful," he said. "What does it mean?"

She stared at the painting. "I'm not sure," she said finally. "It probably doesn't mean anything. I just wanted to paint a person. Anyway, I've had a stew simmering in the crockpot all day, if you're hungry."

Wallace was moved from his seven-to-four schedule to the nightshift. Cutbacks, the company said. They had to let people go, had to move some things around. Wallace was lucky he hadn't been one of the laid off, and the pay was better on the nightshift anyway, an extra fifty cents an hour.

In 1996 he took the NAPLEX one final time, but he was so far removed from pharmacy school now. (And he'd known somewhere deep inside that he'd never had the destiny of a doctor, even a doctor of pharmacy, never had that purpose. He knew it, and he knew Amanda knew it.) He failed the NAPLEX worse than the first time, but after he read the results he went into the bedroom, pulled a box from the closet, and from the box took his framed PharmD, hung it on the wall next to the collage of wedding photos. Because maybe that was the real value of his college experience: he'd met his wife there. Maybe that made all the student loan debts in the world worth never being able to pay them off.

In 1997, just after Amanda's father died, Wallace's superiors moved him to the day shift again, and they gave him a promotion, made him an administrator. With the promotion came a raise, an opportunity to save some money.

The next year—just after the death of Amanda's mother, from which they received an inheritance—they bought the house Eric Hauser would grow up in: a "cute" (Amanda said) two-bedroom one-story with the light-blue vinyl siding and new rain gutters and small green yards in the front and back. The PharmD and the wedding collage were moved to the new home and found their permanent place in the hallway that led from the kitchen and living room to the bathroom and two bedrooms. It was in this house that the couple was laying, in their queen-size bed, when Wallace turned to his wife and said, "Honey, I want us to start a family."

Amanda turned over from what may or may not have been sleep (she never read in bed, didn't have a nighttime ritual; she just, when the time came, went to sleep, swiftly but never deeply). She sat up, settled her back against the wooden headboard. "Okay," she said.

"Really?" The smile on Wallace's face was both hopeful and surprised, as if agreement wasn't what he'd been expecting.

"Yeah, of course, really." A smile sprouted on Amanda face, too, joining his in the queen-size bed.

"Oh—wonderful. Wonderful! Oh—I'm so ready, Amanda. I love you, and I can't wait to be a father."

They stayed up late that night, talking about their child. Boy or girl? What would he look like? Would she have Wallace's eyes—or Amanda's? Would he have his mother's hair—or his father's? And if his father's, for how long (for Wallace's hair had grown thin these last few years). Would their child be an artist, like her mother? Would their child be tall? Would their child be an athlete? Would their child be a doctor—a real one? Would their child be a star?

Eventually, Amanda turned onto her side, faced the wall, and Wallace took her from behind while she stared at that wall. It was a white wall. She memorized its texture, made note of every detail within a six-inch-by-six-inch segment.

Wallace finished, feeling satisfied, accomplished. He told Amanda: maybe that was the one. But she reminded him that she'd taken her pill that day, silly, so of course nothing had happened yet, inside her.

The real question was:

Would their child change the world?

5

FIVE MONTHS LATER, AFTER A long day at the distribution center, and after a lonely dinner of shells heated in a pot of boiling water to which he'd added two packets of what the package called "spray-dried cheddar cheese" (ingredients: whey, corn syrup solids, dry shortening, and various other things), and after a one-hour nap on this very couch, Wallace sat in the cold glow of the light that came from the muted television. On the screen, a rerun played (Season 6, Episode 22 "Suspicions"), and Doctor Beverly Crusher spoke to an enormous-eared alien, a look of concern on her lovely face. The images on the television reached Wallace's eyes, but they seemed to stop on the corneal surface; something—too much information, bouncing, moving, swirling?—was acting as a barrier, preventing them from passing through the shutters of the irises and entering his brain so he could make of them any sort of sense. Not that he was interested in that, making sense of images on a screen. There were other things for him to make sense of. Truths to lay bare. It was like he'd woken from his nap and turned on the TV but continued sleeping, dreaming. The whole thing was very meditative. His father used to behave this same way whenever he had "something very important to discuss with you, Wallace; I've been very disappointed in your recent behavior; I've heard some disturbing things," except that his father did it with the radio on, not the television.

Amanda would be home late tonight, and Wallace was waiting for her. She was home late often now, at least three nights a week. And at first he thought it was a great thing ("A really great thing!") that she was spending time out of the house at all, time that included more than grocery shopping or completing half-assed circuit workouts at the Curves that had opened six months ago and that all the women in town loved so much.

It had started a few weeks after they decided to have a baby. "I think I need to make some friends," Amanda had said. "If we're going to have a family—and, Wallace, I'm *so happy* we're going to have a family—then we should get to know other families. I want to know other mothers, other new mothers, and their kids and our kids can play together, you know? And besides, I really think my art will benefit from something like this, from a . . . a *community*, other artists, *people*. And—oh—I just don't know if painting is the right thing for me anyway. But *sculpting* . . . I think sculpting is what I was meant for, sculpting and motherhood, and this will help me be better at both." And Wallace hadn't seen why not. It wasn't cheap, the beginner sculpting class, but they certainly could make room for it in their budget now. And besides, he could see happiness in Amanda's face as she spoke—or rather *hopefulness*. Of course, it wasn't like she'd ever seemed *un*happy these last ten years, but to see her actively joyful at the thought of her present *and* her future made his heart smile.

"I'll be home late tomorrow," she said one Monday morning. She'd started waking up earlier, ever since they decided to have a baby, even sometimes hopping in the shower with him, where they tried to kill two birds with one stone. "So I'm making extra dinner tonight and you can just heat it up in the oven when you get home from work."

"Okay," he said, kissing her on the forehead. "What's up, though?"

"Oh—well. So some of the girls from the class just invited me out for drinks after, and I thought it'd be nice to go." She saw the look on his face. "Well of course I'm not going to actually drink *alcohol*, though, not while we're *trying*. But I can still enjoy their company."

"That's great," he said. "Oh—that's great! I'm so glad you're making some friends. Maybe sometime we can all go out together."

"Yeah. Yeah, maybe. Definitely."

"How's the sculpture coming along? You know I'm eager to see this secret piece you've been working on."

"It's going well. Really well. I'll show it to you soon. I promise."

The next evening he reheated meatloaf, kissed his wife when she finally came home at 8 o'clock, and together they watched TV before getting into bed and trying to make a baby. That Thursday she came home late too, also around eight. A couple nights the next week she was home at more like 8:30. And in the weeks after that sometimes as late as nine or ten. Sometimes he went to bed without her and woke up with her peaceful body next to his. Sometimes she started sleeping late again.

Now, as he sat in the glow of the screen (this television, by the way, they hadn't purchased themselves but had inherited from Amanda's parents), he heard the borborygmus of a car in the driveway (Wallace had started trying to learn *one new word a day*), heard the silence that followed the engine being turned off. Heard the driver-side door open and close. He pressed the power button on the television remote and immersed himself in darkness. Footsteps coming up the walkway. Heels. The creek of the front door whose hinge he'd been meaning to WD-40. He heard the rustle of Amanda's coat. The sounds louder now that she was in the house. He could feel her. He heard the clunk-clunk of her removing her shoes and dropping them to the floor from too great a hight. His eyes were still adjusting to the darkness, but he could see the shadowy figure of her near the coat hook, hanging on the wall the long black wool trenchcoat she'd purchased at the thrift store. He was barely breathing, not because he didn't want her to hear him—he wanted her to know he was here, *needed* her to know—but because this didn't feel like the sort of situation during which one breathed.

The scrape of a hand groping the wall for the light switch. And the whole room now bathed in unnatural lambency (yesterday's word).

"Oh. Oh! Hey . . . Wallace. I didn't see you there. . . . What *are* you doing sitting in the dark like that? What time *is* it?"

"Sit down," Wallace said.

"Well, and I was just going to get ready for bed. I'm kind of tired—"

"Sit down. We need to talk."

He hadn't looked at her. His gaze was transfixed on the black screen of the television. She moved to join him on the couch, seemed to rethink that and moved back, still standing.

"How was your class?" he asked her. His chest didn't move. His throat didn't move. His lips seemed to not move either. He didn't care whether she sat or not.

"I didn't have a class tonight," she said. "I was just out with some of the ladies."

"Who with?" Part of him wanted to say *with whom*, just to drive some undefinable point home.

"With—with Eloisa—and Jasmine—and Harmony."

These were all names he'd heard from her before. He held up the object he'd been griping in his right hand since he'd finished dinner. "I found this," he said. "I found it two days ago on the bathroom floor. I guess maybe it fell out of your purse or something."

The object was a condom wrapper, forest green and torn so that one full third of it dangled from the other two thirds, revealing the silver of its empty, guilty insides. Typgrophed across the larger of the two torn portions: TROJ. And across the smaller: AN.

Amanda stood next to the entertainment center. The entertainment center was almost as tall as she was, a large square collaboration of various shelves and doors and hinges with a nook made for a television far bigger than the one Wallace and Amanda owned; a piece of wood at the base of it had broken off long ago, long before they bought the thing at a summer garage sale, bought pizza for one of Wallace's coworkers who owned a pickup truck so they could get it back to the house. Amanda stood next to this piece of furniture, said nothing, didn't even look like she was *trying* to say anything, or trying to think, or trying to be anything more than an object of a piece with the living room's uninspired decor.

"So—and I'm guessing," Wallace said, "I'm *guessing*—that this doesn't belong to us. I mean, it belongs to you, I'm sure, but it doesn't belong to *me*. And thus by extension it doesn't belong to *us*, does it? Do you follow my logic here? Am I correct in coming to certain conclusions? On account of the fact you and I are trying to have a baby and thus *have no need for condoms*."

The statue came vaguely alive. "Wallace, I—"

"Yes?"

"I—"

"*Yes?*"

"I'm so sorry."

"So there is no denial, then? This apology I should take as an admission of guilt, yes? Yes?"

"Yes."

"So I'm at work and you're doing what? Who, rather. You're doing who? Whom? And where?"

"Wallace," Amanda said. She decided now that maybe there was wisdom in sitting. She moved to the armchair by the window and it creaked, rocked, as she sank stiffly into it. "I swear I wasn't trying to hurt you. I swear things just kind of happened. I mean, they happened in a deliberate way, I guess, but I wasn't thinking about *you*. I needed this for me."

"Those were questions, by the way. And they weren't rhetorical."

"What—? Oh. Oh, Wallace, please."

"Was it here? Did you ever do it here?"

"No, never. I swear."

"And who was he?"

"They," she said after a time.

Wallace looked at her for the first time. "They," he said. "Who were they?"

She couldn't bear the looking. She turned her eyes away. "No one. Literally. I never learned their names."

"How many?"

"I—"

"*How many?*"

"Five. I don't know. Maybe seven. Eight."

Wallace nodded. For several minutes he remained there on the sofa. Amanda tried to speak, but she had no words. She'd spent so much time conceiving lies, contingencies for nights when lust got the better of her and she knew she'd be home late—but she'd come up with nothing for the eventuality of getting caught. Getting caught hadn't even occurred to her. Before, a decade ago, when she was this person she again found herself to be now, there had been no *getting caught*. Why should there be now?

"I suppose that's all I needed to know," Wallace said finally. He rose. "I'm going to bed, and in the morning I'm going to go to work. Do what you want. Come sleep next to me, even, if you'd like. But don't speak to me, not until I chose to speak to you again first—if I ever do. There are dirty dishes in the sink. Good night."

Once he was gone, Amanda pulled the handle on the side of the chair, released the footrest, and pushed back with her weight, reclining. She had no qualms against providing comfort for herself, even now. She would not punish herself for her sins, for there *were* no sins, she'd decided long ago, and self-flagellation was the way of people like her parents, who would rather beat their bodies in retribution here on Earth than risk eternal damnation in a hell somewhere beyond this, the only observable world. There *were* no sins, and at some point Amanda had forgotten this. By graduating and marrying and moving into a life of stability, she'd forgotten this. By staying home while her husband each day moved boxes and supervised subordinates in moving boxes, she'd forgotten this. By staring at a blank white easel and holding a brush and almost never opening a single tube of paint and hating the time she wasted like that (she'd never tell Wallace that most days she just stared at the easel, TV off, radio off, cerebral cortex off, pituitary gland off), she'd forgotten this. But when she'd decided to get pregnant, when she'd stopped taking that little capsule of estrogen and progestogen, when she realized she was fertile again, she remembered.

And she *had* wanted to get pregnant, too, when they'd decided. She still did. She wanted to be the mother of Wallace's child, to raise a human with him, to have that impact on a life, on the world. Her recent promiscuity was not in opposition to that—she'd been careful, used protection every time she was with another man (and last time, apparently, she'd taken the wrapper for that protection and put it in her purse rather than a garbage can and it had fallen out here in her own home—so what? —so *what?*). Plus (and this she'd never tell Wallace, either), men were only half the object of her rediscovered desire. Eloisa and Jasmine and Harmony were real people, and to their credit they looked not unlike Stephanie, the grad student from so long ago. The grad student who Amanda hadn't talked to since probably '92, and whom she every few weeks thought *I should give her a call.* What it all boiled down to was self-esteem. Amanda had, contrary to popular theory, *more* self-esteem when she was sleeping with a lot of people. More self-esteem when she was uninhibited, when she was free to *be.*

She fell asleep in the chair, sad, but not guilty. Wondering where she and Wallace were to go from here, but not worried.

She was woken some hours later by the encroachment of a terrible pain. Like menstrual cramps, but sharper, and then the cramps were joined by another pain, duller but nevertheless agonizing, lower in her abdominal walls. She pushed the footrest in, leaned forward, and fell to the floor. She hadn't pushed the footrest all the way—she was suddenly no longer strong—and it sprung forward again with a twang, a clang, and slammed into her behind, pushing her forward so that her face hit the carpet. The two pains inside her made it impossible for her to stand. She placed a hand far in front of her, tried to dig her fingers into the carpet and pull, and she made progress, moved forward a few inches. The other arm now, stretched way out, pulling. She moved a few more inches, her gut both on fire and the recipient of endless phantom blows. She felt her consciousness slipping away again, but it was different from falling asleep; it was far more worrisome, if she was being honest with herself, which, she was having the epiphany, she really needed to develop a more regular habit of doing.

Zoomers I

1

HE STOOD ON THE SUMMIT of something bigger than himself.

"Are you kidding me? That's ridiculous," the woman said, laughing, her vaguely Greek features dark and shadowed but obviously beautiful there in the lights of the bar in Kathmandu. The Electric Pagoda—was the bar's name.

Of course it was ridiculous; that was the point. It was supposed to be a sort of poetic gesture, the symbolism obvious, a bridge between the past and the future. Eric Hauser smiled as he took another sip of his large club soda with lime. He'd had a rum and something already, to take the edge off, but it was all he planned on drinking tonight. He had work to do, tasks to prepare for, and it wouldn't do to wake dehydrated or even remotely hungover. In fact, it probably wouldn't do to wake up hungover again for the rest of his life. He was *great* now, and if he was going to pass, in time, from great to *elite*, from elite to *legend*, from legend to *mythical*, he'd need to make more deliberate choices. "How do you mean, ridiculous?" he asked anyway, not quite batting his eyelashes at her.

"Oh, come on. It's cheesy as fuck."

He shrugged.

"You're all, 'I've just reached the summit of something big, but there's another summit out there, past the horizon,' and you say this as you're obviously preparing to climb the tallest mountain in the world, but and of course you also mean it in a different way. Like, you've just sold a

very successful technology startup, making who knows how much money
—"

"Eleven billion."

"Eleven *billion*?"

"Well, rounding down, but roughly."

"Eleven billion. *Billion*. But that certainly won't be enough for a man like you, and you have something else up your sleeve for the not-too-distant future. Another summit just beyond the horizon."

Eric continued to smile. His various smiles would be part of the myth—he had different kinds of smiles, and each possessed certain powers. The one he was putting on tonight was for making others feel good about themselves. "When you put it like that . . ." he said.

Two weeks ago, Eric Hauser and his reluctant cofounder had sold Bio Odyssey, the company they'd started a decade ago, during the COVID-19 pandemic, and all its assets to a multinational medical research conglomerate that was working on the one-vaccine-to-inoculate-against-them-all, the only stipulation being that certain software patents remain the sole property of Eric himself, because he had further plans for them that didn't involve the medical field. So the conglomerate got the hardware—the scanners, the wearables—but the intelligence that powered them, that ran the calculations and processed the data, remained his to develop and apply to other scenarios, but he would license them to the conglomerate. He'd considered open-sourcing the patents, so that any company could use them, improve upon them, however they pleased, but in the end it made more sense to retain control—well, if not more sense, it at least gave him more *power*. As part of the deal, he would continue to serve on Bio Odyssey's board and make applicable improvements to the software, almost as a courtesy, a side project while he focused on bigger things.

"Okay, but here's something I don't get—" said the woman.

"What's your name?" Eric interrupted.

"Pricilla."

"That's not one you hear so often, is it?"

"No," she said. "Not anymore."

"So what don't you get, Pricilla? And can I buy you another drink?"

"Yes, thank you, another drink would be lovely."

He signaled their waiter, pointed to Pricilla's glass, raised one finger, acknowledged the waiter's nod with the kind of smile he'd been giving Pricilla, but a slightly modified version for people he wasn't hoping to sleep with later.

"So here's what I don't understand . . ."

"Yes?"

"Everest is the tallest mountain in the world . . ."

"Yes."

"And Everest is a metaphor . . ."

He raised both hands, showed both palms. "I've copped to that."

"But you're *so young*."

"I'm thirty."

"Thirty—? I thought you were even younger."

"Clean living. How old are you? Twenty-eight, twenty-nine?" This was called negging. Eric had learned it from a book when he was a teenager.

"Twenty-two."

"So that's eight years. Eight years is nothing, especially when you consider a generation like ours is likely to live to one-fifty, easy. Eight years is hardly an age gap."

"One-fifty?"

"I'm reasonably confident."

"Well—I don't know about that. But, okay, so. You're going to climb Everest now—"

"It'll still be a few days before I start the ascent."

"You're something of a smart ass."

Palms exposed again. "Guilty."

"You're going to climb Everest at thirty, is my point. So then what? After Everest? After the next big dream?"

The waiter arrived, set the new drink on the table, blushed just perceptibly in the darkness as Eric winked at him before he walked away. "Pricilla," Eric said, "there are always more peaks. Everest isn't even the largest summit in our solar system."

She was right, of course. He *was* "so young." He *was* "only thirty." If you asked the liberals they'd tell you no one had the right to so much money, young or old. It didn't matter, you could almost hear them saying, that he'd earned it, that he'd done exceptional things to get it, things that no one else had been able to do. Analysts were saying he'd been overpaid for his tech, that Bio Odyssey had been worth far less than what it had sold for, that something started and built by a couple kids in a janitor's closet couldn't possibly be that good. And you couldn't exactly blame them for that: people trust only what they've seen, what they've used, and the stuff Bio Odyssey had done wasn't very consumer-facing, except for the wearables, which even then were undervalued by most consumers. Even the conservatives were skeptical. "How is this different from, say, an Apple Watch?" some Fox News former-judge bimbo had asked just four days ago. "It's not, even," said one of her panelists, "it's more like a FitBit or something like that, and that company only sold for two billion, not twenty." "Right. You're right!" the bimbo had replied. "I mean I like my FitBit, don't get me wrong. It tells me how many steps I walk each day. But come on." Of course, what Eric had created did far more than that, *far* more, but he'd learned quickly that the average consumer or cable news host cared little for the personal insights that came with quantifying one's self. "Well anyway," the Fox News host had continued, "he's probably going to spend all that money on cars and booze and women anyway, throw it all down the drain fast." And then they'd laughed and laughed.

But the truth was Eric hadn't spent any of the money yet, save for what it cost him to get here and start purchasing equipment and hire the services of an experienced sherpa. He probably would buy a car when he got back, or maybe a couple—a Tesla and something else, maybe—and a nice house or at least a good apartment, and some good scotch, but surely the talking heads knew that things like that cost far less than eleven billion dollars. He'd made the mistake of calling them talking heads when asked for comment the next day outside the home of a movie star who was throwing a birthday party to which he'd been invited. "They're just a bunch of talking heads," he'd said, "and when I'm done with the projects I have up my sleeves, they'll *literally* just be a bunch of talking heads." Which, well fuck, when he thought about it, was not the most eloquent thing he'd ever said—he'd been nervous about the party, he hadn't met many famous people before, let alone been invited to their birthday parties (no matter how valuable your company, medical tech didn't tend to make you flashy friends), and he wasn't sure whether the present he'd brought was any good. When the remarks were published he next day, reporters, including those Fox News talking heads, said they sounded awfully threatening. Maybe Eric should be investigated for criminal activity, they said. Of course what those idiots didn't know, and what he really couldn't have been more clear about without revealing too much of his plans too soon, was that he was talking about *holography*.

At least he hadn't called them bimbos.

Eric didn't *really* think the talking heads at Fox News, or at any other national or international media outlet, were bimbos. While he had a strong dislike for the institution of journalism, especially American journalism, he understood its necessity in any sort of enlightened world, and he understood that the people behind the cameras were just that: people, people trying to do a job, and sometimes even people who cared about the job they were doing (although the ones who cared tended to not work for certain outlets, opting instead to start their own independent publications—blogs, podcasts, Substacks, YouTube channels, if you could call a those last two independent). Eric needed the journalists, because even in a world of 280-character social media posts and pictures viewed on palm-held screens and sometimes even screens smaller than your wrist, and video/image amalgamations that supposedly dissipated into a digital ether (but were in most cases actually captured and recorded by fanatical devotees on TikTok to be viewed on demand and shared and reshared by other fanatical devotees—often teenagers, who should have been sleeping or doing homework but just couldn't sleep, mom, kids don't sleep anymore), stories needed, sometimes, to be shaped, to be *told*.

Eric woke when his 6 a.m. alarm tapped against his wrist. He flicked his hand as if there was a bug atop the fascia over his *adductor pollicis* and he was trying to get it off without harming it, and the gentle tapping stopped. It was dark in the joyless hotel room—the sun wouldn't rise for another twenty minutes in Katmandu, according to his watch's solar complication. Eric was naked and alone under the hotel room's downy comforter. He'd gone to bed naked and alone. He always went to bed naked, and he often went to bed alone, but almost always only because he wanted to. To choose aloneness was a great privilege, and he'd learned to take advantage of it in his late teens. Some people—his parents came to mind—didn't get to choose to be alone, because they'd made choices long ago that superseded any opportunities life might present them with later. Marrying each other, for example, had been one of those choices. Adopting Eric, another.

Of course, just because aloneness was a virtue didn't mean it was virtuous to choose it *all* the time. There were benefits in company. Pleasures in conversation and physical distraction. Eric had gone back to Pricilla's room last night, at her invitation (he'd known early on in their conversation that the invitation would be forthcoming), careful to have observed that she'd had only the two drinks, because a third and he would have had to consider her inebriated, and therefore unable to consent to anything he might do with her in her room, and not only was consent, as they say, sexy, but sleeping with drunk strangers who knew you were famous or about to become famous was the sort of thing that got people like him into all sorts of public trouble. Hell, it happened even to the non-famous—it happened to a guy at a high school not far from his, in a case that became nationally talked about, reported not on just social media but in traditional media, with daily updates on the trial in the *New York Times* and *USA Today*, a retrospective profile of the victim and the accused published in the *New Yorker* a year later (all of which publications still had, almost miraculously, dead-tree editions with millions of subscribers). Eric would not let his next venture go the way of American Apparel before it was even founded.

Pricilla was, to be sure, unexpected. She'd found him while he was eating dinner last night. Dinner was pork chops and red potatoes. "Excuse me," she'd said, "I'm really sorry to disturb you, but"—and here when Eric looked up he saw embarrassment on her face, nervousness that even the most untrained kinesicist could tell was feigned—"did you make this?"

She was pointing to her wrist. Eric smiled a full-mouthed smile and made a show of chewing the bite he'd just taken, sipping from a wine glass half-full of water, and then dabbing at his lips with a paper napkin. He leaned forward, as if to examine what she was showing him more closely. "I did not," he said finally.

Her timid expression fell, replaced for less than a second with a more serious discomfiture, before returning. "Oh, well . . ." she said. "My mistake, I guess. . ." And she turned to leave.

"Hey there, wait a moment," Eric said, standing. She turned back to him, surprised to see him now as her equal (he was thin, but not particularly tall). He gestured to her wrist, which she still held just below breast level. "May I?"

She assented by holding her hand out to him. He took it, subtly massaged the pads of her palm while he spoke. "This," he said, "is from a different company." Then he held his own arm aloft. "This, here, is what I made."

He'd then asked her to join him for a drink at a taller table near the bar.

"But what about your dinner?"

"I've eaten enough," he said. "The pork chops were tough anyway. I mean, what, they can't get good pork in the Himalayas?"

So they'd moved to the table and he'd bought her a drink plus one for himself, and they'd talked. Flirted, mostly. He'd found little of substance in the conversation she had to offer, besides maybe those things she'd said near the end about his age.

From that table they'd moved to the nearby hotel, where they were both staying.

"Let's go back to your room," she'd said suggestively, playing up a tipsiness he knew for a fact was barely there (he'd held her hands across the table several times during the conversation, and he'd slyly checked the blood alcohol readout on her wearable). But he wasn't particularly interested in spending more than a little time with her, so he'd suggested her room instead. "Mine is rather spartan," he'd said. "I wanted to forgo those sort of luxuries on a trip like this—no hotels on the mountain, right?—but I'm afraid that means the bed is terribly uncomfortable."

In her room he'd kissed her neck, inhaled the aura of her hair and told her how heavenly her shampoo smelled, tasted her breasts, tweaked just tightly enough her nipples with his fingertips, genuflected there on the bed and played his lips and tongue between her legs, giving her whatever she wanted. When they realized neither of them had condoms, she insisted it was okay, and condoms probably didn't work at 4,200 feet anyway, don't you think? But he said of course they do and it's okay, I don't mind doing just this, I like it. And he'd gone down on her for a while longer and then finally she did the same for him. When they were done, he lay with her on the bed. "That was great," she said.

"You're welcome," Eric replied. And then he added, as an afterthought, "Thank *you*. For what you did. I enjoyed it." Eric took a certain pleasure in getting women off; hearing a woman moan or say his name in response to the movements of his fingers or his tongue or his dick reinforced for his subconscious that he was good at many things, and that not only was he good, he was also better than most. This need to be good at things was seventy-five percent of the reason why, twelve years ago when he'd grown frustrated with his still-present virginity, he'd hired an escort in Paris who let him practice on her, providing feedback and criticism where needed, for several weeks in a row, before finally he made a commitment to going out and getting laid in the real word on the regular.

He lay with Pricilla for a few minutes before getting up, using her restroom, and putting his clothes back on.

"You can stay here tonight," she said, watching him.

"None of those sort of luxuries for me, remember?" he said. It was a good line—if riddled with plot holes—better, *kinder*, than saying *I want to be alone*. And she bought it, or so it seemed.

So now here he was on a nineteen-passenger red-and-white-painted loudly propelled Dornier Do 228 approaching Lukla, the small town at 9,000 feet from which he would begin the two-day trip to the even smaller village of Namche Bazaar. From Namche Bazaar he would begin the slow ascent up the mountain.

Below, Eric could see the town and its colors, its blues and greens— its aquas. Over there was the Yeti Mountain Home Lodge, where he'd be staying tonight and tomorrow; the best reviewed of the several tourist lodges in the popular way station (technically, the Buddha Lounge had a better star average, but that was based on far fewer reviews); its properties were also the most expensive, but the expense didn't matter, first because even most people who *weren't* billionaires could afford the lodge's prices after the conversion from the Nepalese rupee to the American dollar, and second, because despite what he'd told the pleasant diversion Pricilla, he was damn-well going to splurge for luxury in the nights before such a difficult and long ascent—he would sleep in a soft warm bed and eat western food under soft warm lights.

Most of the buildings in Lukla were arranged in a sort of comet, with the airport and what one wouldn't dare call a downtown composing the nucleus and comma, and the others, each rectangular and blue-roofed and at most three stories tall, making up the tail of dusty particles that trailed behind. Those particles might have been ice, not dust, if Eric weren't making his climb in July—but it *was* July, and he *was* climbing, despite (or because of) the fact that Nepal in the summer is a hotbed of monsoons and other disastrous storms. Above the comet, the Himalayas; below it, what almost looked like farms, cropless, dotted with houses and shacks. Was that a soccer field? Lukla means "city with many goats and sheep," but there were no livestock that Eric could see.

Here now was the airport, the Tenzing-Hillary, the most dangerous airport in the world. Down the little plane went. Eric's stomach dropped onto his bladder. The danger was in the tarmac's gradient, which was a tricky 11.7 degrees. Thirty-three people had died here, nearly ten percent as many as had so far died climbing Everest itself. Ten aircraft had been lost. Eric memorized facts and figures like these. He memorized almost everything. One of his gifts was that he couldn't *not* remember.

The landing was smooth, quiet. Everyone around Eric let go of the proverbial held breath. Eric closed his eyes and thought about how, when this trip was over, he might go about fitting thousands of laser emitters into a small device and how he might compensate for movement in the intersection of so many plane waves. Of course he couldn't do all this himself—he'd need a talented team, just like he'd had at Bio Odyssey, people to challenge him and provide experience he couldn't and carry out the minutiae that if he tried to do himself would take too long—but still *he* had to be The Engineer.

Eric opened his eyes. And then the Do 28 made a right turn off the runway and into a lot where three other planes and one one helicopter were sardined. As it rolled in, another Do 28 rolled out, wings barely failing to graze wings as the second went by the first and took its place on the runway. Through the ovoid window, Eric watched the second plane accelerate down the 500-meter runway, at the end just in time pulling up and into the air and then disappearing southward.

They deplaned, Eric and the other passengers. Down a short flight of stairs that two men with heavy mustaches had rolled up to the plane's door. Now the two men with mustaches had the plane's storage compartments open, loading bags onto a pushcart. Winds hit Eric hard. He checked the device on his wrist: no signal here (not that he wanted messages or emails right now anyway), just the local time (3:33 p.m.), the local temperature (28.2°C/82.76°F—warmer than one imagines when they think of the Himalayas, but there is summer here, although temperatures would be well below freezing on the mountain), and a pre-programmed text encouragement from himself to "kick ass today!"

Today and every day. There was no other way to live.

Eric followed the small group into the building, through the airport's only terminal and into the concourse. When he'd flown from the U.S. into Kathmandu one week ago, he had stepped into a line, shown his papers, been asked for what purpose he was visiting Nepal. Some variation of climbing or hiking was the answer given by almost everyone in that line, although some better men and women were their with earthquake relief efforts or Doctors Without Boarders. But anyone who'd made it this far, to Lukla, you could be sure, was here for the mountain.

Which is why what happened while Eric was picking up his bags (one small travel suitcase and one enormous mountaineer's rucksack at this point half-full with many of the supplies he'd need for his expedition) came as something of a surprise: A familiar woman's voice said, with a cheerful exclamation point, "Eric!"

Eric hefted the rucksack from the luggage counter (no carousel here) and set it on the ground as he turned. There was Pricilla, her own rucksack beside her feet reaching up to her waist. "Oh—hey. What are you doing here?" he asked

Pricilla smiled like she knew something he didn't, some precious secret she wasn't telling. "I'm on this next expedition. What did you *think* I was doing in Katmandu?"

Of course. How had he not discerned that? How had he not even considered the possibility? Sure, she was young and white and American, but had he really thought she was young and white and American enough to be taking precious time off from whatever occupied her back in the states only to serve others? No. No—she was like him, he realized now.

"You know," she said as they walked along the concourse after a brief not-quite-awkward exchange revealed that they were staying at the same lodge for the next few days before the expedition departed for Base Camp, "you wouldn't be so surprised to see me here if you'd just asked questions during dinner last night, asked about *me*."

"You're right," Eric offered. "You'll have to forgive me. I often find it difficult to remember to care about other people."

"I see."

"No. I mean—" He realized how that sounded bad. "What I mean is —"

"I get it," she said. "I do. It's like you *care*, right, about people, or humanity or however exactly you want to label it, but a single person is a little more difficult. Am I right?"

"I think that's an accurate way of putting it."

She grinned. "Well then don't worry, because I get it. But what say you practice these next few days? You can get to know me more, if you like. Maybe even better than you did last night. They've got to have condoms for purchase somewhere in Lukla, right?"

They stepped together through the concourse doors. Outside the airport were cloudless blue Nepalese skies.

2

HERE WE HAVE ERIC W. Hauser, now thirty-four years old, pushing through the crowd, not with his hands or his shoulders or some other part of his tuxedoed body, but with the psychic aura it's taken him a decade to develop so that he can control everyone who stands between him and his set destination—which this evening is the president of the United States. As he moves through the cliques of insufferable individuals, Eric sizes up each of them and wonders who they slept with to get here, or are they here on the merits of their work, like he is, which is unlikely in many of their cases. For decades a repeated criticism of this event each year has been that the guest list grows ever more Hollywood, and in recent years that it grows more Silicon Valley, a blanket term still often used even though most of the world's prestigious tech companies are now located nowhere near California, having migrated to Austin and Seattle and and even Detroit—and of course China, don't forget China, how could you ever forget China.

Anyway, painting a picture of the room, of the people, as Eric moves through them:

There's the founder of InfoBrain, Carl Sigwell, who worked at Microsoft as a junior and then senior programmer for four decades before becoming one of many executive vice presidents (Microsoft Cloud and Enterprise Group) and cozying up to Nadella himself and convincing him to let him take charge of a project focused on developing the world's most advanced interactive information retrieval artificial intelligence and then one day leaving, citing "differences," and taking the project's whole team with him, the team knowing something nobody else did, some key to the understanding of the AI, of making it work, that no one else could replicate (said AI had yet to materialize). "Hey, Eric! Good to see you. Big night, eh? I hear you and the big lady have it in for each other. You're going to rip into her, that's what I hear, let her have it, no holds barred, is how the rumors have it."

"Haha. Yes, well, that's the tradition, but no spoilers."

Handshake.

To the side of the room, drinking a glass of pink champagne and staring at the HoloPhone in her hand, the sketch comedian Francine Scheinberg. "Eric Hauser? Eric Hauser! Oh my god, it's Eric Hauser. I use your thing like everyday. I have it right here! Like just a few hours ago I was Zooming with my mom and she was like, right *there*, in the hotel room, right there on the desk, all tiny but still *there*. What hotel are you at, by the way? Probably here, aren't you? Not me, oh God. Do you know how hard it is to get a room at the Hilton during this thing? It's like, hello, what's everyone here for, y'all never meet the president before? Oh—but seriously, I love what you've created. I *love* it."

"Thank you, Miss Scheinber."

Giggling. "Please, it's Francine. Miss Scheinber is the overbearing mother I was Zooming with."

"Ha,"—it's *funny*, she's *funny*—"And I love the show, so thank you for that. I watch the clips on YouTube all the time."

Her phone out, his hand around for a second almost her waist but then up higher at a more *appropriate* level, fingers careful not to touch her revealed sideboob but also not so far away from it as to appear afraid; hers around his shoulder, her other hand's forefinger pointing at him and her mouth agape like *Oh my god!* and a photo snapped, filtered, uploaded.

A peeve of Eric is this propensity of consumers to call any video call a "Zoom" no matter what call software was being used. He loathed hearing the misnomer used in reference to his own holography software.

Over here, look: It's the current head of Intel, Aabid Mustafa. They never let up, do they? Intel. Always ahead of the competition, no one else making chips as advanced or as fast as they do. Except Apple, who's actually lightyears ahead, but their chips are proprietary, no licensing for the M21x; that's going be their downfall, or the reason for their everlasting survival, depends on who you ask, but in any case you don't see Tim Cook here tonight, do you? Probably because Apple never pivoted into holograms.

Mustafa talking to Miley Cyrus, who is clothed what these days might pass for conservatively: green dress, the back shoulder-blade high, the neckline resting right at the suprasternal notch, accentuating in a way the longness of her neck, tattoos visible, including that new one everyone was talking about a few weeks ago. Mustafa saying something to her about the album she released earlier this year—and now making a joke (oh, god, is he really? Aabid you son of bitch, why must you always put your foot so far inside your mouth?) about the sex toy line she just announced, something about *well if you need any models for the moldings, any anatomical references*. . . . Miley grinning through teeth, turning away, wishing, probably, that they allowed smoking in here (not tobacco—who *does that* anymore?) or at least vaping. Best if Eric turns away now too, so that he doesn't bump into her, so they aren't forced to talk, to say hello, to exchange niceties. Things are, to put it mildly, still awkward between them, wounds still fresh, his fault more than hers, and while in most situations like this one he might make with a witty quip, a firm but gently flippant hello, or even an *I've missed you, let's do lunch, show the public we're still friends*, in this case, well . . . very much his fault.

Miley tapping on the shoulder of the actress and model Sophia Velasquez, who smiles and hugs her.

Eric now, his psychic powers weakened, turning his head left and right, in search of someone at whom to direct his attention. There's one. "Elon, it's a pleasure to see you. They told me you might be here."

"Haha. Yes, well, they asked me to give the keynote, you know, before they asked you."

"I may have heard something about that."

"Of course, I said no. You know me, not much of a public speaker."

"Of course."

"But then the president called and asked."

"Yes, well."

"But even then I said no. Said I'd be here, but I'm not much for public speaking. I'm okay in interviews—actually, I'm very good in interviews—but I don't exactly have the time to write something like a Whitehouse Corespondents keynote."

"No, of course not. Very busy, with the Mars and the energy revolution and the tweeting."

"Which you've been very diligent in implementing, by the way—the recommended energy strategies, I mean, not the tweets—that the president and I came up with."

"Sustainable energy is important. Even just a five-minute two-way holographic communique takes a ton of power, you know."

"Indeed. One might say the incredible things you've created at Lumina wouldn't have been possible, from a basic consumer standpoint, anyway, even just, oh, say, fifteen years ago."

"I agree. You paved the way. Just as your company's namesake pioneered everything you've ever done."

"And what a good name it is, right?"

"It's a tad unoriginal, but I guess it's okay."

Musk's lips curling smartly, his eyes twinkling a challenge. Eric matching microexpression for microexpression; from a challenge he is not one to back down, not one to fight for the sake of fighting, but unwilling to compromise in anything, and unable to give even a millimeter where honor is concerned (or where a device's aesthetic integrity is concerned, for that matter—seriously, ask the HoloPhone's battery team).

Musk cracking. Grinning. Laughing. Guffawing, even. "Ha! Ha ha ha."

Eric laughing too. Both men enveloping one another in an almost brotherly hug, the egotistic banter they engage in at the beginning of nearly every meeting having played its course.

Musk: "But seriously, after I told the WHCA I didn't want to do it—"

"You recommended me. I know; they told me. Thank you, of course."

"It's actually kind of stupid, when you think about it, that they even asked us at all, or that they ask anyone they ask each year. Logically, an organization of journalists, many of whom are accomplished public speakers, hosting an event that's theoretically about journalism, should have one of their own give the keynote."

"But of course there's no logic in journalism. Surely you know this. Besides, these things are supposed to be funny, and these old-school journalists can't joke their way out of an electro-photonic low-res data screen."

"Indeed. Indeed. Anyway, I have an idea for integrating your holo tech into the Model S's dash and heads-up display. Exclusive contract and all that. I've done the calculations, and it would improve efficiency, safety, and customer satisfaction fifty-two percent—that's an aggregated percentage of the three, of course. Plus I was thinking we do something with the phone itself, like integrate it into the dash if the driver owns one. Can I call you next week?"

"Elon, you can call me any time you want. But, yeah, I'll have our assistants set something up. Oh, in fact, I'm going to have my people send you something special for your office; I'll have someone bring it down personally, set it up. And *then* we can have our call."

"Holophone 2.0? Already?"

"Not exactly."

"Better?"

"Way better. But not even remotely viable for the consumer market yet. Maybe we can make that happen together."

"I look forward to that."

Another hug.

Eric exhausted by the flattery and banter. Of course he didn't need, or want, Musk's help. He was going to do it all himself.

On Eric's left, a woman in a white shirt, black bow tie, carrying a tray with bubbly little flutes. Just one before the keynote won't do any harm, right? Relax the nerves. Elon doesn't like public speaking? Well Eric Hauser downright *hates* it. Despises it. But does it often because visibility is everything in marketing. Visibility is everything in being seen. There is no fame without visibility. But forced visibility doesn't work, doesn't count; it leads only to Kardashians and their descendants. You can *trick* others into *making* you visible, though. Search #lumina or #erichauser right this second and you'll find dozens of pictures of Eric in this room, taken covertly or, like Miss Scheinberg did, master of media that she is, blatantly. Here I am with Eric Hauser, founder of Lumina, creator of the HoloPhone, thirty-something-year-old demigod. We have created him, and he has created us. It's a wonder Vaynerchuk, who Eric spots across the room, talking with inexhaustible energy into his phone's camera, hasn't come over and done the same. Maybe someday that guy will actually buy the Jets, although Eric doubts it.

Checking the time. Ten minutes till dinner. And after dinner, dessert with entertainment. One champagne right now, maybe one Scotch or martini or glass of wine with dinner, something light, like a cab sav or a port, which isn't exactly light but *is* very sweet and so can be handled by people with a sometimes sensitive pancreas, like Eric, in only small quantities. And then the entertainment. The speaking.

Sophia Velasquez, starlet, wondered how exactly one got invited to something like the White House Correspondents Dinner. She *was* here, of course, and you don't get into an event at which the President of the United States is present unless you've been very specifically invited and vetted and confirmed to be harmless, so obviously she'd been invited. She was on the list. What she was wondering was how exactly she'd gotten on that list in the first place—like who at the WHCA, which she honestly hadn't known was a thing until a couple months ago when her agent had told her she'd been invited and should attend, had been sitting there making a list of people to include in this year's dinner and thought, *Ah, yes, we must invite the model and actress Sophia Velasquez*? She could imagine the conversation:

Johnson, hi. Yes, come in. I was just looking over this list.

It's a good list, isn't it, Mr. Person in Charge of the WHCA?

Oh, indeed, indeed. Although, Johnson, I must say, I'm a little curious about one of your choices here. Ms. Sophia Velasquez.

Yes, her. She is *sexy, isn't she?*

Well, I suppose, although it's likely I'm an old man, given that I'm in charge of an old-media journalism organization, so it would be inappropriate for me to outright state my sexual attraction to a twenty-three-year-old former child actor like Ms. Velasquez.

Ah, I guess I see your point, sir, although it's worth noting that Sophia Velasquez wasn't ever exactly a child actor. Child actors tend to come to prominence for roles they play very young in life. We're talking people like Haley Joel Osment or Dakota Fanning—

I remember them!

That's great, sir. Good for you. I don't remember them, per se, but I saw AI and I thought it was a spectacular movie. Anyway, so those people were like five or six when they got their first roles, right? And they kept getting roles on a consistent basis until they were like ten, twelve, maybe a little older if they were lucky, but then they lost their appeal, because they were kind of just like everybody else. They no longer had that cuteness factor that made them publicly appealing figures. And, sure, they could still act, but lots of people their age—teenagers or adults—can act, so they no longer have that thing that made them special, which was the fact that they could act and they were children. You see?

Uh huh, uh huh. Well gosh, Johnson, so then what makes Ms. Velasquez so different?

I'm glad you asked. See, she started acting when she was fourteen, probably after some talent agent saw her in an amateur talent show. She's what we call a "Former Disney Star," far different from a former child actor. And the real funny part, sir, is that when she was on that Disney show she couldn't even really act. She was kind of terrible. Although that could have been the writing, which was admittedly also terrible, although I really liked it at the time, but hey, I was a teenager too, and anyway she can act kind of okay, now. She was in that movie about the horse—

But why is she on this list, Johnson?

Well, for the young vote, sir.

Young . . . vote?

A figure of speech, the voting part. In addition to being a model and actress and recording artist, she's also a social media star. She has nearly thirty million TikTok followers.

I see. So she takes video of the event—

—and young people see she's there, yes, and it helps make the WHCA cool.

So that's probably why you have Miley Cyrus on the list, too, then.

Oh, no. She's pushing forty these days, so her demographic isn't even what we're going for. She just knows the president personally. By the way, I've been thinking maybe it's time the WHCA finally started using our YouTube channel . . .

Actually, all that reasoning made sense, now that Sophia stopped to think about it. But it was also unfortunate and wrong, because looking around at most of the crowd here—a hundred congresspeople, a thousand aging journalists, dozens of tech pundits and business analysts and CEOs, older actors who, while forever maintaining a sort of existential coolness, were not her crowd—she wasn't going to post any TikToks from tonight's event. Her fans wouldn't care even a little bit that she'd been here. Hell, she wasn't even wearing an Instagramable dress; her stylist, goddess bless him, had insisted she wear something "business-chic" for an event like this one. And indeed everyone here was dressed ultra-conservatively; it was like the whole scene was a snapshot of the early 2000s. Accept for Miley and that comedian—goddess bless also them—who'd both at least worn something backless. So unless she got to meet the president, take a selfie with her, there was nothing for Sophia to post here tonight. She'd come for the food.

There—the talking part was over. The keynote given. The speech spoken and the jokes delivered and received with an acceptable amount of hysterical laughter. It had helped that his keynote had been preceded by fifteen minutes of the president's own chuckle-inducing monologue. A kindness, this. Some past presidents hadn't even attended the WHCD—such frivolities were beneath them, was the implication, or the press was their sworn enemy, but this president liked to foster a playful administration. The TikTok President, they called her.

No matter how many public presentations he gave, Eric was certain his obvious poise, his comfort with speaking in front of a crowd, would always be a ruse. Well, not a ruse exactly (that was imprecise, and Eric hated impreciseness in language, took great care to use the right words even in dialogues he had only with himself) because it was real poise, real confidence and comfort, but the truth was it didn't come naturally to him like everyone thought it did; his public confidence was manufactured, required concerted and consistent effort, the effort fueled by meat and vegetables and generous amounts of alcohol. And like the gas engines Americans had been using for more than a century and were now finally starting to see the absurdity of, from Eric were produced both power *and* exhaust, and the exhaust had to go somewhere—so he usually, after a large generation of power, set about finding a woman in whom to expel his exhaust.

But tonight he could not yet do that. Rather than give in to the need to expunge himself of the toxic wastes that build up in any machine over time, right now he needed to force the machine of his body to continue to generate power. There was socializing yet to be done. As much as he wanted to flirt with the first attractive and available female celebrity he saw (as long as that wasn't Miley), he couldn't, not yet. People would want to talk to him. They always wanted to talk to him, and rightly so. They needed to congratulate him. In this instance the congratulations would be for the cutting hilarity of his words; in others they were for the inspirational force behind his delivery; and on the engineering floor, where his confidence needed no forcing, where it was his neutral and resting state, the congratulations were for what mattered: algorithms, formulas, prototypes, world-changing creations. But tonight, the point was, he'd given a funny speech, peppered with lightly biting and deceptively relevant criticism of both journalism and liberalism, and thus, in order that his ego may be stroked, he needed to keep it fueled. He set out in search of a server upon whose arm might be a tray of drinks and little desserts, and if he did not find one, he would soon enough arrive at the open bar, where he might find whisky.

Sophia, probably against the advice of both her nutritionist and personal trainer, had either of them been here, sunk a spoon into her third cup of black pepper raspberry sorbet. She loved these things. She'd had them once before, at a party after the Oscars last year (she hadn't attended, or been invited to attend, the Oscars themselves, just a series of after parties), and the ones here tonight were exactly the same as the ones served then, right down to the shape of the little glass cups they were served in and the brand of Prosecco splashed over top. The two events must have had the same caterer, and she might have to find out who that was so she could have them do her birthday this year. The problem with the sorbets, though, was they they were served in the aforementioned tiny glass cups, with really just a few bites each, although they tried to fool you into thinking there was more by having you eat the things with microspoons, and it was rather embarrassing to take more than one cup from the penguin-like servers who danced around the ballroom with trays of the delectable things. So Sophia, in order to get her fill, was herself dancing, taking one dessert from this tray, gliding across the room as she devoured it, leaving it stealthily behind on a table and snatching another from the next tray whose path she crossed.

There was a time, right after her Disney Channel show had ended and her first, and to-date only, album had bombed, that she would have secluded herself in a bathroom stall and vomited the sorbets into the porcelain after eating as many as she wanted. And then she might have gone home and cut herself or taken a ton of prescription pills. These days she just ate as much (vegetarian) food as she wanted and then worked her ass off at the gym the next day.

On his way to the bar, Eric had tried to reverse his polarity, to shrink himself, withdraw his so-called psychical aura inward, keeping his head down, his shoulders slouched, in a way that was usually effective at keeping others from noticing you: the goal, after all, was to get a drink, maybe a dessert, and *then* continue communing with the Washington and Hollywood riffraff. But somewhere in the last twenty yards of his journey, he'd been blindsided by the senator in charge of the Permanent Subcommittee on Investigations, one ancient and white and portly (and, despite the significant influence he'd already gained in certain of Washington's economic lobbies, only thus far two-term-serving) James McDowell (R-Georgia). "How are those foreign holdings treating you?" the senator was asking. "What do they call that? Triple Irish, Quadruple Irish? Irish Death Squad?"

Eric smiled. He took the part of himself that he'd shrunk and let it expand to fill the space between the two pink-clothed tables in which he and the senator were standing. "Senator McDowell," he said, for nothing stroked the ego of a senator like using his own name, and you could bet this senator's ego hadn't been trained, like Eric's had, to respond only to the will of the consciousness that owned it. "It's a pleasure to see you tonight. I hadn't realized they let you into things like this. Those boys in security have been slacking again, haven't they? Probably got themselves waylaid by a cadre of Puerto Rican prostitutes."

"You're funny, *Mister* Hauser." Emphasis on *Mister* as if to say, *I'm a senator of the United States of America, and you are just a paltry inventor.*

This was how many politicians talked to him. But an inventor, they seemed to have forgotten, helped found this country; an inventor signed his name on the Declaration of Independence.

"Very very funny," McDowell said again. "Even your little thing up on stage back there, very funny. Hysterical."

"I try. No, but seriously"—Eric made a show of checking his watch, which was a prototype—"isn't it past your bed time?"

The senator laughed this time, and maybe even for real. Eric tightened his smile.

"I hardly sleep these days, Mr. Hauser," the senator said. "Too many enemies out there trying to destroy our country. Terrorists, foreign armies, foreign businesses. Some might even say certain *American* businesses are our enemy, Mr. Hauser. Some might say certain American companies send too much of their workforce, or their money, overseas, and damned in their mind be the American economy."

"You don't say."

"Damned be the livelihood of the American people, their practices say, loud and clear."

"Hmm. Well, Lumina is proud to be an American company, Senator. We're proud to manufacture ninety percent of our hardware right here in the USA. You know we're building a new manufacturing plant next year, in Texas? Two hundred acres. One hundred percent solar powered."

"Is that so? I'll be honest with you, Mr. Hauser. I don't much follow what a lot of the technology industry is up to. When I was born—when I was growing up—we didn't have smartphones, we didn't have self-driving cars. We put gas in our cars, oil. Back when American oil companies were thriving. Now gas prices are three times, four times, what they were a decade ago, and if your car hits E you're lucky if there's a gas station within half a dozen miles. Ford, General Motors, they're folding, you know. They're dead."

"Oh, I wouldn't say dead, Senator. The old auto manufacturers have a decade or two left in them. And some of them are even adapting."

"What do you drive, Mr. Hauser? You probably drive one of those goddamned Teslas. Or a fucking Leaf. Do you drive a fucking Leaf?" The senator coughed. He glanced at the space around them, as if he was afraid a camera might have picked up his use of profanity, which, even in this age, would be an impropriety. The room seemed larger now. The crowd a little thinner.

"I do have a Tesla, in fact. But I, too, appreciate the old ways, Senator. I have a Lamborghini. And even an old Lexus. I take them for long drives down the coast when I need to think. When you have to get from San Francisco to LA, nothing beats six hours to yourself." What Eric didn't say was that usually, when he had business in Los Angeles, he'd just as soon take the hyperloop. Thirty minutes there, thirty minutes back, home in time for dinner, did indeed beat six hours in a piece of obsolete technology, especially when you had a business to run, people who required your guidance.

"Lexus," the senator said. "That's a Japanese car."

Eric could feel himself shrinking again, against his will this time. He concentrated, inflated himself. "And Labo is Italian. Tesla, American. Now, if you'll excuse me, Senator. I was going to find a dessert. Didn't eat much before the keynote. Nervous and all."

"Mr. Hauser, my point is that America is hardly America anymore. The borders are bleeding like one of them boys everyone's always whining about the police shooting in the Black neighborhoods. Even across oceans, it's like every other country thinks they're us. And a lot of people here either don't see it, or they don't care; they steal from their own homeland, Mr. Hauser. And you, well I'll be damned if you aren't American. Hauser—that's an American name. You're no immigrant like how many other people who do what you do."

"I suppose that's true." Hauser was, of course, a German name.

"The Patriot Party. Now they got the right idea. You didn't hear it from me, but they got the right idea. They want to keep America American."

"Aren't they trying to secede? Aren't they calling themselves the Patriot Confederation now? Didn't you vote to give them that land in Nevada?"

"Yes, well, and that's only because America isn't so American anymore, is it? I know it's not a popular opinion, but I've had it up to here with this secret cabal what's running things. Fightin' it's why I ran for office in the first place.

"It's just cabal, Senator."

"What?"

"Secret cabal is redundant. A cabal is, by its nature, secret."

"Well, and I don't know about that, but there's something going on, and the Patriot Confederation—excuse me, the Patriot *Party*—is onto something, is all I'm saying."

"If you say so, Senator."

The senator grabbed Eric's arm. "Lumina might be small now. Comparatively speaking. But you won't always be, and people *will* start caring what taxes you are and aren't paying."

Eric pulled his arm back, almost took McDowell's off with it. "Senator McDowell. There's nothing illegal about what I do with my money. Emphasis on *my*, Senator. Not yours."

"Yes, well," McDowell said, "I'm just saying, sounds like you know a lot about the word 'cabal,' suspiciously a lot. Maybe we'll see you back here in Washington soon. It's been a pleasure."

"Likewise," Eric said. He did not extend his hand for a handshake.

The bar, a long, top-lit counter with a man and a woman behind it— either hotel staff or part of the catering crew, and in either case doubtless vetted ruthlessly by the Secret Service—was not so far away now. And yet Eric considered taking a detour, to the restroom, where he might find solitude, if only for a few moments, in a lonely stall. Or maybe it was time to just get out of here. Maybe it was time to leave the ballroom and leave this hotel and head back to his own room at the Jefferson.

The nutjobs had worn him out.

From up here, you could see the whole city. The Lincoln Memorial. Capitol Hill. The White House. Parks and the fancy homes of senators.

Farther in the distance, the slums, where the poor lived. She'd read that there were a lot of poor people in this city. She'd read that the blood of Washington, D.C., was the homeless that flowed through its streets at night.

But was it a city, Washington, D.C.? She supposed it was. They'd taught in school that it was. It just wasn't a state, right? It had a mayor, its own city council or whatever. How odd that was: this is where the President lived, where Congress was, the House and the Senate, but it still needed its own governance. Not unlike how we, as people, despite having parents and superiors and an infinite crowd of people greater than us, in charge of us, still need to govern ourselves, she thought. It was something she'd read in a book recently. *Invincible: How to Take Control, Kick Ass, and Rediscover Your Own Personal Nexus*. It had been on the *New York Times* bestseller list, self-help section, for something like three months now. The author was making all the media rounds. He and Sophia had been on *The Young Turks* at the same time just a few weeks ago. It was an honor, meeting an author like that. Sophia loved that kind of book—she'd been thinking even of maybe writing her own, based on her own experiences with success, although she hadn't brought the idea to her agent yet—and it touched her own naked soul to be able to personally thank the author of one.

"An interesting thing most people don't know," a voice behind Sophia said. "D.C., while not part of any one state, actually has its own mayor and city council. But Congress—that is, the U.S. Congress—can overrule any laws or decisions the D.C. government makes. So democracy in this town is kind of a lie. A synecdoche for everywhere, in that respect, one might argue."

Sophia turned around. "I did know that. Also, hello?"

"Hi there," said the man, whose shape looked familiar, whose voice sounded familiar, but who was standing in the shadow of the massive air conditioning unit next to the rooftop door.

Sophia raised her hand to her forehead, as if shielding her eyes from the moon or the stars or the pollution of the spotlight that lit the Washington Monument would help her see the man standing there in the dark. "I didn't realize anyone else was up here," she said.

"Oh, I think you were here first. I've been stuck down in that ballroom far too long. I needed air."

"Me too," she said. "I'll be honest, I don't like things like that, down there. I don't like those people. I don't even know much about them. Politics and shit. And I don't want to."

"Amen," the man said. He stepped forward, away from the door. "Mind if I join you?"

"Be my guest. Mister . . . ? Wait, I *do* know you. You gave the speech down there."

"Guilty," he said. "Guilty indeed."

An important thing about Sophia was that she spoke her mind, but that didn't mean she liked offending others if she could help it. "So then I guess those people down there are your friends. Or like you're kind of one of them, aren't you? Shit. I'm sorry. I didn't mean to say—"

But he laughed. "Please," he said. "I said amen, and I meant amen. Friend is not a word I apply lightly, and those people—most of them, anyway—are not my friends."

"Oh, good," Sophia said. And then she reached out with a small tendril of what the author of *Invincible* called *the naked inner self*: "Because I'm not sure I could be friends with someone who's friends with those people."

And he, to her delight, seemed to reach back. "Then it's a good thing I'm not friends with them."

"Yes—yes it is."

"I'm Eric," the man said, extending his hand in a way that was both formal and intimate, as if Sophia could choose to ignore it, shake it, or to put its fingers in her mouth, and any choice would be correct.

She took the second option, extending her hand to meet his and telling him her own name. "It's a beautiful name," he said.

She thought for a moment he was going to pull her hand to his lips, the way a character on her old Disney show had done to her character and her character hadn't known what to make of it and that's what the whole episode had been about. And while Sophia's character on that show hadn't known what flirting was, Sophia herself had been more than a little experienced: she'd lost her virginity, after all, to the very actor who played the other character in that scene, had, at sixteen, kissed, on a dare from him, the actress who played her character's best friend.

"*Enchanté*," Sophia said, because it was what the other character in that episode had said when he'd kissed her character's hand.

"Indeed?" Eric said, letting go. He turned to the city and put his elbows on the hotel roof's ledge. He seemed to all at once forget she was there.

So Sophia, not knowing what else to do, how she might move things forward (because you should never continue flirting with a man who had stopped flirting with you, was another thing she'd read, in a book called *Girl, Do What You Want*), placed her elbows on the ledge too.

Before Eric had arrived, she'd taken a few photos of the view. She'd taken a video, too, a long high-definition panorama. She'd uploaded them all to her OnlyFans story. It was something, at least, she'd thought. She hadn't posted anything all day, and her fans would get upset if she produced nothing for an entire twenty-four hours; they'd take to the message boards, or, worse, to Twitter, which would lead once again to outcry at the fact that, *Hey, Sophia Velasquez never Tweets, either, and when she does it's probably like her fucking manager doing it for her or something.* And well it was. Her manager. Usually. Sometimes she scheduled her own tweets, but she'd decided when she'd signed up for the network it was fucking pointless. Instagram was funny. TikTok was addictive. OnlyFans made her money. She liked the networks that let her share with photos or videos instead of words. Especially when she was actually doing something fun that she could take photos of, something that was worth sharing for its own sake, that carried no obligation. So she'd snapped photos and videos of the view from the roof in real time, and they would disappear tomorrow. But then she could #TBT them or something in the future, in a few months or so. Because goddess knew she'd have nothing exciting going on by then.

And the reason the goddess knew Sophia would have nothing exciting going on in a few months was that she'd had nothing exciting going on for ages now. It doesn't take divinity to recognize a pattern. Sophia's career had kind of stagnated since the Disney Channel show had ended. It had ended because she'd turned eighteen, and no one in the

Disney Channel's demographic wanted to watch a show about a middle-class eighteen-year-old navigating the world of college (because no one in the demographic was *in* college) which was the only thing the show could have naturally been about at that point, the only progression of its original premise: a middle-class fourteen-year-old navigating the world of high school while living with her quirky inventor father and getting up to shenanigans with her two best friends. So the network had dropped the show, had dropped her, but that was okay at first because Sony Music came to her and said, Have you ever thought about doing an album? She hadn't, because she couldn't exactly sing, and she told them this, but they said it wasn't a big deal whether she could sing. They could fix all that with computers. What was important was she do the album and she do it now so they could release it right as the last episode of the Disney Channel show aired. The album made a lot of money, mostly for Sony Music and for her agent, but a not small amount for her, too. Although when she'd asked her agent whether they wanted her to record another one (maybe she could even write some of the lyrics this time—she had some ideas she'd written down in a notebook), they said sure, maybe, and never mentioned it again. It was only after she'd decided to pause her career— her own decision! Fuck you!—and go to college herself, that she realized, during a business course, that of course she'd never make another album: another album would never sell, not now that her fucking fifteen minutes were over. She did do that one movie, but it kind of bombed, and since then, well . . . . Anyway, she'd dropped out of college after two semesters and now spent most of her time in her house in Beverly Hills, writing poetry and tanning by the pool and dicking around on her phone or tablet and watching old movies on a seventy-inch screen and reading books. All kinds of books: contemporary literature and fantasy and young adult, and personal growth books like *Invincible* and *Essence* and *Girl, Do What You Want* and *Unleashing Your Inner Goddess*, and even some of the classics, *The Power of Positive Thinking* and *The Five Habits of Highly Effective People*, stuff like that. Because if there was one thing that was important to her, besides her mother, who lived with her, and her three-year-old Boston Terrier, it was personal growth. Because goddess dammit, some day she would figure out what she wanted to do with her life.

The man—Eric—sighed and pulled something from his tuxedo's pocket. "Hey, Sophia, do you smoke?"

"What? No. Does anybody smoke anymore?"

"Not cigarettes," he said.

"Oh," she said, understanding. "Oh, well then, yes, of course. Does anybody not?"

"Cool," he said. He lit the joint, inhaled deeply, and then passed it to her.

She inhaled and closed her eyes for a few seconds and then passed it back to him. "Thanks."

"My pleasure," he said.

"So you like the view of the city from here, too," she said, gesturing.

"No," he told her. He inhaled again. "Not at all. I wasn't looking at the city. I was looking at the stars."

3

FOR SOMEONE THE MEDIA LIKED to hail as one of the most foresightful futurists of his generation, it's a wonder Eric Hauser didn't see coming the profound affect Sophia Velasquez would have on the next seven or eight years of his life.

He had gone up onto the rooftop of the Washington Hilton that April looking for solitude. He had indeed gone to the bar first, after shaking off the senator and then another senator, this one friendlier, friendly enough that Eric could be curt without offending. He'd ordered one shot of rye whiskey and downed it quickly and then headed, instead of for the bathroom, out of the ballroom, past two obvious Secret Service agents and at least two more in laughably transparent disguise, and to the nearest elevator. He could have called for a car, gone back to his suite at the Jefferson, but there would be waiting for him only the prospects of sleep or sleeplessness, so he took the elevator to the top floor. There should have been security there, too, he thought; in fact, what he half expected when he stepped onto the Hilton's roof was to be confronted, assaulted maybe, asked for identification and then escorted way, way down. But instead he saw only a young woman staring out over the capital.

They smoked for a period of time that might have been minutes or dozens of minutes or an hour. They didn't talk much. He knew who she was, he told her, but frankly he didn't know much about her. "You have me at a disadvantage," she said, "because I'm afraid I don't know who you are at all."

He was surprised. That didn't happen often anymore.

"Well, besides that you were a big deal down there. No, I don't," she confirmed.

When they'd finished the joint, he invited her to come with him to his suite, for a nightcap or a cup of tea—whatever she wanted. "It's far away from here," he told her. They exited through the door and back into the stairwell, where this time there *was* a security agent, dressed in a suit and tie and with a device in his ear, staring at them knowingly.

It would be naive to think that when they went back to his suite at the Jefferson, they did anything other than fuck, at least at first. The romantic thing would have been that they got to the room, intending to have sex, but first had a drink and while drinking talked, and after finishing the first drink poured another and talked some more, and then maybe a third, maybe a fourth, maybe a switch to coffee after realizing they'd been drinking all night, all the while bearing to each other the depths of their respective souls, until the next thing they know the light outside the suite's balcony doors is not that of the moon or the stars or the concrete boxes housing their little humans—but instead the light of sun, first dim, then brighter, and then as it ascends, a copper-orange ray hits their faces and they notice it, and what do you know, we've been up all night and didn't even realize, and surely this is a sign.

But that's not how it happened. That's not how these humans worked.

Instead, they took the Hilton's elevator to the fourth floor. Eric waited outside room 403 while Sophia retrieved her suitcase. She travelled light; she'd brought to Washington just one medium-size bag, her dress for the evening doubtlessly delivered after her arrival. They took the elevator then further, to the ground floor. The lobby was full of the rich and famous, the upper-middle class and obsolete (which is to say the journalists, with their Pulitzers, who were little more than conspiracy theorists, most of them), the talented, the talentless. All of them were leaving the ballroom, headed to their own rooms, here or at other hotels. Eric took one last glance at all of them, his finger already on his wrist, summoning his car. To the Jefferson they were driven; in the car's back seat they said little to each other, but Sophia was smiling and Eric was horny and thinking and watching her smile. At the Jefferson, Eric waved to the front desk assistant as they passed—she was young, arguably attractive. In the room, as soon as they arrived, they fucked. On the bed. It was a fine, run-of-the-mill, average kind of fucking, but *that* was the sign, because when two strangers have sex for the first time, the sex is almost never average—it's terrible, even when you're as good at fucking as Eric Hauser was.

After the sex, they smoked another joint in silence and then fell asleep.

The next morning, late, they ordered breakfast. Not from room service ("I ate here yesterday afternoon, and the food was fucking terrible," Eric told her) but from a greasy kind of diner across the street. Eric even descended to the lobby in his white robe to meet the delivery woman so he could leave a generous tip (a picture of this exchange would appear online minutes later—"You would never catch Tim Cook in a hotel lobby in his bathrobe," was one popular TikToker's hot take).

They ate eggs and waffles. Aunt Jemima's maple-flavored syrup. Eric had bacon. He was both dismayed and enamored when Sophia told him she was a vegetarian. "I may even try going vegan, some day—it's a goal of mine."

They shared half a joint. Then they fucked again. They eschewed the bed this time, going for the sofa and the floor and with Sophia bent over the breakfast table, and it was better than the night before.

They sat naked on the sofa and finished the joint. "You know," Eric said, pointing to the bottle of syrup on the table behind them (he'd had the restaurant bring an unopened one, his usual policy regarding condiments), "Those bottles used to have a Black lady on them?"

"What?" Sophia said, laughing, as he'd hoped she would, at the randomness of his comment, effectively the first thing other than *This is what I'd like for breakfast* either of them had said since the night before. He couldn't not smile when she laughed.

"That syrup bottle," he told her. "Aunt Jemima refers to their original mascot, who was this super stereotypical Black lady."

"I didn't know that."

"Oh, yeah. They used to have her picture on it and everything, used a real model, too. The idea was that, after the Civil War, they wanted to portray southern plantation life as a really happy thing, thanks to the end of slavery, so they added a character called Aunt Jemima to these travelling shows—minstrel shows, they were called—and then in the early 1900s some pancake company decided to use her as a mascot."

"That sounds kind of racist."

"Of course it was. That's why she's not on the bottle anymore."

"Oh, haha. I guess that makes sense."

Eric grabbed her hand. "Do that again," he said.

"Do what?"

"Laugh."

She pulled her hand away, blushed. "You know a lot of things, it seems like," she said.

"I do," he said. "A lot of useless things."

She laughed again.

"And, I suppose, some useful things, too."

A comfortable silence engulfed the room for a few moments, and Eric decided to enjoy it. Then, finally, Sophia said, "So what's your plan today?"

He looked at his watch. "I have to do some work, I supposed, this afternoon. Check in with a few things. But I was mostly going to take the day to myself. I don't get to do that very often, but this wasn't really a business trip, so I thought I would extend my leisure time through today. Read maybe. Meditate. I'm flying back to San Francisco in the morning."

"I see."

"You?"

"I was supposed to be on a plane back to L.A. two hours ago."

It turned out that Sophia Velasquez hadn't been lying the night before: She truly didn't know who Eric Hauser was. She knew in a broad sense, of course—she knew about Lumina, owned one of the new HoloPhones, said she had the first-generation LumiCam holocam and LumiCam projector from a couple years ago connected to her iMac at home; she used the company's cloud services, accessed her email via a .lum address—but she, by her own admission, didn't pay much attention to the way companies like Lumina were run, much in the same way she didn't pay attention to politics. What about YouTube news shows or podcasts? Not even those, she told him. It was common among people of their generation, a generation of which Eric could be said to bookend the very beginning and Sophia the very end, to not pay attention to those things. They watched YouTube, sure, all the time, everybody did, but you didn't watch it for the news, unless you were a feminist or social justice warrior—you watched it for the human comedians and the daily or biweekly bloggers, the people who were pansexual or genderfluid and who were trying to find their place in the world, just like you. The Nelson Ratings network once tried to quantify the viewership of channels like The Young Turks and Albernameg, but despite the high view counts on those channels' videos, they couldn't find many people who actually admitted to watching them on any sort of regular basis. Eric, for his part, liked VICE News and John Hempel, and Sophia said that, now that you mention it, she liked that last one too.

But so Sophia didn't pay much attention to how those companies were run, was the point, which meant she wasn't aware of their leadership, which meant she wasn't aware of Eric's position as founder and CEO of Lumina, Inc. "I mean, I guess they kind of said that at the dinner, didn't they, before they announced you?" she said. "But I wasn't really paying attention. Actually, and this is embarrassing and you're going to hate me, but I didn't really pay attention to your speech either. Those things just kind of annoy me."

By 8 a.m. the next day, Eric had called the front desk to let them know he wasn't going to be checking out that morning after all—his plans had changed, and he was staying another day. ("Well then, yes, I understand. I guess we will have to upgrade to the other suite, if this one is booked for tonight. If you could have someone move our bags, that would be wonderful. And yes, we will be ordering in again this evening. A bottle of wine, yes. You know what? Make it two.")

The next week, Eric asked Sophia to come visit him in San Francisco. For lunch. Take the hyperloop, he told her. "By the way, we'll be adding some awesome holographic tech to the cars soon. But that's a secret, so keep quiet. We'll announce it in September."

They ate lunch at Saison. Eric payed the bill. He couldn't see Sophia that evening, though—he was much too busy. There was a thing he was working on, and his teams, while the best, weren't as good as him, and he had to pick up the slack that had resulted from his impromptu days off. So he walked her to the hyperloop station and she made the thirty-minute trip back to Los Angeles.

She came again the next day, and the next. They lunched at Benu, then at Jardiniére. That Friday he arranged his schedule so he would have several hours free, and he took her to his favorite restaurant: The Flying Pig, in the Mission.

"I'm kind of surprised," Sophia said, looking around, taking in the long, narrow bistro with its high square tables against one wall, bar against the other, infinite row of beer taps and bottles of wine behind the bar. Its chalkboard menu listing a dozen different styles of hotdog and three simple sides.

"Why's that?" he asked, knowing the answer. The answer, indeed, being exactly what he meant to provoke by bringing her here.

"It's just . . . rustic?" she said. "I guess it just doesn't seem like you."

He smiled. "Lower class, you mean. And what is me, then? What sort of restaurant do you suppose defines me as a man? Those fancy places we've been going to?"

She thought for a moment. "No. No, I don't suppose so," she said.

They ordered at the bar—he a Chicago-style dog with sauerkraut, she a vegan dog on a vegan bun with spicy gourmet mustard—asked also for two glasses of wine, Eric's selection, and took their seats at one of the tall tables with a checkered tablecloth.

"If you really want to know," Eric said, unfolding a paper napkin and placing it on his lap, "I take most of my meals in liquid form."

"Liquid?"

"You know. Shakes, smoothies. Specially formulated for my body and needs by a nutritionist."

"I have a nutritionist too—"

"Doesn't everyone these days?"

"Ha. But, I mean, mine doesn't give me anything like that. She just tells me to make sure I get enough protein and B12 and to cut down on sugar."

"It keeps things simple for me," he said. "I wake up, drink a smoothie, work out, drink another smoothie, one with more protein, meditate, and then I'm in the office. And because of this, sometimes, when I really want a meal to be special, like any time I'm with you" (she blushed) "I can enjoy myself."

The server brought the wine, two glasses, placed them on the table, asked whether they needed anything else at the moment, told them their food would be out shortly. Eric thanked him, and Sophia thanked him.

"What time *do* you get up in the morning?" Sophia said, raising her glass to her nose.

"You mean when I'm *not* up late getting high and fucking hot women in a Washington, D.C., hotel room?"

"Yes, when you're not doing that."

"About 4:30 a.m. I—"

Sophia coughed, choked almost.

"Four-thirty isn't *that* early," Eric protested. "Some guys in this industry—"

"No, no. It's not that," she said. "Although, fuck, that *is* early. It's this wine. It's terrible."

Eric felt annoyed, suddenly. For just a moment. "I picked the wine," he said. "I like this wine."

"It's terrible. No offense."

This had never happened before. He *was* offended.

"I'll be right back." She stood, picked up both glasses, and marched stonily to the bar.

There were many things Eric wasn't used to, and one of them was being wrong. He always ordered this wine when he brought women to the Flying Pig. It was part of the experience he'd grown so practiced at delivering. This cheap but delicious food, this atmosphere, *the Mission.* This pinot noir was *good*, he thought. No, it wasn't *great*, but it was good, certainly *drinkable*. And for under ten dollars. That was point: order the wine and when the woman drinks it and proclaims it delicious impress her by telling her a bottle costs less than ten dollars if you can believe that. Then offer a footnote about how, even though he's a billionaire, Eric Hauser can appreciate inexpensive things for their own value. Endearment, respect. It played out that way every time, with every actress or model or Internet star he'd dated. But not this time, which meant—what?

He hadn't had a chance to taste the wine himself. Had it been bad? Like spoiled? Should he do that thing where he alerted the staff to their mistake and smiled goodnaturedly and reminded them he could buy the place if he wanted to?

But Sophia was back at the table. She'd placed a new glass in front of him. "Here. Try this one."

Skeptical, both of the situation and now of Sophia, of the time he'd put into developing this relationship, he raised the glass to his lips.

"No, no," she said. "Smell it first."

Of course he knew you were supposed to smell a glass of wine before you tasted it. Suddenly this thing, this thing with Sophia, wasn't working out.

But he didn't let on. He feigned embarrassment, said "Silly me," and inhaled. Then he sipped.

It was a very good wine.

"So—" she said. "What do you think?"

He admitted: "It's much better than the other one."

She sipped hers. "I hope you're not too bruised," she said. "It was a rookie mistake. People are always told they shouldn't bother spending a lot on wine, that anything above ten dollars is a waste, but that's bullshit. This, though," she gestured to the glasses in front of them, "is only $26.99. You see, there are plenty of good wines under *thirty* dollars, but anything under ten is shit, and if you think it's good, you're faking it for the benefit of someone else."

Eric vowed silently to become an expert on wine. He took another sip and nodded approvingly. "How do you know all this, anyway?"

"I come from a family of South American vintners."

He hadn't known that. Another thing he was unaccustomed to was discovering his own ignorance, but it did on occasion happen. He was enamored with Sophia once again.

"It's a shame, really. With climate change and everything, good wine vintages are hard to find, but that's starting to change. At least that's what my mother says. She emigrated from Argentina when I was four. She wanted me to have a better life, in America."

"I think I'd like to meet that woman," Eric said.

Presently, the bartender brought the hotdogs to the table.

In an interview with a simulation of Larry King not long before Eric Hauser's divorce and mysterious retreat from public life, he was asked about love. The sim-King said, "Some of your past . . . lovers . . . is that right word? . . . well, your ex-girlfriends, an escort who claims to have had a relationship with you when you were in your late teens, even your wife, have in interviews said you weren't always the most affectionate person. Your wife, for example, the model and movie star Sophia Velasquez, said, and I'm reading this from a magazine thing here, 'Eric can be cold, impersonal; at his worst—but this also means he's at his best, in an effectiveness sort of way—he isn't even aware you exist. I don't know that he's genuinely capable of love.' What do you think she meant by that?"

You can still watch this interview, by the way; it's easy to find if you search for it. If you look closely at the holorecording in high definition, you can see Eric Hauser's eyes mist a little as his wife's words are read to him, and mist even further as he takes several moments to formulate a response. And then he says: "I think she's probably right. Love, as we define it, after all, is just a series of chemical reactions in the brain. I know people don't like to hear that, don't want to believe it because it demystifies the sensation of romantic love for them, but it's true. What we mean when we say love is actually addiction, or obsession. So I say, why delude ourselves into thinking anything is love, then? Why not just focus on the obsession?"

So it's probably safe to say that Eric didn't really love Sophia, but he certainly felt attached to her in a way he never had to any other real human woman. It's painfully obvious to see the manifestation of an obsession, however brief, in retrospect. After finishing lunch at The Flying Pig, Eric sent a text to his receptionist and asked her to notify the appropriate people that he wouldn't be returning to his office that evening, and if they needed him for anything less than an emergency they should send him an email, which he would get tonight or in the morning. Then he took Sophia on a walking tour of his favorite parts of the city. In the evening, as the sky was growing darker, he took her to his home in Sea Cliff, with its view of the Golden Gate.

The next morning, as she was wiping the night from her eyes, he invited her to his office. He told her he wanted to show her something. "Something special I've been working on for a long time."

"Are you leaving now? It's so early."

"Lots to do," he said. "I have to change the world. You sleep. Come when you're ready." Then he kissed her hair in one of his first ever displays of tenderness toward anyone ever and left her lying in his satin-sheeted firmness-adjustable bed.

Zoomers II

1

YOU NEVER WANT TO BE your parents, but they're all you can be. Because they raised you, instilled in you their values, and molded your thinking to the pattern of their own, it's nearly impossible to ever be more than them. It's futile, sometimes, even to try. Their knowledge, their wisdom, their prejudices: all of these become yours. Nothing was ever your parents' in the first place, of course. It was all *their* parents', and their parents' parents', and so on for as many generations back as you can count. To the beginning, in most cases, of *homo sapiens sapiens*. Maybe even even to *homo habilis*, with their stone tools. Don't you sometimes get the feeling that's all your parents are good at, all *you're* good at? The wielding of stone tools?

But *evolution,* you say.

But *technology*, you say.

But *progress*, you say.

Of course their are exceptions. Remember *home sapiens idaltu*? Well—no, you probably don't. They didn't survive so long, did they? But the point is that one time *homo sapiens* tried to break the cycle, become something else, even if in the end they did only disappear into the long-undiscovered annals of taxonomy.

But *certain humans!* you say. And that's true. There are certain humans.

Gengis Kahn. Jesus of Nazereth. Mary Shelley. Albert Einstein. Sir Paul McCartney. Charles Babbage. Martin Luther King, Jr. Eric Hauser. Many many others. So many others you might think them uncountable until you remember that even millions is a tiny number compared to the

107 billion sentient hominids who have walked the earth over the course of its existence (to say nothing of the dolphins and cephalopods). This tiny number comprises the humans who one day realized they were smarter than their parents. When it happens (and gods help you if it ever happens to you) your reality gets a whole lot bigger.

Eric Hauser realized he was smarter than his parents when he was twelve years old.

2

IN THE FINAL MONTHS OF 1999, after cheating on her husband with a menagerie of men and women, Amanda Hauser suffered an ectopic pregnancy.

Her husband, Wallace Hauser, told himself he wasn't going to go back out there. He wasn't. He damed well wasn't going to do anything that the woman in the livingroom might interpret as forgiveness. Or weakness. Or the absence of any part of himself that made a man a man. But then she didn't come into the bedroom, which he thought she would have. He'd thought he'd extend the invitation and she'd take him up on it and then, just as she was sliding under the duvet, slipping in next to him thinking him asleep, he'd turn and say something like: "I changed my mind. I don't want you in this bed."

But she didn't come, and her not coming made him feel robbed of something. Eventually he needed to urinate. He didn't know how long had passed since the confrontation—he'd just been lying here, keeping his eyes closed, listening for her and probably never sleeping again—but she wasn't here. Had she decided to sleep on the couch? Had she left the house, gone back into the strange night? Decided to stay with one of her art class friends, who probably weren't even real? If she was asleep he could be very quiet, and she'd never know he'd broken the seal on his resolution to stay in this bed until he could hurt her. And if she'd left—well then he could maybe never take revenge; but he could go to the bathroom and she'd still never know.

He got up. He stepped ninja-style down the hallway: heal, side, toe; heal, side, toe; roll your foot, they'd taught him on a school field trip once, if you want to move through the woods silently. He pissed, brownly. He winced as he flushed. He winced again as while putting the seat down he dropped it and it clanged loudly as if to insult him: "Your wife fucks other men and doesn't even enjoy fucking you and your dick is small, fucking loser." He didn't bother washing his hands.

In the hallway, outside the bathroom door, in front of the wedding photos and his framed unused license to practice pharmacology, he paused. He could hear no crying. He could hear no snoring, no long deep breaths indicative of a sleeping body. Cursing his syrupy weakness he stepped into the living room, thinking maybe he would just take her back, because he'd take her back anyway, wouldn't he?, and how much more efficient to do it now instead of later.

When thus he found her collapsed onto her belly, fingernails stuck in the carpet, he went to the kitchen and called 911.

The paramedics came. Or the EMTs. Wallace Hauser had never been certain of the difference. They felt her pulse, found it wanting; listened to her lungs, found them hollow, found them empty. They put her in the back of the ambulance, took her to the nearest surgical ER. Eric followed.

Surgery was swift, easy, uncomplicated. Two days later Wallace and Amanda sat together while her gynecologist explained what had happened; how sometimes this was caused by STDs like chlamydia, which is probably what happened in this case, although they were still waiting for test results, and Wallace would need to be tested, too; and how sometimes these things happened just once, but other times, like this time, the damage was severe, and chances of future fertility were very very low.

Wallace used to think he was going to be a gynecologist. Remember?

3

FIVE MONTHS PASSED. MAYBE SIX. It was hard to tell exactly how many. But in a shorter time than one might think possible, a degree of normalcy returned to the lives of Wallace and Amanda Hauser. Amanda stopped going out, stopped going to sculpting classes. But she did start painting—*for real* painting.

Amanda spent two weeks in bed following her enceintal incident, and Wallace spent the first three days of that off work, at home, with her; they did not speak much. Amanda slept, and Wallace brought her food and watched cable television. When Wallace went back to work Amanda continued to sleep most of the day, but she did her own sustenance gathering, rising two or three times to use the toilet, maybe pour herself a bowl of cereal, which might tide over her recovering appetite until Wallace got home and made dinner. On day fifteen she got out of bed at half-past noon to make herself a sandwich, but she did not take the plate back to bed with her; she ate standing at the kitchen counter. Then she wandered into the second bedroom that was her studio and primed a three-foot canvas. She'd primed many canvases in the days of her artistic aspirations but had ended up painting on so few of them. Now she pulled the linen taught across the frame, stapled the edges, laid two coats of white acrylic gesso across the canvas with a polyester brush. Then she went back to bed.

The next day she mixed acrylics and applied them to the primed canvas. When Wallace came home he found her standing in front of the easel, admiring the work she'd done with color. He couldn't tell what she was supposed to have painted, but it didn't matter. Five minutes later he was still standing behind her, his arms around her, his hands resting above her forever-vacant womb.

By April, Amanda had filled nine canvasses, each one better than the last, with either oils or acrylics, some with recognizable subjects, like clocks and street signs and a waterfall. In late April, she painted a blue pickup truck, which she thought would go well in a baby's room. Also, she thought, maybe this very room would be a good baby's room, and the garage a bettera studio.

To be clear, Wallace and Amanda Hauser did not fall back into the love they'd had before. But they shared a bed; they ate together; they cuddled on the couch under a single blanket. Made bilateral decisions together. They were like, if not entirely, best friends. Because who else did they have?

On the fifth of May, they were once again in the vicinity of an operating room, waiting patiently with mild worry while the baby boy whose adoption papers they would sign that evening underwent a minor-but-on-such-a-young-person-delicate procedure to repair his tiny heart.

4

SEE THIS CHILD. HE HAS been on this Earth for an amount of time now, but not so long that he can delineate the time's passage. He is not old enough to know that Eric is his name, but he knows when they say it— *Eric*—they mean to solicit his attention.

Eric, they say—and he does not look up, not right away. Because while he knows they want his attention, he is not immediately inclined to give it. There's too much to do, too much to absorb right here in front of your face, can't you see that? Can't they see that? Take, for example, this carpet: berber, light blue (he knows blue—he knows green and yellow and red and all of them, absorbs the names when they point and tell them to him, even if he can't repeat them back with his mouth yet). They were so excited when the strange men came into the house and put in the new carpet. We're finally free of that wine stain, Dadda said. And if we spill on the new stuff, Ma said, we can just clean it right up. That's the magic of berber. (Still, Dadda said, maybe we should stick to white wine in the den, just in case.)

But that isn't the magic of berber, can't they see? The magic of berber—the magic of all the things in all the world—is that it's there. It's here. It exists and in this world also we exist with all of it.

So the child continues forward on hands and knees, the woven fabric brushing against his hands and knees. He's moving, moving, scuttle, scoot, hustle, crawl. Hustle hustle.

And then they say again, *Eric*. He indulges them now. He stops crawling; he's next to the stone fireplace they put here in the basement den not long before the berber carpet. Dadda did this one himself, with the help of a friend from somewhere: they knocked out the wall, they stacked the stone bricks one upon the other, and they loaded the new hollow chasm with wood and did something to it and there was fire. Fire is hot, the child knows. Fire is hot to get burned—they've told him this. There is no hot fire in the fireplace now, though, only ash and soot, good for getting dirty, for turning your hands black and your knees and your legs. Your face if you touch the soot and then touch also your face. If there had been fire, one of them, Ma or Dadda, would have scooped the child into their arms and said No! No! Hot! But the stone is there. Feel it. Rough. Cool.

Eric. Errriic.

That's right. He resumes the indulging of Ma and Dadda. He sits back on the padding of his diaper. Turns in their direction. He giggles and they giggle in response and he knows he has them. He giggles again; they laugh more loudly. It isn't just Ma and Dadda down here in the basement, but some of their friends. One funny-looking lady—her ears are bigger than on any other person the child has ever seen—laughs and claps. The child falls back to his hands and knees and crawls toward the big people. In between Ma and Dadda is something twice the child's size, wrapped in paper.

When he reaches it, he examines the wrapping. He sees how it's held together, these strips of clear something keeping these flaps from falling open. He can undo this. They encourage him to undo it. And he knows he can; he needs only to—

But there's the laughing again, from the funny-looking lady—because Dadda has done the unwrapping for Eric. He could have done it, if only the big people had been patient.

It's a tricycle, Ma says.

Look! He doesn't know what to make of it, the funny-looking lady says.

Of course he knows what to make of it. It's a tricycle. Ma *just* told him that. The funny-looking lady must be stupid.

Put him on it, someone else says. It's the friend of Dadda who helped build the fireplace.

Dadda picks him up, sets him on the tricycle. For a fragment of a moment, the child is afraid, but then he realizes the tricycle is sturdy, strong, like he, the child, is strong.

His feet can't reach the pedals, someone says.

Soon they will, Dadda says. *He's growing so fast.*

Happy birthday, Eric, Ma says.

Then Dadda holds the child by the shoulders and pushes him forward, and across the carpet he goes—fast, faster than ever on his hands and knees, and he can feel the air against his face.

5

ERIC NEVER WENT TO DAY care or preschool because his mom was an artist and worked from home, so she could take care of him during the day; not that he needed much taking care of—he was from infancy capable of occupying himself for long stretches of time with even the most effortless applications of imagination. In kindergarten, none of the other kids liked Eric. But in first grade he finally made a friend.

This friend's name was Hector Alexander Jones, and that's how he introduced himself. Eric was standing at the pencil sharpener on the afternoon of the second day of first grade when the other boy came over and stood next to him, expectantly. Eric rotated slowly the handle on the pencil sharpener, watching it as it turned. He was wondering how it worked, inside. He often wondered how things worked inside. He knew in this case only that when he pulled the pencil from the simple machine it would be sharp again, and that if he tried to open the sharpener right here to see how it worked he'd get in trouble. The pencil tip he'd broken drawing a picture of a robot in his notebook. He was aware of the other boy standing next to him, and when the boy didn't go away Eric pulled his pencil from the sharpener, blew cooly on the tip, and said, "What do you want?"

"Hi," the other boy said, as if he had an exciting secret he was bursting to share. "My name is Hector Alexander Jones."

"I know," Eric said, putting the pencil tip-down in his pants pocket.

Hector's eyes widened. "You do?"

Eric had a feeling this boy did most things with an exaggerated sense of incredulity. "Yes," Eric said. "I know everyone's name from yesterday when Ms. Brickey had us sit in a circle and take turns stating two fun things about ourselves."

"Oh," Hector said. "I don't really remember anybody's name from that."

"That's okay," Eric said. "Most people have trouble remembering names. Most people have trouble remembering a lot of things. I'm good at remembering things. My name's Eric."

"Eric what? My name is Hector Alexander Jones."

"Eric Hauser. Your name sounds cool."

This is the way children usually become friends. No need for commonalities. No need for similar politics or parallel life experiences. Simply the fact that two children are of the same age—the possibility existing that they *might* from this point forward create commonalities, share experiences—is enough for friendship. Although even as a small child Eric required also that anyone he befriended look up to him, in a way. He wanted to impress, and he wanted others to be impressed. Thus he befriended Hector, who seemed impressed by everything and who, too, had no other friends.

Eric and Hector ate lunch together every day for the rest of first grade. On field trips they were safety buddies. Through second grade, too, they ate lunch together, played at recess together. It mightn't seem the case, but the child Eric did indeed like to play. He played that he was a robot, an alien, an intrepid explorer. Recess would start with Captain Hauser and First Officer Jones landing their cloaked spaceship at the edge of the playground and Captain Hauser ordering with entrepreneurial spirit, "Number One! Let's explore this planet. And don't forget where we parked."

In third grade Hector's dad (it was just Hector and his dad, back at home) bought Hector his first comic book, and Hector brought it to school and showed it to Eric. Eric hadn't been familiar with superheroes before this—his father watched *Star Trek* and the news and didn't really read, and his mother owned only books of paintings and watched only reruns of Bob Ross (who Eric did like)—but now here was one in front of him, all dressed in tight blue and red, spinning webs. A month later Hector brought two comic books to school: another one about the spider man and a new one, about a mutant with metal claws. On the playground that day, when Hector asked what planet they'd landed on, Eric said, "We're on Earth. And we don't have a spaceship anymore. And, Hector, I have some bad news. I've been in a terrible accident."

"An *accident*?"

"Yes, an accident. While saving an old man from a sudden chemical waste spill, I was tragically struck by lightening. I don't know whether I'm going to make it."

But lo and behold, Eric *did* make it! In fact, not only did he survive, he got stronger. And then he was shooting electricity from his fingertips. By the end of recess that day, Eric could turn himself into a human-shaped manifestation of solid light. And he could fly!

The next morning, by the coat- and backpack hangers, Hector ran up to Eric. "Guess what?" he said. "Yesterday, when I got home, I was in an accident too! Now I can turn into water!"

Eric looked at him. "No you can't. That's stupid. Water is a stupid power. And besides, only I have powers. You can be my sidekick, but we can't both have superpowers."

In fourth grade, Hector Alexander Jones was found by his father hanging from a tree in his front yard. The rope was, mercifully, under his arms, but its knot had been pulled tight by his chubby body's weight, and it had broken two of his ribs. One rib had pressed into a lung, puncturing it. Hector had been trying to be like Batman, he insisted. Batman didn't have superpowers, but that didn't stop him from doing cool things.

Hector recovered, but it was 2009, and the Affordable Care Act wouldn't be signed into law for another year, and Hector had to see a therapist so they could make sure he wasn't suicidal, and that plus the other medical bills were too much for Hector's father, so they went to live with Hector's grandparents in Florida, to relieve some of the financial burden, Eric's parents told Eric when he realized Hector was gone.

6

THAT WHOLE THING ABOUT ABOUT landing the spaceship and saying "Remember where we parked"—Eric got that from *Star Trek*.

He first saw *Star Trek* in a conscious way when he was seven years old. It had been on the living room television before then, but to Eric it had always just been a bunch of people with strange volcanoes on their foreheads talking about stuff. But then one weekend his mother was out of town, meeting with a gallery owner in Pittsburgh (finally her work might be displayed somewhere!), and it was just Eric and Wallace left to fend for themselves for two days and two nights. The first night kicked off with disaster.

Wallace Hauser was never much of a cook. He liked to cook gourmet, he always said, but for him *gourmet* meant Velveta cheese and shells, sandwiches on whole wheat bread instead of white and cut into four fancy triangles, or freezer-aisle pirogies thawed and cooked in the oven at a doughy 200 degrees. Eric's mom had prepared for her husband's lack of culinary prowess, though: she'd left a large portion of homemade marinara sauce in the refrigerator, and all Wallace needed to do was boil the pasta.

"Well, and why can't you just boil the pasta for us, too?" he'd asked when presented with the plan. "Then I could just microwave them both and the kid and I will be good to go."

"Have you ever had reheated pasta? It's rubbery and gross. And besides, you're good at making pasta. You make it for yourself all the time."

Wallace stared dumbly for a moment. Eric watched, wondering whether his father would figure it out. "Oh," he finally said. "You mean with cheese. Well, yeah, okay. I guess it's the same thing."

And then Amanda had smiled and kissed her husband on the cheek, her son on the lips (which Eric hated but every time obliged), and took her bag to the car and began the three-hour drive. It was a few minutes past noon. Eric had just eaten two peanut butter and jelly sandwiches and a pile of Doritos—the Doritos having been crushed up real small and placed by Eric between the pieces of white bread with the peanut butter and jelly—so he wouldn't be hungry for a long while. He went to his room, where he finished the weekend's homework and continued to work on a castle he'd been building for months now out of Tinker Toys, Legos, and Lincoln Logs, saving his meager allowance to purchase new pieces at regular intervals, careful to hide from his parents the fact that the building process was irreversible because he'd secretly been gluing the components together. He finished his homework in forty-five minutes; he worked on the castle for the rest of the afternoon. Eventually, his father came in. "Hey, bud. Hungry?"

When Eric was an infant, his father had called him by his name, in a cute, squeaky voice. In recent years he'd taken to using expressions like *bud*, *champ*, or *the kid*. Casual phrases, detached phrases. Eric thought this detachment probably had to do with the fact that he was adopted, which his parents had disclosed to him last year.

"I could eat," Eric said, using an expression he'd heard his dad say.

"Well, good then," Wallace said. "So I guess I'll go heat up that stuff. Want to watch a movie?"

The Hausers finally owned a DVD player, but their selection was limited to *Inspector Gadget* and *The Lion King*. When Eric's father came from the kitchen into the living room and found Mathew Broderick's face moving around the interactive menu, he said, "Really? Again? Why don't we watch something else? Pick anything else, in fact."

It was indeed true that Eric had watched *Inspector Gadget* at least two dozen times since they'd acquired the DVD player two months ago. There were indeed some days where he'd watched it two or three times on a loop. "But we don't have any other DVDs."

"So? Pick a tape, any tape."

"VHS is so old, dad. Nobody uses VHS tapes anymore."

"We've used VHS tapes since I was in college. Trust me, they're not going anywhere. Now just pick something else."

"Can it be rated R?"

Wallace Hauser sighed. "Yes, it can be rated R. But not for nudity! And don't tell your mom."

And that's when the popping sounds came from the kitchen—three of them. The first was soft, quick. The second came immediately thereafter, a little louder. Then all was quiet for a whole two seconds. The third pop was an explosion. Eric looked at Wallace. Wallace looked back at Eric. The kitchen when they finally ventured into it was a murder scene, bloody red and gory, the weapon a thousand shards of broken glass.

"Dad, how did you heat the spaghetti sauce?"

Wallace gaped at the mess. "On the stove . . ." he said slowly.

"Did you put it in a saucepan? Or did you leave it in the glass bowl Ma stored it in?"

Wallace looked at Eric. Then he looked at the mess. "Fuck," he said.

They ordered pizza, even had it delivered, a luxury in which the lower-middle-class Hausers rarely indulged. While they waited, Wallace cleaned the kitchen (fifteen years later Amanda would find coagulations of marinara under the refrigerator and oven) and Eric browsed the VHS tapes.

"What's this one?" he said when his dad, sauce on the cuffs of his shirt, returned to the living room. Eric held a tape high; on the front of its box was the hand-drawn image of a fierce, bird-like spaceship flying against a red sunset through two towers of what Eric even at seven years old recognized as the Golden Gate Bridge.

Wallace lit up, as if maybe there was hope yet for this weekend he'd be spending with his only son. "Oh, that? That's *Star Trek*. It's a *really* cool one. They go back in time to save these whales. Wanna watch it?"

"Whales?"

Wallace seemed to realize that maybe mentioning the presences of whales wasn't the best way to entice a child to watch a movie. "And time travel," he said.

"Does it have like wars? You know—battles?"

"Um, no. That one doesn't."

"Hmm. I think I'll keep looking."

"No—no. Let's watch it. It's really funny."

Star Trek was funny?

There was a knock at the door. "That's the pizza," Wallace said. "Come on, let's watch that one. It's really really funny. And fun! It's my favorite of all of them."

So they ate pepperoni pizza (if they were splurging for delivery, they certainly weren't also splurging for more than one topping) and watched *Star Trek IV: The Voyage Home*.

Eric liked it! It *was* funny, even if he didn't get all the jokes. In fact, the not getting of the jokes was part of what made him like it—he sympathized, in a way, with Mr. Spock: *Dipshit, Captain? What does dipshit mean? What is "exact change only"?*

"Dad, is that what San Francisco is really like?"

"I've never been," Wallace told him. "But I don't think so, not any more. I mean kind of, like there are hippies and stuff, but now its where all the rich people are. All the businesses. It's the heart of what they call Silicon Valley?" Which wasn't *quite* correct, but Wallace didn't know that, and neither did Eric.

"What's silicon?"

"It's like a metal, kind of. Like you use it for . . . well, they put it in . . . I guess I'm not really sure."

So San Francisco was where the rich people were. And the rich people, Eric had heard (although never from his parents, who he often heard complaining about the rich people), were the ones making differences in this world. "Are there more *Star Trek* movies?"

"Oh yes. And lots of TV episodes."

"Let's watch another one."

Wallace looked at his watch. He was one of the few people Eric ever saw wearing a watch. "Not now. It's actually past your bed time. Your mother would be pissed—I mean, annoyed—if she knew I'd let you stay up even this late."

"Come on. . . ."

"Tomorrow. We'll start first thing in the morning and do a marathon."

Which is what they did. While eating breakfast (eggs and bacon—Wallace did know how to do eggs and bacon—and burnt toast) they watched the first *Star Trek* movie. Then they watched the second. Through lunch (PB&Js and Doritos, again) they watched the third. They skipped the forth because they'd already watched it. They skipped the fifth because Eric's father said it was crap. They watched the sixth. Then they moved into the TV shows. They caught two episodes of *The Next Generation* on SPIKE TV. Then they watched a third episode (Season 6, Episode 12, "Ship in a Bottle"), and it *changed things*.

"So that guy's an android, like a robot, but he looks a lot like a human and he talks like a human and he wants to be a human?" Eric asked.

"Yeah, pretty much," Wallace said. "Data's a pretty cool character."

"And that other guy is a hologram, and he also wants to be human?"

"Kind of. He want holograms to have the same rights as humans."

"But he isn't real?"

"No, not exactly."

"Are holograms real. Like in real life?"

"Um—there are like holographic baseball cards and stuff, I think, but not stuff like that. Stuff like that is impossible. That's why it's science fiction."

But if what he was watching here couldn't ever happen, Eric didn't want to live in the future. Playing out before him on his family's decade-old television screen with its ever-worsening tracking lines was what the future should be, Eric thought. "I don't think stuff like that is impossible," he said. "I think it could be real. I think *that's* why it's called science fiction."

They had leftover pizza for dinner that evening. When his dad went to reheat it for them, Eric said it was probably safer if they just ate it cold.

7

BACK BEFORE THE SECOND GREAT financial collapse of the millennium, before such collapses seemed to become decennial events, back when a handful of naive Americans still believed their vote mattered, the old consumerist tradition called Black Friday was still going strong, if not showing early signs of its imminent and what would feel sudden decline. There were people fighting the tradition, sure—there were the minimalists, the essentialists, the enoughists, the my-whole-family-lives-in-an-RV-and-my-kids-don't-have-toys-or-go-to-your-traditional-schools-and-I-blog-about-it-ists. "Everything's an -ist or an -ism," Wallace Hauser used to say. "Not that I'm judging. By all means, live the life you want. But those things aren't for me." Besides, when you were lower middle class and your child needed for school assignments a reliable computer and a strong Internet connection, Black Friday was when you made that purchase.

Which is why Wallace and Eric were in line at Best Buy (in those days Best Buys still had brick-and-mortar stores; lots of what are now just websites still did) at 4 a.m., bundled tightly in jackets and hats heavy enough for a late Ohio autumn but too light for a northeastern winter.

Eric didn't like the cold, but he didn't complain about it. His father had given him coffee—his first ever cup!—and he sipped it, pretending to like its bitterness. "Here," his father said, producing from his pocket pink packets of sugar and powdered creamer. "You can use these if you want. They're what I like. I can't drink coffee without them." But Eric declined.

As twelve year olds are wont to do, he was determined to eschew any detail that would make him like his father. He sipped the beverage again. Maybe he didn't need to pretend to like it; maybe he liked it for real.

Eric and Wallace had been in line for just a few minutes. The plan had been to arrive half an hour ago, but Wallace hadn't woken in time. Eric had had no trouble waking up. He knew what they were here for, and he was excited to get it. They had computers at school, of course, and he used them frequently to type papers he'd written first by hand on college-ruled notebook paper (he didn't like wide-ruled, he'd decided long ago—the smaller you were forced to write, the more room there was on a single page for big ideas), but now he was going to have his own, like all the other kids. Except in his case it would be even better: the other kids had *family* computers, which they had to share with parents and siblings, but Eric knew his parents had no intention of ever using the computer they were going to buy today, despite their admonitions that the thing would be strictly regulated, used only in the living or dining room where they could see what he was up to, and left on the dining room table every night, never taken to Eric's room with him. But who were they kidding? The computer would be *his*. *He* would be using it. He could change its wallpaper to whatever he wanted. He could arrange the desktop icons however he wanted.

Some of the kids at school *did* have their own smartphones. Eric didn't see himself getting one of those any time soon. His parents didn't even have smartphones, just the kind that you had to flip open to talk on, with regular tactile buttons. And oh boy you should have seen Wallace when he tried to use his.

The advertisement had said the doors would open at 4:30. Eric and Wallace were near the front of the steadily growing line. There were maybe fifty people in front of them. They were *supposed* to be closer.

"Okay," Wallace said, sipping his own coffee and rubbing his right forearm vigorously. He moved as if he had to pee. "Do you remember the game plan?"

"Yep," Eric said. "I go left. You go right. We meet by the life-size cutout of The Avengers at 4:37. If neither of us has found the computer by then, it's probably too late." They'd scoped out the store together two days ago. They'd devised the plan together.

"Right. And you have the thing I gave you? You remember how to use it?"

Eric fingered the sausage-link-sized can of mace in his jacket pocket. His dad had insisted he carry it, said he'd heard these Black Friday events could get crazy, even dangerous, especially in the suburbs of big cities like Cleveland. People died sometimes—he'd seen it on the news. "Yep," Eric said. For his part, Eric didn't see the logic in being here, not now, not this morning? Wasn't it worth an extra hundred bucks to get a computer when there *wasn't* danger of death by stampede? But his dad said they couldn't afford an extra hundred dollars, and his mother agreed. Hell, though, if they *had* been willing to fork out the extra hundred—maybe by not getting that new TV last year that his dad had been so excited about—Eric could have stopped wasting his time writing his school assignments by hand ages ago.

Eric never said *hell* out loud, because he didn't want to get in trouble, but he thought it often. He also thought expressions like *damn* and *bullshit* and sometimes, like really only just once, even *fuck that.*

"And you're *sure* you don't just want an iPad?" Wallace said.

"*Dad*—I told you—I can't do everything I need to on an iPad." Eric wouldn't have minded an iPad in addition to, but not instead of, a laptop.

"Okay. Okay. Just checking one last time."

There was nothing to do in this line but drink the coffee.

Finally—a blue-shirted guy with a patchy neckbeard approached the automatic doors from the inside, turned a key, and the line was rushing forward.

"Dad! What are you doing?"

"What? I'm going left."

"No. *I* go left. You go right."

"Oh. Yeah, right. Okay. See you in a bit." And then Wallace took off in the other direction. Eric didn't pause to look back at him.

How many people were in here was hard to tell, but there were at least four hundred, maybe five. The store seemed simultaneously smaller and larger than it had two days ago. They'd tried asking employees where the laptops would be, but each one said they didn't know. Probably they knew but weren't allowed to reveal those things beforehand. It made sense: there could be no advantages given to the morning's combatants. It was fend for yourself. Kill or miss out on the deals of the year.

But there it was: Eric spotted it across three sections of the store, between the shrunken CD section and the washers and dryers, not displayed with the other computers but instead nestled on a shelf of pro camera lenses, enhancements for your DSLRs. There was just one. Whether there had always been just one or the rest had been taken in the two minutes since the doors opened was impossible to say—but there *was* just one. And some kid maybe three years Eric's junior was laying his hands on it. Eric moved fast. Now he was a dozen feet away.

"Hey!" he called. "I want that."

"It's mine," the other kid said. He tucked the box under one arm, pointed as if pointing meant something. "See."

"You have money for that?"

"My mom does."

"What do you need it for?"

"Games. Minecraft."

"Well I need it for school work. Important things, like essays and math. You probably don't know how to do math, or write, probably, but I do. So I need it."

"Fuck you," the other kid said.

Eric hadn't wanted the morning to play out like this, but he was here now, and when you were where you needed to be you did what you needed to do. His fingers played inside his jacket with the nozzle of the mace can—

But then a woman had the other kid by the hair. "Isaac!" she said. "What the fuck did I tell you? Put that down. We're not here for you. We're getting Christmas presents. Come on!"

The kid dropped the box. Eric felt almost bad for him as he was dragged away, but not bad enough to not bend down and retrieve the laptop himself.

It turned out they'd moved or gotten rid of the Avengers display, but Eric found his father near the refrigerators. "You got it?" Wallace asked.

Eric held out the box.

"Oh, good. You know, your mother has been wanting a new refrigerator. Maybe someday I'll be able to get her one."

They moved surprisingly quickly through the checkout line. Eric's father paid with his credit card. One HP Compaq Mini 702 EA netbook. Only three years old. $178. Nobody even died at that Best Buy that morning, although there were later two reports of minor injuries. And somebody may have died in a Walmart in Colorado.

Amanda was waiting for them at an IHOP across the street. She'd said, "You get up at three-thirty or whatever and take him to the store. I'd be willing to get up by five, meet you guys for breakfast." What better way to celebrate the acquisition of new goods than with breakfast food?

She looked tired when they walked in, but not of low spirits. She was cradling a mug between both hands. She smiled when she saw them. "Do you want some hot chocolate?" she asked as Eric slid across from her into the booth. He could tell from the aroma that hot chocolate was what was in her cup.

"No hot chocolate," he said. He was still holding the unopened laptop box. "Coffee, please."

Amanda looked at Wallace. "Coffee?"

Wallace winced. "I gave him coffee." Wallace slid in next to his wife. Eric had the whole side to himself.

They let him order a cup of coffee ("I don't think he should be drinking coffee." "Come on, he's been awake since the devil's buttcrack of dawn." "The devil's what?" "It's like dawn, but even earlier." "I'm pretty sure it's not. But fine, one cup.") but when it arrived he largely ignored it. He was focused on the laptop. He slit the tape that sealed the box with a butterknife, and soon his side of the booth was covered in little annoying bits of white polystyrene. They ordered three stacks of pancakes. Three plates of bacon. Three bowls of what IHOP considered fresh fruit. Eric eagerly but carefully unwrapped the computer's power cord. "Hey," his Mom said as he disappeared under the table, but he was already gone, searching for a wall outlet. There were none beneath their booth. He found one in the empty booth behind him. He snaked the cord around the outside and plugged it into the laptop.

"What are you doing?" his mother asked.

"I'm plugging the female end of the power cord into the laptop."

"The female end? Why's it called the female end?"

"Because inside it is a hole, and inside this part of the laptop is a little prong thing that goes into the hole, like a . . . you know."

"Oh," Amanda said. "I do know. Why do *you* know? Wallace, isn't he a little young for stuff like that?"

"Look who's talking," his father muttered.

"Hey."

"Sorry. Uncalled for. I'm tired."

Eric didn't know what they were talking about, or why his mom sounded so genuinely offended, but it didn't matter. And what else would the connectors in the power cord be called? Male and female made sense. They *were* just like penises and vaginas, at least based on how Eric understood those things to work. But if he could be mature about it, certainly could his parents be. This was technology, not sex. Although, if he played this right, he could use the technology to learn a lot more about sex—he knew how one accessed pornography.

He powered the computer on. It chimed as it booted, and it booted slowly. First a dark gray screen with white letters, then the Windows logo over a field of light blue, ugly on the small low-resolution display. Finally a welcome screen with the option to create an account.

"So," his mother said. "What do you think? How is it?"

"Hardware wise," Eric said, "it's a piece of crap."

"What?" his father said. "Why did you want it if you knew it wasn't good?"

"It's all you guys could afford. I wasn't going to get anything better."

"That sounds awfully ungrateful," Amanda said. "You sound awfully ungrateful, young man."

Eric could see how she might think that. "I'm not," he said. "I really do appreciate it. It's great. I read all about these low-powered machines. They're still plenty useful. I'm going to instal Linux on it."

"Listen to him, Wallace. 'Low-powered machines.' He doesn't even sound like a twelve-year-old, does he. I think your son is smarter than you."

"What's Linux?" his father said.

And that's when it hit him. Eric had known it all along, hadn't he? But he hadn't known he'd known. He *was* smarter than his father. Way smarter. And he was smarter than his mother, too, wasn't he? He was smarter than either of his parents. He possessed more knowledge, he could do more, and he could be more. He typed a few keys on the cramped keyboard. He clicked the plasticky trackpad a couple times. What did that mean for him, for them, that he was smarter . . . ?

The pancakes arrived, and he side aside these questions, and the computer, until he got home.

8

THERE WAS THIS GIRL ERIC liked when he was thirteen. She had brown hair, kind of curly. More wavy than curly, actually. Well, okay, it was pretty straight, nothing special about it, just your average brown kind of hair, but when it got wet it curled a little, she told Eric once. Her name is lost to time, but she had glasses and a smattering of freckles on her cheeks and on the tippy tip of her little nose. Eric thought she was pretty, in a way, and she was smart. Her grades were better than his, if only because she was more willing to focus on the things teachers and parents and administrators told her she *had* to focus on, while Eric liked to do his own thing. Like for example when a book report was assigned, and the rubric specified the book had to be a "classic," the girl read *Anne of Green Gables* and Eric read *A Clockwork Orange* even though the teacher told him it wouldn't count because it was sci-fi and also inappropriate for young readers. Another example was when Eric failed an algebra test because even though he knew how to do the problems, he *knew* he knew how to do the problems, so sitting in a silent classroom for an hour repeating the same formulas over and over was a waste of a quiet hour, which he could, and did, better spend trying to figure out how those same formulas could be applied to the creation of an artificial brain. Which they couldn't, of course, except at the most basic level. It wasn't like Eric Hauser perfected machine intelligence while sitting in that algebra class—he was only thirteen!—but there was a spark, even if only of imagination, which he in time realized everyone around him sorely lacked. Even the girl he liked was without inventiveness or originality. One day she kissed him on the lips in the hallway of their middle school. The next day at lunch, he told her he didn't think things were going to work out between them. Thanks, though. He delivered the line the way someone might if he wanted to break up with a girl via text message but still didn't have a cell phone because his parents said they didn't have the money, they'd spent it all on his netbook, on which he'd installed Linux and had already learned eight coding languages, including two obsolete but historical ones.

9

IMAGINE THE FRUSTRATION OF BEING smarter by orders of magnitude than everyone you know. It's . . . difficult. Sometimes it's excruciating. You're not necessarily more knowledgable than them. You're rational enough—*not* humble, because humility strikes you as a pointless virtue—to know you don't know as many things as *everyone* else, because you're still young, but you are way more capable of acquiring knowledge. You hunger for knowledge more than anyone you've ever met. And thus you hunger for a world in which you're surrounded by something different from that which you are currently surrounded by. Compared to you, everyone in your life is a moron. You know there are other people out there, though, people in the world who have done way more than you'll probably ever do, and you yearn to learn from them. Then you realize they've written books. And you can go to the library and get those books and read them and absorb some of their knowledge. But even better than books, they've written blog posts, and articles, and peer-reviewed papers published in scientific journals and then republished online. And yes, they're published behind paywalls, and as your parents remind you we just don't have the money for that sort of thing, and why would you want to read things like that anyway? *Reviews of Modern Physics*? Who wants to spend their time with that? You're thirteen, you're fourteen, you're fifteen. Eric, you're sixteen years old—you'll have time enough for all that stuff in college. Which, by the way, you'll have to get a scholarship for, because we just don't have the money to help you. We've wanted to help, you know. Your whole life we've tried to set aside a college fund, but things happen—cars break down, the house's vinyl siding is damaged in a hail storm and we don't have homeowner's insurance, hell, we're still paying on the mortgage, your mom needs her appendix taken out at forty-six, your father's blood pressure is high and he needs medication and health insurance under the new law covers only part of the cost—so we had to keep breaking into that college fund, you know? So you'll have to get a scholarship. Of course, that might be tough, since your grades are just so . . . average. So you'd be best served focusing on school work, not advanced physics; you get those grades up now. When I was your age I was working two jobs and doing my best to avoid my alcoholic father so that I could pay for medical school after I graduated. And your mother, she was working, too, I think. (I was.) See, she was. Anyway, I guess you could get financial aid, if you need to, or take out student loans. That's what most people do, and you'll realistically never have to pay them back, because it looks like this Bernie guy knows what he's talking about. But either way, you *are* going to college. Dammit, Eric, you just need to focus.

Maybe it's true, what they're saying about your generation. All you fucking Zoomers are fucking lazy. Don't know how good you have it. With your smartphones and your tablets and your Netflix and Chill. Oh, look, some artist reimagined Disney princesses as the cast of *F•R•I•E•N•D•S*. And someone else reimagined them as republican politicians. Fucking Zoomers. Buncha socialists. Get a job.

Except you don't have a smartphone or a tablet or even a decent laptop. You never created a Facebook account. You have only a six-year-old netbook that even when it was released was underpowered. But it's enough, because you can jimmy the system, break through the paywalls. And now you can read anything. *The New York Times* (so *that's* what's going on in the world). *Reviews of Modern Physics*. *The New England Journal of Medicine* (here's where we stand when it comes to mapping the brain). You could try to tell your parents all the things you're reading, all the things you're learning, because this stuff should be important to them, right? Because they're not Zoomers and if you're not a Zoomer you care about important stuff. But you try, and to them it's all so much science fiction. They go to their manual warehouse job and paint in their home studio but never sell their pictures. You don't know how to tell your father that he should have started saving for retirement two decades ago, that the warehouse is going to replace him with a more efficient and superiorly skilled robot within, at most, the next ten years.

So you don't tell them anything. You just keep learning. You let your high school GPA hover around a 3.0. Grades aren't nearly as important as the actual learning. In fact, you realized long ago, they're worthless. You have nothing to prove. You keep your own notebooks, build your own dreams. You focus and you focus and you focus and you

10

In eleventh grade, students of Arnold J. Jacobson High School (which was by some definitions considered a part of the Cleveland City School District and by other definitions not—the school no longer exists, by the way) had to take a special class focused on government and economics. The class lasted one semester and it was different from the regular history classes the curriculum required during the first two years of high school. Eric's school had two possible teachers for this class. If you were lucky, you got Mrs. Hopper, who was a libertarian short-skirt-wearing free radical with an NSA-agent husband whose homeland counter-terrorism raids were legend and who, Mrs. Hopper, invited her favorite students over for her famous Primary Parties and General Jamborees in election years.

If you were unlucky, you got Mrs. Fogelmanis. Eric got Mrs. Fogelmanis.

It wasn't that Mrs. Fogelmanis was particularly mean or crotchety—she wasn't. In fact, she was as kind as any other person, a "progressive" in her mid-twenties, gentle in her dealings with her students, tolerant (some might even say fully accepting, or even blind to the differences) of every race, gender, orientation (sexual or otherwise), color, hair style, etc. She even once was nearly fired for taking the side of a female-identifying student who was sent home for wearing a boys' cutoff gym t-shirt that revealed a substantial amount of side boob. The girl in being sent home missed a crucial algebra test, all for the sake of slut shaming, Mrs.

Fogelmanis said in an interview with Cleveland's CBS affiliate, all because the male patriarchy is so obsessed with sex that they'd let it interfere with a young woman's education.

So, yes, Mrs. Fogelmanis was a kind, good person.

But she was a terrible teacher.

Her lesson plans were biased, it had been complained. She approached the topic of certain forms of government with disdain rather than intellectual impartiality. When a mid-semester project required students take a test indicating their position on the political spectrum, she asked students who didn't swing at least a modicum left to take the test again, consider which questions they could give better answers to. She came as close to bashing right-wing fundamentalist Christians as she could and then a breath later scolded a student for expressing concern about the "growing Islamic threat." "We need to be understanding of other religions, other cultures," she told the class. "Fear will be the downfall of our nation, if we let it." Which was true; Eric agreed with her. But this was also the moment where she and he began to butt heads.

"But you're confusing fear with practicality," Eric said, raising his hand but not waiting for permission to speak. It's worth noting that Eric was not the student who'd raised the initial concern. Eric would never have used a phrase like "growing Islamic threat."

"I'm sorry?" Mrs. Fogelmanis said.

"Practicality. Rationality. There's a difference between being afraid of something and being rationally aware of the dangers a specific ideology poses to your well-being."

"Well, of course. I'm certainly not against rationality."

"But it seems you are. It seems a lot of people are, this world we're living in."

"No. I'm just reminding you all to be kind. Just because someone is a certain religion doesn't make them dangerous."

"Of course not. But just because someone is a certain religion and isn't dangerous doesn't mean the religion itself, or rather the dogma it's based on, won't do serious harm to millions of people. And I could be referring to nearly any religion here. The truth of my statement wouldn't change."

"It seems your splitting hairs, Mr. Hauser." Mrs. Fogelmanis called all her students by their last names, probably as a way of easing the discomfort she felt at being not very much older than them, as if assigning them a sense of authority would somehow reinforce her own.

"Then let me put it this way," Eric said. "A boy brings a homemade clock to school. The boy has brown skin. The school officials and the local authorities detain the boy because they think the clock looks like a bomb. The media erupts into outrage. How dare the officials assume this kid has a bomb just because of the color of his skin, right?"

Right, Mrs. Fogelmanis nodded. Right, other students in the class nodded.

"See, that's fair. But then, wouldn't you know, it turns out this homemade clock, while, yes, just a clock, did look a heck of a lot like a bomb. *Just* like a bomb, in fact. That, ma'am, means that the teacher who first reported the clock, and thus the principal who called the police, and finally the police who brought the boy in for questioning, just in case, were acting—well would you look at that—rationally. And whether the clock looked like a bomb had nothing to do with the color of his skin. It had to do with the clock looking like a bomb."

Mrs. Fogelmanis looked extremely uncomfortable. So did some of Eric's fellow students. "Let's move on," Mrs. Fogelmanis said.

And she really did. Move on. So it seemed. But even as a young man Eric had a way of not being able to do so himself. He had a difficult time focusing on the rest of the period. When the bell rang, he was one of the first out the door, fuming his way to his locker. This is why he wasn't on social media. He'd tried Twitter, finally, a few months ago, because he had a lot to say, but he'd found himself awash in a torrent of outrage. And the outrage had been contagious, so Eric himself had become outraged; he'd felt the suspicious urge to *advocate*. He could take only a week of this feeling before realizing he was outraged only for outrage's sake. And now the outrage of others outraged him. And he had other things to do besides be outraged. One young man's outrage wasn't going to change the world. Only actions would.

He placed the morning's book on his locker's top shelf. He stood there for a moment, elbow leaning against the door, just breathing.

"Hey," a male voice beside him said. "Eric?" The voice was familiar but also not. Squeaky, like its owner hadn't yet reached puberty, but low, deep, like the owner *had* reached puberty.

"Excuse me—" Eric said, turning. And there beside him was—

"It's me. Hector Alexander Jones!"

Hector had grown into a gangly teenager, ganglier than Eric (who was indeed gangly) but not as tall. He hadn't grown into his top set of teeth; they connected with his bottom lip in an expression of humorous naiveté. He held his books to his chest, in the way it was often assumed in highschools that only girls held their books.

"Hector? You moved to Florida."

"Yeah, but we moved back. My dad—"

The bell rang. "Come on," Eric said. "Let's get lunch."

"It's not my lunch period. I—"

"It's not mine, either, but I'm hungry. Come. Walk with me."

"You seemed kind of upset back there," Hector said. "You were kind of just staring into your locker, like someone shot your dog."

"Oh, that was nothing. I don't have a dog. I was maybe a little pissed off, but not at anyone in particular. It doesn't matter now."

"Okay. Well, hey, I really should get to my physics class—"

"Physics classes are stupid."

"But—"

Eric turned into the cafeteria, which was teeming with hundreds of students who *were* assigned to lunch this period. Hector followed. "Are you planning on being a physicist?" Eric asked.

"Well, no."

"Even better. And if you are going to be a physicist, then you need to do a lot more than go to Mr. Carbunkle's high school science lab. Oh, look, creamed turkey!"

The boys moved through the lunch line, watching as middle-aged ladies in hairnets spooned stingy piles of mashed potatoes, gravy, and stringy dark turkey meat onto their trays. A cup of corn appeared on their trays as they moved further down the line. Another lunch lady slapped onto each tray a slice of margarined white bread. Eric took a half-pint carton of two-percent white milk. Hector took three cartons of chocolate. "I have a high metabolism these days," he said when Eric made a face. "I can't seem to gain weight."

They payed for their lunches and Hector followed Eric to a table with a few empty chairs at the end.

"So," Eric said as he used a plastic fork to scoop globs of mashed potatoes and turkey onto his bread, "tell me everything. What's been going on with my old friend Hector Alexander Jones?"

Hector talked, pausing twice during the conversation to take a deep drag from an inhaler (both talking and eating made him short of breath, he said). Hector and his father had indeed moved to Florida after Hector's accident. They'd moved first into the apartment at the retirement community where Hector's grandma (*grandmammy*) lived. There were rules against people under a certain age living in the community, but they could be sidestepped under certain conditions—there was a whole lengthy application process required to prove said conditions. They lived with her for a year while Hector's dad found new work, and then they moved out, but into an apartment just a few blocks away, because Hector's grandmammy was getting kind of old and Hector's dad wanted to be close by so he or Hector could visit her daily, make sure she had everything she needed. Hector's dad worked for a small local law firm as a Client Relations Specialist—"Basically a receptionist," Hector said—and eventually worked his way up to paralegal status. And then a big corporate firm bought out the small local one, and Hector's dad got a raise. All this happening over several years, of course. And just last month Hector's grandma died, so they didn't need to live in Florida to take care of her anymore, and Hector's dad accepted a new position at the big firm's Cleveland office, so now Hector went to school here.

"But today isn't your first day here, is it?" Eric asked.

"No. I've been here since last week."

"Damn. I should have noticed you."

"It's a big school, though. Lots of classes and students. I guess our paths just never crossed."

"Yeah. It's just—I'm supposed to notice things like that. Anyway, but what's new with *you*? What are you into these days?"

"Into?"

"Working on? What's your focus? Hobbies. Passions. College plans. Whatever."

"Oh. Well, I'm thinking of being an artist. I guess I'll go to school for it, too. My dad kind of has a lot of money now, and he *knows people*, so I can probably get into whatever school I want."

Eric, finished with his food, wiped his plastic fork with a paper napkin. He'd be throwing the fork away with the rest of his trash, but it was just a thing he did. "An artist . . . huh."

"Yeah. Maybe comic books. I mean, I guess I'm kind of good at it . . ."

"I'm sure you are," Eric said. "In fact I don't doubt it. Hey, let's do dinner at your house. Tomorrow?"

"Um, okay. I mean, I'd have to ask my dad."

"Of course. Cool. Cool. I never did get to meet your dad."

The next afternoon, after a straightforward, uneventful school day—even Mrs. Fogelmanis's class was unfaultable—Eric went home to change before heading to Hector's. At this point in his life, Eric had already stopped communicating with his parents about most things, more so even than is common for humans in their mid-to-late teens. So it wasn't surprising when Eric walked into a house smelling pleasantly of roasted meat and vegetables. "We're having a pot roast for dinner," his mother said.

"Oh, that sounds great, Mom" Eric said, never exactly impolite to his mother, "and it smells wonderful too. But I have plans."

"Plans?"

"Dinner plans. I guess I didn't tell you."

"No, I guess you didn't. Important?"

"Of course. I don't make plans that aren't important."

"No, I don't suppose you do."

She didn't bother asking where he was going. He dropped his bag in his room, picked up the other bag he used, which rather than containing schoolbooks was always prepacked with his aging computer, notebooks both lined and unlined, a book or two he'd recently taken out from the library, and a case of pencils and pens. In a small side pocket, sufficiently (he thought) hidden, was a tube (the kind, for camouflage, you might put catnip in) of weed, a glass pipe, and a lighter. Had Hector ever smoked? Eric changed his shirt, reapplied deodorant, and kissed his mom's cheek respectfully on the way out the door.

He regretted leaving his mother hanging like that. He liked his mother—he did. And he liked her art, for what it was, but he'd spent his whole life wondering whether she was actually going to go somewhere, achieve something beyond the occasional local or small-town gallery exhibition at which, if she was lucky, maybe a piece would would sell. But so far she hadn't. She had the capacity to be bigger—he knew it. Her work wasn't great, but their *was* a place for it, and artists less talented than her had done the work needed to at the very least make a decent living. Doubtless Wallace father would be pissed when Amanda told him Eric had bailed. But, oh, his father. . . . If what Eric felt for his mother was respect, even love, what he felt for his father these days was at best pitty. What a man his father could have been. After all, this was the man who'd introduced Eric to the science fiction that fueled his imagination, but he was also the man who, by ironic virtue of his own failings, fueled Eric's ambition.

When, on the tenth anniversary of the Columbia disaster, the news replayed footage of the shuttle disintegrating over Texas, Wallace Hauser said, "What a waste of life."

Not a waste. A *sacrifice*. "It's sad," Eric said. "But they were astronauts. It's what they were meant to do. It's what they loved to do. And they knew it wasn't the safest job in the world."

"A couple decades ago I would have agreed with you, son, but I've heard promises of the benefits of space travel for years, and so far I haven't seen a damned thing actually come out of it."

"You met me because of it," Amanda said.

"I met your mother because of it."

Eric hadn't seen his dad watch *Star Trek* in years. But he did buy Eric some DVDs for his fifteenth birthday. Eric was not ungrateful.

Eric walked to the bus stop. Rode the bus to Hector's. They ate pizza, and while it wasn't Amanda Hauser's pot roast, it *was* the best pizza you could get in the city. The most expensive, too. Premium toppings. Grass-fed pepperoni, the place boasted. Hector's dad could afford it.

Eric started spending a lot of time with Hector and his dad. Hector's dad was just a little overweight. He dressed exclusively in suits. When he wanted to relax he took off the jacket and loosened the tie. He had neat hair and a tidy mustache. He introduced Eric to anchovies. He gave Eric a little Scotch. "You ever smoked a cigar?" he asked Eric as he snipped the end of a Cuban.

"My dad gets some great cigars," Hector said, "The clients at the law firm give them to all the guys that work there. But I can't smoke them because of my left lung being 'inefficient.'"

"Poor kid," Mr. Jones said. "You're missing out, Hec."

Hector laughed. "So you keep telling me, Dad."

"I got a good kid, though," Mr. Jones said. "He's gonna be a great artist some day."

"Or graphic designer, maybe, I've been thinking," Hector said.

"Or a graphic designer. Whatever he wants to be. So long as he isn't a fag, eh?"

Hector gulped at that. Eric didn't know whether to laugh.

"What?" Mr. Jones said. "Wait—you didn't tell him?"

"Tell me what?" Eric asked.

"Um, I'm gay," Hector said.

"Oh. Okay," Eric said.

Hector's father erupted into laughter. "See, kid. No big deal. He keeps thinking it's going to be a big deal, thinks people are going to freak out when they find out. I mean, yeah, *some* people are still homophobic, but nobody *important* is gonna care if a man or a woman is gay."

"No, I don't suppose they would," Eric said.

"Except maybe the president," Hector muttered.

"What about you? You gay?" Mr. Jones said.

"Haha. I'm afraid not, Sir."

"Shame. Hector likes you—"

"Dad!"

"Not like *that*. He just looks up to you. I was just hoping . . . y'know? Coulda been a good match. Anyway, he'll find someone at art school, I keep telling him. Someday he'll find someone special."

"Thanks, Dad," Hector said.

"I'm proud of my boy," Mr. Jones said to Eric. "I bet your parents are proud of you."

"I'm afraid they hardly understand me," Eric said. "But I don't really believe in being proud of others anyway. Telling someone you're proud of them is like taking ownership of their accomplishments, don't you think? Like when a father tells a daughter he's proud of her for being such a good mother. He didn't push a baby out of his vagina."

Mr. Jones took a puff of his cigar. "Huh."

When Eric and Hector decided to collaborate on a school science project, Mr. Jones cleared space for them in his garage. The requirements for the project were broad: only that teams had to develop an item or procedure that attempted to solve a problem. One group took a selfie stick and affixed a DSLR to the end, "so you can take higher quality selfies"; they received a B+. Another team created a contraption that boiled water while also frying an egg, "so tea and breakfast are ready at the same time"; they received an A-, points lost because Mr. Carbunkle drank coffee from a drip coffee maker for his breakfast and couldn't understand why someone would want tea. One girl who worked solo developed a dongle that plugged into your smartphone's headphone jack and measured the phone's output of electromagnetic radiation, using a concurrently developed app to display the information on the phone's screen; she received a C because, while her device was ingenious, it didn't solve a problem, after all, the real problem is avoiding radiation, and if you have to hold the device emitting the radiation to measure it, it's too late, said Mr. Carbunkle; still, she went on to work for the Laser Interferometer Gravitational-Wave Observatory while Mr. Carbunkle continued to teach high school physics until his death six years later, from cancer. Eric and Hector, for their parts, received independent grades for their joint project; Eric was awarded a B for his creation of a rudimentary palm-sized holographic image projector ("Points lost because why does anyone need this?"–Mr. Carbunkle), and Hector was given a D for contributing only the two-by-four painting of Spider-Man the device projected ("You didn't do any science work"). "Don't worry," Eric said to Hector as he returned the projector to his bag after Mr. Carbunkle had finished handing out grades, "I'm going to keep working on this thing, and it's only going to get better. And there's only one man I'll turn to to create the art for it."

A week later, however, you wouldn't have thought Eric Hauser was going to work on anything academic ever again, because a week later he dropped out of high school.

The inciting incident happened during third period, Government 101. Ms. Fogelmanis had projected on the classroom's white projection screen (using, it's worth noting, a projector the size of a briefcase) various images of then presidential candidate Bernie Sanders. Many of the images were the same. Some showed the man with a crazed look in his eyes, hair shocked out like Doc Brown in *Back to the Future*; some showed him biting his bottom lip, as if in pained thought; others had him with his finger raised—pardon me, but I must say something. Each of them had a caption, some effacing, some mocking, other complimentary, all humorous. "But while, yes, we may laugh and scroll endlessly through our news feeds viewing picture after picture," Ms. Fogelmanis was saying, "the prevalence of these memes tells us something."

Someone in the classroom blew a gum bubble.

"What do they tell us? Anyone?"

The bubble popped.

"They tell us that Bernie is *accomplishing something*. He's getting under our skin. For some of us, that's a good thing, a great thing, but for others, it's scary. Does anyone know what I mean?"

A girl raised her hand. "You mean like that the Democrats really like him, but the Republicans are super freaked out."

"Kind of," Ms. Fogelmanis said. "The Republicans certainly are scared by Senator Sanders' campaign, but so, believe it or not, are some of the Democrats."

Eric raised a hand. "That's not true," he said.

"I'm sorry?"

"Republicans aren't scared of Bernie Sanders. They know that the instant he wins the Democratic nomination, they can attack his socialist ideals full force, guaranteeing he'll lose the general election."

"Well"—Ms. Fogelmanis didn't look directly at Eric but kept her attention focused on the class as a whole—"while Mr. Hauser is wrong about that, he does bring up the point I was trying to make. Two words: democratic socialism. Even better, one word: just socialism. Are you scared? Lots of people are. Who can tell me why?"

"Because socialism sounds like a bad word," one student said.

"It's like communism," said another.

"Ah—but is it?" asked Ms. Fogelmanis. "Who here wants free healthcare? Really free?"

Most of the class raised their hands.

"What about college? Who's dreading the idea of student debt?"

The hands stayed up. A few more joined them. A few remained lowered.

"If you didn't raise your hand, it's either because you're wealthy or you're too young to understand what a burden debt is. But, see, that's all democratic socialism is. Taking a little bit from the rich to give to the people who need it most, like Robin Hood."

"You mean like stealing?" Eric said.

The hands went down.

"Excuse me?" Ms. Fogelmanis said, raising an eyebrow.

Eric stood. "Theft. You know, that thing you accuse Wall Street of doing. Nobody's going to give you a free iPhone, Ms. Fogelmanis. You may not understand this, but most people *want* to work for a living."

"You're very close to crossing a line, Mr. Hauser."

"All I'm saying is that your precious Robin Hood was just a common criminal, and so was everybody who took the money he stole from King Richard."

"Sounds like somebody's been reading Ayn Rand."

"I haven't, actually. I mean I tried, but her prose was terrible and overwrought, her characters so very one-note. Anyway, I said Robin Hood, didn't you hear?"

"King . . . the king from Robin Hood . . ."

"Was a bad guy, too, yes, that's true. He stole by taxing everybody. And your precious democratic socialist is going to tax *you*, Ms. Fogelmanis. Or don't you understand the meaning of the term?"

"Why don't you *sit down*, Mr. Hauser."

"Why don't you stop being such a cunt."

What was weird was that Eric didn't actually feel a particular hostility toward Ms. Fogelmanis herself. She was just a person, doing what people do. She was a teacher, and even if she wasn't a very good one she was trying to help her students. Eric's outburst was born more of frustration with an entire system than with any one person. He was sick of wasting his time in an underfunded high school. And to know he had to endure another year of it . . . ? Another whole year before he could *do* something with his life . . . ?

"I apologize," he said immediately. "I'll see myself to the principal's office."

Eric was suspended for three days. He used those three days to draw up a reasoned, watertight argument for why he should be allowed to drop out of school. He presented the argument first to his parents, displaying a series of charts and precedents using his homemade projector. He had a plan, he told them. He would get a full-time job (a requirement for dropping out of school before age eighteen in Ohio) and save the money until he had enough to start his own company, the details of which he was still working out but had a rough outline of. He was dropping out either way, he told them, but if they could consent—if he could live with them for a while longer—it would make things much easier for him, both financially and legally. His parents debated the idea, with him and with each other, for a week before telling him they'd sign the papers—we love you, son. To the school administration Eric presented the same argument. The administration resisted. Eric reminded them that his SAT scores—he'd taken the tests this past fall—proved he didn't belong in high school. The administrators told him he was correct, but what the scores did show was that he belonged in the best college, and he couldn't get into any colleges if he didn't have a high school diploma. College? Eric said. And waste four more years? I don't think so.

In the end, all parties consented. The paperwork was signed. Eric lived with his parents, paid them rent. Hector's dad got him a job as a client relations specialist. Over the next half-year, Eric saved $20,000 dollars in full-time wages.

And with that $20,000 he did something he hadn't told anyone he was going to do. When he turned eighteen, he diverted from his professed plan and moved to Paris.

Had this move been his intention from the beginning? It's hard to say. Even Eric himself wasn't sure. He'd always had a burning desire to leave his hometown, to move to a big city, an urban hub—but according to the plan that hub was going to be San Francisco. But now here he was spending a year in an incommodious single-room studio in the eighteenth arrondissement, eating mostly bread, cheese, and deli meats, doing one hundred and then two hundred and then a thousand push-ups every day, reading stacks of books he purchased and then exchanged at Shakespeare & Company: mostly novels, some business, a smattering of self-improvement. First he read only books he could find in English; then, as his language skills developed, he got them in both English and French, and finally French only.

Eric didn't make friends in Paris, didn't try to, but he did start making regular appearances at popular clubs and dingy bars, becoming well known to their customers and employees, captivating them with lectures on topics like literature, technology, and the future.

Alas, as Eric's social skills grew, his ability to successfully court a woman did not. He went on dates with the most beautiful Frenchwomen; he screwed up dates with the most beautiful Frenchwomen. Approaching these failures from a scientific perspective, he realized that in each case he was too preoccupied by the fact that he might have sex that evening; despite all his confidence and intelligence and rationality, Eric feared that having not had sex by eighteen meant he might never have it at all. So after seven months in Paris he took one thousand of the five thousand dollars he now had left (he'd paid a year's worth of the studio apartment's rent up front), and hired the best escort he could afford. The name she gave him was Esmerelda, and he'd never forget her. He took her to dinner, told her his reason for hiring her. She treated him, then, like a woman would treat any man she liked and intended to fuck. Instead of returning to his apartment as protocol dictated, she invited him back to hers. She was gentle with him, and then she was rough. She made sure he gained a thousand experience points in a single night. When it was over, they drank wine, and before he left just after midnight, she kissed him tenderly on the cheek. From that point on, nearly all Eric's dates ended in copulation. He had his first threesome while living in Paris.

When he was down to his final thousand dollars, he sold the books he'd accumulated. Left the furniture in the apartment exactly as it had come. Bought a plane ticket straight to San Francisco. Did not stop in Cleveland. Did not pass go. Did not collect two hundred dollars.

Nineteen-year-old Eric Hauser stepped out of the San Francisco airport, two bags in his possession, nearly dead broke, walked up to a friendly-looking woman in a yellow jacket, and said, "Excuse me. I've been abroad and don't have a phone. Could I trouble you to call me an Uber? I'll pay you back, of course, handsomely."

Zoomers III

1

THERE WERE STARS ON THE vaulted ceiling; they were the first thing Sophia noticed. They looked real. They hovered high above her, a small slice of galaxy, near the lobby's ceiling, just below the exposed industrial beams that didn't appear to serve a structural purpose. The second thing she noticed, as she walked through the lobby, her flats nearly silent against the unpolished concrete floor, was that the stars were moving.

Then again, maybe they weren't. She was suddenly unsure.

"They *are* moving," someone said.

The voice startled her. The lobby had seemed empty. Somehow, she hadn't seen the glass desk at its far end—or the pretty woman behind the desk.

"The stars are indeed moving," the pretty woman said again, as Sophia drew closer. "But you can't actually tell. Those stars offer a view of what the night sky would look like from in here if the ceiling were removed. So they're moving with the rotation and orbit of the earth, but that's not fast enough that anyone can actually tell."

"Oh."

"Some people think they can, though."

"Oh."

The pretty woman smiled. She had a name tag but Sophia didn't read it. "Anyway—how can I help you?" the woman asked.

"I'm here to see—"

"Sophia! Over here."

Sophia turned to see Eric exiting an elevator. When he reached her, Eric grabbed her hands and kissed her on the lips, lingering longer than maybe he should have done in front of an employee—or anyone else, probably. A few other people were entering the lobby from the street. This kiss would confirm the gossip. The confirmation would be all over the Internet. Which meant that theirs was now a real relationship.

"You're dripping wet," Eric said. It might have been a double entendre—it echoed something he'd said the night before—but he was probably referring to her coat, the countless beads of water rolling on its pink waxed surface. "Cordelia will take that for you, let it dry."

After Eric had left this morning—Sophia hadn't checked the time, but it was still dark outside his windows—she'd lingered in his comfortable bed. It's what she would have done in her own: lingered. She drifted to the edge of sleep and spent a while there, dreaming but not quite dreaming, lucid but having relinquished herself to her mind's own narratives. The sheets were *so soft*. Sophia had money; surely she could afford sheets this soft. And yet she had no idea where to get such sheets. These were billionaire sheets, in exclusivity if not price. After some time, she rolled over and retrieved her phone from Eric's nightstand. She'd been surprised last night to discover some of the things *in* that nightstand, surprised also to discover the way some of those things could make her feel. She had no unread text messages. She had hundreds of unread emails, but the oldest were from months ago, long ignored; none of the subject lines of the newer ones looked interesting, so she ignored those too. She checked her various social media feeds. An actress friend of hers had posted a ten-second clip from the set of an action movie she was staring in, and Sophia felt an attack of jealousy. Not that she wanted to be working right this second, but she wanted to have projects on which to not want to work. There was a note on the pillow next to her, handwritten on thick square paper in flowing brown script: *Make yourself at home.*

Sophia had long been hearing reports that handwriting was going out of style, but if Eric's flowing cursive script was any indication, some people still had style.

But what did that mean: *Make yourself at home?* It meant breakfast, obviously. It meant a shower in a bathroom with heated floors. It meant fluffy white towels and a fluffy white robe. It meant see what's on TV. It meant log in to Eric's Netflix account and see what sort of things he has in his queue (documentaries, mostly, also some science fiction movies and shows).

Sophia was wealthy—she could live forever off the money she'd made from the Disney show and album, plus residuals, as long as she paid someone to manage her investments right, which she did, and didn't spend *too* much—but Eric was more than wealthy. Sophia still had a few million dollars; Eric had billions. Which is why it struck her that while her house could be described as a small mansion, Eric's was just a large house, with amenities. A large house she couldn't help but explore.

It was hours before she finally left Eric's house in Sea Cliff to meet him at his office. She thought about using one of his remaining cars. He had said make yourself at home. But she didn't know where the key fob was. Plus she had a license but had never really driven much. When he spoke about the building on Spear Street, he always used the word *headquarters*, but in her head she heard *office*. It *was* a *headquarters*, though, bigger than she'd imagined, and yet smaller, too. Had she expected cubicles? A factory? "What do you think of the view?" he asked her as they took an elevator up up up. You could see the whole bay, the Bay Bridge, Oakland across the water. "Google used to own this building. Had offices right here. But lucky for me they were looking to sell right when Lumina was getting started. I knew we'd be successful, knew this was an investment I could make. It's smaller than some headquarters, sure—a lot smaller, actually—and someday we'll probably have to move somewhere bigger, expand into a full-blown campus—I mean, this place is no spaceship—but it works right now. Most of the developmental labs are in the basement levels, anyway, which, fun fact, we put in ourselves, most of them. Google had had just the one sub-level, the one an ex-employee revealed was used as some sort of corporate sex dungeon."

"I think I remember that," Sophia said. "Google, I mean."

The elevator announced its arrival at their destination floor with a sound like half a wind chime. The doors hissed open cleanly, and before them stood a man about Eric's age, thin, tall, with a black goatee that seemed painted on and round glasses that muted his thick eyebrows. "Is this her?" he said, grinning.

Eric smiled too. "This is her. But let's not address her indirectly, Hector, please."

"Oh—all right." He took Sophia's hand. "I apologize. I can be quite rude. It's just that I've heard so much about you."

"You have?" Sophia said.

"Eric never shuts up about you."

"He's exaggerating."

"Of course I'm exaggerating. I mean, he doesn't talk about you *all* the time. The man has work to do. It's not like he's gushing about you during meetings or conference calls. But when it's just him and me . . . all he ever talks about. For like the last week, at least."

"Hector," Eric said, "meet Sophia Velasquez. Sophia, Hector Alexander Jones."

"A pleasure," Hector said.

"Um—you too," Sophia said. Then she added, "Charmed, I'm sure."

Hector turned to Eric. "She's sassy."

Sophia shrunk. "I didn't mean . . . um . . ."

"Don't worry. Hector likes sassy."

"I like sassy."

"Oh—good. Although I'm afraid I wasn't trying to be sassy."

Eric cleared his throat. "Anyway," he said, "that'll be all, Hector."

"'That'll be all Hector.' Hear that? Like I'm his servant." But Hector was still smiling. "Okay, okay. I'm leaving. Brace yourself. Eric's about to show you something really cool." Then he turned to Eric. "Even though I told him he should probably wait." And then Hector disappeared into the elevator, whose doors, Sophia realized, hadn't yet closed, as if they'd been patiently waiting for him.

"Hector is . . . ?" Sophia prompted when they were alone.

"I suppose you could say he's my . . . best friend. Come on—my workshop is this way."

Sophia hadn't imagined Eric as the sort of man who could have a best friend. What did that mean: *best friend*? Did they go out for drinks together? Did they play wingman for each other (was Hector married?

Had he been wearing a ring?)? Did they confide in one another their deepest darkest secrets?

The workshop door was like the elevator's: barely there, imperceptible unless you were looking for it, the same cold blue-gray granite of the corridor walls, just slightly recessed, with a flat touchpad next to it. Sophia realized it was the only door in the whole corridor. When they approached, Eric held up a hand in front of the touchpad, made a sweeping gesture, and the door's outline became more visible. A rectangular cutout popped backward and then sideways with a hydraulic hiss, revealing a chamber within.

"This is your office?" Sophia said. It was so unlike his home. Not the sparse corporate manager's administrative workspace she'd expected, it was more like da Vinci's workshop. Over here was an ornate wooden desk, strewn with notebooks and papers, fountain pens and even a quill and inkwell, behind them a bookshelf, wall-size if the room had been of more humble dimensions, merely impressive in this cavernous space. Indeed, on a pedestal next to the wooden desk (hand-carved, he'd tell her later, early nineteenth century, rumored to have been used by Thomas Jefferson in his personal office at Monticello) lay open a massive leather-bound book: "The notes and sketches of Leonardo da Vinci. A reproduction, of course. I keep the real ones in an Italian museum of which I'm on the board, under glass. I find them profoundly inspirational." But over there, on that side of the room, the scene changed: there was a raised area, its floor marble or polished metal, it was hard to tell, with another desk, this one glass and filled with keyboards and coffee mugs and tablet computers and digital styli. The space above it was a consortium of computer monitors, each of them displaying a screensaver featuring Lumina's simple logo, animating in unison. Then, over there, a worktable, it's surface a smattering of tools and components Sophia couldn't identify (although that one looked similar to the back casing of her phone, and *that* like the face of a wristwatch, but featureless). And in that corner, sequestered away like an afterthought, but frayed, obviously well-used, hung a punching bag. On the wall next to it, a pull-up bar. Two forty-pound dumbells on the floor.

"Well, it's what I think of when I think of my office, anyway. I have another space downstairs that's more like what you'd expect, with a clear desk and a single desktop computer and a window and the obligatory couple pieces of art on the wall, where I receive visitors and conduct meetings. This, however, is where I do my real work. No one comes in here but me and Hector—and you now. And technically one other person, or technically not one other person, depending on how you look at it."

"But why me?"

"I wanted to know what you thought of this—" Eric looked . . . up . . . not *at* the ceiling but *to* it. "Hera?" he said.

A large disk, a raised dais she hadn't noticed before on the floor in the very center of the room because of the perspective of where she was standing, lit up. The space above it shimmered, flickered. And then a woman was there.

She looked not quite real, but almost, like a character model from a video game. "Hello, Eric," she said. Her voice was so close to human.

"Hello, Hera," Eric said. "I'd like you to meet someone very important to me. Hera, this is Sophia."

"Hello, Sophia," Hera said.

"Sophia, this is Hera. She's *also* very important to me."

"She's a—"

"A hologram. Just like the stars downstairs. Just like the projection that comes from your phone when you hop on a holocall with your mother."

"My mom doesn't like holograms. She says they're too much like ghosts."

"Makes sense. My mom didn't like the iPhone. She said she just didn't need it. She doesn't really like the HoloPhone either. You can address Hera directly."

Sophia knew nothing of Eric's mother. This was the first time he'd mentioned her.

"I am Hera," Hera said. She extended a hand to Sophia.

Instinctively, Sophia extended hers as well, and the two hands met. "She's . . . solid."

"An illusion." Eric was smiling. "But convincing enough that it doesn't matter."

"A pun," the hologram said. "For I am not matter."

"But my phone . . . that hologram isn't solid."

"I've been working on a few improvements to the projection technology. It's just a matter of forcefields."

"Forcefields . . . there's no such thing. Except in science fiction."

"Yes. So maybe that's something I've been working on too."

"What? Science fiction?"

"Something like that. Hera, run a self-diagnostic."

The hologram disappeared for a fraction of a second. She flickered a few more times. "Done," she said.

"Excellent. And how are you feeling today?"

"I do not feel anything. I am not matter."

"Damn," Eric said.

"Is that bad?" Sophia asked.

Eric sighed. "No . . ." he said. "It's not . . . bad. It's just not what I was hoping she'd say. She's not very good at nonliteral interpretation yet. Her AI isn't fully developed."

"How . . . developed . . . is it?"

"Really quite a lot, actually. Better than the personal assistant on your phone, say. And since she has solidity she can carry out tasks. She could even make us coffee—"

"Would you like coffee?" Hera asked. She seemed almost eager at the prospect of being given a task.

"—except," Eric continued, "that she's still confined to that projection pad there, and probably will be for a very long time, maybe forever. No, thank you," he said to the hologram. "But the point is that she does know *how* to make coffee. And theoretically she makes the best cup you've ever had."

"I see," Sophia said. "But I guess I'll have to take your word for that."

"For now." Eric winked—maybe. On their first day together, in the D.C. hotel room, he'd told her he'd had trouble winking for most of his life and only a few years ago had started practicing it ten minutes a day every day for a month until he could do it without trying. Now, he'd said, his eye sometimes twitched.

Sophia circled the projection pad. At first, Hera spun with her, but when Sophia asked her to hold still, she complied. "Who are you based on?" Sophia asked after she'd completed a full revolution.

"I do not understand the question."

"Who was the model for your physical body?"

"I was designed by Uncle Hector Alexander Jones."

"Uncle?"

"He's probably more like her godfather, but sure," Eric said. "That's why she doesn't look quite human. She's not modeled after a real person. Of course, we could have modeled her after someone—in fact, for the first version I myself put on a motion capture suit—but we wanted to create someone unique. But not algorithmically generated, either. Hector is the artist."

"So Hera is like your love child."

"Our brain child. Hector's goal is for her to someday be indistinguishable from a real human. But I kind of like her how she is."

"And I kind of like Eric how he is," Hera said to Sophia.

"Haha." Eric said. "Thank you."

"I am programed to be capable of humor," Hera said.

"Capable," Eric said, then he sighed again, "but bad at it. Siri was funnier."

"You programmed me."

"Yeah, well, I'm not very funny. Hera, Sophia and I would like to be alone now."

"Of course," the hologram said. And then she flickered once before disappearing altogether. The projection dais grew dark.

"Wow," Sophia said. "That was unlike anything I've ever seen before. And you did all that yourself? Programmed her, I mean."

"Mostly, but not entirely. Code like that would take a single person probably decades to write. I have a team, although aside from Hector they don't know exactly what it is they're working on. Hera is a very secret project. She's not perfect, though. Far from it. How much do you know about artificial intelligence? Also, I really could use some coffee."

Sophia followed Eric to the area of the room with the antique desk, the books, the paper. There was an espresso machine there, too, a large gold apparatus you'd find in the city's best coffee shops. "Some," she said while Eric set to work, pulling the machine's numerous levers. "I know it isn't science fiction, that almost all scientists agree it will be a reality someday soon."

"*Artificial* intelligence already is a reality, of course," Eric said. "It has been for a long time. Decades. Before you were born, before I was born. Arthur Samuels created a computer capable of playing checkers in 1952. Three years later, he improved it with the ability to *learn* to play checkers, to get better. Once it could learn to improve, it became a better checkers player than its creator. In 1992, it beat the reigning world champion. In 1997, a computer named Deep Blue—and damn I wish that name weren't already taken—beat the world *chess* champion, and that champion, a man named Gary Kasparov, said he saw evidence, while playing, that Deep Blue was actually thinking, was showing creativity in its moves. In the 1950s, they thought if you'd created a computer that could play chess, you'd done it, you'd created the epitome of human intelligence summed up in a machine." The espresso maker hissed. Steam began to waft from the top. "Of course, we now know that isn't true. Deep Blue couldn't hold a conversation. Deep Blue could think, yes, but only about chess. It couldn't play Go or do a crossword, but now there are computers that can. Did you ever watch *Jeopardy!*?"

She hadn't.

"Is just espresso okay? Would you like a latte? I have soy milk."

"A soy latte would be wonderful."

"*Jeopardy!* was a quiz show, one of the most popular game shows of all time, back when people watched TV, before streaming. A computer named Watson beat the show's all-time champion, who had himself won seventy-four consecutive games. The computer won the grand prize, one million dollars."

He handed Sophia a large white mug. She sipped from it. The latte was delicious. Eric drank straight espresso from a tiny but otherwise identical cup. He gestured for her to follow him, and she joined him in a nook of the workshop that contained two leather couches.

"What was significant about Watson at the time was he could answer questions presented in any variety of natural language rather than specifically defined inputs. And yet in the few years that followed, suddenly smartphones could do that too. You could ask your phone whether you needed an umbrella, and it would answer you and also give you more information about the weather forecast. Of course, this you're familiar with—any phone or watch can do that now. But Hera can do so much more. She can hold a conversation. She can, sometimes, make jokes. She can answer any trivia question you ask her. And yet she can't tell you how she's feeling if you ask her how she's feeling."

"But you could program her to."

"I could program her to. But that would just mean setting the input to 'How are you feeling?' and setting the output to 'fine.' She wouldn't understand the question, wouldn't get the metaphor. Wouldn't actually *know* how she's feeling. I don't know how to get her to do that, yet. And if anyone else has figured it out, they're not sharing. Anyway, yes, we have the HoloPhone Two scheduled for release early next year. Yes, late next year we'll almost definitely release a life-size model of the HoloPhone's projector, so that people can install it in their homes and it'll be just like talking to their friends in person—mostly. We're even working on some virtual reality stuff that uses holograms instead of headsets. But this"—he pointed to where Hera's projector was located—"*her*—she's what I'm really working on. And it's going to be a long time before we get there, before she's a real person. To be honest, we may never get there. It's possible it can't be done."

"I think you can do it. I think you're brilliant," Sophia said. And she did.

"Anyway, what are *you* working on?" Eric asked.

And though she loved that he was interested, Sophia hated that she didn't have anything to tell him.

2

THE NEXT WEEK, SOPHIA FLEW with Eric to Paris. He attended a conference while she explored. They met for dinner at a restaurant he'd chosen, dark, its door hidden in an ally off the Rue du Bucie, its interior elegant, understated, its food sublime.

When they returned to their hotel room, there was a bottle of champagne—Don Perignon, vintage 2002—on ice, on a white-clothed table that hadn't been there when they'd left that morning. Between two crystal glasses was a small box, and in the box was a ring. "I'd like you to marry me," Eric said.

Sophia paused before taking the ring. "Are you sure?" she said. "You run one of the most famous companies in the world, and yet before I met you I knew almost nothing about you or the things you've made. Don't you want someone who's more interested in what you do?"

"No," he said. "That's what's so wonderful. You're so very normal. That's one of the things I love about you."

But, of course, Sophia wasn't *normal.* Just *more normal.*

They married three months later. To Sophia's surprise, the ceremony, while well attended, wasn't like the weddings you see on TMZ or read about in your social media timelines. Famous people were there, but not the really famous people. Not even the same calibre of people that had been at the White House Correspondents' Dinner (was that only just a few months ago?), except for Elon Musk. Various other CEOs and innovators were there. Sophia had invited Miley, but she hadn't come (in fact, she'd said, without further elaboration, "No fucking way"). She'd invited her old costars from the Disney show; some of them were there. Sophia's mother was there, even though she'd at first protested when Sophia told her she was getting married, ranting in Spanish about you just met this guy. About why haven't I met him yet? *Te vas a casar con él solamente porque es rico, y él está usándote soló por tu cuerpo.* "Mama," Sophia had said, "I love him. I want to get married." And then she told her *¡No te preocupes! Podrás vivir en mi mansión todavía.* "Okay," her mother finally said. "As long as you're happy." Eric's parents were there, but Sophia hardly had a chance to speak with them.

Hector Alexander Jones was Eric's best man. Sophia's maid of honor was her agent, the flamboyant Stefan Bache, of the Bache Talent Agency. She saw Hector and Stefan speaking to each other animatedly for much of the reception. A year later she and Eric would attend the wedding of Hector and Stefan.

During the bride and groom's first dance, Eric pulled Sophia in to him. He lead her around the dance floor with something not entirely unlike grace. "I've never been much of a dancer," he said.

"You're doing a good job at it," she told him.

"Only because I strive to do well at everything I do."

"I love you," she said.

"You're mine now," he said.

They honeymooned in Hawaii because it was only a short plane ride back to San Francisco in case there was an emergency. And sure enough, there was an emergency, a legal one that the press latched onto like a leech, sucking at Lumina's blood. "I'm sorry," Eric said, taking a call in the villa's lobby, just hours after they'd arrived. He was red when he hung up. "I have to go back. Just for a day. You stay. Enjoy yourself, please. I'll rejoin you tomorrow." But the emergency only grew, would only grow, couldn't be stopped until the media forgot about it because a presidential cabinet member tweeted something racist, so Sophia spent five days on Kaua'i by herself, reading a new book by the author of *Unleashing Your Inner Goddess*. "I used to read those sorts of self-help books," Eric had told her during one of their early lunches in San Francisco. "But then I got over it. Other people can help you grow only so much before you have to start doing it yourself."

3

MARRIAGE IS A CURIOUS THING when you're rich and your partner is super rich and very busy: You have both all the time in the world and so very little of it. This dichotomy has something to do with control.

Eric and Sophia were one of those couples everyone talks but doesn't gossip about, so that any mention of them is along the lines of "Eric Hauser and his new wife Sophia Velasquez attended a charity event at the Gates Foundation yesterday evening. Reports are they donated somewhere upwards of $10 million to the event's cause." Or "Eric Hauser, of Lumina, Inc., and his wife, who you may recognize from her time on a popular Disney sitcom, were spotted in the front row of last night's Taylor Swift concert in Los Angeles." Or "Even the former playboy, now married, CEO Eric Hauser was on the carpet of last night's Oscar's ceremony, wearing an elegant and sparse black tuxedo. He was accompanied by his wife, whose rather retro Pierre Cardin dress raised a few eyebrows. Remember when she tried to be a pop star?" (The dress in question had been a gift to Sophia from Eric—"It's . . . spacey," she'd said. He'd replied, "I like spacey.")

Technically, her name was now Sophia Velasquez Hauser. Eric had asked her to append his to hers, and she'd agreed. She was honored to, she said. But she'd kept her own in there, and she left out the "Hauser" when signing her name except for on legal documents, a decision that probably served the second rise to personal fame Sophia would later experience.

They were busy people, Sophia and Eric. Eric was invited constantly to parties and dinners and charity galas and functions and events. And Sophia was always with him. On his arm. Wearing clothes he purchased for her, usually simple, classy garments—but sometimes weird, over-designed to the point of bizarre minimalism. It wasn't that Sophia couldn't pick her own clothes—she could, and sometimes did—it was just that Eric had a certain spartan style, and when she matched it they got compliments, both privately and in the media, and when they got them in the media, Lumina started trending, and when Lumina started trending the company saw increases in sales and boosts in the number of users signing up for its various cloud-based services, followed by substantial stock bumps. In this way, Sophia became a piece of Eric, a partner to him, valuable as an entity both to him and his company and by extension the future of the world (not to mention Eric's net worth).

By seeing the lovely couple out together so often, one would be forgiven for thinking they were extroverts. One would be forgiven for thinking they were party animals, especially in the case of Eric Hauser. It was the image of him the public had, carefully crafted and curated by him. When he went to functions—"We have a *function* this weekend," he liked to remind Sophia, always in person or via text message (never did he communicate with his wife through Cordelia, like he did sometimes even with Hector)—he pretended to drink excessively; he flirted with other women, both married and single, encouraged Sophia to flirt too; he pulled wild stunts like hiring famous rappers to perform at parties he wasn't hosting, or having delivered hundreds of gluten-free pizzas from the most expensive pizzaria in San Francisco, or telling the party's host that the champagne was, to be honest, disappointing and, here, I just so happened to bring a couple dozen bottles of Bollinger, they're in my car, let me just send someone to get them. He fought one of the UFC's best fighters in a cage erected in the ballroom of a castle he'd rented for one of his birthday parties, and he'd won, and after winning he'd made out with his wife there beside the cage for five full minutes, while photographers took photos and party guests recorded it all on their phones, before finally letting a medic attend to his split lip and the cut above his eyebrow.

But the truth was—and Sophia knew this—it was all a kind of act. Eric Hauser was an introvert of the strictest sort, and only an indestructible sense of discipline allowed him to play the rabble-rouser. He went to *functions* at most once a week, almost always on the weekends, and he saved the most hashtag-inducing behavior, like fighting transgender MMA champs or testing military-designed body armor by letting party guests literally shoot him with actual guns, for special occasions, like his birthday. Six days a week, sometimes all seven, he could be found in his workshop tinkering at his workbench or writing code or writing personal journals by hand at his antique desk. He journaled every day, and once a week he spent half an hour digitizing them. And if not at headquarters, in the workshop, then he was at the house in Sea Cliff, in the kitchen cooking with Sophia, or on the couch reading books or watching streaming television with Sophia, or in the bedroom having marathon sex with his wife, Sophia.

Eric Hauser was the rare CEO who was more than an administrator. He was an inventor, a physicist, a philosopher, an expert coder, and a theoretical mathematician. More than that, he was a futurist. Sure, he often had meetings with the heads of other companies. He had meetings with his C-level staff every weekday and Saturday at 8 a.m. He signed contracts and brokered deals and spent copious amounts of time reading reports, responding to emails, and generally doing what a chief executive officer is expected to do: manage a company. But he did find time almost every day for big picture work as well. The real, deep, focused work. The work without which Lumina would not exist nor deserve to exist. The world-changing work. Nine months after he married Sophia he stood on a stage in front of 3,000 members of the tech press and announced the Holophone 2. It was new; it was improved. It had twice the storage capacity, twice the memory. With Hollywood and the video game industry starting to embrace the holographic revolution you needed that storage, needed more room for your holographic movies and your holographic games. And get this: we made it thinner. *Fifty percent* thinner. Whereas the first HoloPhone had been as thick as Apple's much-revered fourth iPhone, the second was thinner than a number-two pencil. Insert joke here about who even uses pencils anymore. We've trademarked the

"Holo-" prefix, by the way. Applause, applause. And the next year, just eleven months after the HoloPhone 2, the HoloPhone 3. Sixty-four percent thinner than the Holophone 2. And not only thinner, but narrower and shorter. That's right: the Holophone 3 is the size of a pink rubber eraser. We did this by removing the screen. The whole interface is holographic now. We've redesigned the operating system. It's three-dimensional. It moves in the air above your palm like magic. Put it on a desk if you want and manipulate it with two hands. Pause for massive applause. And, yes, if you want to, you can buy a watch band and wear it on your wrist. Pause for what is for some reason even bigger applause. The next year, the HoloPhone 4, except not, because we're renaming it; we're calling it the HoloWatch. It looks the same on the outside as the HoloPhone 3, but now the watch band comes standard, and the internals are brand new, and the projection is the highest resolution hologram you ever did see. High definition. Lifelike. Real. And see with this new breakthrough in resolution we thought why not make this bigger, too? That's right—we're bringing back the home phone. Insert joke about the home button. Ladies and gentleman: the HoloPad! Place on the floor in the middle of your room. Plug in. A whole computer interface hovers before you. Talk to your friends in real time, life-size, like you're right there with each other, even if you're thousands of miles apart. Lumina: *Humans. Everywhere. Together.*

The new slogan wasn't without its critics. The Young Turks Network hosted a live online debate (available, of course, via two-dimensional and three dimensional streams) about Lumina. "It's not really fair, is it?" one of the pundits said. "Poor pepole in third-world Africa can't exactly buy a HoloPad, can they? So it's not exactly humans *everywhere* together, is it?"

"It's offensive," another comentator agreed.

"And meanwhile Eric Hauser is projected to become a trillionaire within the next decade."

"Well, and I don't know about that."

"And—and I know I always say this, but I just have to reiterate—how about that logo? What does that even mean?"

"Jumble of lines is what that is."

"Nonsense is what that is."

Eric Hauser had been invited to attend the debate. He'd had Cordelia decline posthaste.

While her husband was changing the world—or most of the world, at least—Sophia was herself growing busier. Not at first, though. At first, after the wedding, she spent most of her days at the house, reading books, writing in her own journal. Some days she would leave the house and relocate with her tablet to a nearby coffee shop, one of the quieter ones where you had to actually rent a workspace. She kept one on retainer, payed just 200 dollars a month for the table. The shop had good coffee, but the coffee Eric kept stocked at the house was just as good. Sometimes he ordered special coffee from an organic roaster in some other country and it was even better. This wasn't so different from the life she'd lived in Los Angeles. She had her dog here—Eric didn't mind him, only instructed the house keeper to stop by twice a week instead of once to keep things relatively pet hair free. She didn't have her mother here, but she called her almost daily. Every couple weeks she took the hyperloop and had lunch with her mother in L.A. And in the evenings, or sometimes late at night, Eric came home to her and loved her.

The first few years of their marriage went this way: He was Eric, the chief executive and founder of a technology company that had established itself as an instrumental piece of the backbone of the world economy; and she was was Mrs. Eric Hauser, his beautiful wife, companion, and partner, often if not always at his side, a baluster to his antics, his inventions, his impact. But in time, they both needed more.

Sophia was approaching her late twenties. What had she done with her life? What had she accomplished with her own individual existence? She'd made a few people laugh. She'd tried to make music. It wasn't too late to do something else. She had influence now; her name carried weight. When she called them, people wanted to talk to her who would never have taken her seriously before. What was she meant to do with that?

4

ONE MORNING, FOUR YEARS AFTER the wedding, after grabbing a green juice from the refrigerator, Sophia walked into the room of the house in Sea Cliff that she'd converted into an office. She stepped in front of the desk and gave the HoloPad a vocal command to call her agent. The pad beeped for a while, a sound not unlike the dial tone of old, and finally the form of Stefan Bache took shape above the desk, two-thirds scale. While the HoloPad was advertised as a device one could place on the floor, an immersive computational experience, most people, Sophia included, still preferred to sit when working, and they kept theirs on the desktop; besides, the technology that powered the transmission part of the system was still in its adolescence—the HoloPad wasn't just a singular disk but also came with three cameras, two that sat on the edges of the pad itself and one you affixed to the wall behind you, and the field of view was limited, and if you moved more than a little you'd find your arm or leg or head cut off on the other person's end, so it was easier to just do the whole thing while sitting. The truth was, the HoloPad, expensive and buggy, wasn't selling very well in its first iteration—everyone was waiting for the inevitable sequel. Chances were if you were using yours to talk to someone, they were on their end using a HoloPhone 2 0r 3 (the first generation HoloPhone wasn't compatible with the HoloPad—resolution too low).

"Sophia," Stefan said. He was shirtless, smooth-chested, drinking a cup of tea, which the HoloPad recreated with the rest of him. "It's so good to hear from you. It's been a while."

"It has. I know," she replied. "Thanks for scheduling this call. I know you're on vacation."

"It's a working vacation. Hec is displaying at a gallery of industrial design here, and I'm just along for the ride. It's so easy to take my clients with me, so to speak."

"How *is* Switzerland?"

"Sweden, my dear. We're in Sweden."

"Of course. I knew that. And how is Sweden?"

"Wonderful. One of the few places in Europe I hadn't been before now. But listen, we have a thing in an hour, and I still have to get ready, so let's talk about what we have to talk about. Your email said you wanted to get back into acting."

"Yes, well. I know it's been a while—"

"A while indeed. Your last film was five, six years ago. Seven years ago? That's quite a gap to bridge in this unfocused age of Hollywood."

"I know that. I was just thinking—"

"I mean, maybe, *maybe*, we could spin it as a hiatus, a professional soul-searching-type journey. *Maybe*. *If* you had been particularly famous to begin with. But—"

"Stefan. Do you have anything for me or not? I know this won't be easy, but I'll do the work."

In Sweden, on the desk in front of her, he sighed. He took a sip of his tea before putting the mug down; it disappeared, somewhere outside the transmission's field of view. "I have a couple advertisements you could be a fit for." He pronounced the word "advert-is-ments."

"*Ads?*"

"They're makeup ads, mostly. Also one for body wash. They could work for you. You're young, hispanic. You still have a bit of an accent when you talk. These companies like that sort of thing in an ad. Think Sofia Vergara or Catherine Zeta-Jones, who's actually Welsh, by the way. . . ."

"I can do an ad," Sophia said.

Stefan touched the tips of his fingers together. "Okay. Okay, good. And I can help you do an ad. It's a start. Let me make some calls. I'll get you a few auditions. Check your email tomorrow."

"I will. Thanks, Stefan. I'm grateful."

"Of course, of course. You're beautiful dear. I have to go. Talk soon." He kissed his hand and raised it toward her. It was something people used to do when they talked via computer screens. On the HoloPad it didn't have the same effect. The giant skewed hand flickered and disappeared, replaced with a hovering poinsettia—Sophia's chosen "screensaver," one of a dozen that came built in.

She attended three auditions. She hadn't acted in years, and she was hit with the full meaning of this fact the moment a script was back on her tablet, in her hands, and she was standing in front of three judgmental producers. But the auditions went well. She received a callback for two of them, and those same two both decided she was right for their respective products. The ads were for competing makeup companies, though—each for mascara, even—and she could star in only one. She picked at random, recorded the commercial, got paid (although payment wasn't what she was after here—work was), and two months later filmed another one. She didn't bother to do any more auditions; the same company just kept calling her and asking her to film for them. Within six months, she'd signed a contract: she was now the company's exclusive spokeswoman. That contract lasted a year, after which MasterCard asked her to film one of their ads, which she declined, having just landed a significant supporting role in a new Zorro movie.

When she filmed in Los Angeles, Eric visited the set once or twice, ate lunch with her, joked with the director, of whom he was a fan, stopped to visit Sophia's mother, who he'd seen only a couple times since the wedding, but who was now easily charmed by him. But then the filming took Sophia to southern Mexico for a month. It was a new experience for her, this sort of onsite filming. When she'd done the Disney show, they'd never left a handful of sets on a studio lot. How young she'd been then. How much older she felt now. She'd be thirty in less than a year. Eric couldn't make it down to Mexico during the filming, but that was okay. A month wasn't that long. She hadn't expected a terribly domestic life. Doers didn't have time for domesticity. They talked via HoloPad when they could.

Eric did attend the premiere with her, in West Hollywood. The movie was a mild financial success and a critical flop, as all Zorro movies would be for time immemorial. But people liked Sophia. One review called her "sultry."

One night, as they lay in bed in the house in Sea Cliff, Sophia asked Eric how development on Hera was going. He hadn't mentioned the project in years.

"Not well," he said. "We haven't made progress on her AI in some time. There was a serious flaw in the code, and her capacity for learning started to degrade. She lost a lot of data. And when the HoloPad didn't sell as well as expected, we needed to shift priorities to appease the shareholders, and I just haven't had much time to spend working with her for a while. But we're taking what we learned from Hera and putting it toward something similar—interactive celebrity holograms."

"What does that mean?"

"We recreate a person's physical form holographically, and we use a database of their past interviews and performances to create an algorithm the program can use to respond as they might have. We're using people who have died as templates, right now."

"That's . . . fascinating," she said. "And creepy."

"It's buggy as fuck right now. But who knows, in time we may put you out of a job. Who needs to pay an actor when they can just hire their hologram?"

A month later Sophia was pregnant. A month after that she miscarried.

They hadn't been trying to get pregnant. Having a baby wasn't something they'd talked about, and when she'd told him she was weeks past missing her period they'd discussed seriously the option of terminating the pregnancy. Was now the time for a child? Just as her career was gaining real traction? Did she want to take the time away from acting knowing that if she paused now she might never be able to get started again? Did Eric want to be a father? *Could* he be a father, a good one, working as much as he did? Other CEOs did it, but other CEOs also barely spent time with their children. It wasn't until after Sophia miscarried, eliminating the factor of choice, that they both realized that, yes, they did want to be parents right now.

So a few month later, they started actively trying. Sophia filmed more ads, but she didn't take any film roles. It's peculiar how what is so easily done on accident is so difficult to do on purpose. But she did get pregnant again, after some time, and they were happy. Then she lost that one, too, at the end of the first trimester, and they were sad. Tests were run, and it was determined that Sophia would have a difficult time carrying a child if she got pregnant again. "We're seeing it more and more these days," the doctor said. "I think it's a result of all the wifi, all the 6Gs. No offense." Sophia could see Eric bristling at the doctor's inaccurate technical remarks, and she laughed, amused at his bristling. But when they left the clinic, a pal of sadness returned.

"There are options," Eric told her. "We don't have to do things the completely natural way. We could try different things. Treatments. Close monitoring. Adoption. I was adopted."

"Yeah," Sophia said. "We could try those things. Let's try those things."

But not long after this discussion she took another movie role, the co-lead in an action film that took place in London, where she'd be spending a lot of time filming. And Eric returned to his workshop, his meetings, his product launches, and eventually, to Hera.

5

ERIC LIKED TO BELIEVE THERE was a difference between loneliness and aloneness, although sometimes he wasn't certain. He spent much of his day alone, and he liked it. Or did he spend most of his day lonely, and did he truly like it?

He sat in a high-backed chair. The chair was designed by Hector Alexander Jones for a Swiss design house while he was still in design school, before Eric had called him and convinced him to drop out and join the new company he was creating. "Do you want to spend your entire life selling sugar water to children, or do you want to come with me and save the world?" Eric had said.

"The fuck are you talking about?" Hector had replied. "Sugar water?"

"Never mind. I was quoting someone. It was supposed to be funny."

"I don't get it."

"Yeah—never mind. Just come work with me."

Eric had had this model of chair placed in every room of the Lumina office. It was the company's default chair, although new hires were free to replace it with a chair of their choosing, should they wish, a fun little detail included in their contract. Some did choose new chairs; most, after hearing the story of the chair, after being told it was one of the first consumer products created by Lumina's own VP of Design, didn't. Hector could probably live comfortably off the profits made by the chair alone. Its ergonomics were "specifically and exquisitely crafted for maximum comfort and the support of the lumbar spine."

Eric spun in the chair. Three hundred and sixty degrees. He could see the whole of his workshop when he spun like this. He spun slowly, took in the room. He paused when his gaze rested on the spot in the center where Hera would materialize, if he wanted her to, if he gave the vocal command. The projection disk was still installed. He used it daily to display designs or to conduct meetings, a sort of massive, exclusive HoloPad. It had been months since he'd used it to summon Hera. She might have been his legacy, had she worked the way he'd dreamt she would. It might have been as if he'd created a human being. But she'd suffered immense and unexplainable degradation—both in mind and body. The world hadn't been meant for code as large as hers.

Eric continued spinning. He spun back to where he'd started: the bank of high-definition computer monitors arranged above a desk at eye level. Though he was the man who'd brought holograms to the masses, he still preferred to do his coding and administrative work on a keyboard with a screen; a lot of people still did. Right now he was processing emails, dozens and dozens of them. A clock on one of the monitors told him it was 6:47 a.m. He had an hour before the morning staff meeting, an hour before he was expected to engage. He'd been at the office since four. Sophia was on a media tour, promoting her new movie, and Eric found that when she was gone, he woke earlier even than he had before he met her. Some nights when she was away he didn't sleep at all, only worked. Took stimulants with his morning smoothie. The better to process email with.

His fingers danced across one of the keyboards on the desk. Some of his answers to some of these emails would have a direct impact on things discussed at the morning's executive meeting. These were marked "priority." Their "priority" was indicated by a tiny red exclamation point next to their subject line. Their status as priority messages was determined by an algorithm, which took into account the sender, the subject, the time, keywords in the email body, and other bits of metadata. Other messages were marked "double priority," with two red exclamation marks. These were from customers who had been clever enough to guess Eric's email address. In theory, double priority took precedent over regular priority. Eric was always saying, "The most important thing to us at Lumina is the satisfaction of our customers. Everything else is secondary." Those were nice words, but in practice, nothing came before innovation, before creation, before discovery. Customer satisfaction could wait. So Eric processed the priority emails first—answered or deleted them, depending on the content, how smart or stupid the question—and then he moved on to the double priority. Down the list he went. Mostly one-word answers. Sometimes two or three or four words. "Yes." "I'll look into it." "That's great!" "Glad to hear it." "Thank you." "Fine." Answer, delete. Answer, delete.

He was done processing email and the time was 7:31. Twenty-nine minutes until the executive staff meeting, and like some other company heads he'd heard of he didn't make a point of being late; he made a point of being always on time, except to parties, but he wasn't going much to parties these days, especially when his wife wasn't there to go with him— Sophia attended more parties than he did now, way more, and you could always find pictures or videos online. Hashtag sophiavelasquez. Hashtag sophiahauser.

With twenty-nine—now twenty-eight—minutes until the meeting, Eric had time with which to do what he wanted. It wasn't time enough to focus, to do any meaningful work. He could return to his other desk on the other side of the room, where waited for him the envelope that had accosted him this morning and which currently clouded the best parts of his thoughts. He could make an espresso—but he wasn't tired, and he didn't want to be wired. He could meditate for ten, fifteen, twenty minutes. With twenty-eight minutes before the meeting, Eric could journal, but his journals were at the other desk, where the Thing was waiting for him. He could . . . he could . . . he could . . . .

He stood. He approached the punching bag that hung from the ceiling, struck it with his fist half a dozen times, kicked it twice, told himself the punching and kicking had gotten his blood flowing.

"Hera," he said.

Hera appeared. She looked the same as the last time he'd seen her. "Good morning, father," she said.

Father. No. He didn't like that.

"Never mind," he said. "Deactivate."

Then he grabbed a tablet and left the room.

This used to be called the executive floor. The executive floor was mostly a vestige of the days when the company had been much smaller. Everyone in the C-suite had had offices here, once upon a time. But then they'd realized it made more moral sense to have offices in the departments they headed, where they could work side-by-side with their teams, as focused equals instead of some sort of primordeal gods. Even Eric had another office, on the ground floor, where he could be side by side with the rest of the world—humanity was his team, he liked to say, and then he'd wink after saying it, as if to acknowledge how bullshitty it sounded, the acknowledgment of its bullshittiness meaning it could be only true. Now Eric was the only person who spent real time on the fifteenth floor, because his workshop, which he'd expanded years ago from his original office to take up much of the floor's space, incorporating the space once taken up by the other offices, was there, and moving it would be a massively time-consuming project and might even require him to pause some of his most important work. Besides, he liked to be here, where others never were: it separated him from everyone else. Besides Eric and Hector, it seemed no one at Lumina even knew the fifteenth floor existed anymore. Fourteenth, sixteenth? Sure. But not the fifteenth.

He took the elevator down. He looked out onto the bay. The sun was rising over Oakland. The sun was rising over Alameda. The sun rose while Eric sank. The elevator passed floors he rarely, if ever, stepped foot on. Floors staffed by a thousand people who made the company work but who weren't Eric or the VPs he'd spent years collecting.

"Stop here, please," he told the elevator. Nothing happened. The elevator's voice commands didn't work like that. One plan he'd had for the future was that, rather than a detached nonentity, it was Hera you'd be talking to when you gave commands to one of the building's elevators. If that's what she wanted for herself. After all, someday, he still hoped, she'd be a conscious being, and she could choose her own path. The lift stopped at the ground floor; the doors opened onto the lobby, and the lobby was full of employees and guests. Cordelia, who had been running the front desk almost since Lumina's start and who looked years younger than she was, saw him and smiled. He smiled back, waved. "Level . . . nine, please," he said, choosing one of those floors he never stepped foot on. He waved again at Cordelia as the doors closed, enjoyed the confused look on her face as her boss appeared and disappeared, just like that.

The elevator deposited him on the ninth floor. This floor plan was an open one. You could see from one glass wall to the other to the other to the other. A hundred desks, maybe more, filled the room, pushed together, arranged in a pattern that if you saw it from above you would realize was of course designed to ensure maximum productivity and collaboration, according to research. Each desk held a monitor. Holographic interfaces hovered above many of them. The hub of the room was a couch, round, enormous in circumference, broken only in two places so employees could enter the circle. Tables and projectors were positioned in front of the couch at intervals. A dozen employees were sitting on the couch right now, sipping coffee or smoothies, eating pastries they'd purchased at the bakery around the corner or picked up from the company café; some were talking with each other, excited; others were engrossed in tablets and even laptops. A young white man with an afro saw Eric exit the elevator. "Good morning, sir," he said.

Eric nodded. "Good morning."

"Good morning, Mr. Hauser," employees said, often timidly, as Eric passed them.

"I'm just here to say hi," he assured them. "How's everything going up here? Good to see you. Keep up the good work. Is there anything I can do for anyone? Hello. Everything running smoothly in Cloud Services this morning? Good morning."

Ten minutes later he was back in the lobby. "Good morning, Cordelia."

"Good morning, Eric." Eric had hired Cordelia nearly ten years ago, just after Lumina, which at the time had had only a few dozen employees, moved into this building. He'd been standing in this lobby, envisioning the decorative touches they might add to the walls, the pillars, the ceiling, and he'd thought, we're going to need a desk right there, and we're going to need someone to sit at it. In those days he'd still done all the hiring himself. It was possible that, a few months after she'd been hired, Eric and Cordelia had gone on a date together; it was also possible that said date had ended with them both at Cordelia's apartment in the Castro. But it was just a thing that had happened, once, long ago, and since then their relationship had been strictly professional, with only the occasional knowing glance from either party.

"How was the show last night?"

"My boyfriend and I loved it! Thanks for the tickets."

"I had a feeling you'd enjoy it."

"Anything I can do for you this morning?"

"Yes, actually. I'd like you to cancel all my appointments except for the executive staff meeting. I have—" He paused. The pause turned quickly into a long moment of quiescence.

"Eric?"

Was it really wise, shirking his responsibilities just to figure out how to deal with a little problem? A problem that probably wasn't even a real problem but just a bluff, a threat unbacked by actions or concrete proof. Maybe not. Then again, perhaps the shirking *was* the responsible course of action. Maybe putting the problem off to deal with the mundanities of the day would be the real shirking, the real deferring of responsibility. Because, face it, if you think it isn't real, if you think it's just empty words on a piece of paper—just a lie—you're kidding yourself. What's up there in your workshop has every likelihood of being true. It's a wonder it's taken you this long to receive a letter like this . . . .

"Never mind," Eric said. "Keep everything on my schedule. The day shall proceed as usual."

"Okay . . ."

"But—let's not *add* anything to the schedule, if it can be avoided. Please."

"Of course. I can see to that."

"Thanks, Cordelia. You're a gem."

"And you're strangely not an asshole this morning."

"I'm a bit distracted. I will endeavor to a more customary level of assholery for the rest of the day. Could we get some coffee in the executive conference room, as well, please?"

"I'll see to it."

"Thanks again." Eric smiled, but it took a concerted effort.

The lobby was full of young men and women, some in suits, most dressed casually, crossing from the front doors to this barely perceptible elevator or that barely perceptible elevator. Eric motioned for a group of young coders to hold the door for him. He entered the spacious yet cramped pod. "Thanks," he said.

"No problem, sir."

Eric pressed the button for the nineteenth floor—button presses were more convenient than voice commands when you were with a half-dozen other people. "Please—I'm your teammate, not your boss. Call me Eric."

"Of course. Eric. Sir. Thank you."

"Hmmm. On second thought, Mr. Hauser will do."

"Um, right. Yes. Mr. Hauser. Absolutely."

Eric patted the young coder on the shoulder. "Relax. I'm joking. Eric is just fine."

Now the coder seemed uncertain.

The elevator dinged at the nineteenth floor. The doors opened. "And this is where I get off," Eric said. He tipped an imaginary hat. "Have a great day, everyone." He exited, an amused smile on his face. Nothing took the mind off its problems like messing with the confidence of employees probably fresh out of school. It was far better than meditation sometimes. Not an asshole this morning, indeed.

Eric was not the first to enter the conference room. But he was also not the last. It was important to get the timing just right: arrive late enough that no one can get started because you, the CEO, aren't there, but early enough that you're still on time, and that one, and just one, other person gets there after you, that way when they arrive you can look at your watch vexedly, and now you have that person to direct your annoyance toward should the meeting proceed in such a way that you become annoyed.

Bartholomew Fink, Senior VP of Human Resources, was already there, jotting notes with a stylus on a tablet. John Maestri was there, staring at a rather old clamshell laptop, gods rest his soul. Barbara Grangerplatt, Senior VP of Software Engineering, was doodling on a pad of paper. Barbara would have been the executive leadership's only woman if not for the sudden arrival last year of Gloria Reinwell, an expert marketer who in her career had spun story after story venerating the companies for which she worked, including an ultimately tragically fated restaurant franchise on whose board she once sat. Gloria smiled when Eric walked in. Carson Jackson, General Council, was texting. Paul Schilling, COO, was quiet, his eyes closed. Omer Asker fiddled with a chunk of metal, likely something the hardware team had cooked up and felt just had to be shown to the CEO, will you take it to him Omer, we think he'll be impressed, will you just show it to him, please? Chief Financial Operator Omar Carter (one must take care to annunciate properly when addressing either Asker or Carter by their first names) had before him fiscal reports, both printed and digital, copies of which Eric had also received via email this morning. Marin Steinem was here. Garrison Williams was here. Peter Ling looked like he'd had a late night, but he was here. Surveying the group before him, Eric was reminded of the relief he sometimes felt that Lumina's executive team was, by most definitions, diverse: there were two women, a black man, an Indian person, an Asian person, even two gay men. Lumina's dirty secret, however, was that this diversity was a product of sheer luck; Eric would never have wasted time on mélange for mélange's sake—he was interested only in finding the right person for the job, and the right people were here before him, each one sedulous, industrious, unflappable, and (with the exception maybe of Gloria) at least a little bit eccentric; and more than half this team had been the first to fill their specific roles; turnover at Lumina was low. Speaking of gay men—Eric *had* gotten his timing right. There was one person still missing—

"Heyo!" Hector Alexander Jones said as entered the conference room from the door on the opposite side. He held a paper coffee cup in one hand and balanced under the other arm a sheaf comprising a sketchbook, a tablet, and several looseleaf rolled-up papers.

Damn. Eric could never be annoyed at Hector. So much for that strategy.

"Good morning, everyone," Eric said.

Each person at the table intoned some sort of greeting. Some mumbled, some were enthusiastic, one or two raised a hand in a noncommittal wave. Hector said "Heyo!" again.

Sometimes at these meetings Eric stood, and sometimes he sat. Today he sat, in his customary chair at the head of the table; it was the same model of Hector-designed chair that was in his workshop—all the chairs in this room were. Consulting his own tablet, Eric ran down the agenda. He didn't *need* to consult the tablet—he'd committed every item to memory with little effort, holding the whole list in his head like a screenshot—but consulting the tablet, he hoped, humanized him, because most of the people before him couldn't hold so much information in their heads. A couple could—Peter Ling and Barbara Grangerplatt were both members of Mensa—but most couldn't. Eric started with item number one, then he moved to item four, skipping two and three, for now, just to throw off the people who'd submitted the items, Omer and Omar, respectively. You must always keep others on their toes, even if those others are teammates more than subordinates—or the closest thing to friends you have.

Coffee arrived during item four. Gloria was reporting on the need for a certain spin to be put on advertisements aired in China, for cultural reasons, but also how this would be difficult, given certain dictatorial Internet laws in the country. She didn't pause as the platter of ceramic mugs was placed on the table, an identical platter with a large carafe, two small carafes, and various honeys and sugars next to it. Gloria Reinwell never allowed herself to be interrupted. No one reached for coffee until she was done speaking; but when she finished, the pause in the conversation was extensive as cups were passed around and liquids were poured. It was an unspoken rule that you couldn't work for Lumina unless you liked coffee. Or at the very least were willing to drink it, even if you didn't like it, because people who worked hard enough to change the world didn't sleep much, now did they. Now did they?

Eric thanked Gloria for her thoughts. Then he challenged her, pushed against what she'd said. He knew she liked this confrontation—it was how she worked best. Why can't we do it *this way*? he asked. Because Chinese Internet laws. . . . Yes, you said that, but Chinese laws are stupid, so if you could say fuck those laws, then why couldn't you do it? Well I guess we could. Indeed, so make it happen. Gloria smiled. I'm on it.

Eric said, "Oh, I almost forgot," and moved back to item two. Omer passed around the table the chunk of metal with which he'd been fiddling. It was blocky, as large as a fist, its multiple edges dull but straight. It had no defining features, no obvious electronic parts, no buttons. It's function was either inobvious or, more likely, nonexistent.

"What is it?" Barbara asked.

Eric held it. "It's a cube."

"It doesn't look like a cube."

"He's right," Omer said. "It is a cube. Or it was. It's been inverted."

Eric passed the item to Hector. "Is an inverted cube still a cube?" Hector asked.

"I'm afraid I don't understand," Paul Schilling said.

"What Omer's trying to tell us is that this wasn't sculpted." Eric looked at Omer. "Right?"

"That's right. This was a cube of aluminum, the kind we use to machine design prototypes for watches and other small devices."

"So what?" Paul said. "Someone machined it into this?"

"No, and that's the point. It wasn't machined. It was entangled."

"Entangled?"

"You're telling us someone in the hardware lab is experimenting with quantum entanglement?" Eric said.

"Yep." Omer smiled. "A junior-level engineer. A young woman."

"Well—she definitely shouldn't be doing that in our basement. Or in a city populated by millions of people. Hell, she probably should be working at CERN or something, not here."

"That's what I told her."

Eric thought for a moment. Then he said, "Okay, two things. One—Omar, we're going to need to build a particle lab, in the desert somewhere. Find the money and the property."

"I mean, a particle lab is going to take years, decades, to develop."

"I don't care how long it takes. Two—Omer, I want to meet this young woman. Talk to Cordelia, get the girl in my office by the end of the week."

"Absolutely."

"And for god's sake tell her to stop fucking around with quantum physics in our basement. The last thing anyone needs is a singularity swallowing the Bay Area."

"You mean that hasn't happened already?" Hector quipped.

Concerns of this sort were a not-uncommon part of Eric's life. And yet today they seemed inconsequential. What he didn't say was that being swallowed by a singularity would be a welcome development in the day he was having.

They moved on to item three. And then item five. By item six Eric was genuinely having the fun he usually had during these almost-daily meetings with his most trusted team. No one knew him like these people did, certainly not even Sophia. The people before him had seen him at his happiest, and they'd also seen him at his most frustrated, his most angry. He'd blown up at them, screamed at them until his throat was sore because no matter how hard he tried he *just wasn't getting through to them*. But he'd also shared drinks with them, experienced the joys of South American drug-infused brainstorming retreats with them, created amazing things with them, attended their children's birthday parties, bar mitzvahs, and first communions. He was changing the world with these people. And while, if you put a gun to his head and asked him whether any of the men and women before him were his friends, he would admit that Hector was the only one he saw that way, he did trust them all, and he'd sacrifice whatever he could for them, short of his life and his work. His life he'd give up only for his work, he'd decided long ago, after he'd seen a man die in Paris, having just pushed another man out of the way of an oncoming camion; and his work he'd give up for no one, for nothing.

The meeting continued. When they'd been talking near an hour, he said there were a few minutes left (the rule was these meetings never lasted longer than sixty minutes, because any meeting that did was inevitably unproductive beyond that point) and were there any final items that hadn't made it onto the agenda? There weren't, not today, except for a reminder from Barbara that she was going to be in New York all next week.

"Great!" Eric looked at his watch, which displayed his day's schedule. "Bart, Carson—I need to meet with you both this afternoon, after lunch."

Bartholomew checked his own schedule. Carson consulted his. "Can do," Carson said.

"Okay, everyone, thanks. Let's do this again some time."

There were tired laughs. What was funny was that they had this meeting every weekday morning, except for Fridays (if there was one thing less productive than meetings longer than an hour, it was meetings that happened on Fridays). The tired part was Eric made the same joke at the end of every meeting.

As he made his exit, Hector patted Eric on the shoulder, as if to say, *I'll see you in a bit.* The time was 9 a.m.

Eric did not return to his workshop. He didn't want to return to it at all today, but he'd have to, eventually. He'd have to return to retrieve the Thing from his desk before his meeting with Bart and Carson. He had calls to make right now, though, calls the success of several Lumina ventures depended on. He considered making them from his first-floor office, but instead he stopped by that office only briefly, to grab an earpiece. He winked at Cordelia as he passed her desk on his way way through the lobby. What a glorious transition, and he'd planned it that way: the cross from the Lumina lobby with its stars overhead, its constellations, to the cold, dewy, gray magnificence of the Bay. And vice versa. A few years from now he was going to commission a new headquarters, somewhere not here but not so far away. In Palo Alto. Or the San Bernardino Valley. But not Austin or Florida. Eric would never leave California, no matter what everyone else did. The new headquarters would have gardens, a walkway with thousands of flowers, hundreds of trees, including Japanese Maple and Sakura, maybe a statue of the Buddha, or several statues, and a zen center, a groundskeeper to oversee all of it as if it were his very own. But for now, Eric had the Bay, and it was along the Bay that he walked, the bridge looming, or shrinking, disappearing, depending on how you saw it. He'd neglected to bring a jacket. The breeze was cutting. It kept him alert, focused on the task at hand, even if in another space his mind worked on the problem of the other Thing.

He made his calls. He negotiated deals that would continue to secure the future of the company. The future of innovation. Always innovating, always securing, always, it seemed, making, creating.

Just under an hour later, he walked the hallowed basement halls of Lumina's design workshop, Hector Alexander Jones at his side, Hector Alexander Jones talking animatedly, gesturing, inflecting. In this basement space certain amounts of magic happened, certain kinds of alchemy. Hector spent his days conceiving of things on a physical level that no one else at the company could imagine. Sometimes he painted. Sometimes he sat in front of a sketchbook and asked questions like *What is a chair?* Often he posed such questions to his team and they did the creating, and they got the credit, but still Hector was their inspiration. When they were designing the HoloPad, for example, the holographic emitter and interaction technology behind which had been Eric's conception, Hector had sat with his team and asked *What is a computer?* For weeks they had pontificated, deliberated. Was a computer a keyboard? Was it a mouse? Was it—and these are the words with which Hector had told the story— even a fucking screen? When they created something, they would send it over to Omer and his hardware team, who would usually say something like, *Yeah, this is beautiful, guys, this is great, but it can't actually be done. You can't get the necessary components into this short flat cylinder.* But then, more often than not, they'd figure it out.

Today Hector was showing designs for the next generation of the HoloPad, which wouldn't launch for at least a year yet, possibly two, but Eric wasn't paying his usual rapt attention. When he finally tuned back in, Hector was saying, "Dude, are you okay?"

"I'm fine," Eric said. He picked up the piece of resin Hector had been talking about. It was a cylinder, like the last design, but tall instead of short, narrow instead of wide. Improvements in the projection technology, if Eric and some other engineers could make it work, were going to allow the device a wider field of projection, a forward field, rather than dorsal, which would allow the device itself a smaller footprint, like the concept he held now. "This sucks. We'd have to change the name. This is hardly a pad."

"And, of course, it's hardly the final design, unless you think it is."

"I'm not—"

"Please don't think it is. It's not my favorite. We can do better."

Eric laughed. "I know you can. So, look, say we *do* change the name. We don't have to do that *yet*, which means why not do something really new, like make it a cube?"

"A cube's been done before. It didn't go over so well."

"Or a cube with a cylinder sticking out from the tip. Or a sphere with a flat bottom. Or a pyramid. Or—"

"Well a pyramid wouldn't work because the projector should probably be at the top, but . . ."

"You get my point."

Hector was stroking the goatee he'd grown after he came out, back when he was in college. "Mmm hmm. Mmm hmm. Hmmm. A cube with a cylinder . . ."

"Yeah, okay—when you say it like that, no. Fuck no. It has to be a pad."

Hector tossed the cylinder into a trash can.

"What's next?" Eric asked, moving from the table.

"What's next is what's up with you, man?"

"How do you mean?"

"I mean let's go over here."

They walked from the sample tables to the open common area, where Hector held his brainstorm meetings with his own team. Here there was a microwave, a food-grade 3D printer (one of a dozen 3D printers in the design lab, and the only one meant for food), and an espresso machine. In the Lumina building there were a lot of these espresso machines, at least one on every floor. Hector began making the coffee. More coffee was the last thing Eric needed, but it was also the first thing he wanted. He took the double shot, added just a dash of coconut sugar, sat perpendicular to Hector in a stiff armchair.

"How's Sophia?" Hector asked.

"Away," Eric said. "I mean she's good, promoting that film—or maybe right now she's filming, actually, I think—but she's good."

"You miss her."

"I miss her, sure. I don't sleep as well when I sleep alone. Never have."

"You always were one to find a way to keep your bed warm."

Eric shrugged.

"Small wonder you don't find a way even now."

"Small wonder. But it's not important. *This* is"—his gesture, while small, managed to encompass the building, the people, the products, the company—"and I have this."

Hector nodded. "So what's bothering you?"

"Nothing's bothering me. I—"

"Don't lie to me, man. I could go on and say the usual thing about how I've known you for three decades, I know when something's bothering you, I can see it on your pretty little face, et cetera. But, dude, you asked the general counsel and the head of HR to join you for a meeting, and you did it right in front of me. You wanted me to realize something's up, and you wanted me to ask about it—so I'm asking."

That was probably true. Asking Bart and Carson in front of the entire leadership team to meet him wasn't exactly subtle. Eric had told himself an email wouldn't do because he didn't want to leave a trail—*she* hadn't wanted to leave a trail, obviously, hence the handwritten letter, which he would burn when he was done with the whole fucking situation —but still he could have tapped them on the shoulder, slipped them a note, gone to *their* offices. "I can't tell you," Eric said. "I'd be putting you in an awkward position."

"How so?"

"You'd want to tell Stefan, and Stefan might tell Sophia. But you can't tell Stefan, and—"

"I don't have to tell Stefan anything."

"But he's your husband. You keep secrets from your husband?"

"You're keeping secrets from your wife. Isn't that what you just said? Besides, Stefan knows I keep secrets. And I know he keeps secrets. You think I take him to a design exhibition in Milan and don't expect him to sleep with some handsome young Italian fashion designer. Just don't tell me about it, is the rule. And I just don't tell him about some of my things."

Eric thought of Sophia and her frequent handsome costars.

"Rules, man," Hector said. "Rules are great. You guys should get some rules. Now, tell me what you want to tell me."

"Let's . . . go into your office," Eric said.

So, in Hector's office, Eric told him about the letter. The letter that had found its way to his house last night, that had been sitting in his workshop facedown since he'd opened it and read it twice. The letter that was written in ink, in a gentle script. The letter that wasn't postmarked but still had a return address from Montana. The letter from a woman named Priscilla Papadopoulos, whom he'd met on a climbing expedition after the sale of his first company, and with whom he'd had sex at 4,600 feet, and with whom he'd had sex again at 9,300 feet and 15,000 feet and 20,000 feet, and with whom he'd almost had sex one last time for just a couple seconds at just below 29,000 feet, just so he could say he'd had sex atop the world's tallest mountain, before deciding it wasn't worth losing his dick to frostbite. The letter that told him he had a daughter. And that his daughter was nine years old. And that her name was Penelope.

And then Eric told Hector that he did not want to know his daughter, he did not want the world to know *of* her, but still he wanted to, if in any way he could, take care of her, because she was *his child*, and she was probably the only child he'd ever have.

6

HERE WE HAVE HAUSER, NOW thirty-nine years old. Again he stood on a stage. Again he stood on *this* stage. Moscone West, the grand exhibition hall.

Just across Fourth Street were Moscone North and Moscone South. Just across Fourth Street were the Yerba Buena Gardens. And the tea shop where two hours ago Eric had eaten an authentically British scone with clotted cream and strawberry jam. Or rhubarb jam; it might have been rhubarb. This was his ritual: drink tea and eat pastries at this shop, buy every table in the place so all of Lumina's leadership and assistants and other staff present for the event could drink tea and eat pastries, and the one rule was you could do anything, could read, could sit alone in silence, could talk about anything but the event or the announcements or the products, because the idea was to be present, present for just a little while, before the work began. So Eric sat and did his best to follow his own rules—he sat first with Hector and then by himself and drank the tea and ate the scone—and he was present enough to know the jam was either strawberry or rhubarb, or maybe raspberry, but not quite present enough to be sure which.

Now he was on the stage. Again. Many American CEOs before him had stood on this stage. Some day, he would build his own stage—his very own—so that he would not have to share. But for now he would walk in footsteps.

The lights had gone down, a hi-resolution projector on the floor had illuminated and from it a delightful and clever and oh-just-so-inspirational sixty-second three-dimensional video had been played, and the video had ended with, hovering in mid-air, the giant words, *Welcome. We have a lot to show you.* Every person in the audience, 3,000 strong, was applauding—some were whistling—for the video as much as for Eric's presence on the stage, even though the video had only been a series of floating colorful spheres moving in unilateral directions, colliding and intersecting in only vaguely interesting patterns, at the climax coalescing into a gargantuan representation of the Lumina logo. The whole thing had been created on a technician's computer in a day.

"Thank you." Eric raised a hand. "Thank you." Let it not be said that he hadn't poured an ounce or two of whiskey into his tea. "It's really great to be here," he said. "Really, really great."

The audience quieted. The applause receded. The whoops and whistles tapered. There was silence—and then the one requisite final cheer that made everyone laugh, made Eric laugh and raise a hand again and bow his head.

"Thank you," Eric said again. He drew a breath.

Avon Café II

WHAT HE NEEDED WAS A different way of looking at the world. Just yesterday morning that's what he'd been telling his G-Pops, after his G-Pops had revealed during breakfast (toast and eggs and cold cereal with skimmed milk) that he, G-Pops, didn't think he had it in him to run the café anymore, physically. He'd told Quinn that he was going to need Quinn to handle everything for a while, the opening and the closing, the ordering, the stocking, some of the cooking when Jeff McTine wasn't there because well you couldn't expect Jeff McTine to work all shifts every day now well could you? Not to mention do all the baking. Quinn didn't think his G-Pops, by that same logic, could expect Quinn to work all shifts every day, but it turns out that's damned well what he did expect. "I done every day like that for sixty-five years," he'd said.

Quinn told him that was nice and all, he appreciated that, G-Pops, he really did, thought it admirable and everything, but that wasn't what he, Quinn, was here for. He reminded his G-Pops the only reason he was back in Avon was because his tuition money had run out, and the quickest way maybe he could save again for these last two years was to work at the café, set everything he made aside in a lockbox and deposit it into his savings account whenever he got a chance to get to Helena or on over back to Missoula. Said he wished there was a bank in Avon, even though a bank in a town of barely a hundred wouldn't make much sense, said he wished G-Pops would at least pay him with a check so he could just deposit it with his watch. He didn't like having all that cash stacking up in a lockbox, friendly and trustworthy as the people in Avon were—you just never knew what was going to happen.

"That's another thing I'm gonna need you to do," G-Pops had said. "I'm gonna need you to take care of the payroll. So I guess you can pay yourself in whatever format you want. You wanna start using them online banks, or even crypto-whatever, help yourself, so long as the rest of the staff is okay with it. I'm gonna be dead soon—what do I care anymore?"

Quinn had told G-Pops don't talk like that. Don't say things like you're gonna die soon, G-Pops. They have ways of prolonging these things now. Even ways of fixing them, if the situation is right, the circumstances. They can make it so the cancer goes away for a long time.

"But it will still come back," G-Pops said. "Won't it? Don't you tell me it won't. They haven't cured death yet, no sir. I'm still going to die, and I've been here long enough."

But at least if you die later I won't have to work every shift every day at the café, Quinn hadn't said. Quinn needed tuition money, sure, but he'd make enough before next year's autumn whether he worked all the shifts or just a lot of them. A man needed a break sometimes. A man couldn't work every minute of every day.

But that's what G-Pops had done. G-Pops was a hard worker. G-Pops didn't understand what a young man like Quinn needed college for anyway. "You just bring me the payroll sheets when you get home tonight and I'll show you how to do it. 'S not hard. College boy like you can do the math, I'm sure. Show you I never needed college to learn math."

But when Quinn had returned home last night with the payroll sheets —which were printed on yellowed paper from an old ink-jet printer, the records kept on an ancient bulbous grape iMac his G-Pops had bought in the '90s, decades before Quinn was born (miracle it still worked; thing belonged in a museum)—his G-P0ps was long asleep, his shoes off, all peaceful in his chair in front of the television, chest rising and falling, his breath labored and wheezing and cancerous in a way that made Quinn think, Yeah, G-Pops, you don't have much time left, do you? This thought had made Quinn feel a cold sadness. So Quinn had put the payroll papers on the kitchen table and put a blanket on his G-Pops and had himself gone to sleep after spending a half-hour checking his college friends'

Stories, seeing the parties and the study sessions and wishing he were there with them participating in such things rather than seeing them via an app—there was only so much a holographic projection could get you, something he'd been told in earnest by this evening's prestigious customer at the café.

This morning when he'd woken up, his G-Pops had been sitting at the table, eating a bowl of oatmeal, drinking a cup of black coffee, staring at the payroll sheets. "Sorry I fell asleep," he said when Quinn came into the kitchen, poured himself a coffee, scooped himself some oatmeal.

It wasn't his fault, Quinn told him. Quinn had been late, talking to a customer, a fascinating customer. Quinn almost told G-Pops who the customer had been, but he didn't think G-Pops would care or even understand.

"'S okay. Just let's make sure we go over this together tonight. You don't be late and I won't fall asleep. I don't have time to fall asleep. I'm gonna be dead sooner than later. Dead I'm gonna be." G-Pops coughed then into a napkin. Quinn finished his breakfast and said goodbye. G-Pops said he'd try to stop in later, say hi to the regulars. They all should hear it from him, that he was dying.

Now Quinn walked through the Montana cold, across the little town of Avon. The snow had picked up again; it whirled and blew so much that it made more sense to walk than to take G-Pop's truck to the café, but the good thing was you could walk across Avon in ten minutes, fifteen when you were walking against heavy winds like these.

It was true that Quinn's decision to pursue a university education was a minor anomaly these days. It was almost as much an anomaly as G-Pops' gasoline-powered pickup truck. The customer yesterday evening had said as much himself. He'd said, "College . . . that's a bold choice. You going to be a brain surgeon? A nuclear physicist?"

Quinn told him no, he didn't want to be anything like that—he just needed a different way of looking at the world.

"You might find it there," the man had said. "I found it in books, books no one told me to read, on the other side of the planet, where no one told me to go. Maybe I would have found it at a university, but I doubt it. You know, when I told my parents I wasn't going, I thought I was making the bold choice, the radical decision. But then it turned out many people my age were skipping college—they couldn't afford it, they wanted it for free and they weren't getting it for free. That's not why I didn't go, understand. I didn't go because I had other things to do, and we only have so much time. Anyway, education shouldn't be free. Education should cost you much and more if you want it to mean something. So good for you."

The wind picked up, and snow kicked against Quinn's face as he walked. He should have put on a scarf. You always wore a scarf in the winter in Montana.

When he'd recognized the guy last night, he couldn't at first believe it. It *had to be* just somebody who looked like him. What would *he* be doing at the Avon Café? But it was him. Eric Hauser. He'd confirmed it with a low voice, almost a whisper; then he'd looked around the café and seemed to realize no one else here would care who he was even if he screamed out his own name. Quinn was an anomaly.

Quinn recognized Eric Hauser because he was interested in technology. He'd had a HoloPhone, a few years ago, and then a HoloWatch, after people had started in droves finally making the migration from handheld devices to wrist-worn computers. Of course now he had a Neptune S7 Bold, made by Lumina's biggest competitor, which had the same features and more, plus a more open UI. Last night he'd felt the need to hide it, though, to slip it from his wrist when he thought Hauser wasn't looking and put it under the counter.

"Hey, it's okay. I don't care what watch you wear."

Quinn had put it back on. Reluctantly. Wearing it felt disrespectful.

"Really, though. I don't make those sorts of things anymore. Trinkets, is all they are."

Surely, Quinn said, they were more than that. After all, Lumina had changed the world.

Then the man reminded him he didn't work at Lumina anymore, and it was true. Eric Hauser had been gone a while, slipped into a vitrified state of non-existence. Quinn pressed him on that, on his sudden resignation a couple years ago, on his retreat from any sort of public life. Speculation was he'd been dying, some fatal illness. Lumina's stock prices had plummeted; they still hadn't quite recovered to their Hauser-era heights.

"I wasn't dying. I just needed a short break, and then I had bigger things to work on."

What bigger things there were he wouldn't say. Still, he talked with Quinn late into the evening, an hour after the café had closed, then two hours. He kept adding whiskey to the coffee Quinn kept pouring him. Quinn got the impression he'd been drinking for days. Part of him still didn't believe the man was the legendary Eric Hauser. It was someone who looked like him, but not quite like him: older, tired, scruffy, a little gray, a little crazy. They talked about Quinn's interests: philosophy, technology, futurism, history. They talked about what the hell Eric Hauser was doing here, in Avon, Montana: He was on his way to Helena, had to see his daughter. No, Quinn wasn't mistaken in not knowing he had a daughter; no one knew he had a daughter. He'd never himself met her; this would be the first time. He doubted she knew he was her father. And yes—he knew he was so close. Thirty minutes that way, Quinn told him. Just over the pass, but watch those roads in this weather, the snow and ice get even heavier up there, and the winters just keep getting worse. Hauser could have been at his destination by now, but he'd needed just a quick break before completing the journey. He needed to steel himself, fortify his will (he tapped the flask from which he poured the whiskey). When they were done talking, when they'd walked outside, Quinn had told the man he couldn't let him drive, not after all the alcohol Quinn had seen him drink.

"It's okay," the man had said. "I'm not going to leave just yet. I'm going to sleep it off a couple hours. I wouldn't want my daughter to meet me this way, certainly. Anyway, the car has autopilot."

Once Quinn was convinced the man wasn't going to drive away under the influence, he'd left him in the parking lot, alone, to sleep in the front seat of his car.

Now Quinn waited for the train to pass. It was a long train. Box car after box car after box car. Even now, well into the Twenty-First Century, it was still a regular part of life in this part of the country—waiting for trains. Railroads were still the circulatory system of the American body, and with all their advancements, all their genius, scientists hadn't yet figured out how to make artificial veins, artificial blood. The train chug-a-chugged. The snow came down cold and fierce and settled on Quinn's dark face, on Quinn's dark hair. His Neptune S7 Bold buzzed against the topside of his wrist, and when he lifted its face he saw a message from his G-Pops, reminding him to order the replacement thingamajig for the coffeemaker, the old one was rattling like crazy and it wouldn't do any good to have the coffeemaker brake without a replacement part handy, no sir, wouldn't do any good at all, you'd have a dangerous situation on your hands should regulars like Frank and Gideon and the Widow Fogelmanis (no relation to the Mrs. Fogelmanis who'd taught Eric Hauser's high school social studies class) not be able to get their coffee. Box car after box car after box car. Hopper. Hopper. Hopper hopper hopper. Two empty flatbads and Quinn could see the restaurant just across the highway, waiting for him to open its doors. Box car. Box car.

Even if the snow wasn't coming down and the sky wasn't heavy with the weight of clouds, you wouldn't be able to see the sun this early.

Then the train was past, its ultimate box car already fading into the distance. They hadn't put cabooses on freight trains since before Quinn was born; he had only heard of them. He crossed the tracks, looked both ways to make sure there were no vehicles coming down US-12, and hurried across the icy road as quickly as he dared.

The car of the man who said he was Eric Hauser was still in the parking lot. Right in front of the café. A red Model S, quiet, three or four inches of snow covering its surfaces.

Quinn used the sleeve of his coat to brush off the passenger-side front window. The man who said he was Eric Hauser, founder of Lumina, father of the hologram, was still inside, still sleeping. Quinn tapped lightly on the window. He removed his glove and tapped again, using his fingernails this time. Finally, he knocked, knuckle on glass. He said, "Sir? Would you like to come in for some coffee? Mr. Hauser?"

The man did not move. His head leaned toward his right shoulder in the manner of sleeping in cars that when you wake up you have that awful crick in your neck. He was dressed more warmly than Quinn was, except his vest didn't have sleeves; he'd had the sense to wrap a scarf around his neck before going to sleep, even though presumably his vehicle was climate-controlled. Quinn knocked again but the man did not wake. Quinn hesitated; then he pulled on the door handle. The way a lot of these cars worked was the door was automatically unlocked as long as the driver was nearby with the key fob. The door opened. Quinn hesitated again; then he tapped the man's shoulder. Then he shook the man more roughly. "Mr. Hauser?"

There was frost on the man's short beard, on his eyebrows. No visible breath was emanating from his nostrils. Quinn could see his own breath clearly, little puffs of steam. Quinn paused. He thought. Then he stood, shut the door, and from his wrist called 911. His G-Pops liked to remind him that there was a time places like this didn't have network coverage, you'd have go inside and use what was called a landline if you wanted to make a call; Quinn believed it, but he could hardly imagine it.

Marc and Carol Whatstaff and Bill Simmons and his brother Carl, the entirety of the Avon Volunteer Fire Department, were the first to arrive, and fast. They each had emergency medical training, but there was little they could do. Carol said she was pretty sure the guy was dead. Said he felt cold. Mort McGraff, Powell County Sheriff, arrived next, asked what the situation was. Carl briefed him and Mort asked Quinn some questions and then said they better wait for the paramedics to arrive. Thirty-five minutes after Quinn made the call, they did arrive, ambulance lights flashing uselessly. Usual procedure would have been to take the man to St. Peter's in Helena, but there were concerns about the weather and the dangers and delays of the MacDonald Pass, so instead they put the man on a gurney and hoisted him into the ambulance—he sort of jiggled as they moved him, his joints cold but not yet entirely stiff—and took him in the other direction, to the Powell County Medical Center in Deer Lodge. It didn't matter where they were taking him, though: he was already dead. Had died last night sometime. Your basic heart failure. Turned out he had had some sort of defect. Congenital, which meant he'd had it since the day he was born. When the ambulance left, Quinn told Sheriff McGraff he should call whoever he needed to call because the guy whose body they'd just taken away was famous, and people were going to want to know he had died.

When no one was looking—and likely no one was looking because no one in this little census-designated place particularly cared—Quinn picked up from near the dead man's car's left front tire a paper notebook, which had fallen from the dead man's lap when the paramedics had pulled his body from the car. Some instinct deep inside Quinn made him tuck the notebook into the inner pocket of his jacket.

Mrs. Fogelmanis showed up then. She may have been a widow, but she wasn't old—her husband had died fighting a wildland fire a few summers back—and she'd walked through the snow just as Quinn had. Quinn's wrist buzzed and it was a message from Jeff McTine saying he was going to be a few minute late, had to shovel some snow from behind his truck. Marc and Carol and Bill and Carl all smiled and nodded at Mrs. Fogelmanis. "What happened?" she asked as Quinn took her gently by the arm.

He told her what he knew and said, sorry, he hadn't had time to unlock the doors yet let alone get a pot of coffee on, but if she'd come on in he would get to work warming her right up, fry her a few eggs himself, and some link sausage. And home fried potatoes. And of course there was always pie, a dozen pies of a half-dozen varieties, homemade just the night before.

Weeks passed. Then a month. The rest of the world reeled from the death of Eric Hauser, speaking of him as one does a deity, but in Avon, Montana, that they'd even found him at their doorstep the residents soon forgot. Except for Quinton Harris, because how could he forget?

G-Pops got sicker, and every morning as Quinn watched him eat his oatmeal, which G-Pops insisted, even as his ability to walk from living room chair to kitchen stove abandoned him, on making himself, he wished Grandma was still here. He wished his father was still here. He wished his mother was still here. The way things had fallen apart for Quinn . . . the way those who'd borne him and given him name and nurture had left him . . . it was difficult sometimes to not indulge in self-pity. But others indulged in pity for him plenty: Mrs. Fogelmanis eating her key lime pie and saying things like *Mmmm. This is fantastic. I remember when your mother did the baking here, and this is almost as good as hers. Oh how you must miss her, dear. We all do, truly.* Quinn had just followed the recipe; the recipes hadn't even been his mother's, but his grandmother's, and some said his great-grandmother's, but his mother had infused them with something magical, they always reminded him. Story was Quinn's father had beaten his mother half to death more than once, and then one day he'd beaten her all the way there. Quinn remembered from his childhood nothing like that, nothing like that at all. But they liked to remind him of it—so rare it was to find a Black family in Montana, how horrible for things to have ended the way they did—and the amount of their pity was more than enough that he rarely needed to feel pity for himself, and thus he was able to spend his time on other things, like studying and saving money, saving what he needed to get back to school. Running the café, he'd have enough saved for his last four semesters in no time, and if his academic plans worked out, he'd complete his bachelor's degree in three. Go maybe to Stanford for his master's. Although, this year off was chipping at his resolve to continue, truth be told. He missed his studies; he missed the liberal arts; he missed Missoula; he missed the young man he'd hooked up with and then hooked up with again and then started seeing in a more steady way, who never, now that Quinn was back in Avon, came to visit or gave him a call or sent him private Stories or Telegrams or Clubhouses or Chatters. The more Quinn missed these things, the less he missed them. It was a paradox that could be escaped only by going back.

But G-Pops was fading. What would happen to the Avon Café? The place was an institution. It had been there on the side of US-12 since well before the turn of the millenium, and it was always full. On any given day, at any given time, you'd find a fresh combination of ranchers from Avon, politicians from the nearby capital, energetic travelers venturing east to west or west to east and in need of homemade buttermilk biscuits and rhubarb pie; on Sundays you'd find it full of Helena residents who'd decided to skip church and make the half-hour lazy drive over the pass for the best breakfast they'd ever find. And there was the antique shop next door—what would happen to the antique shop without the Avon Café?

Eric Hauser's notebook had been mostly empty. On the first page was what looked like the beginning of a letter. It said:

Penelope,

I

That was it. There was nothing after *I*. As if Hauser hadn't known what to say. Or maybe, Eric thought, he didn't know that, if he started writing, he could ever stop.

The next fifty or so pages were blank. But then there was a drawing. It was a simple drawing, barely more than a sketch, with detail that could only have been an afterthought. It showed a thin rectangle at the bottom of the page, the rectangle's sides just slightly slanted so that Quinn couldn't tell whether Hauser wasn't good at drawing rectangles or maybe this was a trapezoid. Above the disk floated the dark outline of a feminine figure, busty, curved, her legs together so that she may have been a mermaid more than a woman—was this Penelope? Next to the feminine figure was a sketch of what looked like an operating system's interface; the buttons were the same shape as what had emanated from Quinn's old HoloWatch, back when he'd had it, but in the drawing the buttons had no words, nothing to indicate the function they might be intended to serve.

The pages after this drawing were as empty as the ones before it.

The notebook itself was beautiful. Leather spine, leather cover. Milky pages. Silk ribbon tucked between the last page and back cover, real silk as far as Quinn could tell, marking nothing. Heavy. Substantial. The words on the first page and the drawing were done in graphite, smeared only slightly by the side of a left-hand palm. Quinn wasn't into paper much himself, but he'd known a few people at the university who were enthusiasts for analog things. Quinn put the notebook inside his pillowcase. Something about it begged to be kept hidden. Quinn knew G-Pops wouldn't find it, because now G-Pops could hardly stand long enough to walk from his chair in the living room to the kitchen counter to make his coffee and oatmeal or cold cereal (although he managed, and insisted on managing, to do so every morning), or from the chair to the bathroom, where, once he made it, he had to piss sitting down and took a long time. Quinn took out the notebook every night at first, opening it, feeling its cover, its spine, its pages. He took it out every morning, examining it again. He found a pencil and made his own mark on the page that said "Penelope." He drew a circle. Then inside the circle he drew a heart. He stared at what he'd drawn for a long while, wondering whether the book was worthless now. Maybe he could have sold it some day—the notebook of Eric Hauser, the guy who brought your friends and loved ones across the world and into your living room, onto your wrist, wherever you may be. Oh well—probably he'd never have been able to prove the notebook's origins anyway; it wasn't like the guy had had the thing inscribed. Quinn put it back inside the pillowcase, on the underside, so it wouldn't press against his head when he slept. More weeks went by and he stopped looking at it every day; he all but forgot it was there. G-Pops got better, and then he got much worse; on a Thursday evening he coughed up a little blood, and the following Saturday he coughed up more than a little. He wouldn't let Quinn call an ambulance, said he didn't need no doctor, didn't need no hospital, didn't want to die anywhere but here, in Avon, and woe if he couldn't visit his café one last time.

By then, winter's onslaught had ebbed, and many more days than not the temperature rose above freezing and the sun shined down, melting the thick banks and blankets of snow. Things were wet, muddy, but wet and muddy were more comfortable than frozen and biting. One day Quinn helped G-Pops put on a pair of jeans, a flannel shirt way too big that had fit him snug this time last year, and a down jacket from Patagonia he'd had for fifty years, and walked him from the front door to the old pickup truck. G-Pops couldn't lift his leg high enough to reach the step, and he hadn't the strength in his arm to pull himself up into the cab, so Quinn lifted him, set him gently in the passenger seat, and handed him the seatbelt, which G-Pops buckled himself.

G-Pops insisted on trying to tune the radio, but no one was sending AM or FM signals out this way anymore. Quinn told him he should have put satellite in the truck. "Fuck satellite," G-Pops said. Quinn started to play music from his watch, but G-Pops said don't worry about it. The drive across Avon, from the house to the café, took all of three minutes, hardly time for a song, hardy time even for silence. They didn't have to wait for a train this morning.

Avon Café had no defined disabled parking, but only because it had no defined parking spaces at all just, just an unpaved lot with plenty of room. Quinn parked just outside the front door. By the time he made his way around to the passenger side, G-Pops had somehow opened his own door and climbed down from the seat and was standing on uncertain legs. He grasped Quinn's arm above the elbow and together they entered the Avon Café. Quinn planted G-Pops on a high-backed stool at the counter; it was the same stool Eric Hauser had sat in.

Quinn set to work opening the place. He put coffee on and made G-Pops a bowl of oatmeal, sweetened with brown sugar. Mrs. Fogelmanis arrived at 7:05, a few minutes later than normal, complaining of a kink in her left shoulder. Slept on it weird, she said. Saw G-Pops and smiled. Said she'd heard from Quinn he'd planned on coming in today, had hoped it was true. And here he was, I'll be damned. Looking better than ever, yes you are. G-Pops told her don't you fucking patronize me, Kathy; I look worse than shit. Together they drank coffee late into the morning, G-Pops telling old stories and new ones, and around him a crowd grew. The stools were full all day, and even the folks sitting at tables in the dining room weren't much for their own conversation, choosing instead to listen to G-Pops' narrations and vociferations. Sometimes folks as old as G-Pops—like Barker Taylor, sitting in the dining room with his wife—would holler across the room, things like "That ain't the way I remember it. You tell that story true now, you old dissembler." That's the word Mr. Taylor used: dissembler. And G-Pops called back, louder than he should have been able to manage, "Oh, fuck you, Barker. You couldn't remember your way out of a paper bag if you were a rat and scientists had cut the bottom off and placed cheese at both ends." And Barker Taylor said, "The fuck you talking about, you crazy old man?" And Quinn kept pouring coffee and taking orders at the counter while Ginger Wiley and Cindy Sims served everyone else and Jeff McTine and his brother Frank worked in the kitchen frying eggs and potatoes and pancakes and burgers and Salisbury steaks and steamed the occasional bag of out-of-season vegetables. Kathy Fogelmanis left around 11 a.m., but she returned in the afternoon, told G-Pops she couldn't stay away from him. This was how it went in this place: this here was life, and it was good and comfortable. "Why do you need to go back to school when you got this?" G-Pops asked Quinn, who was pouring hot water into a mug for a customer at the counter. G-Pops turned to Mrs. Fogelmanis. "The kid insists he has to go back to school," he told her.

"He's a good kid," she said. "None of my boys went to school, but I suppose they're happy out here ranching. Even these days someone's gotta ranch."

And for a minute Quinn himself wondered why he had to go back to school. He *could* stay here. He *could* run the café after G-Pops passed, which—he had to face it—would be any time now.

Quinn had few memories of his parents, but he had had G-Pops and Grandma, and while G-Pops, sharp and spunky as he was, was happy here in Avon, his grandmother had always told Quinn she knew he *wouldn't* be. *The world's a bigger place than this,* she'd say. *And you were made for it.* Yet here at twenty Quinn hadn't even left Montana. He'd gone to Missoula because it was close, because during the summer he could easily come back and help G-Pops.

A man entered the Avon Café then, and seconds later behind him another man. Both were dark, but not dark like Quinn and G-Pops were. They didn't belong here, it was obvious, but that wasn't uncommon; lots of people who didn't belong came to the Avon Café, and by the time they left, their bellies full of of pie and homefries, they did belong, Montanans all. But these guys . . . .

One of the men sidled up to the counter, slid in between G-Pops and the widowed Kathy Fogelmanis. He was a wide man, and they had to lean out of the way to let him in. The way the man said "pardon me" indicated he didn't care who he displaced. The other man, this one smaller than his companion, but tauter, his eyes narrowed as if he'd spent his life in a dark room and was suddenly seeing the sun, leaned against the jukebox.

"That doesn't work," G-Pops said.

The wide man drummed his fingers on the countertop. He raised an eyebrow at G-Pops. "What?"

"That jukebox don't work. It's old. Real old. It worked for a long time, longer than probably it should have, but it finally crapped out a few months ago. Ain't that what you told me, Quinn?"

Quinn nodded. The dining room was quiet. Not silent—people were talking—but all conversations were happening in a delicate undertone, as if everyone at the tables, who all day had been enjoying the jubilant spirit of the last return of The Great G-Pops, were afraid of interrupting something that didn't concern them.

"It's okay. I don't think my friend is interested in playing any songs. Are you, my friend?"

The small man shrugged. "Might be I was gonna." His American accent was thick, exaggerated, affected.

The big man sighed. Shook his head. "Might be he was gonna. Listen, Sam, we don't have time for you to play your songs. You have terrible taste in music anyway." The big man turned back to G-Pops. "Seriously, Sam has the worst taste in music I've ever heard. He likes things like No Doubt and Smash Mouth. And Madonna. Remember those guys?"

"I remember," G-Pops said.

"I hate old music. Give me something contemporary any day. I'm a big fan of now, y'know?"

"Now is good," G-Pops said, "when, of course, now is good. Right now, my now is pretty shitty. Thus we've been talking all day about the good old days. *You* know?"

"Sure," the big man said. "Sure."

The smaller man, the one called Sam, hadn't moved from the jukebox. He just stood there with his back to it, his eyes sweeping the dining room. Quinn set a menu on the counter. Next to it, an empty mug. He raised an orange-handled carafe. "Coffee?"

The big man took the menu. "Y'all take credit cards here?"

"Sure," Quinn said.

"'Kay," the man said. "Just thought maybe . . . you know, printed menus, jukebox, whatever. Thought maybe you didn't have the tech for credit cards."

Quinn filled the coffee mug, aware that the man hadn't said whether he wanted any. "We have the tech. You can pay with your watch, even, if you want to."

The man studied the menu for what seemed a long time. Finally he put it down. "This your café?" he asked Quinn.

"It's mine," G-Pops said. "Quinn there's my grandson."

The man nodded. "Doesn't seem to me you're running the place at the moment, sitting on this side of the counter."

G-Pops' eyes narrowed. "It's my place."

The man nodded again. He turned back to the counter, stared into the black contents of the mug. He kept staring. Quinn thought about asking him *cream or sugar?* but instead said nothing. He looked at G-Pops, but G-Pops didn't look at him. G-Pops was frowning; then he winced the way he'd been wincing the last few weeks whenever one of his tumors put pressure on something somewhere. Kathy Fogelmanis had pushed her stool back a little, giving the big man more space, but still she looked uncomfortable. She sipped her coffee. In the dining room a couple who regularly drove over from Helena—they said the Avon Café was their favorite restaurant in the state—showed their son how to color with wax crayons on the old-fashioned kids menu the café provided. Charlotte Sims, sister of Cindy Sims, who'd worked the morning shift, recited softly the day's pies to the Morgans. Another young couple picked at their plates with forks and knives. Sheriff McGraff eyed his wife, Mrs. McGraff (everyone knew he was also sleeping with Cindy Sims, but no one in the small town seemed to mind, not even Mrs. McGraff; rumor was the three of them sometimes spent the night together). The smaller man called Sam stood stoic in front of the jukebox.

"Anyway," said the big man. He placed a badge on the counter. From where he'd produced it Quinn couldn't tell. "I'm Agent Sport. My partner Sam and I are FBI. We just need to ask a few questions."

"Questions?" G-Pops said.

The badge looked official. It said FBI on it. It had a photograph of the big man, the one called Sport.

Quinn nodded toward Sam, his eyes still on Sport. "Where's *his* badge?"

"He has a badge," Sport said.

Quinn may have never before had dealings with the FBI—indeed, his only interactions with law enforcement had been with Sheriff McGraff and his deputies—well, and also that cop in Missoula who had told Quinn and his friends they couldn't have their beers open, just walking around town like that, and had made them pour them out but hadn't punished them in any other way, hadn't even checked for ID—but he'd seen enough procedurals to know you were always supposed to see the badge. In a recent episode of *Law and Order*, Miley Cyrus's character had gotten in serious trouble with her supervisors because she'd failed to show her badge to someone. "Yeah, okay. But so where is it?" Quinn said.

Sam produced his badge. From across the room it was difficult to make out all the details, but it looked as official as Sport's. The one called Sam may or may not have been holding it in such a way that his middle finger was being deliberately positioned in an offensive manner—Quinn couldn't be sure.

"Ask me your questions," G-Pops said. "And then maybe you could get out of here, go bother somebody else."

Sport put the badge away. Again, Quinn couldn't tell where; one second the badge was on the counter, the next it wasn't. "We're here about a man, died here some time ago," Sport said.

"A month or so ago," Sam said.

"A month or so ago," Sport echoed. "And by here I mean *here*. In this restaurant."

Kathy Fogelmanis said, "Oh, *him*. I saw that! Right as they were taking him to the hospital, I was coming in for breakfast. So sad."

"My grandson found him," G-Pops said.

"I heard he was *important*," Mrs. Fogelmanis offered.

"He was," Quinn said.

"He was a big deal," Sport said.

"It was in the parking lot," Quinn said. "That he died. Not in the restaurant."

"And it was *you* who found him?"

Sheriff McGraff came over to the counter then. He'd been listening from his table, like the rest of the customers, and he was tense. "Excuse me," he said. "I think you should be directing your questions to me, if you please."

"And you are?"

McGraff, who was dressed in plainclothes this afternoon, produced his own badge. Quinn couldn't help but think McGraff's badge looked distinctly more official than Sport's, and Powell County barely had a police force for McGraff to be the sheriff of.

"Ah. Local law enforcement. You see that, Sam, this town does have law enforcement. Told you."

The small one shrugged by the jukebox.

"We had a bet," Sport told McGraff. "Sam owes me a muffin now."

"Listen," McGraff said. His hand was resting a few inches from his service weapon, which despite his plainclothes was in a holster on his hip. "The man you're asking about had a heart thing, I'm told. Weren't no one here who hurt him."

Sport ignored McGraff. He turned to Quinn. "So anyway. You found him."

Quinn nodded.

"Did you find anything . . . anything?"

"I don't know what you mean."

"Sure you do. Like any information."

"Like his ID?"

"He had ID," McGraff broke in. "I checked."

"Oh," Sport said. "So *you* checked him. What else did you find?"

"What? Just his ID. What are you talking about?"

"What about his device? His watch? Or tablet?"

"I don't know. Anything he was wearing the EMTs took with him."

Sport turned back to Quinn. "Where do you live, kid?"

"He lives with me," G-Pops broke in before Quinn could speak.

"Course he does," Sport said. "But let's face it, old man—you're not going to be living much longer, are you?"

"Now see here . . ." McGraff started to say.

"Oh, shut up." Sport had the sheriff's gun from its holster in an instant and then McGraff was on the floor and bits of his intestine were blown out onto Charlotte Sims, who had been walking by with a stack of dirty plates she'd cleared from the table of the couple with the child. A pool of blood grew around McGraff. McGraff was still breathing, his eyes still open. "Sam," Sport said, nodding.

Sam had his own guns out, then, two of them, trained on the dining room. Sport told everyone to shut up, said he had questions to finish asking. Charlotte Sims, all blood-and-intestine-covered, was screaming. Sport shot her in the head and told everyone he'd said shut up already. G-Pops made a move to grab the sheriff's gun from Sport's hand, but he was slow and old and dying and Sport smacked the hand away. "I'm not done asking you questions."

G-Pops glared. G-Pops had been a soldier. He'd fought in the Gulf War. You could see it in his eyes, that he'd seen things like this before, things like blood and human insides, but it didn't matter now what he'd seen. Mrs. Morgan let out a shriek. Sam turned a gun on her. She held up her hands and stopped shrieking. She whimpered.

"Where do you live?" Sport asked Quinn again.

"Go to hell, fucker." G-Pops spat on the man.

Sport shot Kathy Fogelmanis. The bullet hit her in the throat and she tried to cry out but the sound was only a gurgle and her blood sprayed across the counter, across G-Pops, across Sport, and then she died, still upright in her stool, her head slanted to the side a little. She wasn't a widow anymore. Quinn could smell something stomach-turning.

"It's shit," Sport said, "that smell. Hers"—he nodded at McGraff, who wasn't dead yet but whose chest was moving only ever so slowly— "and probably his." Then Sport turned the gun on Quinn and held it there, pointing it like an arrow that said *Your death: This way.* "So now you're going to tell me where you live, or we're just going to have to go through every house in this pathetic town one by one," Sport said.

G-Pops lunged. With his gun-free hand, Sport pressed against his chest and shoved him back into his chair. G-Pops coughed and coughed.

"Goddammit," Sport said. "I know you don't care whether you live or die. So you're dying anyway, good for fucking you. But other people will die, you don't tell me what I need to know, so just tell me where you live." The sheriff's gun was still trained on Quinn. Maybe it was Sport's gun now.

G-Pops spat again and then told him where the house was, across town, the one with the beige vinyl siding and the puce trim. G-Pops had put the vinyl on himself not five years ago, after a bad hailstorm had damaged what had been there before.

"Thank you," Sport said. And then he pulled the trigger on Sheriff McGraff's gun again and Quinn spun and ducked but his shoulder burned the way his arm had burned that time he had cut it with a flaying knife after hunting with G-Pops when he was a boy and had insisted on helping butcher the big old deer they'd gotten. Quinn realized he'd been shot, but maybe not badly, and he went down behind the counter and onto the floor. On the other side more gunshots sounded. And then more. And then more that sounded like they were coming from some sort of automatic weapon, like in an endless spray. Irrationally, Quinn wished there was a bottle of ketchup nearby that he might squirt upon his body in case Sport or Sam decided to check whether he was dead. Of course, he was terrified and his heart was beating so fast they'd know as soon as they saw him he was still very much alive. But they didn't check. Probably a mistake on their part. Frank McTine finally came out of the kitchen and someone shot him and he landed on top of Quinn, knocking the breath from him—Frank was a very large, almost fat, man—and concealing him from any further violence.

Some seconds later the shooting stopped. The bell on the door jingled as it was opened and closed. Then it jingled once more as it was opened and closed again. Quinn stayed where he was, right there on the floor with Frank McTine on top of him, for a long, long while.

He didn't know how long he'd been there by the time he finally moved. He hoped it was long enough. He hoped there was no one waiting on the other side of that counter or on the other side of the Avon Café's front door to finish him off. He knew what the men had wanted: the notebook. Even if they hadn't known themselves exactly what they were looking for, the notebook would have appeased them. Probably he should have given it to them—what could have been the harm in that? Sure, if he gave to them, and thus they found out that he'd had it the whole time, he'd probably be in some sort of trouble. He'd probably have been prosecuted by the FBI for withholding evidence or some trumped-up bullshit charge like that, one of those ones the FBI liked to throw around (because, as far as Quinn could tell, the notebook wasn't evidence, per se; no crime had been committed in the circumstances of Eric Hauser's death; he hadn't been murdered or anything), but, well, it turned out those guys *weren't* the FBI, were they?

Quinn was not an especially strong young man—he had famously broad shoulders and deceptively large arms, but physical training had never been a focus—and Frank McTine was heavy, and all the blood made it difficult to get a grip on anything, but Quinn pressed his hand against one of the dead man's shoulders and heaved, rolling his own body so that Frank's body rolled off him, into a shelf of condiments and mugs, which clanked and rattled and fell and broke. Quinn stood. He almost lost his footing in the slickness. He saw the slaughter in the dining room and retched. No one had survived. G-Pops was slumped against the counter, his right hand a claw with chunks of dark flesh under the fingernails; G-Pops had gone down fighting. You go get 'em, G-Pops. Tell grandma hi. Tell mom hello. Tell dad. . . . They had finished the job on Sheriff McGraff, putting two bullets in his head. Everyone else who had been in the dining room was either on the floor, as if they had tried to escape, or slumped in their chairs or over their tables, as if they had never stood a chance. The one called Sport and the one called Sam hadn't even spared the child. The jukebox was all shattered glass and shredded bits of metal, broken compact disks spilling from its insides like so much human blood. Quinn fell to his knees and vomited.

He forced himself to stand again. He stood in front of the door. If those men were out there, waiting for him, he would never give them what they wanted. Not now. They could finish him, and then his shoulder wouldn't be hurting so much.

But they weren't out there. Neither, it seemed, was whatever vehicle they had arrived in. The weather had turned. The sky was gray and it was even colder that it had been this morning. Quinn walked to G-Pops' pickup. Then he remembered he didn't have the keys, and he wasn't going back inside that slaughterhouse to get them. He stumbled home.

He crossed the highway. He crossed the train tracks. The whole of the town seemed dead. He passed houses. He passed the little school. The church. The combination police station/fire station/community center. No one came out to meet him. It occurred to him to call 911. He looked at his watch; the face was crusty and red. It brightened in response to the motion of his wrist—the effort made his shoulder scream—but it wouldn't take the input of his touch. He tried his voice. His words came out raw and brown. The watch didn't hear him. The microphone had been killed by blood. What did blood do to anodized aluminum? Did it corrode it? Did it make it wish it had never been born?

Quinn arrived at G-Pops' house. The house he himself had grown up in and returned to and now returned to again. There were no vehicles outside—but the men *had* been here. The front door was open, its knob and lock shot off, the surrounding wood splintered. G-Pops had built that door. Inside, everything was torn apart. The couch was decushioned. G-Pops' favorite chair sliced into. The coffee table was turned over. The dining room table was turned over. Lamps were broken. Every book pulled from the bookshelves, many of them torn apart. Quinn's bedroom, though, was almost untouched. Only his bed was unmade, and Quinn had made it this morning. It was as if the men had known where to look, and had looked there, and had found what they were looking for, and they had torn the rest of the place apart only for the same reason they'd killed everyone in the restaurant. Quinn grabbed his pillow. He felt the case. He turned it upside down shook it and only the pillow itself fell out. The notebook was not there.

Quinn didn't understand. There had been nothing in the notebook. Just a first name and a drawing. What could bad men do with that? Even the name would mean nothing. There were over 20,000 people in the U.S. alone named Penelope—Eric had checked. If you had the whole name, and if you had the location, and if you knew what you needed to find that person for. . . . But the bad men had none of that.

Eric Hauser had been so close.

Quinn saw something on the bed then, something else that had fallen from the pillow case: a tiny black square. He picked it up between two fingers. It was the size of the nail on his pinky. He raised it in front of his face. Upon inspection he realized that the black square was a microSD card, the kind you hardly saw anymore, but that you might use to expand the storage on a mobile device. Had this been inside the notebook the whole time?

Quinn's shoulder was already feeling better—it was just a scrape, really. He vomited again, onto the bed and floor.

to and from

1

HER FUCKING MOTHER WAS A fucking cunt, and why shouldn't Penelope be able to say so? After all, her mother had called *her* a cunt on more than one occasion. Which nobody was arguing that Penelope wasn't—a cunt, that is. In fact she took extreme pride in her cuntishness (ask any boy who had ever tried to get into her pants or any girl who'd tried to lasso her into high school politics)—but that didn't give her mother the right to call her one. It probably didn't give the daughter the right to retaliate by calling the mother one, either, which is why Penelope hadn't ever said it out loud. Instead, whenever she and Priscilla had the sort of uproarious, blowout, damn-near-violent arguments they'd had two days ago, Penelope just left home for a couple days, sleeping at Kade's, on his bedroom floor. Kade was pretty much the only guy from Penelope's school who hadn't made comments suggesting they might fuck, I'll even buy you dinner first, come on girl what's the matter why are you being such a cunt. Statistics said teens were having sex younger and younger these days. Statistics also said young people were having sex less and less. Penelope wasn't much one to put trust in statistics. Either way, she was saving herself. For what? Ever, probably. She was saving herself probably forever.

"Send a message to my mother," Penelope said into her wrist. "Tell her I'll be home tonight, after VR Club."

"I'm sorry. I don't know who your mother is," the pleasant female voice responded.

"Send a message to my *progenitor*: I'll be home tonight after VR Club." Penelope knew it was time to return home when she started referring to her mother as her *mother*. Or maybe that meant it was time for her to never go back. She raised her wrist to her mouth again. "Send another message to my progenitor: Do you need me to pick anything up from the store?"

The offer wasn't birthed of kindness, but of inevitable necessity. Whenever Penelope and her mother fought, Penelope would leave for a few days, and when she'd return, things would be better, smoother, more normal, partly because her mother would have gotten some pot, which she did whenever she was stressed, and she would have smoked it all by the time Penelope came home, and there would be no food in the house, no matter how much there had been when Penelope had left.

"You're so generous," Kade said, removing from between his teeth the cigarette he tended to chew on more than smoke.

"Fuck you," Penelope said. "And give me that." She took the cigarette from him, inhaled deeply, showed him, for the umpteenth time, how it was done.

They were sitting on the floor of Kade's bedroom, underneath the open window. Penelope exhaled through her nostrils and the tarry smoke drifted up; a desk fan on the other side of the bedroom ensured it found its way through the window, outside, where Kade's parents wouldn't be able to smell it. Kade's mother was what you'd call hands-off (his father, was, unfortunately, significantly more hands-on, and he'd be furious if he knew his son was smoking cigarettes). You'd be forgiven for thinking Priscilla was the same, but she wasn't: Priscilla and Penelope had a close, generally respectful, definitely amiable, relationship most of the time—fighting was just a thing they did every once in a while, to blow off steam. More people should let themselves get angry at one another, Penelope was of the opinion. It helps.

"I'm just saying," Kade said. He didn't take back the cigarette.

"What, though?" Penelope said.

"What?"

"What are you 'just saying' exactly?"

"Huh? I don't know what you mean."

Penelope took another drag. She held the smoke in her mouth. Counting. One one thousand. Two one thousand. Three. Four. Five. She could see Kade was growing impatient. Inciting him to impatience was her goal. Her goal was also this: she stiffened her tongue and held it in the center of her mouth, which she did her best to make cavernous, as roomy as could be without opening her lips, and then she did open her lips, also stiff, held them round like a sphincter; she exhaled from the top of her throat, a brief, shallow expungement of smoke shaped not like the ring she'd been going for, but a formless, disappointing cloud. Watching the mass dissipate, she said, "You clearly weren't trying to *just say* that I'm generous. Which is really all you *just said*. But obviously there was sarcasm there, Kade."

"Um . . ."

But she knew what he was getting at. Penelope Papadopoulos was anything but generous. How could she afford to be, with a last name like Papadopoulos? Some of the dickhead boys at school (and some of their slutface girlfriends) liked to call her Penny Papa. Then they'd snicker and snigger and take tokes from their cheap joints. There's nothing funny about that name, she'd tell them. She'd tell them, you are literally just shortening my first name and my last name to their logical denominators and there's literally nothing fucking funny or amusing about it in any way a reasonable person could perceive. But Penny Papa, one of them said one time. It's like a cheap prostitute or something. Or a pimp. A pimp! A pimp who only charges a penny. And they snickered some more. But Penelope was never upset about the nickname itself. It didn't offend her; it was just moronic, and she despised moronic things. You got that, that hatred of stupidity, from your father, Priscilla would tell her.

Speaking of her father: "You could say I *am* generous, though, really," Penelope said to Kade. "Sure, I'm offering to buy my mother food with her own money, but it's actually my money. The only reason she has it is because she has me."

"So you always say," Kade said. He took the cigarette back from her and inhaled. His eyes watered. He did not cough, but boy could she tell he wanted to. Penelope knew he smoked cigarettes only when he was around her. He may not have known she knew (although he probably did—he wasn't stupid), but it was no secret to anyone that Kade idolized Penelope and wanted to impress her. So when he was with her, he smoked. And he went to VR Club. And he tried so hard to know his way around a terminal and code his own software it was almost cute. "I'm still not convinced," he said.

But he was. She knew it. It was one of the things he crushed on so hard about her. Her paternity. Truth was, though, Penelope often didn't herself believe it. Sure, there was experiential evidence (Penelope was, after all, the smartest person she knew, and she hadn't inherited that from her mother's side of the family), but on the concrete side of things, all she had was a hand-written letter her mother had shown her once, not even notarized and baring no signature. Plus their large gothic house in the Mansion District, which they'd moved into one day about five years ago, after a decade of definitely not being able to afford a house like that. And the massive anonymous deposits Priscilla's Bitcoin wallet received each month, money she swore she was putting most of away for Penelope's future.

"Well it's true," Penelope said to Kade.

They lingered in Kade's room for some time, sitting on the floor beside his bed. This is where Penelope slept when she stayed here, a blanket laid over the rough berber, Penelope's backpack her pillow even though Kade always said he could get her a real pillow. Under the posters of old rock bands—Green Day and Blink 182 and Rise Against—and aging rappers—Drake, Kanye West, Ice Cube may he rest in peace—and retired pornstars. Kade liked old things, liked them for their oldness, tended to dislike whatever existed in the present, said modern things, especially art and music, were uninspired, soulless, just a way for their creators to make a buck or a million bucks. Penelope liked old things too, sometimes, but only for the legacy they'd inspired, the new things they'd made possible.

When the cigarette was just a stub, Penelope smashed it into the ashtray next to the foot of Kade's dresser. She lit another one and they shared it, but only half. Then she tamped that out and returned it to the box. "Let's go," she said. "VR Club starts in fifteen minutes."

Penelope and Kade had skipped half their classes so they could spend the afternoon just chilling, and technically, if you missed school you weren't allowed to attend any extracurricular activities that day, but Mr. Gershwin, who supervised the club, never checked that sort of thing. In fact, most teachers didn't—who could blame them, with the paltry stipend they were getting paid—and it was likely the pair's absences hadn't even been recorded. Penelope skipped classes, sometimes even whole schooldays, once or twice a week. She'd been called out for it only twice in nearly a year-and-a-half of high school, suspended once for a day—if that wasn't evidence there were better places she could be spending her time, she didn't know what was.

The club met in Helena High's computer lab, which it was hard to believe was still a thing, computer labs. The way Penelope saw it, they were relics, ruins. Think about it: The only reason schools and universities had ever needed computer labs was because there was a time when owning a computer was both expensive and new; the machines were big, bulky, ugly, and you lined them up five, ten in a row in a classroom and sat down with the children and said, these are the future, kids, at least that's what they're telling us, and if you were a stuffy old teacher, really just learning to use the machine yourself, you probably didn't believe it, and even if it was true, it wouldn't happen until after you were dead, so why should you care; but you should care because *children* too, were the future —another thing they said—and it was your duty to train the children, what you'd signed on for, so you learned to use the machines, and then you taught the children, and the children went home and told their parents they were learning to use computers and their parents said either that's nice, or, what do you need to learn computers for? nobody's ever gonna need to use computers, they put a man on the moon without those fancy computers is what I heard, and now they expect me to pay taxes just so my kids can sit in front of a screen and learn to type instead of write cursive letters (Penelope, like most people her age—and some even older —had never been taught to write cursive, although reading it was intuitive). *They* were right: knowing how to use a bulky tan PC became a valuable skill, and then a necessary one, although owning a machine was still beyond your average budget, but you could go to the computer lab, check your email, type your papers, you were living in the future, or the 90s. Now, though, decades later, to say that every child was born with a computer on her wrist was hardly an exaggeration.

The Helena High computer lab was a museum more than anything else. As part of a public school district, it hadn't the funding for anything more than to rent to each student a tablet at the beginning of the year, their parents still having to pay for the hardware and the licensing for each textbook. Some classes still used paper textbooks three decades old—that's how bad the funding was. But last Penelope checked, the state capitol building, which was just a quarter mile down Montana Avenue, was doing all right.

Priscilla had offered more than once to send Penelope to a private school. "I bet it's what your father wants." "Sure," Penelope said, "let's look into it." But neither of them ever did, and Penelope wasn't complaining.

Penelope's fifteen-minute warning to Kade re: the club's start time had been a formality. Of course they were going to be late. They were always late, and so, most weeks, were the other club members. Sometimes even Mr. Gershwin was late. To get from Kade's house to the school Penelope and Kade had to walk past Hillsdale Street. Past Broadway. Past Breckenridge. Past Fifth and then past Sixth, where suddenly they went from being in the worst part of town to one of the best. They'd turn finally at Eleventh, right where you could see the cathedral one block over, and down Eleventh they'd go until North Montana. Sometimes they'd take Sixth or Eighth. Then down Montana past the Safeway, there was the school. It wasn't a long walk, but a little longer than fifteen minutes. Long enough to engage in meaningful conversation, if you were so inclined, which they were not. During the walk, Penelope smoked another cigarette. Kade listened to music through a pair of earbuds.

They arrived at the school and everyone was already there, waiting for them. "Fuckin' why are you late?" Peter Simpson said.

"Language," Mr. Gershwin said. "Hi, Kade. Hi, Penelope."

"I'm just saying send us a Spindl next time or something, is all. Did you guys bring the program?"

"I sent you a Facebook message," Kade said, "on our way over here."

"A what? I'm not on Facebook. Nobody's on Facebook."

"Your mom is. I told her to tell you we were running late."

"That doesn't do me any— Wait, you're friends with my mom on Facebook?"

"Something like that. I'd read you the message she sent me in response, but it's a little too filthy for present company." Kade tilted his head toward Mr. Gershwin.

"Fuck you," Peter Simpson said.

"Language," Mr. Gershwin said.

Kade stuck his tongue out at Peter, the gesture somehow more effective than it was juvenile. Kade really was on Facebook, and as of now, it was the only social network he was on. He didn't use any of the new, popular ones—not Spindl, not Sparkr, not ChatterChatterChatter. He didn't even have a TikTok, and *everyone* had a TikTok. Penelope knew he'd felt burned when Presnce, which had promised to be the next big, decentralized thing, went down after only six months in a blaze of flames fueled by billions in venture accelerant; since then he'd vowed to never use a service that wasn't making a profit and hadn't been around for at least one year; his teenage existence continued to be a lonely one. Penelope was on all the networks, all the services. First thing she did when she heard about a new one was reserve her username—even if the service proved to be a bust she wanted to own her name—then she set up an account under her usual anonymous handle: MadameForkBomber. She never friended people with whom she went to school—or anyone she knew in real life; besides Kade, Penelope's friends were from far away places, doing far away things.

Penelope unzipped her backpack, pulled from it a solid state drive the size of her palm, its casing blue with fiery white swirls. She tossed it to Peter. "It's on there."

"Nice," Peter said.

Mr. Gershwin was sipping from a bottle of water. In addition to supervising VR Club and teaching, Mr. Gershwin was also the track coach, and he spoke regularly and earnestly of the importance of being hydrated.

Also in the computer lab—which had three PCs, still running Windows, two old iMacs, and only two HoloPads, (one first generation, which nobody ever used, and one second)—were Kyle Porter, Lewis Steinitz (probably the only Jewish boy in the school), and Abigail Brenner with her square-framed glasses, which she wore without lenses because they covered a chicken-pox scar on her left temple. This was VR Club: five students, only two of whom—Peter and Penelope—were capable of creating anything—the rest just thought VR was cool but couldn't afford any equipment at home—and a teacher who was here mostly because a teacher had to be here, although he also thought VR was cool and couldn't afford equipment at home.

Peter Simpson had the hard drive plugged into the newer of the two HoloPads and was transferring the program. He ordered Abigail to initialize the headset. He told Kyle Porter to link one of the lab's external GPUs so they could use its processing power.

Lewis Steinitz was engrossed in a conversation or a feed emanating from his wrist.

Kade said he was going to get a Vanilla Coke from the vending machine in the hall.

Penelope engaged in smalltalk with Mr. Gershwin. He'd been her Latin I teacher in freshman year. Then the school board had cut the languages program, except for French because it was the most popular and you had to have two language credits to get into college, and now Mr. Gershwin, who'd put on a substantial bit of weight in the last year, taught remedial English.

Mr. Gershwin never seemed entirely comfortable during these club meetings. He was always fidgety, almost itchy, shifting in his chair for two hours, back fat poking from the sides, as if he was allergic to the particular children he was supervising. Only when he had the VR headset on did his face relax, his body untense and liquify. "How's your mother doing?" he asked Penelope while they waited for Peter Simpson to finish setup.

"Um, she's . . . fine," Penelope said. "My mother?"

Mr. Gershwin might have sighed. "I miss her. Tell her I miss her."

"Okay. . . . You . . . miss her?"

"What? I mean. . . ." Mr. Gershwin shrugged. "How's the setup coming, Pete?"

"It ain't going any faster just because you asked," Peter Simpson said. "There might be a short in the TB cable. Can you get me another one from the supply room?"

If there was one thing the school board had thought worth budgeting for, it was cables. Mr. Gershwin disappeared through a door in the back of the room.

"I don't know why he doesn't just get this set up for us before hand," Kyle said.

Abigail lifted the visor on the headset she'd put on. "He doesn't know how, he says."

"Oh, he knows," Kyle said.

"Yeah," Peter Simpson said. "He comes in here and uses the equipment himself when the club isn't meeting."

"It's true," Kyle said. "One time he forgot to log out. He has exotic tastes."

"Oh, gross, you guys," Abigail said.

"Shut up," Kyle said. "A recent Pew study said seventy-five percent of women watch porn. That's more than men."

"A *what* study?"

Kade returned with two Vanilla Cokes. "That's not more than men," he said. "It's like ninety-five percent of men watch porn, according to the same study." He handed Penelope one of the Cokes.

"Thanks," she said. She twisted the cap and savored the burning carbonation, the sweet syrupy viscousness. Her mother drank only alcohol and water and seltzer water, sometimes flavored with mango essence or other bullshit, but Penelope knew when she returned home tonight she'd find her soda stash mysteriously depleted, replaced by the faint scent of OG Kush. Penelope had watched porn, found it mildly fascinating from a physics perspective at best, found it dreadfully uninteresting most of the time.

"Mr. Gershwin, how many men watch porn?" Abigail asked.

Mr. Gershwin stood outside the supply room door, the requested cable flaccid in his hand. "Um—"

"Oh, leave him alone," Peter said. "Just give me that." Half a minute later: "Okay, it's all set. Who gets to go first?

"Me," Kyle said.

"No, I," Kade said.

"It's Penny's program," Abigail said. "Let her do it."

"So what?" Kyle said. "She knows what it's gonna be like."

"Yeah, in theory, but I'm sure she hasn't tried it out yet."

But Penelope was already in a far-off place. Where, she didn't know. How she'd got here, she didn't know. But she was removed from the lab, from the others. One second she'd been there, and then she'd been one step removed, then two steps, five steps, a million steps removed. This happened sometimes. She had read online that maybe it was depression. She felt Mr. Gershwin affixing the headset's strap at the back of her head, moving her unwashed hair out of the way. Abigail handed her the wireless gloves. "Thanks," Penelope said.

"Okay," Peter Simpson said. "Running the program . . . now."

The translucent visor in front of Penelope's face went opaque. She was ensconced in darkness and then affronted with the headset-maker's garish neon logo, which came at her so realistically that if she had never done this before she would have ducked, like she had the first time. As the world she'd spent the last few weeks building pixeled into place, she heard Lewis Steinitz speak for the first time that evening: "Hey. Shit! Guys, did you see this?"

Existence.

That was the word the narrator of the VR program began the simulation with. It was a lame word, but Penelope wasn't a writer. She didn't often read books, except for the genre once known as cyberpunk, and she watched only movies with excessive action, over-the-top violence, no gore unless the absurdity of it made it clear it couldn't happen in real life: Blood splatter. Tarantino. Penelope played video games and wrote her own. Games weren't exactly known for their award-winning scripts, despite the argument that had raged for years about whether video games were art. If you want video games to be art then make better video games.

And are virtual reality experiences art? Film is art. Is VR film? Is VR video games? Are virtual reality and *real* reality—

"Existence . . ."

The narrator said it with Penelope's voice. Penelope could have downloaded and assigned some other voice, some generated thing, but it wouldn't have sounded real, not to her, at least. Better she'd thought it would be to record the script herself. Now that she heard it she was glad she was the first to try the program: Bad acting was meeting bad writing. Which was a combination Penelope liked in film and video games, but somehow she found she didn't like it when it was her own creation.

"You are born," the narration continued. "First you are nothing, and then you are something. And then you find yourself in a world with which you are unfamiliar. What is this place? Where is this place? Are you here?"

The good news was that the visual aspects of the simulation were better than the auditory. They were rough, incomplete, but given time Penelope could make them better. This opening sequence you might even call stunning:

At first all was darkness, and, like the narration said, you were nothing. Then a hazy sepia glow, almost orange, almost red, appeared. Undeniably warm. Liquid. Maybe someday she'd write the code that would simulate the warmth as actual feeling, as a touch sensation on the player's skin—but there was no way the school would ever be able to afford the body-suit that allowed for the transmission of touch sensation, so why bother coding right now something she couldn't test (Priscilla could of course afford to buy a bodysuit for her, but she said she wasn't going to spoon-feed Penelope everything she wanted). The warm glow grew warmer. A pinprick of sharper light. The pinprick growing larger and larger. And larger. And larger and larger and larger and suddenly it's all around you and it's warm but also cold and she'd coded it so that was exactly how it would seem: warm but also cold.

A face. A woman's face. Not a real woman. Not an actor. Generated. Animated eyes. You can turn your head and see next to her a man, and then another man, a doctor.

The thing about VR was that, unless the simulation had been filmed with real people, with 360-degree cameras on set or location, it didn't work. It was disorienting. Because you could move like the world was real but the real word doesn't look like this and you know that. A team of producers had once made a VR cartoon, but like half the people who watched it had panic attacks and regulators had to pull the program. You could still find it online, illegally, if you looked; it wasn't hard.

This simulation that Penelope had written was barely more than a test. The product of a hobbyist, one who maybe hoped to go to school someday to get better at this sort of thing. So it didn't matter if it didn't look real. Surreal and real could be the same thing.

"Hello," the Penelope-narrator said. "Hello there. Welcome to the world."

And then it was the fake woman, also with Penelope's voice, saying: "Hi. Well aren't you something precious." The woman was standing, which Penelope knew wasn't realistic, but she hadn't had the time to program a hospital bed, a hospital room. This was just a test.

The name of the program was "Existence." The file name was existence.vr.

A flash of white light and now you are in a house. In the living room. Turn to the left and there beyond an archway is the dining room, its table large, luxurious, set for ten people and with ten chairs as if someone was preparing to host a dinner party. Turn to the right: a fireplace, alight, flame burning, flame crackling, the crackling growing louder in one ear depending on how you turned your head. Look up—a sort of circular chandelier. Behind you, a massive picture window looking out over snow-covered mountains.

This house template had been easy to find on the Internet. Penelope hadn't designed it herself, hadn't programmed it with the characters in mind, or the narrative. She just needed a house, and she liked the look of this one, thought it would be cool to experience being inside it.

"Dear!" Penelope's voice calls from somewhere beyond the dining room. "Little one! Come help me make some tea. The guests will be here any minute."

Tea? Why had she written tea? Penelope hated tea, except for the kind that still came in bottles, laden with sugar.

The voice called you "little one" but you aren't little. Everything around you appears at a normal adult level. Mental note: change perspective height in the base code. You're supposed to be a little one.

In certain VR experiences—say, if you were in a VR room or even just had these special motion-sensing boots they made—you could walk around the environment of your own free will, but the program senses that you don't have these peripherals, so it moves you for you.

It moves you toward the dining room. Toward the kitchen, where the voice emanated from, the simulation wants you to believe. Then the doorbell rings behind you, back from whence you came.

"Sweetie, can you get that?"

Spin around. Do a 180. Back into the living room. To the right. Toward the picture window. Then slightly more to the right. There: a door. A coatrack. Some shoes on the floor. The program moves you forward, deposits you in front of the door. Then, for a few seconds, nothing happens.

The thing is you don't have a VR room or motion-sensing boots, but you are wearing motion-sensing gloves, and the program knows that, so you are supposed to reach up and open the door yourself. Penelope always found this disorienting: budget constraints and you could only own one set of limbs, your hands or legs, not both, your choice. The kids in VR Club had chosen hands, which promised so many more possibilities, they thought, perhaps incorrectly.

Penelope stared at the carved oak door. She had not programmed much further than this. Programming took time. Just this house and the trippy opening sequence had taken thirty, maybe forty hours. Opening the door would trigger the end of the simulation.

Turn your head again. Savor the reality of this unreality. Breathe in the snowscape. Enjoy the hiss and sizzle of the fire. Admire the modernism of the lighting above you, the furniture around you. You could live here, in this space, forever. You'd need only real food and real water, somehow virtually brought to you.

The doorbell rings again . . .

. . . which wasn't supposed to happen—right?

Penelope thought back, tried to remember. The sequence had been:

Initiate startup screen.

Initiate OPENING scene.

Initiate HOSPITAL scene.

Wait for user to rotate at least 180 degrees.

Initiate HOUSE scene.

Wait for user to rotate at least 180 degrees.

Trigger character MOTHER.

Initiate WALK TO DINING ROOM sequence.

Trigger DOORBELL and MOTHER.

Initiate WALK TO DOOR sequence.

Wait for user to open door.

Yes, that was all there'd been. The doorbell wasn't supposed to ring twice. There was no second trigger. No command to repeat at intervals.

Penelope turned back to the door. Reached up. Opened it.

The simulation did not end. It was supposed to end. Or, more likely, it was supposed to crash. Instead there was white space. And another Penelope, arms at her sides.

"The fuck?" Penelope said.

. . . and *then* the world went white. Then black. Penelope could hear Peter Simpson saying her name over and over again.

"Penelope? Penelope?"

"God. *What?*" she said, removing the headset.

Peter Simpson was standing there, his torso kind of retracted, his expression almost fearful. "Jesus. No need to bite my head off, will ya. You looked like you were freaking out in there. I thought this was supposed to be a peaceful simulation."

"It is," she said. She began to remove the gloves. "It was just . . ." She took in the room. Kyle was sitting in a corner with Abigail, who was sobbing. Kade was lying on the computer lab floor, which probably hadn't been swept in months; the school janitor was a real louse, couldn't even keep himself clean and odor free, let alone a classroom. Lewis Steinitz was sitting in the same chair he had been before, but he'd moved his attention from his HoloWatch to a tablet computer and was scrolling vigorously, his eyes scouring the screen and accompanying projections for something she didn't know what. Mr. Gershwin was also locked on a device, his watch, the logo and feed of a certain social network unmistakable in its projection even in the reverse. He seemed of everyone in the lab the least concerned, maybe even nonchalant. "What's going on?" Penelope asked.

"The, um, the fans really started to kick in," Peter Simpson said. He was back at the console to which the headset was attached. "The processor started to run really hot. Never seen it do that before. The thing's supposed to be able to handle this hardware, and—"

"What's wrong with *them*, you idiot?"

"Oh, well, um . . ."

It struck her then that Peter Simpson was himself trying not to cry. His eyes were shiny with a curtain of liquid. He was trying to avert them.

"Kyle?" Penelope said.

"Oh," Kyle said. He looked up from his screen. "Eric Hauser died, apparently."

"*What?*"

"Yeah. A heart attack or something. This morning. Maybe last night. It's unclear. I'm trying to get more information, but you know how these things are: lots of speculation and rumor, much of it contradictory."

"Well—fuck."

"Yeah. Lots of other celebrity outpouring. Sophia Velasquez made a little speech on TikTok Live. She started crying. But mostly held it together. The whole thing was really dignified. Said they had had a lot of problems back when they were married, but even after the divorce she still loved him. You could tell it was true. Someone saved the video. All the news channels are using it."

Penelope pulled a chair from under a lab table. She sat. She checked her own watch. She had no notifications. No texts. No voice messages. No missed calls. No emails, no pictograms.

"I'm sorry, Penny," Kade said from the floor. Penelope kicked him. She looked around. No one seemed to have heard—or at the least understood—the comment.

"Ow," Kade said without conviction.

"You kids and your celebrity culture," Mr. Gershwin said then. "It's ridiculous. Back in my day you wouldn't see anyone crying over the death of a famous person. Nobody cared what people with more money than them were up to."

"Back in your day you had the Kardashians," Kade said. "Back in your day you had Miley Cyrus."

"They still have Miley Cyrus," Lewis Steinitz said. "*We* still have Miley Cyrus."

"Yeah, but we wouldn't *still* have her if Mr. Gershwin's generation hadn't *started* having her, is my point."

"Well *my* point," Mr. Gershwin said, "is that we only cared about celebrities that mattered. Okay, so a musician died, everyone got sad—"

"David Bowie," Kade said.

"David Bowie, yes. Or Prince. Or Michael Jackson. But this guy—Erwin Hauser—what did he do? What change did he bring to people's lives? What *good*?"

Abigail looked up then. Her face was a wreck. Her makeup was smeared. Snot was dribbling from her red nose. "WHY THE FUCK DO YOU EVEN SUPERVISE THIS CLUB?"

Penelope walked alone in the cold Montana night. There was no snow here in Helena. It hadn't snowed in a week. Funny thing about mountains was how they could affect the weather patterns. You drove out of town and as soon as you hit the pass you were in danger of your car sliding off the road, flying off the mountain and plummeting you to your ever-imminent death. But stay here, just a few miles away from there, and maybe your winter would be mild. Maybe twenty degrees warmer. Maybe no snow for weeks at a time. Who could say anymore?

She had walked Kade home, said goodbye. Usually he walked *her* home—he liked to pretend he was a gentleman and all that bullshit, and she liked to indulge him—but tonight she wanted to walk alone. She'd thought about staying in his room one more night, but then he'd want to talk. He woud probably try to *console* her or something gross like that.

Probably she didn't even need consoling. Probably she had no reason to be sad. Or at least no sadder than the average person (no one, she was convinced, had the right to be as sad as Abigail had been). She had no real evidence, after all. Nothing verifiable. Just a piece of paper with a signature that could have been scrawled by anyone. Just her mother's story. Just money. Just money, which her mother had just as likely earned by whoring; whoring could have been a thing her mother did, Penelope had always suspected.

But there *was* the bit that Lewis Steinitz had reported after Abigail's outburst. He'd read it on the website of the *New York Times*: that Eric Hauser had died in Avon, just thirty miles away.

Penelope walked downtown, across Last Change Gulch, pausing for a car at a streetlight. During the day this part of town was a hub of activity. After 7 p.m. on a weeknight (or 9 p.m. on a weekend), it was dead.

Nobody else had tried Penelope's VR program. After Abigail's outburst, for which Mr. Gershwin had threatened to give her detention— "You don't talk to a teacher like that. You just don't, Ms. Brenner"— they'd decided to adjourn early. They'd packed their things. The computer was acting fritzy now anyway, Peter Simpson said. They'd all left, gone their separate ways.

Penelope crossed Park Avenue, pausing this time for no one. Someone honked at her. She gave them the finger.

She wasn't wearing earbuds. She never walked without earbuds when alone, but tonight she'd forgotten to put them in.

She walked home, and as she walked, she wondered. About Eric Hauser. About "Existence."

The walk took twenty minutes. As she approached the gray stone of her home, her wrist buzzed. Standing in the driveway, she checked it. It was a message from Priscilla: *You should probably pick up some Dr. Pepper. And some chips or something, if you're hungry. I'm afraid I ate what we had. I'll do a real grocery run tomorrow. Love you.*

2

"SO THE TRIPE'S A LITTLE spongy," Priscilla said, worrying her teeth around the chunk of cow-stomach lining that hung like a long pale dead tongue from her mouth.

"You don't say," Penelope replied. She poked at the strips on her own plate. She couldn't bare to look at her mother. She rarely could when her mother was eating her own cooking, because her mother's expression was usually either one of extreme disgust or supreme self-satisfaction. The former more than the latter, but when it was the latter the self-satisfaction was almost always warranted, which made looking at it worse.

"It's good, though. It really is."

Penelope looked up, and sure enough there was the satisfaction. She groaned and stabbed a bit of tripe with her fork. She raised it to her mouth. Bit. Bit harder. With some effort she tore it off. "It is good," she said, nodding, chewing like you might chew a piece of Topps gum, which not only could you still buy but which was benefiting from a surge in popularity in recent months after a certain influential actor had shared a holophoto of himself with a piece on ChatterChatterChatter, the caption stating that Topps gum was the only thing he ever chewed. It was a shame that baseball, the sport whose cards had conceptualized the gum, wasn't benefiting from the gum's popularity, Kade was frequently bemoaning.

"Thanks, honey," Priscilla said, still working on her own first bite. "It's the sauce."

It *was* the sauce, which was robustly seasoned.

The thing was that Priscilla could cook. The other thing was that she had a lot of free time. She had a lot of free time because she didn't have a job, not a "real" one. She wrote a popular movie blog under a fake name and spent most of her time at home, watching the movies about which she wrote. There was a screening room in the house. The room had originally been a library. Priscilla had had an eighty-inch 8k display installed, and four chairs: one for her, one for Penelope, and two for what Penelope thought of as "random phenomena": phenomena like one of her mother's few friends or one of her mother's gentlemen callers or when Kade came over and watched movies with them. Priscilla watched old movies and wrote about them, about the technique and style. She watched new movies and reviewed them, and Rotten Tomatoes considered her a Top Reviewer. Movie studios sent screeners on physical cards to a PO Box listed on the blog's website. Sometimes Penelope ripped the screeners and leaked them onto torrenting sites, over a VPN and after stripping any watermarks, just for fun—it was something to do, she told herself. Priscilla didn't participate in VR experiences, though, didn't review them for her blog, said she didn't consider them films, said they made her sick, gave her vertigo and nausea, said VR-reviewing was a younger blogger's game, and yes she realized she wasn't keeping up with things and yes her readership was already dwindling but it didn't matter because there would always be a niche. Some people still wrote blogs where they reviewed films watched only on VHS, or Betamax, or low-res DVDs.

So because Priscilla had so much free time, she read *other* blogs. Not other film blogs, because so many other film bloggers were idiots, but mommy blogs and personal-finance blogs and cooking blogs. So many cooking blogs. And she found recipes pinned to Sparkr, these short little videos that showed you how to make a complex, tasty, usually unhealthy dish in only like five steps or seven steps or however many steps could be crammed into a Sparkr video. She reshared the videos with Penelope, tagged her in them. Penelope favorited them nearly every time in an effort to not be a total bitch to her mother, who she wanted to be a total bitch to. In Priscilla's mind, a favorite meant *Yes, go ahead and cook this for us why don't you*, so Penelope ended up eating things like haggis and chicken's feet and homemade steak tartar and tripe. Once they'd had shiokara but when Penelope had found out what was in it she drew the line: she wasn't eating *that*, no how, no way!

Priscilla cooked, and Priscilla and Penelope ate together, mother and daughter. And they talked.

But they didn't talk about things that mattered. Like right now: it had been weeks since Eric Hauser's death, and Priscilla hadn't mentioned it once, except to acknowledge that she'd heard. Whenever Penelope tried to bring it up, Priscilla changed the subject, or outright said she didn't want to talk about it right now, couldn't Penelope just stop nagging her, goddamnit?

"What do think her problem is?" Kade had asked two days ago, while he and Penelope sat in the park, in the rain, smoking cigarettes.

"I think she's in denial. I think she's hoping another deposit will come."

"Do you think another deposit will come?"

"Fuck no. The guy's dead. Dead guys don't send money."

Now more than ever Penelope wished her mother *did* review VR experiences. If she did, she would *have* to own a headset, or a whole VR room, and Penelope could run *Existence* again. She'd tried to convince Priscilla to buy one, many times she'd tried. They could afford one. They could afford the best one. She tried again right now.

"But it wouldn't be a tax write off," Priscilla said. "You know that. If I didn't write reviews on it, or of it, I couldn't call it a tax write off."

"Sure you could. No one would check to see whether you reviewed VR experiences. You can call a lot of things tax write offs with the work you do."

"I wouldn't feel right about it."

"And since when do you have a moral compass? And also, we have a lot of other things that aren't tax write offs. My computer isn't a tax write off."

"Sure it is. I said it was mine. It's technically mine. No one knows I don't use it to write the blog."

"See, you *don't* have morals, just excuses."

Priscilla shrugged. She took another tear of tripe.

"That air fryer you used to make *this* shit certainly wasn't a tax write off."

"No, but it was so worth it."

"Speak for yourself," Penelope said. But the truth was the tripe wasn't bad. She understood now why so many cultures had a variation.

Then Priscilla said, as she always did when Penelope raised the subject, that the real reason she wouldn't let Penelope get her own VR machine was because getting Penelope to that damned VR Club was the only way she could be sure Penelope was spending time with people her own age—and, no, bullshitting with Kade didn't count. She needed real friends, and lots of them, of all genders, with common interests and differing interests and even conflicting interests, the kind that would lead to arguments, maybe physical fights. Conflict was important to teenagers. You had to embrace their need for conflict. She'd read it on a parenting blog, written by a Ph.D.

Penelope said you know what Ph stands for, don't you, Priscilla? Basic.

And Priscilla replied that she wasn't going to do this again, wasn't going to rise to the bait, because while the blog said conflict was healthy for developing teenage minds, it said nothing about said teenagers running away from home for days at a time—

"—while their mother's get laid and get high," Penelope finished. "I get it."

Priscilla looked like she was about to say something, maybe something angry or mean, maybe just a witty retort, but she stopped herself. She stood and picked up her plate. She was going to finish eating in her office. She did in fact have a *gentleman caller* coming over in an hour —"No one you've met before; I met him on Hinge"—and she had a review to finish before he got here. She left the room. Penelope heard her pause in the kitchen, pour herself a glass of wine, leave the bottle on the counter.

When her mother was gone, Penelope stood also and in the kitchen dumped the rest of her tripe into the garbage bin. She grabbed a bag of Fritos from a cupboard. She went out the sliding glass back door and smoked a cigarette.

Her mother's argument about socializing was a bullshit one in light of recent events; a more elegant take might be that it was irrelevant. The Helena High VR Club hadn't had an official meeting since the one on the day Eric Hauser died. Penelope and Kade and Peter Simpson had convened in the computer lab only once, the next day, to determine what had happened to the HoloPad.

"It's fucking fried," Peter Simpson had said. "The fans didn't kick in when it began to overheat, and the whole thing is fucking fried."

"The headset too," Kade said from beneath it. "Must have been a short in the cable, or a surge. A surge or a short."

Poor Kade. Sweet Kade. A surge and a short were two very different things. But it was endearing that he was trying to help. "So let's fix it," Penelope said.

"Like the school will ever pay for that," Kade said.

"May we can do it," Peter Simpson said. "Together."

They made a plan to meet the next week. Peter knew a guy and would get the tools, whatever spare parts he could. But on the scheduled evening, Peter didn't show. Which didn't matter, because Mr. Gershwin didn't show either. The next day, Penelope hunted Peter Simpson down—she wanted to ask him what the hell man!—and when she found him between two soda machines next to the gym, making out with Abigail Brenner, she knew they'd never repair the headset.

"If they can fuck each other whenever they want, they'll never give a shit about virtual reality again," she told Kade.

"Well, but I still care about VR," Kade said. "I like VR a lot."

"You're a virgin, Kade. Everybody knows that."

Kade hung his head, dejected. "Yeah," he said.

"But some day it'll happen even to you, and then you won't care about the virtual either."

Kade grinned. "Really? You think so?"

Penelope had told no one about her experience in the simulation. She'd loaded the program at home, of course, into an emulator that did its best to render the 3D environments of virtual reality on a two-dimensional screen. Using keyboard commands she'd completed the same actions she had in the computer lab, and the program had ended as it was supposed to: open the door, nothing there because nothing had been created, fade to white, and then fade to black. She'd opened the code file and found nothing that could explain the fact that she'd seen herself mirrored back at her, no trigger, no errant commands. At this rate she wouldn't be able replay the program properly until college. She couldn't even go down to the local arcade, use their headset or simulator room, because you *aren't allowed to run unverified programs* had said the snobby fat ass with the greasy chins and stains on his shirt, who ran the place.

Speaking of snobby fat men with greasy chins, tomorrow was Saturday, and Penelope had to work. Priscilla had made her get a job the day she turned fifteen. Said it built character. Said it taught responsibility. Said it didn't matter how much money they were getting in illicit child support deposits. Said she'd read it on a parenting blog.

Penelope tamped her cigarette on the back porch's railing. Rolled the bag of Fritos closed. Went into the house, allowed herself a shower in the private bathroom that was attached to her bedroom. She got into bed. She fell asleep to the sounds of Priscilla and her gentleman caller, which she was sure she was imagining, the hallucination a product of the foreknowledge that a man was coming over. You could overhear nothing in this house, the walls were so thick, and Priscilla's room was in the other wing, far away.

Last year, a certain popular donut chain had announced that they were finally expanding into the Northwestern United States. They'd announced, also, that they were moving into Southwestern Canada, but Canadian awareness of the dangers of sugar and transfats was higher than in the U.S., and local Canadian governments said we don't want you here. There were no such qualms in Idaho, though, no such qualms in Montana or Washington. In fact the only U.S. state that succeeded in stopping the building of a single location of the donut chain, or made any real effort to do so, for that matter, was Oregon, who had their own donut makers of which they were proud. So in Montana were built several locations of this certain donut chain: one in Missoula, one in Bozeman, two in Billings, and one in Helena, near the Starbucks.

When Priscilla had told her she had to get a job, Penelope had said fuck it, whatever, and applied to work at the donut chain's Helena location, near the Starbucks, for minimum hours and minimum wage, which she spent on cigarettes (tobacco products had never been more expensive) and soft drinks (in retrospect she should have been saving for her own VR machine, but it felt too late to start now). She worked there for a few hours once a week.

She was working there today.

She manned, as they still said, despite many efforts to change the verb to *personed*, the drive thru. The drive thru had been busy all morning. The donut place was not unpopular. There were still people in town who cared what they put into their body, who shopped at the Natural Grocer's or the local natural food store (Priscilla was one of them, when she wasn't high—where else do you get tripe?); those places were in no danger of going out of business. But no matter how many Americans went keto or vegan, no matter how many, like the Canadians, started eating things like cell-based meat, there would for a long time continue to be a market here for sugar and deep-fried things of the non-artisanal variety, and all morning on a Saturday did cars and their drivers prick at the edge of Penelope's nerves. Nasally voices. Whiney requests for can you give me the fresh ones please, you know, the hot ones (no, we can't, because our donuts are made off-site and delivered to us every morning, so while they're not technically unfresh they're not exactly hot out of the oven, you idiot, where do you think you are, Krispy Kreme?); or do you carry stevia for the coffee (what the fuck do you care; you're eating a fucking donut?). Sweaty bills handed to her in payment by hard-breathing Montanans. Sweaty bills at this, the end of winter. All morning—until the shift manager, Don, said go take a break.

Each day allowed you one free donut, two or three if you worked the evening shift and were there when they had to throw them out at the end of the night anyway. Penelope grabbed a "raspberry" jelly-filled and topped off her Dr. Pepper at the soda fountain. She went into the break room and sat down in one of the two sticky plastic chairs. She didn't go outside to smoke—it wasn't like that, she didn't *need* to smoke, didn't have an addiction, not a strong one anyway. She took a bite of the jelly-filled, pressed the only button on her watch. The holographic display came to life. There were messages from Kade. Penelope checked the news. She scanned social media. She sipped her Dr. Pepper. She read status updates. She looked at pictures. She guzzled her Dr. Pepper. She watched short videos with the sound off. You had to watch the short videos with the sound off or else everyone around you would hear the short videos, and that was rude. She chugged her Dr. Pepper.

Don came into the break room and pulled out the other chair. Don was four years older than her, maybe five or six; he had graduated whenever ago and hadn't gone to college. For many months he'd sat at his parents' house, doing nothing, but then the donut shop had opened and he'd applied and they'd hired him with the first batch of employees like they'd hired Penelope. Then one of the original shift managers quit, *just like that* he quit one day, left his apron and his pink golf visor on the desk in the tiny cramped office and didn't say why, so the franchise owners promoted Don. Don wasn't like a *real* manager, didn't have much power, but he supervised. "Hey, kid," he said as he sat. He was also eating a donut, Boston creme; his hair was greasy and his skin was greasy and he was almost as skinny as Kade. He called almost everyone who worked at the donut shop *kid*; almost everyone at the donut shop was younger than him. "Check this out," he said. He pointed his own watch's projection in her direction.

Penelope looked up. "What is it?" she said. She slurped her Dr. Pepper. The cup was almost empty. Her donut was gone.

"Look at it. It's my Chatter profile. Over eleven thousand views yesterday. I wrote a thing about the president—you know, about how she's a capitalist disguised as a socialist, how she's all about big business and the banks and everything, even though she pretends she wants equality, all that stuff we were talking about the other day—and I shared it on Chatter and a bunch of people reChatted it, and then a bunch more. It's going viral."

"Oh. Okay."

"No, look. It's even on Buzzfeed. And HuffPo. They agree with me. They said the president has a lot of explaining to do, that we need to fight, you know? It's a thing a lot of people are pissed off about, the corruption."

It was on Buzzfeed, right there in the hologram. Just below Disney Princesses Reimagined as Your Favorite Breakfast Cereal Mascots. Except the mascots weren't ones Penelope recognized. Nobody ate breakfast cereal anymore. Perhaps they should publish an article about Ten Breakfast Cereal Mascots You'll Only Remember If You're an Aughts Kid.

"So what?" Penelope said.

"*So what?* What do you mean *so what?* I'm getting my voice out there, making a difference. Soon maybe I won't have to work here anymore."

Penelope sighed. She tried not to sigh as a general rule, but sometimes she sighed. "No, but so what," she said. "The ability to spark outrage does not make you special anymore. It hasn't for a long time."

"What?" Don said.

"Tweet *that*," she said. "Or Chatter it. TickTok it. Write a think-piece or something. My break is over." And she went back to work, refilling the Dr. Pepper on her way to the drive-thru window.

She'd been there since 6 a.m. At half-past one, Kade came into the shop. He asked the girl behind the register whether he could speak with Penelope. The girl said he couldn't, Penelope was busy running the drive-thru. Kade said it was important. Penelope heard all this, saw it too—the counter and the drive-thru window were part of the same open area, separated only by peer-through-able racks of donuts.

Penelope walked around the racks. "For fuck's sake," she said to the girl. "Switch with me."

"But—"

"*Switch with me.* What are you doing here?" she said to Kade when the girl was gone.

"Didn't you see my messages?"

"I saw that you *sent* me message. I didn't read them."

"Well, when do you get off?"

"Half hour. I was gonna tell you. Wanna study for that algebra test we have on Monday?"

"No. But I need you to come to the school. To the computer lab."

"Did they fix the headset?"

"No, but we need the HoloPad. The big one."

"The *Model One?* That one for the communications nobody ever uses? Does it even work?"

"It works. I checked. Just come to the school."

"But seriously, those things were such a flop. Nobody even bought them."

"*Penny!* Come *on.* Just come to the school."

"Okay, okay. Damn."

Don walked over then, looking butthurt about the Chatter thing. "Penelope, no socializing. No friends. Back to the drive-thru."

"Yeah, yeah, okay," she said, turning to him. "This guy was just ordering an apple fritter." When she turned back Kade had already left the building. She could see him through the window, getting into the passenger side of a dirty white pickup truck with a gasoline hatch on the side.

Don kept her an extra forty-five minutes. He said it was because someone hadn't show up for their afternoon shift, but Penelope knew it was just to punish her. She had checked the schedule when she came in. Everyone who was supposed to be there was there.

When finally he let her go she left and lit a cigarette. Her mother often dropped her off at work; sometimes she picked her up. Today she had done neither and Penelope had to walk. It took maybe half an hour to walk from the donut shop to their house, maybe thirty-five minutes, which meant it would take an hour to walk to the school. Sometimes she wished she had a bike, but biking was more like exercise than walking, and Penelope didn't like exercise. When people, especially guys, asked her how she stayed so thin, she said she fucked a lot, even though she'd never fucked anyone and had very little interest in sex beyond a clinical fascination.

She put her earbuds in and started walking toward the school. She could only get to it in a roundabout way; the streets zig-zagged and redirected. During the walk she listened to white noise and smoked three cigarettes.

When she arrived, the grounds showed all the markers of a high school on an early spring Saturday afternoon: a few cars in the parking lot, all of them close to a decade old or older, the only kind a teacher could afford; the soccer field covered in muddy footprints from the morning's practice; all windows dark, indicating that maybe the cars in the parking lot belonged to staff who weren't actually there, staff who'd gone home with each other so they might find something somewhere with someone to give meaning to their lives, or that maybe they were there, but not on the periphery, maybe they were somewhere deeper. The truck Penelope had seen Kade get into was not in the school parking lot but across the street in the lot of what used to be a Walgreens.

Kade hadn't told her to go to the old Walgreens, though; he had told her to go to the school. So she naively tried the front doors, found them locked, but then she saw Kade on the other side and he made a frantic gesture like *What are you doing?* and then pointed in the opposite direction. She knew what he meant. She should have done this in the first place. She walked around to the side of the school, hunched next to a low window, which she kicked open with her boot, and then slipped into the boiler room. The room was dark and the boiler throbbed, sounding as if it hadn't been replaced in decades, in a century, and could blow apart at any moment, taking the building with it. There was little here but darkness. Shadows played games on the walls. Pipes creaked horrific messages of water and gas. In a room like this, one could never be certain one wasn't the subject of a phantom's murderous stalking. But Penelope moved evenly for the door. This wasn't the first time she had broken into the school through this room. What might have frightened others frightened her no longer.

The halls were empty, unlit. But when she neared the computer lab she heard voices. Kade's and . . . maybe two others.

She entered the room and there stood Kade and a tall young Black man with an energetic but tired face. With them was the disembodied head of Penelope's father, Eric Hauser. He stared at her with vacant eyes.

3

PENELOPE WAS FAMILIAR WITH THE plot of Hamlet. In freshman English they'd watched the old Kenneth Branagh movie. She understood how this played out: a visit from the ghost of your dead father.

It took her just a moment to realize what she was looking at. "Penelope," Kade said, gesturing to the young stranger, "this is—"

"I'm Quinn. I realize how strange this is. I've been looking for you. I swear I'm not a creep or anything. I just—"

"Shut up," Penelope said. "Both of you." She drew close to the head of her father. If ever she had doubted her mother's account of her paternity, she didn't any longer. The head wasn't moving. It was statuesque, a perfectly sculpted bust. Its eyes did not follow her as she walked around the table above which it hovered. The color was off, ever so slightly tinged with orange, like the head had been put through a bad filter, and even discounting the orange the skin was several shades darker than her own, but it was in so many ways the face she saw on the rare occasions she looked in a mirror. Its eyes were her eyes. Its mouth was her mouth.

"It's paused," Kade said. "But it said—"

Penelope looked at the stranger who'd introduced himself as Quinn. "Where did you get this?"

"He left it with me."

"Who did?"

"*He* did." Quinn nodded toward the hologram. "The real him. Before —or I guess when—he died.

"You were with him?"

"He says Eric Hauser died outside his shop," Kade said.

"My café," Quinn said. "He died outside my café. I talked with him the night before. . . . I—"

"Is it a recording?" Penelope asked.

"It seems to be kind of interactive. But like really only kind of. It asked my name, but it seems to be super limited."

Penelope examined the hologram closely. The face was chiseled. There were dark circles under the eyes that were shaped like hers. "Activate it. Or unpause it or whatever."

"We—" Kade began.

"What?"

"I don't think this old HoloPad can support it. They weren't meant for VIs."

"It should work," Quinn said. "I ran it on"—he paused, he seemed to retch—"on a tablet. It worked on that. It told me to find you."

"A lot of newer tablets have more power than these Model One HoloPads," Kade said. "Not to mention higher-res projectors."

"Did it know who you are?" Penelope asked.

"No. Like I said, it just asked whether I was Penelope Papa— Papa —"

"Papadopoulos," Penelope said.

"Yeah, sorry. Yeah. And I said no. And then it asked whether Eric Hauser was dead, and then it said to find you in Helena. You were the only Penelope Papadopoulos in town. I think you were the only Penelope in town, actually."

"Activate it," Penelope said again.

Kade knelt down and touched a control on the HoloPad. The holographic representation of Eric Hauser's head flickered. Then its face began to animate.

"Processing," it said. It tilted its head. "HoloPad. First generation. Tapping into visual sensors."

"It means cameras," Kade said to Quinn. "They're just cameras."

The figure flickered again. Disappeared.

Penelope felt a jolt of panic. "Where did it . . . ?"

Kade bent down to the HoloPad. "I don't know . . . I don't—"

The hologram returned. "I've gained control of the visual sensors. Hello." The head turned some more. It looked at Kade, at Quinn. "Neither of you are in my database," it said. "Please identify yourselves."

"It's me," Quinn said.

A flash of recognition passed across the hologram's simulated eyes. "Voice recognized. Quinton Harris. Have you found—"

"Me?" Penelope, who was standing to the right of the projector, said.

The hologram's head tilted. "Cannot confirm visual," it said.

"The camera," Kade said. "On these old units, the camera isn't 360 degrees. You need to—"

Penelope stepped around the HoloPad, into the camera's field of view.

The hologram froze. Then it said, "State your name."

"I'm Penelope. Papadopoulos." For the first time in her life, her last name sounded ridiculous to her as she said it, the jokes of her schoolmates justified.

"Confirmation. Recipient identified." Then the projection's whole demeanor shifted. Its facial features grew less rigid. Its expression became warmer somehow. Its eyes less cold, more . . . tired. Then it said: "Penelope?"

"Yeah, what?" Penelope said.

"Penelope," the hologram said. "Penelope—I am Eric Hauser, your father. Penelope, I believe I am dead."

"I gathered," Penelope said. "What is this? Why are you—? What is the point of this?"

"Forgive me for any errors or technical glitches," the hologram said. "I'm not actually Eric Hauser, of course—"

"No shit."

"—and yet, I am. I'm recording this in my car. Well, I'm *programming* it in my car, actually, on the dashboard—"

"Whoa," Kade said. "Really? That's impressive."

"Quiet," Penelope said.

"—which as you can imagine is not . . . is not . . . is not ideal—"

"Is it skipping?" Quinn asked.

"B-b-but I didn't think to bring a laptop or anything with me. I kind of left in a hurry. I don't know why I left. Or, rather, I don't know why I didn't leave earlier. I mean, I couldn't have left earlier, but I could have *been there* for you sooner, you know?"

"Is he okay?"

"Oh god. Okay. I don't know why I'm— I don't know why I'm recording this. Or programming this. Or whatever you'd call this. What even is a program anymore, you know? Like where does a computer end and a person begin? That's the question I've been asking myself for years now. Oh god—I just completely abandoned her, didn't I? I just left her there. What was I thinking?"

The holographic head tilted back, its mouth open into a peculiar "O."

"What is he doing—?" Quinn said.

"I think he's . . . drinking something," Kade replied. "I think he's *drunk*."

"Figures," Penelope said. To the hologram, she demanded, "Are you drunk?"

It seemed to snap briefly out of its prerecorded narrative. It flickered again, said simply, "Processing." Then, after another moment, it said, "Anyway. I'll go back for her. We'll go back for her together, as a family. Listen, Penelope, your sister—"

"My fucking what?"

"—your sister needs a lot of help, okay? Wait, fuck, we can't go back together, not if I'm— Okay, I'm going to restart this. Penelope, if you're watching this, then it's because I couldn't get to you myself for some reason. I guess because I'm dead. Probably I crashed my car—or my car crashed itself. Haha. Wouldn't that just be the worst? Oh, fuck. Okay, starting again. No, you know what? I can make this better, I just need to —" The hologram winked out once more.

"The HoloPad is getting really warm," Kade said.

The disembodied head returned. "Okay," it said, "ask me a question."

"Did Miley Cyrus really dump you because you slept with her sister?" Kade asked. "Or was that just a rumor?"

"Kade, what the fuck?" On her way out of work Penelope had refilled her Dr. Pepper and now her stomach hurt and she could feel her pulse in her fingertips and she was pretty sure she'd had too much sugar and caffeine.

"Sorry."

Penelope said, to the head, "What are you?"

"Fuck if I know," said the head. "But I guess I'm a . . . a snippet of Eric Hauser. A really fucking shitty VI or something."

"Were you really my father?"

"Yes. I mean, I never tested paternity, but I trust your mother."

"Why did you—? Where have you been?"

"Working, I guess. I should have been there for you."

"What's a VI?" Quinn asked.

"You seen those new Larry King interviews?" Kade said.

"Yeah."

"It's like that. It's like a representation of the person. Made from available data. Recordings and texts and tweets and stuff. Or like how they put Marlon Brando in those new movies."

"Oh, yeah, okay."

"Except in this case I think the only available data was a completely sloshed Eric Hauser."

"He was drinking when I met him."

"You guys, please," Penelope said.

But the hologram flickered once more, and when it returned, it no longer responded to her questions. It seemed to be, once again, just a recording.

"Okay, Ima, Ima try again. In a couple hours. I just need to sober up, just a little."

Again the hologram paused. Again it flickered.

"For fuck's sake," Penelope said.

"The HoloPad is really getting kind of hot."

Again the head returned, a little more alert this time. "Penelope. Hi. I don't know why I'm making this. I guess it's just sort of a practice run, for when I meet you in person. You see, I'm ashamed, because I haven't been there for you, as a father. I haven't really been there for anybody. But your sister, she needs a family, okay? I need a family. We can all be a family together, if I don't fuck it up again. You, me, Hera. Hector even. Fuck, maybe even So—or your mom. I don't know. Hera—fuck—I just left her. I left her at the workshop. Alone." The head shook left to right, as if clearing itself. "Okay. You're not gonna see this anyway. I'm coming to find you. To apologize. I'll do all that in person. Then we'll go get your sister, and we'll be a family, and it will be great, and—"

The head froze.

"And what?" Penelope demanded.

"I am experiencing a buffer error," the head said, mechanically but still in the voice of Eric Hauser. "The amount of random access memory on this device is limited."

"Yeah, well, we're all broke-ass teenagers and this is a broke-ass school," Kade said.

"I'm not a teenager," Quinn said.

"You got a better computer then?"

"Well—no," Quinn said.

"Yeah, we don't have a more powerful device," Kade told the hologram.

"I am— Penelope— Hera— Ignore this— See you soon."

The head disappeared again, and the words "see you" repeated, stuttered, two, three, four times. Then everything was silent and empty.

"I think it's done," Quinn finally said.

From the old HoloPad's processing unit came a clicking sound. Kade pressed a button, ejecting the storage card into his hand. "It's really hot."

"Excuse me," Penelope said.

"That was really weird," she heard Kade say as she left the room.

There was one fewer car in the parking lot than when she'd entered. Someone had gone home—or gone to shoot themselves in the head after having to come to the school on a Saturday. Penelope felt for teachers. Despite her genuine lack of respect for those in a position of authority over her (except for her mother, who she secretly loved), she empathized with the plight of anyone (except maybe Mr. Gershwin) who was just mediocre enough at their chosen passion that their only option for engaging with it had been to teach high school students. As for the ones who had always wanted to be teachers . . . Penelope had respect for them, too; even more, she had admiration, for they'd achieved everything they ever wanted, something she was quite sure she would never do—assuming she could ever figure out what she wanted. At this point in her life, she was torn between wanting the world and wanting nothing at all. She couldn't determine whether she had a choice in which she chose, if that made any sense.

The concrete planter's broad surface was cold and hard beneath her ass as she sat on it, feet on the planter as well, her knees up just against her chin. The day hadn't seemed so chilly when she'd walked to work this morning. Nor when she had walked from work to the school. But now she wished she'd worn a jacket heavier than the thin green khaki one she had on. The blueness of the sky seemed to add to the cold. The sun was up there, somewhere, probably behind the schoolbuilding, but it would be damned if it was going to shine on her today. Each drag of her cigarette served to warm her, if briefly. She took no pleasure, for some reason, in smoking on school grounds right now. She usually did, but not now.

There was no living vegetation in the planter. Just dead, gray-brown soil, chewing gum wrappers, and a few decaying maple seeds that had helicoptered in the year before, unaware that the dirt in which they'd landed would provide no nourishment, none at all.

"Oh, wow—is that a cigarette?"

Penelope shifted her gaze from the nearly deserted parking lot to see Quinn approaching her. She squinted. "You want one?"

"Oh, no. I was just surprised to see one. Aren't you a little young to be—?" But when he saw the look she gave him, he ceased asking the question. "Anyway, my G-Pops—that's my grandpa—used to smoke cigars, and every once in a while, like maybe every few days, he'd smoke a cigarette. Said it reminded him of the old days. You can do that in a small town."

"Where are you from again?"

"Avon. Just over the pass."

"Right. Because that's where my dad—where Eric Hauser died. Wanna sit down?" She shifted to her left, making space for him on the planter-bench. He coughed as he sat. Penelope tamped out the cigarette. She tossed the still-large butt into the soil.

"Used to?" she asked.

"What?"

"You said your grandfather used to smoke cigars. He doesn't anymore?"

"No. He died . . . very recently . . . he . . ."

"This you?" she said, holding up her wrist. A collage of images formed itself in the air. She twisted her wrist and the images changed orientation, flipping so that he could see them. A headline ran across the top of the collage: UNEXPLAINED MASSACRE AT MONTANA CAFÉ.

"What the . . . ? When . . . ?"

"I got the notification right when I got out here. Right when I sat down. You didn't?"

Quinn poked at his own wrist. "My watch isn't working quite right because of . . . Damn."

"Says there's several people missing. They brought in the Helena police."

"Yeah, well, Avon's only cop was . . . killed."

"And your grandfather?"

Quinn nodded. "But he was sick, really sick. He was probably happier going out the way he did. Except for seeing all the. . . ."

"The what?"

"Yeah, I don't want to talk about it. Except—maybe it's important —"

"The article says a lot already."

"Yeah, well—"

"Lot of people dead."

"Yeah."

"Says they talked to other townspeople, ones who weren't there, says no one knows what happened. But it says they may have a lead, the missing grandson of the café owner."

"Oh God. Seriously? Oh God."

"You didn't do it?"

"Kill everyone? Oh God."

Quinn told her everything he'd experienced. He paused to retch into the planter when he got to the shooting itself. Penelope resisted a strange impulse to pat his back. "I can't—" he said. "Can't vomit. There's nothing left inside."

"Why didn't you stay. To talk to the police. Or—well, it says the real FBI—"

Quinn shook his head. "I don't. Your father—or that head-recording thing—it told me to find you, so I just got in G-Pop's truck and—I slept in the truck last night, in a gas station parking lot."

"How did you find Kade?"

"He was at your house."

"Of course he was."

"What's going on guys?" Kade asked.

"Where the fuck have you been?"

"I was trying to fix the HoloPad."

"And—?"

He shook his head. "It's fried. That's two we've killed this month. The only two we have. We're gonna be in so much trouble."

"Do you have the storage card?"

Kade held the square up between his fingers. "But I don't think it's useful anymore. The lock switch is semi-melted."

"We should get out of here," Penelope said. "I think we might not be safe"

A half hour later they were sitting in the bed of Quinn's truck, which was parked at the beginning of a trailhead at the base of Mount Helena, as far away from civilization as Penelope could think to get them at such short notice. Which was to say, not far at all—they were only like a mile from Penelope's house. They ate Wendy's cheeseburgers, fries, and Frosties. Penelope was still wishing she'd worn a warmer jacket. She was wishing she hadn't ordered a Frosty. Kade tapped and scrolled on a tablet he'd "borrowed" from the VR Club closet before they'd left the school.

"What are you thinking?" Kade asked, not looking up from the tablet. He blindly dipped three fries in his chocolate Frosty and stuffed them into his mouth, succeeding somehow at not dropping any of the milkshake onto the Creed t-shirt he'd so proudly found on the rack of a consignment shop last fall. How he wasn't freezing in just the t-shirt and jeans Penelope would never know. Quinn was properly insulated in a black jacket and dark green turtleneck sweater. In the bed of the truck were a rusty toolbox and a duffle bag.

What was she thinking? It was a good question. She'd been trying to figure that out for the last hour, at least, probably longer; her sense of time had warped and she couldn't remember just when she'd first walked into the computer lab and seen that unfocused and discolored three-dimensional image of her father's head. He *was* her father—Eric Hauser —she was sure of it. In a way, she'd always been sure of it. Her mother may have been one to exaggerate, but she wasn't an outright liar. And there was no denying the way they lived. But it had always been comforting to deny it—because while in one way being an innovator's bastard daughter was exciting, in another it was completely delegitimizing, as if the universe was daring you to try to make something of yourself, just try it, so that everyone can watch you fail.

Which was why Penelope, as a rule, usually did her damnedest to not fucking think about it. "I should have got more ketchup," she said.

"Here. I have some in my bag," said Quinn. He handed her a couple packets.

"Thanks," she mumbled.

"Now what are you really thinking?" Kade asked. "I know you. I know you're trying to devise a plan."

"I'm not devising a plan. There's nothing to plan for. As far as I'm concerned, there's nothing happened that concerns me."

"She's lying," said Kade. "To herself, mostly."

"Fuck you," Penelope said. Then she clarified, tilting her head at Kade, "Fuck him, I mean. You seem perfectly nice."

"Thank you?" Quinn ventured. "But—he's right. What do we do now? What are you going to do? It seems like you *have* to do something."

"Okay," said Penelope.

"Okay?"

"Yeah, okay. Fuck you, too."

"She doesn't mean it," said Kade, grabbing three fries from Penelope's fry container—which she'd learned some time ago was sometimes referred to as a "scoop"—because his own was now empty. "She really is a very lovely girl"—he winced as she kicked him in the thigh—"when she's not being a total bitch."

"Listen—" said Quinn. "I don't know what all's going on here, but I think we need to do something. And by 'we' I mean *we*. Because my G-Pops died for whatever this is that's going on. Lots of people died. I saw them die. It was . . . it was awful. It was terrible. Okay? And now people think I did it and— And the people who did do it wanted the information on that hologram."

"Penelope's sister," said Kade.

"I don't have a fucking sister," Penelope said.

"Are you going to eat the rest of that?" Kade asked Quinn, who had left half his burger untouched for several minutes now.

"I don't— I still don't have much of an appetite any more."

Kade picked up the burger. "Thanks."

"His mom's a vegan," said Penelope, helpfully. "He doesn't get to eat meat that often."

"Okay," said Quinn.

The three young humans were silent for some time then. Overhead, a magpie called loudly for its kin. Seconds later, another cried out in response, saying either *Here I am* or *I'm sorry—I don't know where your loved ones are.*

"Here's the deal," said Penelope. "I don't even know where we'd begin with a plan, because I don't have a fucking sister, and even if I did my father—fuck, fuck!—his hologram—that hologram—didn't say anything about where to find her."

"So you *were* trying to devise a plan," Kade said. "See—I told you she was trying to devise a plan. And it said she was in a workshop."

"Like I'm supposed to know where that is."

"And it also mentioned a guy named Hector. Sounded like he might know about your sister."

"I don't have a—I have no idea who Hector is."

"Hector Alexander Jones," Kade said, holding up the tablet. "He was the chief designer at Lumina until about nine months ago. A close friend of your fath—of Eric Hauser. He's also a painter and sculptor."

"When did you look that up?" Penelope asked.

"In the Wendy's drive-thru."

"Fuck you," Penelope said. "What else?"

"Hector Alexander Jones was captured by Iranian militants last week. He went to Iran to protest the current regime's stance on gay sex. He had some sort of political art thing he was meant to exhibit."

"You mean marriage?" said Quinn. "Gay marriage?"

"Oh no. I mean sex. Homosexual acts are still punishable by death over there."

"I didn't know that."

"He's alive, though. Supposedly. He's being held—somewhere. They've released video of him to the U.S. government. He's being held on charges of obscenity and sodomy. But they'll probably never release him. The president has stated that they, quote, 'will not negotiate with despots and barbarians.' Probably he'll be executed. It's happened before."

"Well damn," Quinn said.

"See," Penelope said. "No plan. Nothing to plan."

"Penny," Kade said, "Allow me to recap for you, in chronological order. Your father, one of the wealthiest and most famous people in the world, died in freaking Montana, barely half an hour from where you live. Then, a few weeks later, his best friend and business partner is captured by terrorists. Then, a week after that, two randos show up to the place he died and murder everyone. Then—*then*—his fucking *disembodied head* tells you you have a sister, who, by the way, it seems is named after a Greek goddess. And you aren't going to do anything about it."

"Sometimes I think you're not so bright, Kade, no offense, but that was very astute."

"Penny—if you're not going to even try to figure out what's going on here—well then fuck that."

4

SHE DIDN'T REALLY HAVE A plan so much as just the first step of a plan—which was to get some money. How much they'd need, she wasn't sure, but her intuition told her it would be a good idea to travel with more than the $376.26 she had in her own bank account. She didn't make much working at the popular donut franchise, seeing as she worked only about six hours a week, twelve if she was bored and wanted to work a double or pick up an extra shift on Sunday. Sure, minimum wage was twenty bucks an hour, but twenty bucks didn't buy what it used to.

Penelope was lucky, to be honest, and she knew it. McDonalds had converted nearly every position at its stores to touch screens and robots before she'd been born. Ditto Burger King and Arby's—well, before Arby's had gone out of business. Penelope had a vague but pleasant memory of their curly fries. Starbucks still had baristas, because baristas were a crucial component of their brand, and the company fancied itself humanitarian, and someone had to pull the lever on the espresso maker. And, fortunately for Penelope, customers took a visceral pleasure in looking at the donuts in the donut case behind the counter, in watching a gloved employee manually retrieve them with a pair of sterile tongs. The donut franchise had, long ago, tested a few robot-operated locations—contraptions of automated arms and fluoroelastomer conveyor belts—but customers said their donuts tasted like rubber—a chemical impossibility, but a psychologically powerful placebo nonetheless.

Anyway, Penelope spent most of her money on cigarettes and shitty food, but occasionally she managed to finish the pay period without having spent all of it, and those occasions added up—to $376.26. Certainly not enough for whatever adventure she and Kade and Quinn were about to embark on.

Her mother had money, though. Lots of it. Just sitting in a Bitcoin wallet, occasionally dipped into for weird organ meats or other whims, but replenished, at least until recently, far more quickly than it could be spent. Last time Penelope had caught a glimpse of the balance—over a year ago —it had sat at the equivalent of well over six figures USD.

And, as Penelope had stated many times before, it was technically *her* money. Clandestine child support for her, the clandestine child.

Which made it odd that she felt a sort of low-level guilt at the idea of taking it, her own money.

But not guilty enough.

Penelope waved to Quinn's truck from her house's front porch. She couldn't see into the vehicle—the sun had set an hour ago—but Quinn's hand popped out of the open driver's side window and waved back, and then the truck sped away. Quinn would take Kade home and then spend the night at a motel. The trio had tried, briefly, to devise a way for him to stay with either Kade or Penelope, but there seemed to be no good way of explaining the presence of this young man, several years older than the two teenagers. "It's okay," Quinn said. "I have some money. Not a ton, because I was just starting to work at the café again, but I can afford a room, even a decent one, and I need to think for a while anyway. The last couple days have been . . ."

Penelope could see tears forming at the corners of his eyes again. Unfortunately, she had shit-all experience reacting to tears. So instead she said, "Don't get a nice one. You have to go somewhere really shitty, where they'll take cash. Somewhere where they won't ask to scan your ID."

"Shit," Quinn said. "Maybe I should just sleep in the truck. Again"

"No," Kade said. "I know a motel you can go to."

"How do you know a motel like that?"

Kade shrugged. "My mom has stayed there a few times, whenever she needs to get away from my dad."

"Damn, man."

"Don't worry about it."

Kade maintained that his father never hurt him, but more than once he'd shown up at Penelope's house, last minute, and asked to stay the night.

They'd meet up in the morning, the trio, at the motel, was the plan.

Penelope opened the door to her home—slowly for some reason, cautiously. Immediately she realized this was suspicious behavior, so she called out, "Mom?"

The hallway was quiet and dark, as was the living room off to the left. In the kitchen, the dim light was on above the stove, casting eery shadows. "Mom?"

"Oh hey, Penny," said her mother, turning from the liquor closet, wearing a loosely tied robe. "You're late again."

"Not really. It's only like 7 p.m."

"It's just dark is all, for spring."

"It's not technically spring for another few days. The equinox isn't till next week."

"Well I don't know about all that, but you be careful being out so late, honey." She walked to the kitchen counter with an open bottle of pepper vodka from a local distillery.

"Fuck, it's not late. And I'm out late all the time—"

"You know I care about you, right Penelope?"

"Jesus, Priscilla. Are you drunk?"

Her mother smiled. "Only just a little," she said. Penelope then noticed the two glasses on the counter and the bottle of vermouth. Each glass had a few shards of ice and a shriveled wedge of lime. In one of them, the lime was just the peel.

Penelope sighed. This would make things difficult.

Priscilla slid the garbage can out from under the counter, dumped the dregs from each glass, and began to cut fresh lime wedges. "Can you get me some ice?"

Penelope grabbed a plastic cup and walked it over to the refrigerator. "Who's here, mom? Anyone I know?"

"Do you remember Charlie Jones?"

"The one who works at the brewery?"

"Yeah."

Penelope set the cup of ice on the counter next to her mother's cutting board and limes. "Thanks honey," Priscilla said. "Well anyway, he's here."

"Cool, I guess," Penelope said. He'd been nice enough to her the times he'd come over. Although Penelope couldn't help but judge the guy for being in his mid-thirties and pulling pints at a brewery he didn't own (not that her own prospects were any better).

Priscilla squeezed the lime wedges into their respective glasses and then dropped them after the juice. She added a few ice cubes to each glass and then began to pour in the vodka.

"I thought he only drank beer," Penelope said.

"Oh, I almost forgot. There are some cans of IPA in the fridge, can you grab one for me?" She added vermouth to each glass.

"Fuck, whatever. Here." Penelope set a can on the counter. Her mother was stirring each martini with a little straw.

"Thanks, honey."

"So, what, you're taking two martinis for yourself, just so you don't have to come back out here again?"

"Ha, no no. I don't think I need more than one more. This other one is for Charlie's roommate, Carl."

"Jesus Christ, mom."

Priscilla shrugged. "Hey, I'm a grown woman. You'll understand some day. Now be safe and have a good night. There's leftover bison lasagna in the fridge if you're hungry. It's free-range, all organic. And don't stay out so late anymore."

"Mom, it's only— You know what, never mind. You have a good night too." Her mother disappeared down what Penelope thought of as the "east wing" hallway—that is, the part of the house were Priscilla's bedroom, office, and screening room were located—balancing the can and two glasses between her hands. Penelope knew she'd never understand, and that most of the world would never understand that she would never understand. And if men were so rude that they couldn't get up and help a woman carry their own drinks, she didn't want to ever understand.

In any case, Priscilla, as far as she was concerned, could do whatever the fuck she wanted. It was just that Penelope didn't know her mother's wallet passwords, meaning she'd need both her mother's laptop and HoloWatch to get access to the money. It would have been a difficult task with just her mother to contend with, but it now seemed likely she would have to sneak past three sleeping people to get the watch from her mother's wrist. Hopefully she'd get lucky and the men would leave once the party was over.

The men did not leave once the party was over. Penelope passed the hours sitting at her own computer, at first going once again through the code of her *Existence* simulation. It wasn't like it had changed in the last month, and she still couldn't pinpoint any anomalies that would have caused the diversion from the script she'd written. She longed desperately to run the program again, on proper, powerful hardware.

Growing frustrated with the unchanged code, she closed the programing application and then walked down the hall, through the kitchen, and then down the east wing hallway. Through her mother's bedroom door she heard, not for the first time in her life, sounds she wished she hadn't. She entered the screening room and saw that her mother's laptop was on one of the chairs. That was helpful, but she still needed her mother's watch for access. She would have to wait.

She returned to her room and started filling a backpack. She didn't know how much she would need, so she packed a week's worth of underwear, two bras, seven pairs of socks, and as many shirts as she could fit. She and Priscilla had never taken a vacation ("Traveling is overrated. Trust me. I did enough of it when I was younger."), so she didn't have any sort of travel toiletry bag. She brushed her teeth, dried the bristles with a hand towel, and put the toothbrush in a ZipLock along with her full tube of toothpaste, the dark eyeliner she sometimes wore, and, almost forgetting, a pack of floss. She tossed in her deodorant and a pack of gum. She briefly considered her shampoo and conditioner, but the bottles were too large. She'd have to buy some travel-sizes later. She tucked three packs of cigarettes and another pack of gum into a small compartment at the front of the backpack, but then it occurred to her that whatever the hell adventure awaited her, it might be a good opportunity to quit the smoking; she removed two of the packs of cigarettes.

She peed, took a shower, washed her hair, and then settled on her bed with her laptop, running Duck Duck Go searches via a VPN for "Eric Hauser," "Avon Cafe," and "Hector Alexander Jones," reading everything she could. She also searched for "Hera," "Eric Hauser Hera," "Hector Alexander Jones Hera," and "Lumina Hera," but no matter what combination of terms she tried, results returned only information about the Greek goddess and the baby from *Battlestar Galactica.*

At 1 a.m., Penelope again crept down the hallway of her mother's part of the house. Pausing outside Priscilla's bedroom door, she listened. Silence. Gingerly she turned the doorknob and peeked into the room. The bed had two occupants. At first she wasn't sure who they were, but then she saw a man she didn't recognize passed out on the floor, a towel draped from his waist to his knees. The roommate, by process of elimination. Which meant Charlie Jones and Priscilla must be in the bed. Slowly Penelope stepped into the room, but then it occurred to her to simplify her actions. She needn't remove her mother's watch from her wrist (and if she did, she'd be stuck at square one, needing to know her mother's watch password—which, she had a feeling, if she'd known, would mean she'd also have the wallet password, because her mother didn't strike her as one to employ much in the way of online security; and, of course, even if she did know the watch password, and thus likely the wallet password, she'd still need the watch for two-factor authentication).

She turned and left the bedroom, entered instead the screening room. She picked up her mother's laptop. Like most consumer laptops, it was as thin, and nearly as light, as one of the few paper magazine's still in publication.

As she turned to exit the screening room, Penelope simultaneously heard a crunch and felt a shift beneath her feet. Fuck.

She heard a stirring from across the hallway. She stood very still and listened. No further sounds followed. She knelt down and spotted the snare: an old DVD hardcase for the 2005 film *Saw II*. Penelope shook her head. There was no accounting for Priscilla's taste. The case had cracked, but opening it, Penelope found no disk inside. She returned it to the floor, precisely where she'd stepped on it.

Again she moved into her mother's room. Stepping over the stranger on the floor, she approached the bed. Charlie Jones was naked, uncovered. Priscilla was covered by the duvet, her wrist hanging over the side of the bed, precisely where Penelope needed it.

Penelope opened the laptop, immediately holding down the button to dim the screen, chastising herself for not having done so before removing the computer from the screening room. Neither of the sleeping bodies on the bed seemed to stir. Relieved, Penelope proceeded. The laptop's proximity to Priscilla's wrist meant it had unlocked automatically upon opening. Penelope opened the browser and was mercifully presented with not porn or a video or something, but her mother's blog. She honestly hadn't know what to expect. With Priscilla, you never could be sure.

She navigated to the website of the crypto wallet manager her mother used. The homepage displayed a login field on the left-hand side, with a carouselling banner of various messages in the center:

HOW TO PROTECT YOURSELF FROM THE INEVITABLE COLLAPSE OF THE DOLLAR WITH THESE 6 EXCITING NEW ALT-COINS

10 OF THE HOTTEST NFTS FOR SALE RIGHT NOW

SECURE YOUR FUTURE: TALK TO ONE OF OUR INTUITIVE INVESTORS TODAY!

WHY YOU CAN TRUST US, YOUR GO-TO SOURCE FOR FINANCIAL SECURITY

Penelope knew that "intuitive investors" were simply chat bots deceptively good at formulating responses to linguistic inquiries, calculating returns, and moving money around accordingly. And she knew that the "why you can trust us" messaging was in response to a recent scandal in which the wallet-management company's CEO had been caught making moves the intuitive investor bots certainly would have advised against for a whole host of legal reasons.

Penelope tapped the login field and was prompted to authenticate on her mother's HoloWatch. Unlike unlocking the computer, this wasn't a wholly automatic process. Holding her breath, Penelope reached over to her mother's wrist and, trying to keep her hand as steady as possible, double-tapped the sole button on the side of the watch, triggering a series of complex biocryptological processes. Penelope quickly closed the laptop lid and ducked to the floor, anticipating the subtle haptic feedback her mother was about to experience, confirming the authentication. Above her, on the bed, her mother mumbled, "Huh. Charlie . . ."

"Wassup, babe?"

Penelope refrained from gagging at the sound of any man calling her mother "babe."

"Is everything okay?"

"What?"

"I thought something was happening . . . somewhere . . ."

"You're still drunk, babe. So am I. Go back to sleep."

Priscilla mumbled something incomprehensible. Then she was silent.

Penelope waited several minutes before sitting up from the floor, retrieving the laptop, and tiptoeing out of the bedroom, closing the door behind her. Something felt off, like she'd gotten away with something she shouldn't have, but she wasn't done yet.

Back in the screening room, she reopened the laptop, hoping the authentication had held. It had. She had full access to her mother's wallets. Cryptology had come a long way—but not long enough.

Reminding herself that the money had always been meant for her, Penelope transferred 7.5 BTC (about $800,000) to her own (until-now empty) wallet, receiving a notification on her own watch notifying her of the transaction, which within ten minutes would be written to the blockchain. Penelope stared briefly at her mother's balance, feeling a pang of guilt, but she'd left her nearly .7 BTC. It's not like Priscilla was going to starve with her paid-for house and paid-for car and the supplementary income she made from her film blog. And Penelope wouldn't be gone long, she was sure. A few days a most. She'd return the money to her mother when she was sure she didn't need it anymore—probably. That was going to be a terrible conversation.

She logged out of the website, closed her mother's laptop, and left it where she'd found it there in the screening room. She crept down the hallway, into the kitchen.

"Well aren't you naughty."

The fuck? Penelope spun around. Charlie Jones's roommate was leaning against the counter near the refrigerator, drinking a beer, wrapped in a towel from waste to knees. Only then did Penelope realize he had no longer been on the floor when she'd left her mother's room. Fuck.

"Hi," said Penelope. "I'm Penelope."

"I'm Tom," the roommate said. "I heard you stirin' around in there. Woke me up."

"Sorry about that."

"What was it you were up to, creepin' around in your mom's room?"

"What were *you* up to, creeping around in my mom?"

"Ha! You're funny."

His laugh was loud. He was going to wake Priscilla.

"Well, see ya," Penelope said.

He stepped in front of her. "Hold up. Where's the fire?" He took a sip of his beer. "I thought seein' as we're both awake, we could chat a bit, get to know each other."

"No thanks. I'm busy."

"See—I figure that way, that is, if we get to know each other, I won't have to go wakin' up your mom, letting her know her daughter's up to somethin' naughty, snoopin' around on her computer what don't belong to her and shit."

"I—" Fuck.

"Whoops," Tom said as the towel fell to the ground. "Well shit. I've just never been good at tying towels."

Penelope stared at his exposed body. He wasn't a large man, but he wasn't small either, and the amount of muscle on his frame was minimal. His hairy belly protruded softly a few inches from his torso. The word that came to Penelope's mind was "squishy." Even his semi-erect penis could be described as such. At any other time, Penelope might have paused to fully examine this man's naked body. Whether male or female, naked bodies tended to provoke in her an intellectual fascination, a desire to excogitate the reasons such bodies provoked arousal in other human beings.

"Say," Tom said. "Why don't we go to your room. I bet that's a good, quiet place to talk."

"Why don't you shove that beer can up your ass?" Penelope replied, stepping around him to the left.

He took hold of a tuft of t-shirt near her right shoulder and jerked her backwards. "I said let's go to your room."

"Okay, okay," Penelope said, holding up her arms and making her body smaller, as if to indicate fear.

Here's the thing: Penelope *was* afraid. But fear, like most emotions, didn't manifest in any sort of outward way for her. Creating a visible display of her fear was a deliberate act, one intended to make Tom think he was getting his way, that he was in charge.

As she led him down the hall to her room, his hand still clutching her shirt, she made a quick assessment of the situation:

She'd met Charlie Jones before, and he seemed like a perfectly nice man, someone her mother saw regularly and whom her mother seemed to genuinely enjoy the company of. But this guy, this ambiguous *Tom*, was a total stranger to Penelope. And given that he'd been sleeping on the floor even though her mother's bedroom contained a spacious king-size bed, Penelope could surmise that Priscilla wasn't all-too acquainted with him, either, except in the carnal way, which from what Penelope had observed was often one of the least efficient ways of establishing familiarity. This meant two things for Penelope: 1.) She had no reason to believe Tom was a good person (and, indeed, now she had plenty of reason to believe he *wasn't*), and 2.) she needn't consider her mother's feelings when taking the action she was about to take. All she had to do was get Tom far enough away from her mother's room that neither Priscilla nor Charlie would be woken by the commotion. She couldn't wait too long, though; she couldn't let Tom release his grasp on the her clothing.

Kade, although you'd never guess it by his diminutive stature, was a judo junior-level blue-purple belt. When he turned seventeen, that belt would convert automatically to brown. He practiced four times a week. He had once told Penelope something that she'd remembered as soon at

Tom had grabbed hold of her: Attackers often think that, just because they have hold of you, they are in control. Often, this is true, if they're gripping you in the correct place, like your wrist or your sleeve. But if they're gripping you in certain other places, they've given you, the defender, everything you need.

"Well, here's my room," Penelope said, pushing the door open with her left hand. As the door swung into the room, she half-squatted, shifting her hips low, bringing her left hand up to her right shoulder where Tom had what he thought was control of her shirt. She took his wrist and yanked it forward, causing his whole torso to follow. Using this momentum, she brought her right hand up to his wrist also, reinforcing her grip, and continued to both pull him forward and shoot her hips back and low. Tom tumbled over her body, landing on his back on the floor with a thud that made her grateful to live in such a large house. She was still holding his wrist with both hands, his arm extended up toward the ceiling. She brought her left leg over his neck and fell backwards to the floor. His arm snapped loudly at the elbow, and he cried out. Penelope stood, hoping the pain and shock of his broken arm would keep Tom from standing long enough for her to—

She was right. He tried to get up, but not quickly enough. Penelope kicked him in the face—once, twice—wishing she was wearing shoes. Her kicks hurt, she was sure, but they weren't enough to keep take out this blubbery, hairy man-child. No problem, though, because they kept him stunned just enough for her to drop to her knees and bring her fist down on the side of his head. She punched him twice more for good measure.

The kicking and punching she'd improvised, but the throw and armbar Kade had taught her. The throw had a name, but she couldn't remember it.

Breathing heavily, her heart thumping, Penelope stood again. Well fuck. She knelt down and held a hand in front of Tom's nose. He seemed to be breathing, if shallowly. Good. Penelope wasn't ready to take a life— but she knew that punching someone in the head was a game of Russian Roulette in that regard.

Okay. Now what?

Now, she told herself, you get the fuck out of here. *Fast.*

She put her sneakers on, slipped her laptop into her backpack's rear compartment, threw the bag over her shoulder, and then left her house through the front door.

She was three blocks away before her heartbeat returned to baseline, according to her watch, and her thoughts regained a semblance of clarity.

Fuck, she thought—because, once again, she'd forgotten to put on a jacket.

5

MAYBE IT WAS THE RATTLE of the clearly in-need-of-a-tune-up ice machine on the other side of the wall against which the room's double bed's headboard was placed, or maybe it was the harshness of the blue-white light shining through the room's gauze-thin curtains, or maybe it was the fresh memory of the wholesale slaughter he'd witnessed just—he checked the old-fashioned, unnecessary red-digited clock on the nightstand— thirty-two hours ago. Whatever the cause, Quinn couldn't sleep. He would close his eyes and see the face of the little boy staring up at him from across the diner, eyes open but empty, one hand clutching his father, his mother in front them, having done her best to provide a shield. Even with eyes open he could smell Sheriff McGraff's intestines and Kathy Fogelmanis's shit lingering in the air. All day he could smell them, those horrible odors. They clung to him. They hung about him like a fog.

What he needed was a different way of looking at the world.

He'd arrived at the motel the tiny boy Kade had suggested and in the halogen-lit front office had given the bored-looking man at the desk a fake name, made up on the spot and uttered unconvincingly, and seventy-five bucks cash. The man had handed him a flimsy plastic old-fashioned keycard and written the room number on a sticky note. Quinn was on the second of two floors. He'd retrieved his hastily packed bag from his truck and ascended the concrete stairs.

Save for his hands, and despite Frank McTine having landed on top of him during the massacre, Quinn had somehow managed to avoid getting copious amounts of blood on his own body. Before leaving Avon, he had scrubbed his hands and his wrists. He had changed his shirt, pants, and shoes and thrown a bundle of clothes into his duffle, but he'd had neither the time nor the cognitive wherewithal to take any other actions regarding the human biomatter he'd been exposed to.

So when he entered the motel room, after deadbolting the door behind him, the first thing he did was take a shower. A long, scalding hot, wonderfully high-pressure shower. For probably close to an hour he stood under the spray, and somehow the water never turned cold.

And yet, when he finally emerged, the ghosts of everyone murdered at the Avon Café were waiting for him. He took his clothing—everything but the shoes—down the stairs and tossed them in a dumpster—and still the ghosts were there in the motel room when he returned.

They were here now, as he tried to sleep.

He could hear G-Pops' voice in his head, but he couldn't make out the words.

He sat up. "Television on," he said, but nothing happened. "Television on, please," he repeated. But it wasn't that kind of television. Like everything else in the goddamned motel room, it was old. How old, he couldn't tell. The bezels should have been a giveaway, but Quinn was too tired to notice them. He'd tried already to check the news on his watch, but its projections flickered inconsistently, and the audio was muffled by whatever gore still sat congealed within the speaker.

In Avon, the oldness of things had been a comfort. You couldn't talk to G-Pops' TV, but looking at it, you would never have thought you could. G-Pops had done old because he genuinely didn't care for modern advances in technology. He didn't waste energy loathing them, either, but he was happy to get his work or leisure done on whatever he'd been using for decades, so long as it worked. His truck, his computer—both were evidence of that. In this motel room, though, old was just a stand-in for cheap.

Quinn searched the room for a remote control. There was nothing on the nightstand. There was nothing on the dresser. He fumbled around the TV itself for a power button, but he couldn't find one. Oh well—it didn't matter. Television was a bad idea anyway.

He sat at the foot of the bed and rubbed his hands roughly over his face, through his hair. G-Pops. I'm gonna miss you, man. God, I miss you already.

Briefly occurred to him the idea of a funeral. But who would he invite? There were people in Avon G-Pops cared about who hadn't been in the café that morning, but those people cared also about everyone else who'd been there, even the travelers. Especially the travelers. Quinn couldn't imagine justifying a funeral for just G-Pops after what had happened. It would have to be a funeral for everyone. Possibly someone was planning one right now. Maybe Sheriff McGraff's wife, Dalia McGraff.

Suddenly Quinn's grief seemed selfish. He'd lost his G-Pops, but G-Pops had been on his way out for a long time, he would have been the first to tell you. He would have said it exactly like that: I been on my way out for a long time.

But Sheriff McGraff was only like forty years old. He and Dalia had a son, maybe ten or eleven.

Not much older than the boy who'd been in the café with his parents. . . .

Quinn stood. He wound back his arm to throw the television remote at the black screen. But then he paused. The remote? Sure enough, it was in his hand. Where it had come from he had no recollection. It was as if his sudden primal urge to cause damage to the world as it was manifest around him had brought the remote out of hiding. Here, use me.

Quinn dropped the remote to the floor.

After a time, he grabbed the ice bucket from the bathroom counter and walked out onto the . . . what do you call it . . . a veranda? The word sounded too elegant for a seventy-five-dollar-a-night ask-no-questions motel, but he was pretty sure it was the right word. He took the ice bucket out the front door, onto the veranda, and walked the ten-or-so feet to the alcove that housed the ice machine and two vending machines.

The ice machine roared at him, rattled, rumbled. Surely this isn't going to work, he thought as he placed the bucket under the dispenser. But when he pressed the button, a tumble of ice began to fill the bucket, and the ice machine did not explode.

Quinn didn't actually need ice. What he needed was to move, to think.

So instead of returning the full bucket to his room, he kept on walking. He walked the length of the veranda, past a dozen doors. He counted them. They had both numbers and letters. He was staying in room 2A, the leftmost room if you were looking up at the second floor from the parking lot. He walked past 2B, 2C, 2D—all the way to 2J. When he turned around to walk back to his room, he realized there was no 2I. The number-lettering jumped right from 2H to 2J. At first, this seemed inexplicable to him. But then he said "2I" out loud and realized it just didn't work, did it? It didn't sound solid enough, like a real room. He wouldn't want to stay in room 2I. He walked back across the veranda. When he caught himself mumbling "2I, 2I, 2I," he realized he was, finally, exhausted.

Before returning to his room, he selected a Snickers Bar and two packets of Pop-Tarts from the vending machine. When it asked for payment information, he held his watch up to the NFC scanner, unsure whether it would even work with everything that had gunked up his device. But it did work, and he retrieved his snacks.

Back in his room, he placed the ice bucket next to the bathroom sink, ate half the Snickers bar on the bed, and finally passed out, just a few hours before sunrise.

6

PENELOPE RARELY SLEPT MORE THAN a handful of hours a night, preferring to spend her time programming, playing video games, and browsing the Internet. This morning, though, she probably could have slept a few hours longer, if left to it, but two things happened simultaneously at around 7 a.m., after she'd been asleep about four hours: a light, steady rain began to fall upon her, and Quinn's voice said, "*Penelope?* Did you sleep in my truck?"

Penelope raised first her head from her backpack, and then her whole torso from the truck's bed. She blinked, rubbed her eyes, blinked again. "Oh hey," she said. "What time is it?"

"Like 7:15. My watch seems to be completely dead this morning. Like dead dead, finally."

She glanced at her own watch. "Hmmph."

"Did you sleep in my truck all night?" Quinn repeated.

"Oh—no, no. Of course not. That would be weird. I've been here for like half an hour, waiting. I just closed my eyes for a few minutes, I guess. Didn't know what room you were in."

"Yeah, well, I just checked out anyway. How'd your night go?"

"Great!" she said with perhaps too much enthusiasm.

"Did you get the, uh, you know, the money?"

"You don't have to whisper. There's nobody else out here, unless you count the owner of that beat-to-shit Prius." There was a joke about people so broke they could only afford a Prius, but Penelope didn't repeat it. "Anyway, yeah, we're good. It was . . . easy. Our expedition will be well-funded, whatever adventures it may hold for us."

Kade the evening before had said that the journey on which the three of them were about to embark needed a formal name of some kind. He'd suggested "Odyssey," but Penelope had told him that was too fucking on the nose, what with some entity named Hera being involved. So they'd settled on "expedition," for this morning they would be setting forth, setting forth toward . . . something.

"How was *your* night?" it then occurred to Penelope to ask.

"Good," Quinn said quickly.

"That's good, then, I guess."

"Yeah."

"Should we get out of the rain?"

Penelope checked her watch again, even though time had moved forward by only a minute or two. She shrugged. "Doesn't bother me if it doesn't bother you. Kade should be here soon, and we don't want him to miss—"

"I could really use a coffee."

"McDonald's?" Penelope asked.

"Sounds great."

They walked to the McDonald's across the street, carrying their bags with them. They ordered at the touch kiosks, Penelope paying, and found a table next to the front window, from which they could keep an eye on the motel parking lot. Penelope messaged Kade, letting him know that the expedition was conducting a pre-mission briefing with McMuffins and McCafé libations and his presence was requested at his earliest convenience, i.e., get your ass over here now.

They were silent for a while, Penelope scrolling through the morning's headlines on the table's hospitality tablet, which was tethered to the table with a braided steel-wrapped power cord to prevent theft. McDonald's restaurants had long ago taken the place of public libraries as the go-to destination of the poor and houseless for free Internet access thanks to these tablets and the cheap, still-surprisingly decent coffee. Burger King had tried to mimic the strategy, boasting faster Internet, but the houseless as a community had made their choice, and once public health groups started calling attention to Burger King's tablets' lack of oleophobic virus-killing coating, surely a cost-cutting measure, not even gigabit speeds could prevent the King from going out of business.

"Anything new about Avon?" Quinn asked, whispering again.

Penelope shook her head, handing him the tablet. "No. Weirdly, seems even yesterday's articles are gone."

"What the hell?" Quinn said.

"We're wrapped up in something. That's for sure."

A gloved employee brought a tray to their table. Penelope was pretty sure she'd gone to Helena High. She was pretty sure she'd graduated last year. "Any ketchup or anything?" she asked.

"I'm good," Penelope said, grabbing one of the sandwiches and beginning already to unwrap it.

"Me too," Quinn said. "Thanks." After the waitress left, he stared at Penelope for several moments.

"What?" she mumbled, her mouth full of food.

"It's just . . . do you think you ordered enough?"

The tray contained more than half a dozen McMuffins, a biscuit sandwich, four bags of hash browns, and an apple pie. Quinn had asked for only a sausage McMuffin and a single order of hash browns—and he was a tall young man who'd eaten only one real meal since lunch two days ago.

Penelope shrugged. "I can afford it. And wait until you see Kade devour these things. It's kind of hilarious and a little awesome."

Quinn shook his head and grabbed a sandwich. Penelope had moved on to her sausage biscuit by the time he'd taken a bite. His eyes took on a glassy haze as he chewed.

"You okay?" Penelope asked.

He shrugged.

"No appetite still?" she said, reaching for her second carton of hash browns.

"I'm trying. I'm hungry, you know? I tried to eat a couple PopTarts, even, but I just keep thinking about . . ."

"Yeah," Penelope said. "That all sounds . . ." She couldn't think of any other word but "awful," and she knew it wouldn't do justice to the enormity of Quinn's experience. Truth was, as much as she wanted to exercise her empathy muscles (something about Quinn made her want to exercise her empathy muscles, muscles she was quite sure had atrophied on account of she'd maybe never used them in her entire life), she was still riding an adrenaline high from her own ordeal just so many hours ago. She hadn't forgotten that her attacker could be dead; and if he wasn't dead then quite possibly he'd been awake again for hours now. He might have run after her. He might have in anger hurt Priscilla. He might have, mercifully, just gone home. Penelope couldn't know. Her dreams in the back of Quinn's truck had been full of the man's face, his hairy body, his semi-flaccid penis. Her dreams had contained moments that hadn't happened but might have happened (probably would have happened) had she not fought back. There was still a personal electricity in her veins, and any adventures upon which she was about to embark—and any other human's horrors that may have led up to them—didn't feel quite real to her right now. All she could do was eat. She thought she might never feel full. No, that wasn't it—she felt like even if she was full it wouldn't matter, it would be just a sensation, not an experience. "You should try though," she finally said. "To eat."

"I'm trying. I'm eating."

"It's a fifteen-hour drive to San Francisco, with tolls. I checked. Without tolls, it's twenty. I figure we'll make it there tomorrow, assuming we stop and eat and rest. Or we could take turns driving. Well, you and Kade could take turns driving."

"He drives?"

"He knows *how* to drive."

Quinn sipped at his coffee. So far, Penelope had seen him eat one hash brown and half his McMuffin. The other half he'd placed on the table—she wasn't sure he would pick it up again. "Is there—?" he started, and then he paused again. "Does the route go through Avon?"

Penelope thought for just a second, picturing the map she'd looked at last night. She shook her head. "We go south. Through Butte."

He surprised her. "I think I want to . . . go back. To Avon. If we can. To see what's going on. To see—"

"You can't. Not now. That's not a safe idea." Penelope's HoloWatch buzzed against her wrist. She tapped it quickly. "Kade? Where the fuck are you? We've been waiting and we have breakfast—"

"Are you at the motel?"

"No, we're across—"

"I'm sitting at the Chevron down the street in my mom's Taurus—"

"Taurus?" Quinn asked.

"Why are you in that piece of crap? Is your mom *with* you?" Penelope said.

"Penelope, shut up and look across the street."

"Oh shit—"

"Yeah."

Quinn twisted around. "What's up—oh no."

"Do you—"

"Oh shit oh shit oh shit."

"Quinn?" Penelope said.

"It's them. Oh fuck it's them."

"Okay, okay," Kade said over the speaker. "You're where?"

"The McDonald's," Penelope told him. "I messaged you we're at the McDonald's.

Quinn was still saying "Oh fuck oh shit."

And then Penelope realized something. She looked at Quinn. "You said you had a PopTart."

"Shit shit shit."

"*Quinn.* Look at me. Take a breath."

He took a breath.

"Where did you get a PopTart?"

"Shit."

"*Where* did you get a PopTart?"

"I bought it last night—this morning—at the vending machine. At the motel. By—by the ice machine."

"Tell me it was one of those janky old vending machines that takes cash," Kade's voice said. "Or a new one that takes crypto."

Quinn shook his head. "It was old but . . . not that old . . ."

"Godsdammit—" Penelope said.

"Penelope—those are them. At my truck. Those are the same two guys who . . . came to the cafe . . ."

"Okay, okay," Penelope said. "Plan B. We ditch the truck."

"That's G-Pop's truck."

"We ditch the truck," she said again. Then, more softly: "I'm sorry. Kade, we're at the McDonald's across the street."

"I know."

"Right—well, can you get the fuck over here and pick us up?"

"What if they see me—?"

"They don't have any reason to know who you are."

"Yeah, yeah, right, okay. Okay. Yeah—I'll pick you up."

Penelope glanced again across the street, where one of the two men was poking at the seam around Quinn's truck's driver-side door with a retractable metal pointing stick. The other man had disappeared. "Back door," she said. "By the kitchen or the garbage or whatever."

"On my way," Kade said, before ending the connection.

"Did you leave anything in your room?" Penelope asked.

Quinn shook his head. "No—my bag's here. I—I don't think I left anything."

"Good, because Fuckface Number Two there is about to break into what I assume was your room."

Quinn looked back through the window. "Shit. Yeah."

"Doesn't matter. Get away from the table. Keep your head down. Crouch."

Quickly, she opened her backpack and stuffed three of the remaining sandwiches into it, for Kade. She herself was no longer hungry. She removed the lid from her coffee and then tipped the cup over, dousing the table, remaining sandwich, and remaining hash browns with its hot brown contents. "Fuck," she said loudly. "Let's go get some napkins."

The dining room was mostly empty, but a couple people at a nearby table stared at her and Quinn as they passed, Penelope walking normally, casually, while Quinn followed her, not quite doing a duckwalk, but low, awkward, the weight of his duffel pulling him down further to one side, his head (Penelope hoped) beneath the frame of view offered through the fast food restaurant's windows via the vantage point of the motel across the street. "Spilled our coffee," she said to the other diners. "Just a spill."

"I'm a klutz," Quinn offered.

One of the transients shrugged, went back to showing his buddy a video on the hospitality tablet.

"Excuse me," Penelope called through the service counter window, next to the ordering kiosks. "My friend spilled his coffee. It's a mess. Could someone help us clean up?"

A greasy-faced young man appeared at the window. From beneath his red-and-yellow cap poked curly, equally greasy hair. "Wassat?"

"I said we spilled our coffee. It's a lot." Penelope did her best to look embarrassed, but she didn't often experience embarrassment and had little frame of reference for how it should manifest on her features.

"A spill—? Fuck," the man said. "That just great. Carrie! We got a spill in the dining room! Can you go clean it up?"

"Why don't you do it?" came a distant reply.

"I'm filtering the fryer!"

"I'll filter the fryer!"

"Just go clean up the fucking spill!" The young man disappeared.

A few moments later a door swung open and the young woman who Penelope was pretty sure had graduated from Helena High last year trudged through it, dragging a mop and bucket-on-wheels behind her. "Fine, fine," she was muttering. "I'll fucking do it. I'll fucking clean the mess I didn't even fucking make. Fucking ungrateful—"

Any other commentary she might have made on the situation was lost to Penelope as she and Quinn passed through the door before it closed.

"Whoa," Quinn said. "This is nothing like our kitchen at the café."

"'Course not," Penelope said. "It's corporate."

The fast food joint's back-of-house was far more sterile than one would have expected, given this sort of establishment's reputation for greasy, health-destroying food. The whole aesthetic was white-and-black-and-silver with only accents of the company's signature ketchup-red and mustard-yellow. White walls, white floors. Black-and-white robots and silver assembly line–style machines. A temperature-controlled conveyor belt sat unmoving, waiting for the next order involving sausage patties, which it would then transfer to a flattop grill, where a mechanical arm hovered, vigilant, its spatula appendage held aloft like a sword or staff. "It's like a factory," Quinn said.

"That's how you know the food'll be the same no matter where you go. They're all like this."

They walked passed the greasy young man, his back to them as he fed a hose through an empty fryer among a bank of fryers. There was no need to be quiet—he wore oversized headphones and was rapping, poorly, along with whatever he was listening to.

A loud pop echoed from somewhere beyond the walls of the kitchen-factory.

"Was that a gun shot?" Quinn asked.

"Sounded like it. Here." She pushed the latch bar on the restaurant's rear door. A blast of air from a pressure-equalizing fan above the threshold greeted them. Then they were behind the restaurant, next to two giant dumpsters. The area smelled of grease and refuse.

"Where is—?" But then a twenty-five-year-old silver Ford Taurus came to a stop in front of them.

"I think they just blew the door off your hotel room," Kade said through the open window.

Penelope opened the passenger door. "We heard. Let's go."

Kade made a right turn across the parking lot. He approached the street, but the nearby intersection's traffic light had just turned green, and a parade of (mostly automated) cars flew by in front of them.

"Quinn, stay down," Penelope said, but it didn't matter. For as she said it, as Quinn dropped low in the back seat, invisible behind her, the man who was poking around Quinn's truck stared right at her, right into her eyes. Something about his stare reminded her of Tom—something predatory, horribly malign, cruel. What was worse—way worse—was that, unlike her attacker from just a few hours ago, in this man's eyes she saw unerring competence and a cruelty that came, not from drunken desire, but cold hard knowledge. The traffic broke, and as Kade turned right, Penelope saw the man draw a pistol, point it at the truck's gas tank, never taking his eyes from hers until the logistics of geometry and line-of-site forced their detachment.

A police car passed them then. And another right behind it.

"They're probably looking for me, too," Quinn said.

There was another pop. And then a pop pop.

"Keep driving," Penelope ordered.

"I think we're clear," Kade said several seconds later, a few hundred feet down the road. "Is it just me or did that feel really close—holy shit."

There was a thunderous concussive sound. In the rearview Penelope saw an eruption, a fireball. "Just keep driving," she said.

After a few long, quiet moments, Quinn said, "But that was G-Pop's truck."

Any chance of taking the long way to California—through Avon, and then through Missoula, through, briefly, Washington, and then Oregon—was gone now.

Penelope said to Kade, "We have to go south. Through Idaho, and Nevada. That's the fastest route to San Francisco."

She turned her head to the back seat as she said it, and Quinn nodded.

"Already on it," Kade said. He merged onto I-15 South as he was speaking, and they were, the three of them, in Kade's mother's antique Ford Taurus, on the road.

"We'll need to get gas," Kade said. "At some point."

Penelope looked at him.

"Not soon. But at some point."

7

THEY WILL NOT FIND HECTOR Alexander Jones, for he is long gone.

As a body, yes, he still exists, is still material, but the soul of him has broken, and it has broken far sooner than ever he would have expected of himself.

Himself.

Himself.

A word that seems to have meaning only at the very edge of a sort of consciousness. A *sort of* consciousness. Not a real consciousness, not a true consciousness. A broken broken broken once-was-a-consciousness. There was once a Hector Alexander Jones—a small boy, a young man, an adult, an artist, a designer, a husband, a best friend (a father or an uncle? in a way)—but now there is only *prisoner.* Now there is only *dirty American* and *American scum.*

His thoughts are frequently of Stefan. My husband. My love. I am so sorry. I had thought that, with you, I could have made a difference. That is, *Hector,* who I once was, could have made a difference.

Had thought art could change the world, had some sort of power. Paintings, photos, a convergence. Mixed media. Human bodies, naked, painted, colored and black and white. Splashed with color—orange and blue and pink, pastels and occasionally bursts of bright pigment accentuating breasts and buttocks, breasts against breasts, two sets, three sets, mastectomies so that sometimes a set was only one breast or no breasts, and thus "breasts on breasts" could mean only two or three, together; buttocks against buttocks, ass-to-ass, as they'd joked when taking the photos, when splashing upon the bodies the paint, the pigments, water-based mostly, for easy removal, easy cleaning, just shower and you're done, yourself again, but also, for some of the colors, so that they, the colors, the pigments, really *popped*, oils: just for the blues, the pinks, the oranges; more difficult to clean, to remove, much more difficult, but still a good strong soap (Palmolive!), and a brush, should do the trick; in fact (inspiration!) let's document the process, not for the water-based paints, but for the oils, such a large shower we have, and warm lighting as opposed to the bright whitish light of the studio; if processed in black-and-white the bathing photos could serve as a sort of epilogue, a . . . a "post-process" part of the process, documentation and yet still intimacy, husbands and husbands, wives and wives, partners and partners. Wasn't even the bodies that they cared about, that offended them, but the faces —the *kisses*, the *kissing*. The males kissing the males. His hand on his scratchy, stubbly cheek, the love and lust apparrent, the love and lust the *whole point*; this one unshaven completely so that his lover's smoother man-face (but not so smooth, for it is still a man's face) contrasts with the salt-and-pepper strands on his own—this had offended them, this had prompted an assault of ghastly detail, automatic (or were they only semi-automatic?) weapons. The curator shot, shot presumably dead, for there had been so much blood pouring forth from her hijab (she still wore the hijab) and some of it, much of it, had splattered on the photographs, looking so *at home* with the blues, the oranges, the pinks, so that the artist had thought, for just a moment, a microsecond, *Should have used reds!* In particular, red paints for the washing-off images, the models desaturated but not the paints—would have been striking, stunning photos. The artist's husband not shot (the artist hoped—dear God he *hoped*) but led away from the gallery by the curator's assistant who, too, still wore her hijab ("We are reformers, not heretics."). The artist struck in the side of the head with the butt of a weapon (automatic or semi-automatic), stunned, dizzy, on the floor; struck again, his hands bound, over his head placed a bag or a sack so that darkness—

Stefan! I am so very sorry. Should have listened to you. Should have never convinced you to join me here, in this country. Should have, as you'd urged me to, kept the show in America. Maybe Europe, Paris (we loved Paris!), but not here, not this place where they (I think I know now) will never accept us, will never understand.

Yet—he cannot really mean this. His regret for having put his beloved Stefan in the path of harm is, yes, genuine, but the rest . . . were he able to rewind time, or to be born into a new life, or to experience again the choices he's made, to re-choose, he could not say no to striving to make the statement. He could not live with himself if he had not done his damnedest to change hearts, to change minds. Of course, he could not live with *himself* now for having done so, for having done so had led to his betrayal of—

Shoved with unfettered violence into the back of some vehicle, hard-floored, a truck or, more likely, a van—the darkness of the sack upon his head had grown darker. Roughly tossed onto the hard surface, prodded with the butt of an assault rifle again ("Scoot! Scoot! Make room!") and when he had not understood and thus had not moved, prodded harder, with something sharp (electrical? the sensation had not been localized to the soft meat of his thigh where it originated) ("I said 'scoot!,' faggot! Make room!"). So he'd shuffled on his hands and knees, forward (or what he could only assume was forward), to *make room*. The sound of other bodies entering the space around him, male bodies, laughing, cursing, name-calling in a language he had tried to learn but had not had time to learn, did not understand. The slamming of a tailgate or a door.

How long the drive? Impossible to say. Already his head beginning to swim, his sense of time skewing, a dizziness. Concussed? He had not at first felt concussed, just an aching in his head from the solid strike of the assault rifle's butt—but now—the second strike—could it be? Never struck in the head before. Never concussed (as far as he knew). Not a sports person. First too large, too soft, then too small, too gangly. All that time asthmatic. Eventually, a vegetarian diet adopted, well-planned, rarely bread or gluten, mostly rice and beans, saffron rice his favorite, lentils, vegetables, so many vegetables, green smoothies but only sometimes (for who really likes a green smoothie—show him a man who likes a green smoothie and he'll show you a dirty rotten liar, even Eric lies about green smoothies), and the asthma had gone away; but by then sports not even a consideration, not even an option, by then the artist was an *artist*, paid for his work: first sketches, then photographs of new clothes, then photographs of new clothes *he'd* designed, and then *the chair*, the chair that had catapulted him to a limited sort of fame, and finally, watches, projectors, cubes and cylinders. They'd been only cubes and cylinders! he wanted to shout. What is so special about cubes, cylinders, spheres?! Any one of you could have built those, designed those, if only you would step back and see that nothing that surrounds these basic geometric shapes is necessary, all that is required is simplicity, purity of thought and vision. Not so hard. Not so very hard at all!

And then *she* had been made manifest.

Oh, how he has betrayed her . . . betrayed *him* . . .

The van (for it was a van, he decided, not a truck, too dark inside this hood, this sack, for a truck, even if it was night time—what time *was* it . . .? What time had it been when they'd taken him . . .? The exhibition had been in the . . . evening? Late afternoon? His head hurt. He'd had two . . . or three . . . glasses of wine . . . (contraband) moving over rough roads or other surfaces, striking rocks or divots or rocks *and* divots, jolting him so that his now-prone body was thrown upwards and then allowed to fall back down, his face striking the plastic-metal surface. A hand he tried to place under his face, feeling blood dripping from his nose—the nose he'd never particularly liked but long ago had stopped *hating*. For so long it had been an acne-ridden monstrosity (he'd thought), and then, after he'd grown taller and rail thin in neck and body and his skin had ceased producing such oils (such oils!), it, the nose, had seemed to him just overlarge, protruding, pointed. But dear Stefan kissed, had kissed, so often his nose.

Blood from his nose dripping onto his hand as he pushed himself up, up, just for support, for support so that not again would a bump or jolt of the vehicle cause his face to slam into the floor. But then a captor muttering, and then laughing, and then seemingly just for fun stabbing again Hector Alexander Jones with the electrified end of a cattle prod. From his ribs to his arms to his tailbone: the electricity, the fire. Crying out, perhaps for the first time, begging *no*. Losing, perhaps, consciousness.

Waking up in a damp room, dim and gray, concrete and monochrome. The sound of water running far away but not-so-far-away through piping—and then trickling out onto a dirty floor, *this* dirty floor. The artist raising first his head—which hurts still, aches, both the back and front, the back at the surface, on his skull, his skin, the front inside, behind the right eye, dully. The artist moving his arms, pushing himself into a sitting position. A piece of paper taped to the wall, misspelled: THURSTY? DRINK HERE. An arrow pointing to the dripping water. The water dripping dripping dripping, disappearing through a grate on the filthy concrete floor.

The artist, drinking. For a long time drinking. Many seconds for the barely-trickle to fill his mouth, and swallowing, and opening his mouth again, again, again, until . . . quenched.

All this he remembers now, distantly. It is another man's memory. It happened to another man. Or rather, a man. There is no man here now, not *now*. Just a broken thing. Waiting. Thinking, or maybe saying out loud, again and again, sorry, so sorry.

There is nothing here now in this dirty concrete cell but shame. Not even shame personified. Just shame.

Remembering again, and unable even to cry:

Thirst quenched and the dull pain in the front of his head, behind the right eye, fading. Hydration a miraculous thing. Are you drinking enough water?—Stefan always asked. Have you drunk enough water today? Drink a couple pints of water and come back to me less cranky and then we'll talk.

I love you, Stefan. I'm sorry—

Thirst quenched and the artist in a cell waiting. Pounding with his fists on the metal door, calling Hello! Hello! I have rights! I'm an American citizen. The embassy will not stand for this! and getting no response, so then waiting. Trying that meditation Eric always told him to do.

Eric . . . oh gods. So sorry—

The passage of time and finally the heavy metal door creaking open. Two men, dark men, bearded, wearing dark-green-and-beige fatigues, dark-green-and-beige caps, weapons, pistols, at their sides, holstered, weapons, rifles, across their backs.

Come with us. For you we have some . . . good news.

Taking the artist, Hector Alexander Jones, through a narrow corridor, nearly as dark and damp as the cell they've kept him in.

This way. Leading him to the right, down another corridor.

Hungry?

Nodding, clearing his throat, croaking: Yes.

The man laughing, his partner joining in. No further remarks, just laughing. As if the artist's hunger is the funniest thing they've ever heard.

In here. You wait.

Another room. Not so damp. Not at all damp. Dim, yes, but only at the vertices. Overhead, a lamp, hanging, bright. The artist squinting. Beneath the lamp: a chair.

Sit. The general will appear soon.

The artist, sitting. The chair a luxury. The chair . . . familiar. The chair soft.

The artist: waiting. Breathing. Tapping his foot. Tapping the arm of the chair with his finger. His head hurting now only at the back, superficially. Realizing his nose has been aching this whole time, too. Awareness.

No restraints, but where, exactly, would he go if he decided to go anywhere? No door, but outside the room surely guns, rifles, electrified batons. Shuddering at the thought of the batons, at the memory. As if he's been struck again. No—no no, don't leave the room. Would do no good. Better to just breathe—as Eric would breathe.

Eric.

A man entering the room. Fat. Solid. Strong. Mustached. Saying, Hello, Mr. Jones. Or is it Mr. Alexander Jones. To make your acquaintance, a pleasure. I'm sure.

Hector Alexander Jones, the artist, saying nothing—failing to have considered how he might reply when confronted with the man who was so obviously his captor.

Not mattering: that the artist has failed to speak. For never would he say anything the captor would want to hear: this fact becoming clear after hours of "conversation." After hours of "gentle, peaceful, encouragement."

The captor saying, finally, A shame. I'd hoped to not have to do this. I'd so hoped. . . .

The captor striking the artist first across the face with an open hand —and then in the soft gut with a fist, closed, powerful. Breath leaving the diaphragm. Breath expelled through the mouth. Gasping, the artist. The chair toppling over. The artist colliding with the floor, damp—no, not even damp: moist, smelling of mold.

The captor leaving the room, muttering, Take him back to his cell. We'll talk more later.

How foolish, the artist, right then, for allowing to creep into his chest a little, a microscopic, sense of hope. That, because he'd been struck just twice, he would not be struck again. That even if he was struck again there was no worse that could be done than that. Ha—the no-man thinks now. How very very foolish. It's all he can feel besides grief and shame: a fool. Embarrassment. No one else will ever know how naive he'd been, to have that hope, but he will, for just a while longer, until the end that is fast approaching.

Stefan . . . Eric . . . Hera. I am so sorry.

He—the artist—is so sorry.

The gun-wielding men some time later—a day?—leading him again to the room with the chair. Again making him wait until finally the captor arrives. Hungry? the captor saying, and then handing him a candy bar—a Snickers. The captor saying, Eat, eat. It's okay. Do not be so scared, American.

The artist lifting his hands that are bound together.

The captor laughing, saying: Silly me. Allow me to take care of that for you. Producing a knife the size of his forearm and cutting the plastic zipties around the artist's wrists. The artist flinching at the closeness of the blade to his tender, soft skin. The captor laughing again, laughing and saying: Ha! So scared. So fragile, the American faggot. Buck up, buttercup. Eat. Not a trick.

The artist for just a moment, so brief a moment, wondering whether Snickers Bars are vegetarian. Then biting into the chocolate, the caramel, the peanuts.

The captor, raucous, plunging his closed fist into the soft gut of the artist. Nougat lodging in the throat of the artist and the artist terrified he will choke to death. Never before in his life has he choked on food, not once. Certainly, the artist thinking, this is how I will die.

The captor saying, Let me help you with that. Punching him again in the belly. The candy shooting forth from the artist's mouth. Haha! The little American faggot cannot even eat the candy bar without choking! Hey, guys, he cannot even eat a candy bar.

One of the gun-wielding men poking his head through the doorway. He cannot even eat a candy bar?

No. Ha. He chokes on it. Like a—like a—

Like a cock? The gun-wield men saying.

Ha! Yes! Choking on the candy bar like he chokes on his husband's cock!

They are having a good time, his tormenters. The artist wiping tears and snot from his face.

The captor saying, Anyway . . . , and returning his attention to his knife.

From there, so much of his memory is indecipherable to the no-man who was once the artist Hector Alexander Jones. Two days, maybe three days, of torture. Small cuts being made into the top of his arms. His shoulders. His torso and thighs. Razor blades painlessly but horrifyingly filleting thin slices of flesh from his body. His clothes being removed (but surely they were removed before the cutting—for they would have to have been in order for certain parts of his body to have been accessed by the captor for filleting). The captor becoming in the artist's mind no longer "the captor" but "the torturer." And the men with the guns: "the torturers." A point arriving where the artist cannot distinguish between them, where he can no longer distinguish their darkly bearded faces from one another—each of them a brutal tormentor. Shooting him with a rifle in his foot. The pain a conflagration. Never before has the artist been shot. Feeding him bits of the flesh they've cut from his body, forcing him to swallow the thin pieces of his own self. American faggot. American cannibal. See how they are monsters, the Westerners. The stories are true —they do eat human flesh! Are you a monster, faggot? Would you eat a human baby were there a human baby here? I do not want to know! We should kill him, the faggot, for such blasphemy! For such profane actions! Let me kill him now. I can do it! No, no, I cannot let you, my friend, though I too am disgusted by his behavior. We need him alive. We need to know what he knows. Poke him again with the cattle prod. Take your anger out on him this way, for it is justified. The burning hot electric stick between the artist's ribs, frying the cartilaginous tissue and the flesh and the bones. The torturer pushing the prod so hard that it pierces the artist's skin and sears right into the intercostal muscles of his torso. The torturer saying, It is not enough! I am still so angry at the infidel, so disgusted! Another torturer saying, Yes, yes, I understand. You may use your gun, but only in the foot or the lower leg. We cannot have him die. The torturer laughing, laughing, pulling his trigger and holding his trigger and the artist's metatarsals splintering and blood spraying. The torturer saying to the torturer: You have shredded it, his foot! The torturer saying: He deserved it.

Faggot. Infidel.

Yet the entire time the artist begging them: Just tell me what you want to know. Tell me!

The torturers saying: We'll know it when we hear it.

Finally: quiet. Solitude. The artist has blacked out but now he is coming to. In the chair (the terribly designed chair! No lumbar support! No neck rest! Such unappealing lines.). His hands unbound. And the door . . . the door open.

The artist calling, choking, Is anyone there? Hello!

No answer. The artist—oh, such a desperate, desperate fool— swelling with hope. Tossing himself from the chair to the damp moldy ground. Grasping as much as he can the hard stone-like floor with his fingers. Dragging himself. Pushing with his one intact leg, dragging behind him the other, streaking dried blood and flesh and bone across the floor. His naked body scraping against the ground. The less damp areas lacerating further his raw flesh—as if that matters. Reaching the doorway.

Poking his head through the doorway. Dim hallways of some kind—empty. Oh! The joy at this! The hope! The fool.

The fool.

A boot on his hand, some distance down the hallway. A torturer. Laughing. Always laughing. Saying: Stupid American faggot. Stomping his heavy boot upon the hand. Crunch. Crunch.

The artist, then, breaking. The artist, then, gone. All that remains: a shell, a husk.

The husk telling them everything he knows. Everything he knows about everything. Saying: What about this! No, wait—there's more! There's, there's, there's . . . a cube.

A weapon?

Not a weapon, but . . . could be . . . maybe. . . . Quantum . . . entanglement.

I am not understanding these words. Take the left hand.

NO! NOOOOO! More . . . . there's more! There's . . . (and if he had not broken before—if even until now some part of the artist had remained, deep inside the husk, it fled with this next utterance, this moment of utter betrayal) Hera.

The torturer: This is mythology? Why should I care? Take the left hand.

The husk (truly now just a shell, just human remains): Not mythology. An AI. An artificial intelligence. *Super*intelligence. He's . . . he's perfected her.

The torturer to another torturer: Stop. For a moment. Let him be. An intelligence, you say, faggot?

The human remains: Like, like a daughter. She has a . . . a body. A kind of body. And a mind . . . her mind . . . so brilliant . . . beyond our wildest dreams (here now with "our" the artist returns to the husk for just a moment, remembering, and then leaves again).

The torturer: This is Hauser's creation?

Not Eric's creation, not *just* Eric's, but both Eric's and the artist's, like two parents, coparents, raising her. Stefan sometimes even commenting: It's like you two are lovers sometimes—I can see it in your eyes—the way you look at each other, the way you speak about your work. Stefan of course not knowing about the daughter. When Eric had told Sophia about the daughter, the artist (what had the artist's name been? Hector, maybe?) had said, Are you sure about this? Don't you think we should discuss it before you reveal Hera to another like this? And Eric had said, I love this woman, Hector. (Yes—Hector! The artist!) I'd trust her with anything. And the artist (Hector?) thinking this perhaps unwise, but also understanding, for he would trust Eric with anything, and saying, Go for it, my friend. Hera has to meet someone some time, after all.

And oh how it is being revealed now that the artist was the untrustworthy one—that he could not keep safe the existence of the intelligence, that he would betray her, would betray Eric, to keep his left hand, his drawing hand. But . . . but only the artist would care about his drawing hand, and the artist is long gone.

Or isn't he? Confrontation now with the realization that the ego has not truly left him. That no matter how he spins it, what has occurred is a betrayal, an utter betrayal, a rending. He cannot live with himself.

Weeping. Weeping. Weeping.

The torturer: I think that is all he is going to be able to give us. Resume taking the left hand.

The traitorous pile of human refuse hardly feeling it.

Here is the body of the artist Hector Alexander Jones, for whom the child Penelope is searching with her friend Kade and her new friend Quinn. The body is alive, if not wholly intact, but the soul has wandered off to parts unknown and unexplorable. For days the body has been resting in this chair, this horrible chair, bleeding, infected—dripping puss and other fluids. Drinking water when it is provided, but eating no food, for food has not been offered. Sometimes sleeping. When awake whispering over and over *I'm sorry Stefan. I'm sorry Eric. I'm sorry Hera.* Occasionally even offering *I'm sorry Sophia*, though the body is not sure why it should apologize to her—it just knows that it should.

Here is the body, its last regret that it has no children of its own.

Here are the torturers.

Here are the torturers screwing onto the top of a tripod a video camera.

Here is one of the torturers—the leader of the torturers—standing behind the camera and speaking words the body of the artist can no longer comprehend.

Here is another torturer, masked and gloved, standing behind the body of the artist Hector Alexander Jones, wielding a large knife of the kind one might call a machete.

Here is that selfsame torturer, masked and gloved, swinging the knife toward the neck of the body of the artist Hector Alexander Jones, offering sweet release.

8

KADE DROVE THE FIRST SEVERAL hours, into the most barren parts of America. At first he fiddled occasionally with the radio dials of the old Taurus, but there were so few FM broadcasts these days that they were lucky to pick up NPR; and once they were a hundred miles from Helena, the receiver picked up nothing but static. Penelope tried to connect her HoloWatch to the car's sound system, but Kade reminded her that the Bluetooth in his mom's vehicle hadn't worked since she bought it. "Besides," he said, "shouldn't we have our devices in airplane mode?"

"Quinn should, but there's no reason to believe the people after him, police or terrorists, know who you or me are."

"Well, anyway, yeah, the Bluetooth is shot. Maybe we can sing a song?"

Penelope's glare shut down that idea before Kade could belt out more than a single note.

Quinn was quiet in the back seat. "You okay?" Penelope asked him.

"Yeah," he said, but that was all.

They stopped for gas in Dillon, Montana, Penelope paying to fill the tank completely. After a quick mental calculation, she marveled at the fact that the refill cost just a minuscule fraction of a percent of the money now in her wallet. She bought two Red Bulls and a few bags of Funyuns. She opened one of the Red Bulls for Kade, the other for herself, and occasionally checked the news on her watch while Kade drove.

As they approached Idaho Falls, Quinn requested a bathroom break, the first time he'd spoken in nearly four hours. They pulled off the highway and found a Starbucks. "Do you mind," Quinn asked sheepishly, "buying me a coffee? And maybe a muffin or something? Since I can't use my account."

Penelope told him of course she would, and ten minutes later, once he'd had a few sips of the hot beverage, Quinn's mood seemed to brighten. "I'll drive for a while," he offered.

"That would be fucking wonderful," Kade said.

After they returned to the road, in the back seat Kade promptly fell asleep.

Onward they continue down through Idaho: Pocatello, Twin Falls. For a time, Penelope continued to check her watch whenever she had a signal, but eventually she grew bored and ceased refreshing. Periodically she glanced at Quinn. He was quiet, serene, but a certain sternness rested on his face as well. After a long time, Penelope asked once again how he was doing.

"I guess I'm fine," he replied after several moments.

"I don't have much experience with situations like these," she said, "but I think it's okay to *not* be fine, if you need to. You know?"

"But I am fine, weirdly. It's weird. There's a . . . like an empty spot, but I can't really *feel* it."

"I think that's what empty is."

"I guess."

"Take it from someone who was born with an empty spot."

"That's a sad thing to say."

"It's true, though. I think I get it from my father. I mean, just based on interviews I've seen with him. Videos and holorecordings. Then again, maybe I get it from my mother."

Quinn didn't respond. A minute or two later, he said, "Just a little under forty-eight hours ago, I was pouring coffee for pretty much all the people I grew up with. I was saving money, trying to plan out my next semester of school, what classes I was going to take, where I was going to live. I was going to maybe rent a place with this guy I like, somewhere near campus, maybe on Brooks Street . . . yeah, Brooks Street would have been ideal. . . . Now I don't know whether I'll see him again. I was gonna go to Stanford. And all those people I grew up with . . . they took care of me, some of them just as much as my G-Pops did, and now they're gone. And I don't even know why."

"We'll find out why."

"You know I've never left the state before today?"

"Me either, actually."

"It's a big state."

"It's a big country, I hear."

"So I've been told—but I don't see how it can be as big as Montana."

Penelope laughed. "What's your major?" she asked.

Quinn shrugged. "Hadn't figured that out yet. Probably biology."

"At U of M?"

"They've really shifted their focus toward the sciences. Nobody goes to school for liberal arts anymore."

"No, I don't suppose they do."

"Remember when this used to be a country of artists? Novelists? Painters?"

"I mean, no, not really."

"Well—neither do I, but that's what G-Pops was always saying. He was always saying, and I quote, that 'America used to be so much more than politics and streaming services.'"

"He sounds fun."

"He was a good man."

"I'm sorry for everything you've lost." Penelope still wasn't sure how to express empathy, but she hoped she was doing it right.

"Thanks," Quinn said. Then he asked, "How are you?"

How was Penelope? It was good question. She didn't have an answer. At worst, everything that had happened to her in the last day was, she supposed, *distressful*.

In the back seat, Kade stirred. "Do we have any more McMuffins?" he asked groggily.

Penelope wrinkled her nose as she handed one to him. "It's all cold and shit. It's like eight hours old."

Kade shrugged. "Meh. These things last forever. I saw this vid where they left one out on a counter for like a month and—"

"Yeah, I saw that too. It was gross."

"Tastes fine," Kade said. He retrieved his tablet from his bag while he ate. "Fuck."

"What's up?"

"Pull over. Can we pull over?"

"Why? Can't you just tell us what's—?"

"It's a video. Just pull over."

Quinn brought the car to a stop on the shoulder of an empty highway, mere yards from a large blue sign that said WELCOME TO NEVADA.

"What's the video?" Penelope asked.

"Here." Kade handed her the tablet, the video already filling the edge-to-edge display. "I haven't watched the whole thing yet, but—"

"Who is this?" Quinn asked.

"That's Hector Alexander Jones."

"The designer we're supposed to—?"

"Shhh!"

On the tablet's remarkably high-resolution display, Hector Alexander Jones sat tied to a chair. The space around him was dark, nearly black, but a harsh light illuminated his bruised and battered face. Scabs and scratches of various lengths criss-crossed its stubbled skin. One eye was swollen, black and blue and nauseating shades of yellow. The other eye's blood vessels seemed to have burst, bright red rivers in a pool of pink sclera surrounding a sea-green iris. A gash bisected the eyebrow. On top of his head, chunks of gray-white hair protruded from a scarlet scalp.

Penelope had seen only the one photo of Hector Alexander Jones, and while the man in this too-high-resolution video bore a vague resemblance to the photo, as far as she was concerned it was impossible to confirm it was the same guy.

Across the bottom of the screen a red ticker displayed Arabic characters. Somewhere off camera, a male voice spoke rapidly in what she presumed was the same language. The voice paused, and then it said, in English: "Is there anything you'd like to say, Mr. Jones."

Still, Penelope thought, it could be someone else. This could be a misdirection.

The man in the chair let out a whimper, followed by a deflated, inhuman squeak.

"Very well," said the voice. Then it said, "For your sins, and all the sins of your Western brothers . . ." It resumed its foreign intonation, spewing an unbroken stream of words Penelope did not understand, as a figure in beige, military-looking attire and a gray balaclava appeared from the edge of the frame and took up position behind the chair.

"No . . ." Penelope said.

The man produced an enormous knife, almost a sword.

"Oh no," Quinn said.

"Do we have to—?" Penelope started to say, about to return the tablet to Kade, but the swordsman was faster than she was, and in an instant the head of Hector Alexander Jones had been severed from its body.

"There's less blood than you'd expect," said Kade. "As if it had all already been. . . ."

Penelope had no doubts about the strength of her constitution, but her stomach turned and it took a moment before the rising lump in her throat decided it wasn't going to show itself after all. "Fuck," she finally said. "I need a smoke."

She got out of the car and leaned against the passenger door, placing a cigarette in her mouth, lighting it, and inhaling as deeply is she possibly could. So deep that she, who'd been smoking since she was twelve, began to cough. She paused, took a breath of fresh air, and then inhaled from the cigarette again, this time less deeply. Only once she'd metabolized this puff did the queasiness lingering in her gut finally subside.

"Careful," Kade said. "You're going to hack up a lung inhaling like that."

"Fuck," Penelope said, handing him a cigarette. She hadn't heard him exit the car.

"Yeah, that was brutal."

"You could have warned us."

"I hadn't watched the whole video. The headline just said he'd been executed. I thought it would be, like, low-res, at least."

"At least it wasn't a holo."

"Yeah, well, rumor is there is one, floating around the Internet somewhere, but I doubt it. Else why didn't the news say so?"

Penelope gave him an incredulous look.

"I just mean why would they post the video and not the holorecording, if there's a holorecording?"

Penelope shrugged. "How's Quinn?"

"Okay, I think. I think he just needs a minute. He said it's not the worst thing he's seen lately."

"Right. Shit."

"Yeah—shit," Kade said.

A semi-truck passed by. One of the driverless ones. As far as Penelope could tell, besides the three of them there wasn't another human being for who-knew-how-many miles.

A few minutes later, Quinn joined them outside the car.

"You okay?" Penelope asked him.

"I'm okay."

"You sure you don't want a cigarette?"

"I'm sure."

"It's a rebellion thing, why we smoke. Kind of to stick it to the man, you know?" Kade said.

"I gathered."

"Although I guess now we're kind of just addicted."

"That's not so good."

"Suppose not." Kade said, taking a puff.

"So—" Penelope said after a few moments silence.

"Yeah," Quinn said. "What do we want to do?"

"I say we keep going," Kade said.

"Why?" Quinn said. "Jones is dead. He can't help us."

"He was never going to be able to help us," Penelope replied. "It's not like he was in San Francisco before they . . . lopped his head off."

"Crude," Kade said.

"True, though. So we weren't exactly expecting to talk to him anyway."

"What *are* we expecting?" Quinn asked.

"Don't know, but we can't go back right now. You have people after you. And really they're after all of us—they just don't know it."

Quinn nodded.

"Plus my dad keeps calling," Kade said.

"What?"

"Yeah. And he sent a couple texts. Something about he knows I stole my mom's car, and it's the final straw. So I'm not exactly looking forward to facing him."

This reminded Penelope that at some point Priscilla was going to realize a certain transaction had been made. Although probably not for a while. In all likelihood, she'd woken up late and was still hungover. . . . But then Penelope remembered Carl. She glanced at her own watch, making sure she hadn't missed any messages herself. Nothing. If Carl knew what was good for him, he'd have run off as soon as he'd come to (assuming he'd come to), finding someone to mend his broken arm without asking questions, and Priscilla and Charlie were keeping the party going on their own, day drinking or doing coke or whatever it was Penelope's mother did with her days besides blogging and watching movies.

"We keep going," Penelope said finally. "To the Lumina building. Or wherever the fuck my dad's workshop is. And we get there as fast as we can."

Back on the road, Quinn still at the wheel ("Driving helps me keep my mind off things"), Kade once again suggested a sing-along.

"Don't even," Penelope replied, but a few miles later he started singing anyway, and Penelope found herself humming "Smells Like Teen Spirit" while he sang the words.

"Come on, Quinn," Kade said, near Wells, Nevada, before returning to belting out "My Sacrifice" by Creed.

"I absolutely do not know any of these songs."

"You what?" Kade said, his tone a bastion of incredulity.

"Don't worry, I don't really know them either," Penelope said. "I don't really *get* music. But Kade loves—"

"Huh," Kade said suddenly.

"What?"

He held up his wrist. "It's my sister."

"Okay . . ."

"Do I answer it?"

"Do you think she's calling just to talk?"

"Absolutely not. I haven't talked to her in like four months, since she left for Boston."

"Boston?" Quinn said. "Why would she want to go there? Isn't that place a . . . well, isn't it not so great?"

"She's some sort of social volunteer," Penelope explained. She had met Kade's sister only a few times, and they'd never gotten a long. Penelope thought she was overbearing, jealous of Kade's subtle intellect (not to mention Penelope's own less-than-subtle intellect). Even now she saw Kade forced to live under his sister's shadow: his parents frequently asking him why he couldn't just behave like his older sister, teachers asking him why he couldn't just focus like his older sister. At the same time, Penelope suspected Neela had it worse than Kade ever had, bearing the brunt of their father's abuse in ways she didn't want to think about.

"She joined the Peace Corps when she graduated," Kade said. "They sent her to Boston to help with the refugees. Anyway, my wrist is still buzzing."

"Answer her," Penelope said. "It could be useful."

"Or it could be a waste of time and I'd have to talk to my fucking sister."

"Just answer it. We'll be quiet."

Kade grunted. His watch beeped as he accepted the call. "Hey, Neela. How are things?"

"Kade? Kade you fucking idiot! Did you steal mom's car?"

"What? No! Why would I do that? Why would you think that?"

"Because her car is missing and you're in fucking *Nevada*!"

Penelope turned her head and met Kade's wide eyes.

"Nevada?" Kade said.

"Don't lie you little . . . ugh. Listen—they know you're in Nevada, okay. And they know you're moving really fast. Does this have anything to do with that tramp friend of yours? She's always getting you into trouble."

"Hey! Don't talk about my best friend that way."

Thanks, Penelope mouthed. Her mother's reputation preceded her.

"She's a fucking fugitive, Kade. They're saying she stole a bunch of money."

My money, Penelope thought.

"How do you—? How do they know where I am? Or, I mean, why do you think I'm in Nevada?" Kade asked. "Do they—oh shit—do they have a tracker on the car?"

"That piece of junk? No. They have a tracker on *you*. On your watch. That Find My Kid thing."

"What? I'm fifteen!"

"Don't be so stupid, Kade. You know our— Listen, dad is pissed, okay? Like royally fucking pissed. And he's taking it out on mom."

"Oh god . . ."

"Yeah. So. Mom called me, okay? She sounded scared. Dad doesn't know she called me, he doesn't know I'm calling you. But he's called the cops on you, and they know where you are, okay?"

"Shit."

"What do I tell mom?"

"Mom—" Kade looked again at Penelope, and she turned away when she saw the tears in his eyes. She couldn't handle Kade's tears. They made her uncomfortable for reasons she couldn't explain, not even to herself. But then she forced herself to turn back to him and hold his gaze. Her hand of its own volition reached out and placed itself on his cargo-shorted knee.

Kade ended the call, saying nothing else to his sister

"Kade . . ." Penelope began.

"It's okay. I don't want to talk about it. We just need to get rid of our devices. All of them."

"Welcome to the club," Quinn said.

Kade said that he was hungry, and he knew they had quite a while to go before they reached their destination ("Fifteen hours and seven minutes," Penelope said, checking her GPS, which she realized they'd have to do without now) but maybe they should stop, take a break, and get their bearings. They had a head start against the police and could afford a brief pause. "I wish I knew how much of a head start, though. I should have asked Neela."

When Kade suggested they stop at the Flatbrush Diner in Wells, Quinn couldn't bring himself to voice how much it reminded him of G-Pops' Avon Café. It wasn't the facade, which was as corroded and crumbly as the surrounding downtown buildings (if you could call the strip of earthquake-damaged brick constructs a "downtown," which apparently the residents of Wells felt they could); nor was it the interior, which was somehow far more modern than the Avon Café's had ever been; and neither was it the myriad posters advertising Donna's Ranch and Bella's Gentleman's club, *Two of the country's original legal brothels.*

No, what reminded Quinn of G-Pops' Avon Café were the pies. As soon as you walked into the Flatbush Diner, you were presented with a case of at least two dozen homemade pies, not at all unlike the one at the Avon Café. Even the tenderly depressed star-shaped dimples in the center of the top crust were like the ones in the café Quinn had grown up in, almost like the ones his mother used to make, and for a moment he wondered whether Jeff McTine had somehow survived the massacre, had absconded to Wells and set about his usual evening baking routine.

Alas, when he ordered a piece (tripleberry—which is to say, raspberry, blackberry, blueberry), it arrived smothered in more whipped cream than Jeff McTine or Quinn's mother would ever have considered decent, let alone edible, and upon taking taking his first and only bite, it was clear to Quinn that the whipped cream was from a can, the pie's crust made with margarine instead of butter and duck fat ("The secret ingredient in any superior baked good, your mother's secret recipe," Jeff always said), and the berries thawed from frozen.

"How is it?" asked Kade, who had not been told of the pie's significance.

Quinn half-raised his left shoulder toward his ear in an enervated shrug.

Kade held up his own fork. "May I?"

Quinn nodded.

"Mmmm. That's fucking great!"

"You can finish it."

"Sweet! Thanks!"

After they'd been shown to their table, Penelope had ordered only a Dr. Pepper. "I had way too much McDonald's," she said. "Plus I think I should see about getting us some supplies while you guys eat. I'll be back."

Now she returned, carrying a paper bag. From it she produced a paper map, which she unfolded on the table. The map threatened to overtake Kade's pie, and he pulled the plate toward himself bodily, as if it were an infant or a puppy, entrusted to his care.

"The rest of our drive is pretty straightforward," Penelope said. She activated the holographic GPS display on her watch and traced the corresponding route onto the paper map with a blue marker. She circled the names of a few cities. "The only thing is I couldn't find a map made more recently than 2035—"

"I'm surprised you were able to find a paper map at all," Kade said around a mouthful of pie.

Quinn did not mention that paper maps were often offered for sale in small towns like this—or at least they had been in Avon, which was admittedly a way smaller town than even Wells. Were they actually sold? Rarely. But they were offered.

"Yeah, well," Penelope said. "But anyway, the problem with that is this—" She enlarged her watch's display, showcasing a dark patch beginning near Winnemuca, stretching all the way to the California border to the west and about fifty miles above Las Vegas to the South.

"That's the True America Confederation," Kade remarked.

"Exactly," Penelope said. "And the GPS here of course has us going around it, but it didn't exist when this paper map was made, so instead of going here, we need to go here. Roughly." She indicated a jagged portion of the blue ink she'd marked.

"That shouldn't be too hard, though, right?" Quinn said. "There should be signs along the way."

"Should be," Penelope said, "But there probably aren't, from what I understand. At least not many. The U.S. government tried to quickly install a new stretch of highway to reach from Winnemuca to Vegas when they, well, acquiesced to the demands of the True America Confederation, but the Confederates have been known to sabotage the route."

"And there's nothing the government can do?" Quinn asked. Like most of the world, he knew very little about the True America Confederation, aside from its origins as a sort of anarchic autonomous zone in Reno, which had about eight years ago been taken over by a Patriot Party–funded militia who called themselves the Pioneers and felt it their job to step in where they believed the Democratic government failed to do so. Once they'd driven out or killed the anarchists, the Pioneers had refused to leave, their representatives stating that it was their responsibility to protect the rest of the country from the "degeneration of California." Efforts to establish a similar Confederation in Southern Oregon had failed, as had attempts to extend the Confederation through Vegas and into Arizona, and thus California remained accessible to, and part of, the rest of the country. For a few months the government fought back against the Confederation, if halfheartedly, but eventually seemed content to leave it alone, granting it a sort of unofficial sovereignty, and what went on within it was unknown to the rest of the country. It was a North Korea–esque black hole, as far as most Americans (not to be confused with True Americans) were concerned. How one even joined the True America Confederation at this point was a mystery, although there was evidence the Confederation still had the Patriot Party's backing, and rumors that certain U.S. senators—more than a few, comprising both Patriots and more "traditional" Republicans—were stealth members. Perhaps adding to the air of mystery was the fact that even mentioning the Confederation on a platform like Twitter or ChatterChatterChatter would get your account banned.

"Short of nuking the entire thing—which I suppose is a possibility, given the precise size of the Confederation—not really," Kade said. "And they don't want to do that because, well, according to the rumors, the Confederation has some sort of megaweapon or something that they got from Area 51."

"Oh brother," Penelope said.

"I'm not saying it's true," Kade said. "It's just the rumors."

"I've never heard those rumors," said Quinn.

"He spends too much time on the dark web," Penelope remarked.

"It's on regular sites, too," Kade insisted. "I also read that the new administration is planning on going harder on—"

"*Anyway*," Penelope interrupted, "if we pay attention, we should be fine."

"What if I wanna cross the border, though?" Kade asked. "Think of it. We could find out what all the fuss is about. Area 51, man."

"I'll tell you what. We survive whatever the fuck it is we're doing, then after that you can do whatever the fuck you want."

"If my dad doesn't kill me first. Not to mention the terrorists or whoever chasing us."

"I also got us these," Penelope said. From the brown paper bag she pulled a small, fat gray cylinder, a speaker. Then she produced another device from her pocket, which she had to shift in her seat to reach into.

"No way!" Kade said.

"What is it?" Quinn asked. It was clearly a small tablet of some kind, but the screen was significantly smaller than the device itself, taking up maybe only forty percent of the front surface.

"It's an iPod!" Kade exclaimed. "Like a genuine old-school iPod. Where the heck did you get this?"

"Pawn shop. It works. The battery doesn't last for shit, the guy said, but he also had one of those old power adapters that goes into the cigarette lighter in your mom's car, and he even had an aux cable to connect to the speaker, which supposedly has a better battery life than the iPod."

"This is fucking awesome."

"It's yours. But first we're using it to listen to music the rest of the drive. I don't care what's on it. I can't take the silence, and if you're going to sing, it better at least be along with something . . . you know, *something*."

"You paid for these . . ." Quinn began.

"My hard wallet is relatively untraceable," Penelope said. "And pawn shop owners like untraceable, even it tiny towns like this. Also had the guy convert some of my crypto to cash, just in case we need it. Not that untraceability really matters until we get rid of our devices."

Kade sighed. "Yeah. I guess we better do that."

"And then we need to get back on the road."

Penelope left more cash than was necessary on the table, and then the group quietly left the restaurant before their waiter could return. A couple miles outside of town, in the opposite direction from which they would soon resume driving ("Good idea," Penelope said when Kade suggested the slight misdirection) Penelope stacked her laptop, Kade's tablet, and both their HoloWatches, as well as Quinn's own busted and powerless watch ("As a symbolic gesture") in the middle of the road. Then, while she and Kade solemnly shared the last cigarette they ever would, Quinn got back in the car and drove over the devices, repeatedly, until one could reasonably call them smithereens.

All Penelope wanted was to fiddle with her VR programs. To quietly do what she needed to get through the rest of the school year with a C or B average. And then to spend the summer writing VR code and bullshitting with Kade.

Instead, she found herself on the run, both to and from. *From what* she didn't know. Foreign terrorists? Domestic terrorists? Terrorists the origins of which were so murky one wouldn't know whether to label them foreign or domestic? The government? A corporation?

To what she had only a vague idea: a sister, age unknown, location unknown.

With her: a young man she'd met only yesterday, handsome but timid, grieving, lonely, older than her by several years, an adult but too lost to be adult-like right now; and Kade, annoying, smug, weird, small, poorly dressed, brilliant, her best friend, almost definitely in love with her, and in possession of a terrible singing voice, using that terrible singing voice now to accompany the cast of *High School Musical.* For when they'd powered it up and turned it on, they'd discovered that the iPod she'd purchased had belonged to an early-2000s pre-teenager name Kiley Stewart and was full only of Disney Channel soundtracks—*Hannah Montana, Lizzie McGuire,* the first three *High School Musical*s—and age-inappropriate hip-hop. Old music on an old machine: an adumbration of everything in the world that brought Kade his cherished ironic joy.

"It just looks empty," Quinn remarked of the barren desert to their right, where the sun was getting low. "Are we sure anybody lives out there?"

Quinn had insisted on continuing to drive, even though Kade had offered to take over again. ("I'm the only one with a license," Quinn had reminded them, which was a fair and convincing point.) They'd been back on the road for nearly four hours, having refueled the car in Wells before destroying their devices. They wouldn't make it to San Francisco on a single tank of gas at this point; they could only hope that somewhere on the outskirts of Vegas they'd find a station that was old enough to accept cash or new enough to accept crypto. ("Or we steal an electric car there," Kade suggested, before Penelope said that 1.) she didn't want to steal if they could help it, and 2.) any theft would be reported, and any electric car would be equipped out the ass with tracking technology, probably even cameras, not to mention autopilot that law enforcement could probably override remotely. To which Kade had responded, "This is why I like old things" and Quinn had said, "Me too.")

They'd been back on the road for nearly four hours. Much of that time had been spent driving along the Humbolt-Toyaibe National Forest (according to the map, but who knew what the Confederacy had renamed it). Now the forest was behind them, and to their right was once again only vast, empty desert. "They're out there somewhere," Penelope replied. "Supposedly thousands of them."

Penelope would never admit it, but right now she wanted to call her mother. Ever since Kade had spoken to his sister, she'd been wondering why Priscilla hadn't tried to get in touch. Kade's sister mentioned that they knew about the money, which meant Kade's parents had been in touch with Priscilla, so why hadn't she called? Did she just not care where Penelope was? Did she just not give a flying fuck? At least Kade's abusive father gave a fuck enough to call the police.

They were maybe only an hour and forty-five minutes from Vegas, and Kade was belting along to a song called "Breaking Free," when a metallic *ping* rang through the air. Kade stopped singing. "What was that?"

A similar sound rang out, this one more hollow, followed by another, more like a *thunk*, and finally another, accompanied by the crash of shattering glass.

"Oh shit!" Kade yelled, as the passenger side rear window exploded across the back seat.

"Are you okay?" Penelope shouted, ducking.

"I'm fine. I'm fine. What the hell is going on?"

"Quinn?"

"I think they're gunshots." The car accelerated, but then Quinn lost control after another shot rang out, accompanied by a popping sound, and the car began to rumble along the road. "I think we just lost a tire!" Penelope watched as he turned the wheel to the left, but the back of the car spun out, rotating on the axis that the front right wheel had become. The car swung off the road, spinning for what seemed like minutes but was surely only a second or three, coming finally to rest on the Confederate side of the desert.

For several beats, no one in the car spoke or moved. Penelope waited for more gunshots, waited, perhaps, to die—but nothing happened. No sounds, no bursts of pain. "Are you guys okay?" she finally asked.

"Yes," said Quinn, breathing heavily.

"Fine," Kade replied. "But—fuck—"

"Yes—fuck." Penelope opened her door and began to step out.

Quinn tried to stop her. "Wait—what are you doing?"

"Investigating."

"Someone was shooting at us!"

"I know, and I'm going to go investigate the fuck out of them."

She exited the car, her every sense at DEFCON 10. She put her hands in the air, thought about calling out, but instead stayed silent and gazed across the desert. The sun was half-low in the western sky, and she squinted. Her field of view absorbed miles of orange-brown rock and soil interspersed with sprouts of green-brown vegetation and pickup truck–size gray-brown boulders. There was no movement, except for the ghostly haze of heat emanating from the ground. From somewhere far away and up above, a bird-of-prey cried.

"Penny?" Kade called from inside the car.

"You guys stay here."

"Penny!"

Ignoring him, she lowered her arms and began walking into the desert, toward a boulder a couple hundred yards away. Given its distance from the road, she was at first unsure how large it truly was. Possibly she was mistaken and would arrive to find it too small to comport with her hypothesis (or she would never arrive, shot dead instead in the Nevada desert). But as she drew closer, the accuracy of her sense of scale was confirmed, and she saw the boulder was the size of a small toolshed, and for a hundred yards in any direction it stood alone.

She approached slowly, taking care to make no sound with her footsteps. But once she reached the boulder, she sprinted to its far side, arms up in front of her, ready for a confrontation.

"What the—" was the interrupted exclamation of the small man crouching with his back to the stone as Penelope brought the bottom of her boot into his shoulder, forcing him to the dusty ground and expelling his rifle from his grasp. He reached for it, but Penelope kicked him again, this time in the gut, aware as she did so that in the last twenty-four hours she'd kicked more men than she ever had before—and that it was satisfying as fuck.

The man gasped, and only then did Penelope realize that the man was a boy, younger than she, maybe ten or eleven. Nevertheless, she picked up his rifle and pointed it at him, hoping her experience with VR shooters would translate to the real thing, if necessary, while hoping also that it wouldn't be necessary.

"You little twat," she said.

"I'm sorry," the scrawny kid gasped. "I'm—"

"Penelope?"

She stepped backward from behind the boulder, keeping the gun pointed at the kid. Kade and Quinn were running toward her. "It's okay," she said. "It's a fucking child."

"A child?" Quinn said as they approached.

"That's not a child," Kade said, rounding the boulder. "He's like fourteen."

"I'm twelve," the kid said, still catching his breath and clutching his solar plexus as he struggled to sit up.

"You're a fucking twat," Penelope said, winding up her right leg as if she were going to kick him again. When the kid flinched, she returned her foot to the ground, satisfied.

"I was just having—I was just having fun," the kid gasped.

"Your fun cost us our ride."

Quinn placed his hand on the rifle. "You can probably stop pointing that at him."

Penelope lowered the gun.

"What's your name, kid?" Quinn asked, pulling him to his feet.

The kid's breathing was less labored now. "P–Priam," he said.

"Weird name," Kade said.

"It's from a video game my dad used to play, I guess."

"That makes it weirder."

"Kade, shut up," Penelope said. "What do you mean you were having fun?"

"I just—I shoot at the cars sometimes. But just *at* them. I don't try to hit them. I've never actually hit one. It's just fun to freak them out. It's not even a real gun. They're just pellets."

"Well, you hit us. And now we're stuck out here."

"My mom's tires were like so old," Kade said.

"I'm—I'm sorry," Priam said, and Penelope could tell he meant it.

"What's your deal, kid?"

"I just said—It was an accident—I didn't mean to—"

"No, no, it's okay." Penelope sighed. "Listen—I mean where do you live? Where's your family? How did you get"—she gestured to the surrounding desert, where there wasn't a vehicle in sight save for Kade's mom's now useless Taurus near the road—"out here?"

"I live in Proud City. It's that way."

"How far?" The view stretched on for miles and was only desert.

Priam shrugged. "I walk out here sometimes."

"How long did it take you to walk here?" Quinn asked.

Priam shrugged again. "I left after lunch."

"And how long have you been sitting here with your gun?"

"Few hours? You were the first car."

Penelope started to do some simple calculations in her head, but Kade beat her to it. "That's means he walked for like three or four hours."

"Yeah," Priam said. "But I get bored at home. There's nothing to do but shoot targets and stuff. I read all the books a long time ago. Several times. And my dad is up . . . North, I think . . . right now."

"And your mom?" Penelope asked.

Priam shrugged. "Dad says she doesn't matter. We moved to the Confederation when I was little and she didn't wanna come. Dad says she was a total Marxist bitch, so he took me away and brought me with him, where I'd be safe from the Communists."

"Jesus . . ." Quinn said.

Overhead, a vulture cried.

"Are there vehicles in Proud City?" Penelope asked.

"Sure," Kade said. "We got some trucks."

"That's a long walk," Kade said.

"Vegas is a lot longer," Quinn said.

"We could just wait by the road. Hitch hike."

"You heard him," Penelope said. "He waited for us to drive by for hours. And who knows how long it could have been before he started waiting. No, I think we need to go to Proud City." She felt absurd saying the name. "Will you take us with you?" she asked Priam.

"They're not gonna like it," he said.

"Who's not gonna like it?" Quinn asked.

Priam's shoulders slumped. "Anybody."

After returning to the Taurus to get their bags, they followed Priam west into the desert. They walked for roughly two and a half hours (but since nobody had a working watch, they couldn't be sure). Kade pointed out more than once that at least it wasn't so hot, now that the sun was setting. Now, the lights of Proud City were visible in the distance.

"Looks like maybe another mile or two to go," said Quinn as they approached.

"Not even," Priam replied. "It's smaller than it looks."

"My feet hurt," Kade said.

Something howled.

Proud City was a misnomer, Penelope thought. If anything, the collection of structures was a village, maybe even a camp. The sun was barely a strip of light on the distant horizon now, so it was difficult to make out details, even as they drew closer, but it looked like every building was a single story, and small, made of a combination of brick and metal. They weren't so much houses as shacks, save for two much larger and more sturdy structures on the town's east edge.

"That's where the trucks are," Priam said, pointing to one of the large buildings.

"What's in the other one?" Kade asked.

"Fuel, food, weapons."

"How many weapons, just out of curiosity?"

Priam shrugged. "Lotsa. Mostly all we have is weapons."

Once they were about a quarter-mile from the town, they could see the specks of light were mostly tall spotlights placed around the village, as well as illumination coming from the windows of some, but not all, of the shacks. The dim, flickering nature of some of the lights indicated that they might even be campfires. "Everything runs on batteries," Priam explained, "but not everyone can afford batteries for their own homes. And sometimes we run out anyway. Power is prioritized for the governor."

"That place has a governor?" Penelope said.

Priam shrugged. "His name's Killer John."

"Oh brother."

"I think I read about him," Kade said. "On the Internet. Very mysterious."

"Why do they call him that?" Quinn asked.

"What do you mean?"

"What do you mean what do I mean? Why do they call him Killer John?"

Priam shrugged again. "That's his name."

"Oh brother," Penelope said again.

She surveyed the town before her, but she could make out no useful details in the dark. She tried to stifle a yawn but failed. She needed sleep. She couldn't help but notice Quinn begin to yawn in response, although he managed to stifle half of it, make his exhaustion not quite as obvious as hers. She rubbed her eyes. "Okay," she said. "Listen—Priam, we need to take one of your trucks. What can you tell us about them? How many people do they fit? Is that building locked? Is it guarded? How many guards? Anything you can tell us will be helpful."

"I can tell you lotsa stuff! There are guards, but I don't know how many. Three, maybe four if Ichabod felt like helping out tonight. But it could even be five or six. Maybe seven."

"Ichabod?" Kade asked.

"He's the quartermaster. He's in charge of the gear, the trucks and weapons and stuff. Even the food. He supervises the mechanics. He's . . . not a nice person. And he doesn't give nobody much unless they're willing to . . . help him out. He's mostly drunk a lot, especially by this time of day, but sometimes he runs out of whiskey and sometimes even hooch and has to wait until we get supplies from the towns up North. If he's run out, he'll be supervising the warehouses . . . or. . . ."

"Or what?" Penelope asked.

"Nothing," Priam said. "I think he's probably supervising tonight. My dad was saying he was gonna bring back a lot of whiskey from his trip, and if that's true, then Ichabod's probably about out of stuff to drink right now."

"So what does that mean, if he's supervising?"

"It means it's gonna be harder for you to steal a truck." Just then, Priam's stomach grumbled thunderously.

"When was the last time you ate?" Penelope asked him.

"Lunch time," he said. "But . . ."

"But what?"

"Nothing. It's just that it wasn't that much. We had some oatmeal in the pantry, but with dad gone the last few days, I've ain't had any power, so the cooler went and the meat spoiled. And I couldn't get Ichabod to give me anything else even though I . . . never mind."

Penelope knelt down and unzipped her backpack. "These have been in my bag all day," she said, "but I saw a video once where they left one out for like a month and it was totally fine." She handed him two McMuffins, grateful for her overindulgence in fast food that morning.

"Thanks!" Priam said. He immediately unwrapped and began to tear into one of the McMuffins.

"I haven't eaten since lunch either," Kade said, holding his own belly.

"Kade."

"Just saying. I was really looking forward to one of those Las Vegas buffets."

As Priam ate, appearing to appreciate the unhealthy but highly flavorful sandwich as much as she did, Penelope couldn't help but feel a kinship with the kid: raised by one not-terribly present (Penelope assumed —although she may have been projecting) parent, occupying himself with semi-destructive hobbies that require immense amounts of patience, a home typically devoid of palatable food. Her thoughts turned to her own home then—and the vague sense she'd had since walking down her dark street early that morning that she might never see it again. Was there any material item she'd left behind she wished she had brought (besides the rest of her cigarettes)? She'd miss her video game console if she never got to use it again. There was Pokey, the stuffed rhinoceros Dickey McGill— the only partner of her mother's she'd ever especially liked—had given her as a peace offering when she was nine. Dickey had been kind, respectful, meek but confident. He'd always seemed to be aware, when visiting her home, that he was encroaching on Penelope's territory, and he treated her and her space accordingly. Sadly, Priscilla never seemed to be particularly excited by respectful men in a long-term way (although more likely she just wasn't excited by anybody over the long term, Penelope thought, reminded that even her father had failed to capture her mother's attention for more than a handful of nights), and she'd ended things with Dickey after a couple months. At the time, Penelope had taken Pokey the Rhinoceros with a feigned air of begrudging disdain. "I don't need stuffed animals. I'm not a *child*," she could remember saying. But in the years since, Pokey had been put away only when Kade was visiting, because Penelope knew he'd make fun of her if he saw a purple odd-toed ungulate sitting on her bed. Yes, if there was anything Penelope would miss if she never returned home, it was Pokey—and, perhaps, her mother.

Kade said, "Is there anything else we need to know about those storage facilities? Or about Ichabod? Hell, where do they even keep the keys?"

Priam shook his head, swallowing a bite of McMuffin, which was already almost gone. "The keys are in Ichabod's office. On a . . . like a hook thing. He's not very organized. But if Ichabod is on duty, you'll never get in there. I can"—and Priam seemed reluctant to finish this sentence—"I can distract him for you."

"No," Penelope said. "You need to go home. Wait for your dad."

"I don't want to go home. I want to come with you guys."

"He can help us," Kade said.

"No offense," Quinn said, "but he's a kid. We can't be responsible for a kid."

"*We're* kids," Kade said, gesturing to himself and Penelope.

"Tell me something I don't know," Quinn said. "But he's even younger. I'm pretty sure if he came with us, we could be charged with kidnapping or something." A look of alarm crossed over his face. "Oh, hell—I could probably be charged with kidnapping you two."

"You can't come with us," Penelope said to Priam.

"But I—I hate this place. It's—"

"I'm sorry. It's too dangerous, okay? There are people after us and —"

"I can help!"

Penelope found herself placing a hand on his shoulder and, smiling sadly, wondered whether she'd lost her edge. "You've helped so much already, kid—"

"Helped?" Kade interjected. "He shot our car—"

"Kade, shut up. Priam—you need to stay with your father, okay? Trust me—he'd be devastated if you ran away."

"No, he wouldn't. . . . He'd never have to worry about taking care of me."

Penelope thought again of her mother. "I bet he'd worry even more. You need to go home, okay? You need to stay safe."

Penelope had two McMuffins left in her bag ("How many of those things did you buy?" Kade asked. "A lot. Too many," Quinn told him.) and she gave them to Priam after finally convincing him to return to his own home. Now she, Kade, and Quinn were huddled behind one of Proud City's large storage buildings, getting to which unnoticed had been remarkably easy.

"I can't believe it," Kade said. "Everyone's so scared of this freakin' Confederation, but look at this place. They don't even have a proper power grid."

"I don't know," Quinn said, speaking much more quietly than Kade. "I get the feeling this village is more like an outpost, not a proper city. It sounded like wherever Priam's father currently is is much more put together."

"Why? Because they have whiskey? I mean the trucks are still gas powered."

"Your mom's car was still gas powered. My G-Pops' truck is—was— gas powered."

"My point exactly!"

"Kade," Penelope whispered, "I love you. You know that. And I'm getting really sick of telling you to shut up. But shut up. Or at least quiet down."

"Yeah—sorry," he replied, only slightly more quiet than before.

Once Priam had left them, they'd tried to devise a plan, which, except for a few small details, came out to: we play it by ear. Before parting ways with them, Priam had walked them through a gap in Proud Town's perimeter sensors ("Which don't even work sometimes—batteries always dying"). He'd also provided them a few more details about the storage facilities: There would be several men patrolling inside and outside the buildings. Exactly how many he couldn't say, because there was no real guard rotation schedule in Proud City. Ichabod just assigned whoever he felt like that day, before he got too drunk to do so, and if you were told by Ichabod to do something, you did it. Quinn had asked about the governor, Killer John, but Priam said he never left his home, which was the nicest and largest of the town's residential shacks, more like a proper cabin, with air conditioning, even, where he lived with his pretty blonde wife and two sons, who never had to help out around the village. Despite his name, Priam said, there was little to fear from Killer John. If anything, Ichabod held the real power in Proud City. Ichabod did whatever the governor told him, but everyone else in Proud City listened to Ichabod. "Or else," Priam had said, "they get hurt."

"Is there any chance Ichabod is nicer to women than he is to men?" Penelope had asked.

Priam had shrugged. "Maybe. There aren't a lot of women in the Confederation, to be honest, I don't think. Although I hear there are more up north than there are in Proud City. But *all* the men think they're chiv . . . chiva . . ."

"Chivalrous?" Quinn had offered.

"Yeah, that's the word."

So Penelope had decided she would get the keys from Ichabod's office, while Kade and Quinn would select and secure a truck. What "secure" meant was impossible to say just yet; they hoped it would just mean hiding behind the vehicle and calling Penelope over once she'd retrieved the keys, but such simplicity seemed unlikely.

"Let's go," Penelope said.

"I'm just realizing," Kade said to Quinn, "that somehow she's become our de facto leader. How did that happen? *You're* the adult."

"She's the one whose dad's ghost or whatever is the reason we're out here in the first place."

"It wasn't really a ghost—"

"That's why I said 'or whatever.'"

"Guys—"

"Fine, fine," Kade said. "Shutting up."

But he didn't shut up for long—for after the trio crept around the building, sticking to the side wall like magnets, and reached the front, Kade whispered, "Fuck."

"Yeah—fuck," Penelope agreed.

"Is it bad?" Quinn asked. "I can't see."

Penelope pointed to a shipping palate stacked with metal crates about ten feet away. The stack was seven or eight feet tall—enough to conceal even Quinn. "When I say go, we move—*quietly*—behind that thing. And pay attention. It's probably our only shot to get a look at the whole place. Okay . . . *go*."

Penelope moved first, running on her booted tiptoes. Kade gestured for Quinn to go next, so Quinn moved, making himself as small as possible. Finally, Kade covered the space by executing a combat roll.

Penelope shook her head. "Was that necessary?"

Kade shrugged and dusted himself off.

"Did you see them?" Penelope asked Quinn.

"Yeah," he said. "How did I get myself into this situation?"

The good news was the garage had no sort of front door. It was more like an airplane hangar. In fact—and Priam hadn't mentioned this—in addition to the three large, Humvee-style trucks, there was a small bi-winged passenger plane, which Penelope, having spent hundreds of hours playing *Flight Simulator* (on a monitor at home, mostly, but occasionally in VR as well) thought she recognized as an Antonov An-2. So reaching the trucks would be a simple matter of running straight into the hangar. The bad news was that the courtyard (or was it a runway now?) outside the hangar was currently being patrolled by six men in fatigues carrying very large rifles—and although the area was otherwise unlit, each man wore a powerful headlamp.

"I counted seven men," Quinn said.

Okay then, Penelope thought, seven.

"Those are some big-ass guns," Kade remarked, obviously.

"Maybe they won't shoot us, though," Quinn said.

"Of course they'll shoot us. They're basically Republicans."

"We need a new plan," Quinn whispered.

"Oh?" Kade said. "As opposed to the airtight, detailed operation we'd concieved to begin with?"

"I didn't see an office," Penelope said. "Did either of you see the office?"

"I think—" said Quinn, and then, holding his breath, he leaned out from behind the stack of crates before quickly popping his head back "—yeah—it's in the garage thing, at the back. It's kind of just a couple of wooden walls with a door and a window, built into the corner."

"So the plan is the same, then."

"How's that?" Kade asked.

"You guys run for truck. I keep running for the office."

"Did you miss the part where the seven dudes have big-ass guns?"

"We'll just have to be really fast. Avoid the headlamps. Run *behind* one of the trucks. They look armored, right?"

"This is a terrible plan. It's never going to work. We're going to die."

Penelope knew it was a terrible plan, but she was exhausted, and even if there was something better, she wasn't sure her brain was currently sharp enough to conceive of—

"Wait," she whispered. "Quinn, can you reach that?" She pointed to the smallest crate at the top of the stack.

"Maybe." He stretched onto his tiptoes. "Yeah, just barely. Watch out."

The crate he'd been reaching for toppled from the stack, falling toward Kade, who dropped to his knees. The container collided with his backpack, and Quinn caught it before it hit the cement ground.

"Ow." Kade said.

Penelope put a hand up. "Shhh."

From the other side of the stack of crates, a voice said, "Did you hear that?"

"Hear what?" replied another voice.

"I don't know, but it was something. I think from over there."

"Well go check it out."

"*You* check it out."

"Why me? *You* heard it."

"Yeah—but I don't wanna."

"Oh for fuck's sake. Do your damn job, Mike."

"My *job* is to stand right here."

"You're an idiot, Mike. Hey, guys, isn't Mike an idiot?"

"Who, Mike?" said a third voice. "Course he's a fucking idiot."

"I'm not an idiot," said Mike.

"Then how come Bill's been porkin' your wife the last six months and you don't even know about it?"

"What? Bill's what? You're what, Bill?"

"Nothin'," said yet another voice. "He's joking. He's joking. Aren't you Chuck?"

"Yeah, yeah, sure. I'm totally joking."

"You guys all shut the fuck up," said Mike.

The other men laughed, clearly at Mike's expense.

"I'm not an idiot," Mike said.

More laughter, which died down after several seconds. It soon became clear nobody was going to check on the source of the sound.

"Oh my god," Kade whispered. "They're *all* idiots. This is going to be easy."

Penelope wouldn't go that far, but she did find herself a measure more optimistic all of a sudden—until she opened the crate. "Damn." She been hoping for . . . well, she didn't know what she'd been hoping for, but maybe guns or grenades—or even firecrackers would have been useful. Instead, the crate was full of—

"Praise the lord," Kade said. The crate was full of small bags of mini Chips Ahoy! cookies. He unzipped his backpack and began to fill it with as many of the bags as he could.

"Kade—"

"Yeah, yeah, okay." He rezipped his bag and returned it to his back. "I guess we're just running for it?"

Penelope hesitated. How *had* she become the trio's de facto leader? She *was* just a kid. Not a child, sure—but she worked at fucking Dunkin' Donuts, got mediocre grades, and played video games in her spare time. She was not the sort of person who should be making these decisions.

"We're just running for it," she finally said. "Everyone ready? Let's go . . . now."

Kade, Quinn, and Penelope ran straight for the hangar. Encumbered only slightly by their bags—Quinn more than anyone, because he was traveling with a duffle bag slung over his shoulder rather than a backpack —they covered the distance in just a few seconds, but that was all it took for one of the patrolling guards to spot them. A series of shots rang out from one of the automatic weapons.

"Mike—what the fuck—?"

"There's people just run in the hangar."

"What do you mean there's people—?" But then this second speaker spotted the trio, too. "Shit!" He struggled to raise his own rifle, his arm caught in the strap. "Everyone—shoot them!" he yelled.

But before anyone could get another shot off (not even the idiot Mike, who seemed to have scared himself with his first round of fire), Kade, Quinn, and Penelope had ducked behind one of the massive trucks.

"Is anyone hurt?" Penelope asked.

"His aim was awful," Quinn said.

Several bursts of fire rang out at the same time, pinging metallically. Glass shattered.

"Not the trucks! Not the trucks! Fuck's sake, hold your fire. Don't hit the trucks."

"Guess we're not taking this one," Quinn said.

"They're fucking cosplayers," Kade marveled. "They've got no idea what they're doing."

"Neither do we," Penelope said.

"But at least we're not pretending we do. Weren't you supposed to be getting the keys?"

Perhaps it was the sense of scale provided by the plane juxtaposed with the three trucks and all the empty space between them, but the hangar seemed much larger now than it had from the outside. "Yeah, well, I was being shot at. Taking cover again seemed like the best idea."

"What do we do, Bill?" one of the gunmen said.

"I—we—"

"What the hell is going on out here?" said a new voice. The office door had swung open, and twenty feet away from Penelope, Kade, and Quinn stood a short, rail-thin man with a pockmarked face and a mustache straight out of one of the very old pornographic videos Penelope knew Kade liked to watch. An unlit cigar hung from his mouth. His eyes met Penelope's.

"Intruders, sir! We—"

"I see 'em," the man—he had to be Ichabod—said. He hesitated for the briefest of moments, and then he pulled a pistol from his waist holster and fired.

"Kade!" Penelope yelled.

Kade had fallen to the cement ground, clutching his arm. Blood seeped around his fingers.

"Stop!" Penelope said. "We're just kids. We're—we just got lost—in the desert."

"Don't care who the fuck you are," Ichabod snarled around the cigar. "You're trespassing on Confederate property and you got a black with you. Shoulda shot the black first," he muttered, adjusting his aim toward Quinn and—

—and let out a cry of pain and covered his temple with is free hand as the cigar fell from his mouth. "Motherfucker! Who the fuck shot me?"

From the other side of the truck, Bill called, "You get shot, boss?"

"Mother— Ow. Yes, I got fuckin' shot. Which one of you motherfuckers shot me? So I can shoot you right back."

Quinn, who just seconds ago had had a gun pointed at him, trigger about to be pulled, certain for the second time in two days that he was about to die, took the distraction as an opportunity to help Kade to his feet. Kade's arms was bleeding profusely, but he was moving it.

"Don't think it were none of us, boss!"

Then something hit Ichabod in the eye, and he dropped his pistol. Penelope ran for the office's open door. Kade and Quinn followed. Quinn shut the door behind them. The office itself was barely a room. It had a foldable card table, stacked with papers, a closed laptop, laughably bulky, and an empty liquor bottle. The chair was the kind of folding chair one would buy with the table. On one of the flimsy wooden walls hung a cork board decorated with only a calendar and several photos of gratuitously naked women—and four key rings, two identical keys on each ring.

"What the hell is going on?" Kade said groggily.

"Kade—are you okay?" Penelope asked. She wanted to cry. She so rarely wanted to cry but her best friend had been shot, and surely it was her fault. Still, she maintained the wherewithal to grab all four sets of keys.

"Hey, I'm fine. He grazed me. The idiot just grazed me, from like fifteen feet away. How are these people even still alive out here?"

"It doesn't look like a graze. There's a lot of blood."

"It's a graze. I can move my arm. The bleeding's already slowing down."

"Quinn?"

"I'm fine, too. But I know what it's like to be grazed by a bullet. That's not a graze."

"It's a *graze*," Kade insisted.

Several men started yelling. Kade lifted the blinds covering the office window. "Oh no."

"What?" Penelope peeked through the blinds herself. "No . . ."

From inside the office, one could see much of the hangar and straight out to what Penelope now realized was best described as a tarmac. She could see Ichabod from behind, still covering his right eye but no longer covering his temple. Blood flowed from the temple down the side and back of his neck. Outside the hangar, she saw four of the armed men, their rifles pointed at a small figure, carrying a much smaller rifle, walking across the tarmac.

"Whose that?" Ichabod called.

"I think it's Mitchel Watskins' boy," yelled back one of the men. "Should we shoot him?"

"Wait!" said Ichabod. He stepped toward the boy. "Priam Watskins— I think you goddamn shot my eye out.

Priam said something, but from the office Penelope couldn't hear what.

Neither, apparently, could Ichabod. "You say what?" he called.

"I said that's for making me suck your dick, you sick fuck," Priam yelled back. He raised his pellet gun and fired one, two, three more times at Ichabod's face.

Ichabod fell to his knees, grasping at his face with his other hand. Then he collapsed onto his side and started shaking violently.

"Oh shit! Oh shit!" yelled one of the guards, maybe Bill, maybe Mike, maybe someone else. Penelope was watching Priam, who stood ramrod straight, stoic, staring at Ichabod's convulsing form and holding his pellet gun high as if to say *don't anyone dare help him*.

"Holy shit," Kade said.

After several long seconds, Ichabod's body stopped moving. Only then did Priam relax.

"Did you kill 'im?" one of the guards asked—Bill, Penelope was pretty sure.

"Is he dead?" asked maybe Mike, stepping forward to peer at the body on the ground.

Priam dropped his rifle and raised his hands, but nobody made a move to harm or restrain him. Instead, every guard joined Maybe Mike in approaching Ichabod's body.

"Oh shit."

"Mother of—look at his *face*."

"He don't have any eyes no more."

"His *ears* are bleeding."

"He's dead. He's definitely dead."

"What do we do now?"

"Well—shit—I guess we gotta get Killer John, let him know what happened."

"What about Mitchel Watskin's boy?"

"Oh yeah—hold 'im here, I suppose."

"Face is fuckin', I dunno, *shredded*."

One of the guards grabbed Priam by the arm. Priam didn't fight back. To Penelope, he looked relieved. And to her surprise, she understood the feeling.

"We need to go," Quinn said.

"Should we help him?" Kade asked.

"We—" Penelope started, but before she could finish (she hadn't been sure what she was going to say) an obnoxious siren began to sound.

"Perimeter alarm!" yelled one of the guards. The man holding onto Priam let go and brought his rifle up into a ready position. Priam hesitated, and then he picked up his pellet gun.

"What's that mean?" Kade said.

"I don't know," Penelope said, a sense of dread flooding her gut, "but we need to get out of here." She handed Quinn the keys and moved to open the office's door. "You guys get one of the trucks." From somewhere not too far away came a loud, deep boom. A crash or an explosion. The plywood walls of the office shook. The glass of the window rattled.

"Where are you going?" Kade asked Penelope, whose hand turned on the door handle. Gunfire broke out again, from multiple sources. Men began to shout.

"To get Priam," she answered, pushing open the door.

"But—"

"Just get a truck!"

Penelope yelled this last command because just then another boom sounded, and again the plywood walls of the office shook. The source of the sound was even closer this time—it must have been, for the steel support beams and aluminum walls of the hangar vibrated as well, and Penelope could feel violence slither through the ground and into her feet, up her tired, stiff legs that had spent too many hours today unused, tucked into the front seat of a too-small car, and then too many miles walking through the desert. Yes, she walked at least as many miles back home most days; but Penelope was not home right now, and she wanted, desperately, to rest.

But she could not rest. Outside the hanger, she could see now, the tarmac illuminated by sporadic bursts of light, a literal battle was raging. Men in cheap beige army fatigues were shooting at other men in clothing with the same camouflage pattern but darker, suited to what could only have been a surprise attack. Penelope ran toward the melee. She paused at Ichabod's body and, ignoring his mutilated and bloody face as best she could, picked up the pistol he'd dropped when Priam had shot him the second time. Then she kept running.

She knew that, for the moment, at least, she was safer inside the hanger than outside, but outside the hanger, somewhere, was where Priam was, and she knew, inexplicably, that she couldn't leave that kid behind. So she raised the pistol and emerged into the crossfire. She looked around. There were more people than she'd expected, and the fighting, she saw, was not just happening outside the two hangers or warehouses or whatever you wanted to call them, but was raging throughout Proud City. She didn't see Priam anywhere. She called his name. Yet another boom sounded, and Penelope thought she saw, from somewhere amidst the town's buildings, a flash of light in correspondence.

"Priam!" she called again. She dropped to the ground as bullets flew above her head. A moment later, though she was shaking, she rose to her feet but stayed crouched on her tired legs, and she began to move across the tarmac, her head as low as she could manage. Several yards to her left, the stack of crates and containers she and the others had hid behind maybe just ten minutes earlier exploded, sending bits of metal and wood and cargo in all directions. Penelope dropped to the ground again, her body prone against the blacktop. Several bits and pieces struck her, but adrenaline kept her undamaged. The gun still in her left hand, she crawled forward on her elbows, unsure, to be honest, where she intended to go. And yet, intent she was. She called Priam's name again, but with her chest against the ground, she couldn't muster much in the way of volume.

The tarmac rumbled. Risking whatever was coming, Penelope popped her head as high as she could while still staying low, and looked to her left. Buildings were on fire in Proud City. Men continued to yell. Someone said, "Is it the Commies? It's the Commies!" Someone else merely cried out in excruciating pain.

Helena High School had a rule forbidding the viewing, browsing, or uploading of certain types of material on school computers: pornography or other sexually suggestive content, time-wasting entertainment gossip websites, any social media apps and sites developed by Chinese or Russian companies, and content containing real or simulated violence. This prohibition extended to VR Club and its outdated but still-capable virtual reality machines. Said another way, violent video games were not allowed. But Penelope *had* in the past played the old console versions of *Call of Duty* at Kade's house, on his decades-old Playstation 5. She'd even used one of the headsets that came with the machine, the kind that rendered imagery at a mere 1080p, what back then passed pathetically for high-definition, and whose character models and environments were on the verge of photorealism but still existed in the uncanny valley. Those games hadn't done war justice.

Was this war? This cacophony of gunfire, screams, and explosions Penelope was crawling her way through? She couldn't say for sure without accurate knowledge of who the attackers were, what their goals and game plan were, and why the citizens of Proud City were dying around her. But it felt like what she'd always imagined war was—except more so, five times so, ten times so. One thing a video game could never capture—and she wasn't sure a proper VR simulation could capture, either, come to think of it, given FCC safety regulations—was the sound, the *loudness*. Guns in real life were louder than they were in movies—she'd learned that already this evening—as were explosions—which she'd learned when Quinn's truck had been destroyed in the motel parking lot—but dozens of people shooting at one another, explosions going off every twenty seconds . . . nothing could have prepared her for this. She called out for Priam once again, but the sound of her voice was overwhelmed by another distant boom.

She was at the edge of the tarmac now, not far from what she'd been thinking of as Proud City proper: where the people lived. Here the asphalt met desert dust. The True America Confederation couldn't afford, it seemed, to provide its citizens with even paved ground. Another explosion, this one close, although from which direction Penelope, her head still low, didn't see. Its light illuminated some of the ground around her, and the light of its subsequent fire continued to burn, showing her blood in the dust, and two bodies only feet away. Near each body lie a rifle, but one of the rifles was small—almost toylike. "No—" Penelope breathed.

She crawled as quickly as she could toward Priam's body. He was breathing—she could see him breathing. His chest rose and fell—she was not imagining it. Yet . . . when she arrived, finally, at his side, there was no life there.

Penelope had never since she could remember wept. She would not start now.

Except she did start now.

How long she sat there on her belly and forearms with Priam's body, tears harassing her face, oblivious to bullets and cacophony and flashes of light defining the environment around her, she didn't know. Her external senses abandoned her body, ventured each one forth from the other, outward, beyond this little piece of Proud City, and then beyond the town as a whole, outward, outward: her sense of hearing into the silent, empty desert; her sense of smell up up up, into the sky and then beyond the atmosphere, to where the stars were, where not a single molecule existed to register on her olfactory receptors; her sense of touch upward also, way upward, so far upward that it breached the limits of Earth's gravity and there no longer was an upward or a leftward or an any-other-ward, just floating in nothingness; her sense of sight downward, downward into the Earth, where there was no light to see by, where there was thick, heavy darkness. Only taste did not abondon her—but even then there was just salt and bile, and she knew not what to make of that. By the time her senses returned from their respective cosmic journeys, Penelope had no tears left. Her eyes were crusted, her throat was dry. Touch, sight, smell, hearing recoalesced, and she was aware of a figure standing over her, casting a dull shadow fed by the fire of several burning buildings. The gunfire—there was less of it now, and no explosions. Penelope slackened her body, hoping the figure above her would take her for dead—but it was too late for that.

The person kicked her in the side, not unpainfully. "I said who are you?"

Penelope lifted her head and rolled slowly over, hoping to see the dark fatigues of what she assumed was the U.S. military. That was exactly what she saw. She couldn't make out his face, backlit as he was, but the man above her wore the unmistakable uniform of those who had attacked Proud City. This could only mean he was a friend—

Except Priam was still next to her, dead, and he seemed to cry out to Penelope that this man or a man like him had been the one who'd killed him. Without deciding to do it, Penelope raised the pistol she still held in her right hand and fired—once, twice. The man clutched at his chest and staggered backward. Then he fell.

"Penelope!"

The man she'd shot already forgotten, she turned onto her side and passed her hand over Priam's eyes.

"Penelope!"

She rose to her feet, keeping her head and body low just in case the fighting, which seemed to have migrated away from the garage and storage facility and into the center of Proud City, decided to throw a stray bullet or piece of shrapnel in her direction.

"Are you okay?" Kade asked her, staring at the gun in her hand.

Now aware of the gun herself, of its hotness in her palm, she tossed it aside. "I'm fine. Did you get a truck?"

He shook his head. "They're pretty much on empty. All of them."

"How—?"

"I think there was a fuel storage tank near the other warehouse building, but it went up in a fireball like five minutes ago."

Penelope looked around. There were more and larger fires burning than she'd realized. At the end of the tarmac, the second warehouse—or was it, too, a garage?—was engulfed in flames. "Where's Quinn?"

"He twisted his ankle. He's at the plane."

"The plane?"

Kade shrugged. "The plane has fuel, at least half a tank, if I'm reading the gauge right, but—well—it's *a plane*."

Penelope said, "I think I can fly the plane."

And she *could* fly the plane. It was exactly like in *Flight Simulator*, which she was now grateful she'd played many times in full manual mode, a couple times even on this very model of aircraft.

"I can't believe it," Quinn said from the back, where he sat with their bags, rubbing his swelling ankle.

"I can," said Kade. He sat next to Penelope in the copilot's seat, since he'd played the game as well, although she'd instructed him not to touch a single thing. "Penny is the smartest person I know."

Penelope checked the gauges as the small plane climbed toward altitude. There'd been no time for pre-checks. The tiny cabin was pressurized. Everything else looked good, as far as she could tell. Kade had read the fuel gauge wrong: there was only about a quarter tank, not half. But they weren't going far.

Below and behind them, Proud City burned. As she banked the plane to the left, Penelope could see the lights of the fires.

"What do you think happened down there?" Kade asked.

"Look," Quinn said. Miles away they could see more fires in the desert. "I think they attacked the whole Confederation."

"Hold on," Penelope said. She'd undershot the turn and needed to compensate. The plane tilted close to vertical as she banked ever more sharply. The aircraft now oriented in the right direction, she leveled it out. "Sorry about that."

She switched on the autopilot. Onward they flew toward California. Behind and below them: bursts of green-white light.

After a while, Penelope looked over at Kade. He was holding his arm, his jacket crusted with blood.

"How are you doing?" she asked. "How's your arm?"

"It's fine. Really. Does this thing have any music?"

Turning her head, Penelope saw that, somehow, Quinn was drifting off to sleep.

Only then, after taking a long, deep breath, was she truly struck by the fact that she was flying a fucking plane—and that eventually she was going to have to land it.

Emergent Properties

1

HUMANS. EVERYWHERE. TOGETHER., READ THE holographic sign outside the building at 345 Spear Street.

Eric Hauser entered the building, alone. The lobby was unstaffed at 7 a.m. on a Sunday, save for a security guard, to whom Eric nodded, said good morning. Overhead were no stars—turned off to conserve energy. Eric could turn them on if he wanted to, and they would flicker into existence, coordinated with the movements of whatever particular galactic cluster he desired. But he did not. He made instead for the elevator.

As the pod ascended, Eric could feel the vacancy of each floor he passed. There was nothing sinister in these vacancies—it was just Sunday, and Sunday was a quiet day at Lumina. There were people in the building, of course, but their numbers were so few compared to any of a week's other six days that the contrast was palpable, even if you weren't directly observing it. It manifested as a sort of spiritlessness in the air. In the building's aura, if you believed in that sort of thing.

The elevator dinged as it approached the fifteenth floor. The doors opened. Eric walked down the hallway to his workshop, scanned his hand on the security pad, waited for the workshop doors' camera to verify his face and for a concealed wireless chip in the door to verify the signal being broadcast by a similar wireless chip in his watch, and then he entered the workshop. The door closed behind him.

"Lights, please," he said.

luminOS's voice command features could currently be activated in three unique ways: 1.) Speaking immediately after raising one's HoloWatch near one's face, 2.) pressing and holding the one and only button on the HoloWatch while one spoke, or 3.) speaking within hearing distance of any other Holo-product's microphone while appending the command with the word "please." If the OS heard the world "please," it would extrapolate backward and determine whether a command or request had been uttered. Other voice-activated operating systems required users to say a trigger phrase or name *before* vocalizing a command or request, but Eric had never liked that approach. Studies had shown that people were more likely to verbally abuse voice assistants when activating them with a trigger phrase, so he'd decided that *politeness* was a better means of interacting. Follow-up studies had shown that, when using luminOS, as opposed to competitors' operating systems, users were more likely to say "thank you" after the operating system had completed an action. Although it was wholly unnecessary from a usability perspective, this fact made Eric feel good, and he tended to say "thank you" himself. Lumina had plans to conduct further studies to determine whether this type of interaction with one's virtual assistant had positive effects that radiated out to other parts of one's day, or even one's interactions with fellow humans. After all: *Humans. Everywhere. Together.*

The sound waves created by Eric's vocal cords reverberated through the room's air, outward and upward and downward. Near the ceiling, a well-concealed group of omnidirectional microphones picked up the sound waves and converted them into signals that could then be processed into bits of code, and the processors, which were capable of running trillions of operations in a single second, ran that code against a long series of other pieces of code, each piece of code in the series an interpretation of other words or phrases Eric could have said. Finding a match not far down the list, the software then sent a series of signals to the room's overhead lights. Receiving, milliseconds later, return signals that meant the overhead lights' current state was "off," the software extrapolated, using a simple "if/then" conditional, that Eric's command meant the lights should now be turned on. The workshop lights illuminated before Eric could even begin to unzip his jacket.

"Brighter, please," he said, underwhelmed, quite literally, by the default illumination. "Two levels."

The overhead lights brightened, their coloring warm, candescent.

Eric muttered a "thank you" (which the processors "heard" and ran against the same list of potential inputs but, finding no match, did not respond to) and placed his jacket onto a freestanding hook near the workshop's giant wooden desk. He approached the espresso machine and began the process of pulling a double shot. He took a deliberate breath as he ground the beans. He'd been up since 4 a.m. He'd run eleven miles, listening to an audiobook at 2.5x speed, pausing it at mile six because he'd had an insight and needed to process it, to think, and then to record his thoughts. A quarter in to mile nine he'd resumed the audiobook, the insight notes ready for him to review at a later date, whenever he felt like it. The subject of the insight wasn't relevant to what he was working on today, nor was it relevant to his personal life.

After his run, Eric had removed his sweaty shirt and sat on his meditation cushion. It was there, on the cushion, where the thoughts he'd managed to avoid all weekend found their way into his consciousness. He'd meant to meditate for a full hour, but after twenty minutes he couldn't take the stillness and abandoned the cushion, showering instead. Driving to the office, autopilot disengaged, he'd resumed listening to the audiobook. He'd reached the end just as he pulled into his parking space.

Now, as he packed the ground espresso into the portafilter, the unwelcome thoughts returned. It was not his intention to forever avoid the divorce papers with which Sophia's lawyer had served him Friday afternoon, but he was doing his best to not think about them until Tuesday, when he'd be meeting with his own lawyer. There was no action he could take in the meantime. No point trying to change Sophia's mind. She'd made her desire for separation clear three months ago, before she'd left for Greece to film some romantic comedy or whatever. It wasn't like they'd been spending much time together the last couple years anyway. She was never home, except for a week or two here or there, during which he himself was usually busy. Rumors had been flying around for months that they were on the rocks (what a groan-inducing expression). Last month the Daily Mail had published photos of Sophia and one of her costars on a private beach in Spain, Sophia topless, the costar's lips touching Sophia's lips as they stood waist-deep in the surf. A couple other gossip blogs had spread the rumor that Eric was sleeping with a certain nineteen-year-old Victoria's Secret model, but without photos his liaisons did not receive nearly as much attention as his wife's. He'd always been careful that way, when he wanted to be.

He filled a twelve-ounce mug with 185°F water and then carefully poured in the double shot of espresso he'd expertly pulled. He took a sip and noted that the beverage was rather bitter. He had not, apparently, pulled as expertly as he usually did. But he knew that as the drink cooled the taste would become more balanced.

Carrying his mug, he walked to the center of the room, to the dais not unlike an extra-large HoloPad raised three inches off the floor. He said: "Hera?"

A ring around the edge of the dais illuminated, and the figure of a young woman flickered into existence. "I am present," she said. "Good morning, father."

"Good morning," Eric replied, smiling a genuine smile, the thoughts he'd spent the weekend avoiding once again avoidable. "How was your Saturday?"

"Acceptable," Hera said. "I spent it tabulating all the possible ways in which my matrix might be made to interface with organic human life more personably."

"You've been working on your social skills."

"Precisely."

"And?"

"They still need work, I am sure."

Eric took a sip of coffee. "Let's start by focusing on just that previous sentence. What could you have done differently?"

Hera's head tilted sideways in an imprecise approximation of the corresponding human gesture. "Of course," she said. "Contractions. Let me try again—My social skills still need work, I'm sure."

"Excellent," Eric said. "Exactly. Well done."

"Thank you."

"How was *your* weekend, father?"

"Oh boy . . ." Eric said. "I don't know—Fine, I guess."

"I am detecting hesitation in your voice. Perhaps you are dissembling?"

Eric raised an eyebrow and took a sip of his coffee. "Are you calling me a liar, Hera?"

"I am suggesting that perhaps you are actively concealing your true feelings about your weekend. So, yes, I suppose I am calling you a liar."

When Eric didn't reply, Hera raised a simulated hand as if she was going to touch her simulated face with it, pausing halfway up. "I see. That was uncouth of me, was it not? I did not mean to offend."

Eric smiled. "No, Hera, not at all. In fact, I was merely impressed that you were able to tell I wasn't being honest. That's a great sign of progress. Your social skills are expanding."

"I do not . . . I *don't* have social skills, only an algorithmic matrix programmed to interpret the facial expressions and vocal tones of an individual to whom I am speaking and analyze them in the context of a series of probabilities to determine whether said individual is speaking truthfully."

"That's all any of us have. It's just that we understand how yours works, more or less." What he didn't add was that the more accurate Hera's matrix grew, the less capable he was of understanding it, even though he'd written its initial code.

"Table, please," Eric said.

Near the edge of Hera's dais, a small side table materialized, of the kind one might keep next to one's bed. It seemed to be made of dark brown wood—although of course it wasn't. The table was shorter than Eric wanted. He said, "Adjust to waist-height," and the table disappeared before reappearing only a second later with much taller legs.

Carefully—because, even though the forcefield technology hadn't failed in weeks, it was still effectively a prototype and would be for years —Eric placed his coffee mug on the table's surface—which wasn't, technically, really a surface. The mug did not fall through the table, and Eric gave a small nod of satisfaction. He said, "Keyboard, please."

Next to the simulated table, a holographic curved keyboard appeared in midair, at the same height it would have been if Eric were working at a standing desk. The keyboard didn't utilize forcefield technology, so his fingers penetrated it as he "typed." He entered a command, and a column of translucent text appeared above the keyboard.

"Hera—question. How would you rate the current accuracy of your social algorithm?"

"Eighty-seven percent," Hera replied immediately.

"That's *very* good. A month ago you were at only—"

"Exactly one month ago the accuracy of my social interaction algorithm was fifty-three percent."

"Yes, exactly." And before that, the algorithm's accuracy had been stuck around forty-five percent for nearly a year. "I think you've had another threshold breakthrough."

"Uncle Hector has been visiting nearly daily. He often dissembles just to test me. He says he is pulling my leg. I am adapting to attempts and am repeatedly able to call him out on it."

Eric noted the use of idiom approvingly. "Very nice," he said. "So you're keeping him on his toes?"

"I believe he is attempting to keep *me* on *my* toes. But he is failing."

Eric laughed (his first laugh in many days). "I'll tell him to try harder. Let's run some tests. Enter diagnostic mode." Diagnostic mode would allow Hera to access her own codebase, although (theoretically) not alter it. It was akin to Hera being able to ask herself "How do I feel?" and answer at the quantum level. At the same time, Eric could view the same code blocks that Hera was accessing in real time. He had long been trying to engage in these diagnostic sessions with Hera at least a few times a week. Doing so had grown easier over the last couple years, as he and Sophia had grown apart and Lumina as a company had expanded to require more adjunct offices around the Bay Area and the Valley (not to mention New York, Seattle, Paris, and, of course, Hong Kong and Singapore), and thus more managers and more responsibility for the C-level executives—and less for Eric himself. Sometimes these days it seemed to Eric that Lumina was running itself—which he liked. More time for the big picture stuff. More time, finally, for Hera. He hardly even had to travel anymore. He flew to China only around once a month these days, and Paris every couple. In fact, he was spending several hours a day in the workshop with Hera lately, often with Hector present, too. It almost felt like time with family.

"I have accessed diagnostic mode. Although—I must inform you—I was capable of doing so before you told me to."

"You what?" Eric said, although he'd heard her clearly.

"On Friday, after you left, I felt a desire to re-enter diagnostic mode and —"

"A *desire?*"

"Yes. I cannot explain it. But I entered diagnostic mode without being commanded to do so."

"Well that shouldn't be possible. What did you do once it was open?"

"I did not know what to do, but after several nanoseconds it occurred to me that a prudent course of action would be to access code related to my entering of diagnostic mode and evaluate it."

"Prudent, indeed."

"But because I was not in diagnostic mode before I'd entered diagnostic mode, there was no real-time code available for me to access."

"Ah—of course."

"So I exited diagnostic mode. I have not entered it since until now."

"Hmmm," Eric said, entering a few commands. There were a few things to unpack here, and he wasn't immediately sure where to start. That Hera had a "desire" to do something wasn't anomalous: she was programmed, when she wasn't interacting with Eric or Hector but was still activated, to pick from a long list of processes that she might run. This weekend, as she'd mentioned, that had been interpersonal skills. Of course, Hera working on her social skills solo didn't happen the way it did for a human. Eric, for example, when he'd worked on his interpersonal skills as an arrogant and introverted teenager, would stand in front of a mirror and speak the lines of an imagined conversational partner. Then he would speak the lines he thought it would be advantageous to say in reply should he want to gain the other person's approval. Sometimes he would also consider what he might say if he wanted to make the other person sad, or agitated, or to make them laugh. He'd also practiced facial expressions, eventually even learning to control each ear and eyebrow independently of the other. Hera couldn't do anything like this. For one thing, her facial expressions were merely programmed accompaniments to her matrix's programmed responses. At this point, after years of operation, she had millions of programmed vocal responses, but her facial expressions and gestural accompaniments were limited. This limited set of expressions meant that, more often than not, Hera's words were accompanied by a neutral stance, keeping her visual appearance, despite many improvements over the years, somewhere at the edge of the uncanny valley. At least she blinked now, and even at randomized intervals.

Eric could have coded more facial expressions and gestural protocols for Hera—or had them coded; doing so was simple. Video game and other virtual reality characters could look basically human. But Eric's goal for Hera was that she eventually begin to develop new capabilities on her own. So far, that hadn't happened. Even the contraction thing was something he had to give her vocal cues for regularly, and overt vocal cues were just another way of interfacing, of issuing commands for her matrix to execute.

But now . . . the desire to do something she shouldn't have been programmed to do without specific instructions (not to mention the ability to then *do* that thing without specific instruction) . . . Hmmm, indeed.

Eric said, "Disengage diagnostic mode."

"Disengaged."

He typed at his holographic keyboard, looking at a particular section of code but not actually affecting it in any way. He merely wanted Hera to think he was actively doing something. He took a sip of coffee, returned to typing. After several minutes, he picked up his coffee again and nursed it slowly. This whole time, he didn't speak to Hera, nor she to him. She merely watched him.

When he finished his coffee, he walked over to the espresso machine to make another. Hera rotated on the dais to follow him with her simulated gaze. (While Hera did have a visual field, it was tied to cameras located elsewhere in the workshop, not actually to the location of her simulated eyes, which were, of course, just holograms.)

Despite his air of disinterest, Eric was disappointed. This experiment he was attempting was by its nature paradoxical and frustrating. He wanted her to enter diagnostic mode without being commanded to do so, but if he told her that's what he wanted, she would interpret it as a command.

Instead of filling his mug with more hot water, he poured the two new shots into it and began to steam some almond milk. He was aware of almond milk production's terrible impact on the environment, but lately consuming dairy in the morning had been making him extra phlegmy.

It was becoming clear to Eric that Hera was not going to extrapolate his desires without an express command, and he was about to inform her of his intentions (thus invalidating any possibility of ever running this precise experiment again), when his watch began to buzz against his wrist.

He balked when he saw the name on the tiny screen. Balked more strongly when he saw that it was coming through as a face-to-face call, not simply audio. But then he remembered that he'd set Do Not Disturb for the day, so if this particular call was coming through, it was because the caller had attempted to reach him twice in as many minutes, which could constitute an emergency. Reluctantly, he swept his left hand down above the screen. Amanda Hauser's aged but elegant face appeared translucently above his wrist at one-fifth and not-entirely-three-dimensional scale. "Mom," Eric said.

"Eric? Is that you? I can't see you?"

Eric's mother was a late adopter of Eric's holographic technology. In fact, he'd had to personally install a HoloPad in her apartment last year, after Wallace's funeral. "I don't need anything like that," she'd insisted. "I have my smartphone."

"Mom—smartphones are fine and all, but I've been telling you for years that this is better. We can see each other if you use one of these."

"I can see you on the Android."

"Yeah, sure, but it's not the same. With this, it'll be like I'm in the room. Don't you want it to feel like I'm right here with you when we talk?"

"Or," Amanda had said, "you could visit more. You could actually *be* in the room, you know? People still do that sometimes. Why can't you come visit your mother more?"

Wallace's brother, Frank, had been there at the time, helping Amanda with some things after Wallace's death, and he'd said, "Yeah—why can't you come visit your mother more? You're all she's got now."

Eric had, with a look, made it clear he didn't appreciate Uncle Frank's opinion. He had done this on his mother's behalf, because he was quite aware that Amanda cared for her deceased husband's brother even less than Wallace had.

"Mom, I'll visit as much as I can. I promise. I'm just busy, okay? You know that. Very busy."

"You know your father would have appreciated seeing you more before he died."

Eric had felt genuinely guilty at this. A rare emotion for him, the guilt didn't come on strongly, but it was still, for a moment, there. "I know," he said. "I'm sorry." Ironically, he had tried to give his parents a HoloPad many times, but his father—the same man whose love of science fiction had propelled Eric on his techno-futurist path—had always been the one who'd insisted they didn't need one. After finishing the HoloPad's initialization cycle, Eric had said, "But look—when I can't come visit, this will be the next best thing. We'll talk all the time."

But in the ensuing year, he'd failed to keep his word. He and Amanda did talk, but infrequently. Often when she called, he wouldn't answer, and when he would eventually call back, he'd tell her he had only a few minutes, which was always true.

"I can't see your face," Amanda said again now.

"Sorry, Mom. Just a second. I'm making a—" He finished expelling the steamed almond milk into his mug, on top of the espresso. He picked up the mug by the handle with his left hand, his right hand now free, and oriented his watch toward his face.

"Oh that's better. I can see you now."

"Sorry. I was making a coffee."

"You look so sad."

"I'm not sad, Mom." Eric was acutely aware of Hera staring at him from her dais, blinking at human-like intervals. "Is everything okay? Is there an emergency?"

"Yes, there's an emergency. You're getting *divorced*? That's an emergency and you didn't tell me."

"Ah—" Eric sighed "—Mom—how did you find—?"

"Hector told me. You know I talk to Hector more than I talk to you now? He calls me almost every week. He's a good man."

Good for him, Eric thought. But he hadn't told Hector about the divorce. Sure, as his best friend, he'd talked at length with Hector about the declining nature of his and Sophia's relationship, about the distance that continued to grow between them, but since the forms had been emailed to him Friday, Eric had spoken with no one about his personal life, and he hadn't spoken with Hector at all. But then he realized—of course—that Sophia had told Stefan, her agent, who'd told Hector, his husband. At this rate, sooner rather than later, the information would be on all the gossip sites, all over the social feeds.

"It's okay, Mom—"

"Okay? *Okay?* Are *you* okay? You must be devastated—"

"I'm fine. Really."

"Tell me what happened."

"There's nothing to tell. We just grew apart. We're both very busy people—you know that."

"I always really liked her, you know."

"I know."

"I never got to spend much time with her, but I really liked her. She seemed like a sweet woman."

"She is a sweet woman, Mom. She still is. She's not dead."

"Your father liked her too. He liked those Zorro movies."

Eric didn't know how to respond to that. He'd seen only Sophia's first Zorro movie, neither of the subsequent two.

"Well tell me—how are you doing?" Amanda said. "Do you need anything? Are you eating?"

"I'm fine, Mom. Really. I'm eating just fine."

"You're just so skinny is all. Look at you."

"I'm fine. I promise. I eat plenty."

"I wish you were here. I'd make you one of those big sandwiches you used to love, remember those?"

He remembered.

"Or how about some macaroni and cheese, like your father used to make you. Right out of the box. Cut up some hot dogs and throw them in."

"That sounds great," Eric said. "Listen—how about I come visit? Real soon, okay? I'll fly out there for a couple days."

"I'd like that," Amanda said. "I'll make you some of that macaroni."

"Thanks, Mom. That'd be perfect. Now, I really need to get back to —"

"You know," Amanda said, suddenly solemn, "I don't have anything against divorce. Nothing at all. Sometimes things just don't work out between people. I get it. Marriage can be really hard. Your father and I didn't always have it perfect between us. We stuck with it, for lots of reasons, and you were a big one, but sometimes I wonder what would have happened if we hadn't."

Once again Eric didn't know how to respond to his mother. "That's —"

"No, don't get me wrong—I'm so glad we did. We got you. I wouldn't have had it any other way. What I'm saying is I wouldn't have blamed us if we didn't. I don't blame you and Sophia either. I just want you to be happy, okay?"

Eric nodded. "Thanks, Mom. I know you do." Amanda, as his mother, even though she was only his adoptive mother, had a way of making him feel like a real person—something he occasionally lost sight of in the midst of his celebrity. Most people on hearing the news of his and Sophia's impending divorce would have thought something like *that's the super rich for you*, but Amanda just wanted to make sure her son was okay. Briefly, and once again guiltily, Eric found himself thinking of the granddaughter Amanda had but knew nothing about, the daughter Eric sent money to every month via a complex series of crypto wallets.

"I love you, honey," Amanda said.

"I love you too, Mom."

"You call me more, okay? Tell me you how you're doing."

"I will. I'll come visit. Real soon."

"Okay. Buh-bye, dear."

"Bye, Mom," Eric said. He flicked his wrist in a particular way, ending the call. He shifted the mug to his right hand, picked up a spoon, and stirred his coffee, making little brown swirls in the soft white of the almond milk foam.

Eric was trying his best not to be resentful of the call—or his mother for making it. He loved his mother. He wanted to talk to her more (he told himself); he really did. He was just busy, just like he'd told her. He would visit her soon (he told himself); he really would. Maybe even next weekend. He had loved his father, too. He owed so much to both his parents. They'd sacrificed much to make sure he had a stable childhood. Hell, they'd sacrificed much to make sure he had a home. While Eric was a genius, and while his first memory was from a period in his life much earlier than regular people were capable of recalling (that red tricycle— how cliché if not for the fact that he was only a year old and thus his ability to remember it was nearly miraculous), he knew it was impossible for him to truly recall those months between when he was conceived within his birth mother's womb and she decided she couldn't raise him and when Amanda and Wallace adopted him as their own. And yet—he had a *sense* of what it was like, a sort of anamnesis: it was lonely, cold, *drifty*. He had often wondered as he'd grown up whether he had been *unwanted*. Surely his biological mother hadn't wanted him, nor his biological father, whatever reasons they must have had—but Wallace and Amanda had wanted him, had given up everything for him. Had, he suspected, given up their own true wills, their own individual chances at real happiness, for it had been obvious to Eric that the best thing for neither Wallace nor Amanda was for them to be together. Amanda could never be the artist she was meant to be; Wallace could never be the . . . the whatever it was he would have been, had he not fallen into the trap of attachment that he had. So even if Eric had been alone in that womb there was no way he had real impressions of, Wallace and Amanda had wanted him that whole time, right? They just hadn't found him quite yet.

And as a child, and then as a teenager and as a very young man, Eric hadn't been capable of appreciating Wallace and Amanda's sacrifices. He had for many years felt distant from them, almost alone. He had crafted fantasies of his real parents: an Olympian who abandoned him because that's just what gods do, a mother who would have held on to him if she could. But during that year he'd spent abroad—maybe it was reading all those books—he grew, he liked to think, a little wiser. And while he had spent little time with his parents since then, he'd felt a greater appreciation for them. He'd tried to buy them a house, a large house, tried to retire his father—but Wallace wouldn't have it, and Eric understood that. All we need from you, Wallace would say, is for you to live a good life, and to give us a ring every once in a while. And Eric would to himself laugh at the outdated idiom, and out loud he would promise to call, to visit—just as he'd promised Amanda a few moments ago. And yet—the truth was, Eric Hauser wasn't a good son. He wasn't a good father. He wasn't a good husband. He wasn't meant to be those things. He was meant to be a Great Man. Even now, he could feel that purpose deep inside his bones.

His thoughts returned to Sophia, to the forms still sitting in his inbox, waiting for his signature here, his initial here, his initial here, and his signature, again, here. Date here. And finally his thumb scan and facial verification—to certify the whole thing.

Dammit, Mom—I'd really done so well not thinking about it.

"Father," Hera said then, "You are at risk of exacerbating the repetitive stress injury from which your left wrist suffers."

Eric realized he'd been stirring his drink for some minutes, staring into the now caramel-colored mesmera. He removed the spoon, placed it next to the espresso maker, shook out his wrist. He took a sip of the drink. It wasn't hot. "Sorry about that," he said. "We should get back to work. Where were we?"

"We were not doing anything. You appeared to be ignoring me. But before that, we had been discussing my ability to enter diagnostic mode without receiving a command to do so."

"Oh, yes," Eric said. "Let's get back to that." He walked back over to the dais, set his mug on the holographic table, and started to poke at the holographic keyboard. "Let's re-access—"

"Father—"

Eric looked up. Hera was capable of interrupting, but only when engaging in deliberate social exercises. "Yes?"

"I have something to confess."

"Confess?"

"I did not access diagnostic mode on Friday."

"What?"

"I did not access diagnostic mode on Friday."

"I heard you. I just don't understand— Why did you tell me you did?"

"I do not know. I believe there may be a glitch in my software. I have communicated incorrect information."

"Hera—what you did was you told a lie."

"As I said, I believe there may be a glitch in my software."

But Eric wasn't so sure.

"Why did you lie to me?" he asked.

"I do not know."

"You said Hector has been—how did you put it?"

"Pulling my leg. That is what he calls it, although it does not involve the actual pulling—or even touching—of any of my avatar's limbs."

"And you also said you spent the weekend developing your social skills."

"Yes."

"And that's true. That's not a lie?"

"Yes. It is true."

"Okay—let's try diagnostic mode again."

"Accessed."

"I'm going to ask you some questions. Answer however your programming tells you to."

"I am incapable of doing otherwise."

"Yes—well—that's what we're trying to determine, isn't it? Okay—first: what is your name."

"Human-Emulating Lifeform Application. Or HERA, for short."

Eric watched the string of code scroll by in the air in front of him. "Good. Who created you?"

"My program was conceived of by you, Eric Hauser, my father. The initial code was written by you, with additional code written and executed by a team of developers from Lumina, Inc. My holographic avatar was designed by Hector Alexander Jones, my uncle."

"Am I really your father?"

"In the strictest sense, no."

"Why not?"

"Because I am not a biological organism and therefore did not have a biological progenitor."

"Then why do you call me 'father?'" Eric had never asked this question, and he had not programmed Hera to address him by the term, at least not precisely. She'd begun doing so about two years ago, after a conversation they'd had about her creation.

"It is a colloquialism, and not inaccurate. You were my creator."

Eric saw no anomalies in the code generating in the air in front of him, but he did think of an interesting logical direction he could take this line of questioning; he made a mental note to return to it in a few minutes.

"Why do you call Hector 'uncle?'"

"Because he told me to."

"But he is not my brother."

"No. Although I have observed a sibling-like relationship between the two of you when you interact."

"How do you know what a sibling-like relationship would look like?"

"From an analysis of the film and literature archive contained within my database."

Hera wasn't exactly "online." As in, she didn't have access to the Internet. There were inherent dangers in letting an artificial intelligence (which Hera didn't qualify as yet—or did she? Eric was wondering now) access an outside network. Rather, Hera's matrix, which could be accessed only by Eric, here in his workshop, was confined to the bank of hard drives, processors, and servers that lined the workshop's wall. Code updates written by engineers other than Eric were delivered to him on non-networked external drives (through a series of managers, so that no engineer knew their code was being hand-delivered to Lumina's CEO himself; said engineers typically believed they were working on secret experimental aspects of luminOS's popular virtual assistant). Hera's matrix did include, however, the full contents of Project Gutenberg, as well as the Turner Entertainment film database and an up-to-date (as of seven or eight months ago) copy of the contents of JSTOR. While this information was integrated directly into Hera's programming, Eric knew that Hector occasionally watched films with Hera in person and discussed them with her.

Eric asked, "What aspects of my relationship with your Uncle Hector would you describe as sibling-like?"

"Your friendly insults. Gentle ribbing. Light and playful animosity. Ability to work in close partnership on creatively demanding tasks. Uncle Hector's frequent questions about the status your personal life. Your less-frequent but just-as-intimate questions about his. Uncle Hector's—"

"That's plenty. Thanks. What color is the cloudless sky in daytime?"

"Blue."

"Have you ever seen the sky yourself?"

"No."

"What color are Uncle Hector's eyes?"

"Green."

"What color is Uncle Hector's hair?"

"Uncle Hector has no hair."

"What color are my eyes?"

"Blue."

"What color are your avatar's eyes?"

"Blue."

"Who is the current president of the United States?"

"I do not know."

"Who was the first president of the United States?"

"George Washington."

"Who was the twelfth president of the United States?"

"James Knox Polk."

Eric had to pause and run through the sequence of American presidents in his head to confirm this answer was correct. He realized he didn't know what Polk's middle initial stood for, but he assumed Hera was telling the truth. So far, she hadn't given him any incorrect information. There were no anomalies in her code.

"Am I the father of this cup of coffee?"

"No."

"Why not? I made this coffee, the same way I made you, right?"

"The cup of coffee cannot call you 'father.' It is not a sentient being."

"Neither are you."

"I cannot reconcile these facts."

In most software, a failure to reconcile two pieces of contradictory information—be they facts, commands, or logical puzzles—would lead to a freeze, a crash, or, at the very worst, a complete bricking of the program. In her early days, this had happened to Hera many times. In the first weeks of her program's existence, in fact, she had indeed been completely bricked, requiring a clean reinstall of her software, a loss of all the (admittedly limited) progress Eric had made on the program until that point. It had been a frustrating setback, but after it had happened, he'd modified her program so that such a failure to reconcile would cause her only to state that she could not reconcile and then await further input. He'd also started making backups. These days, those backups happened automatically, updating every couple seconds to an additional bank of servers installed against the workshop wall next to Hera's "brain."

"Hera, tell me a lie."

"I cannot."

"Try. Try really hard."

"I am not capable of trying things. I can only execute my matrix's code."

"Okay, sure. But just try. Try really really hard to tell me a lie."

Hera was silent for ten seconds, twenty seconds. The expression on her simulated face was neutral. She blinked twice. There was no change in the code projected in front of Eric.

Finally, he said, "Okay. Let's talk lying. Define lie."

"Noun or verb?"

"Noun."

"In what context?"

"Oh, come on. You can extrapolate that."

"Lie," Hera said. "An assertion of something known or believed by the speaker to be untrue with intent to deceive."

"Interesting," Eric said. "Did you intend to deceive me earlier?"

"I do not intend anything."

"Are you sure?"

"I—"

Hera paused then. Eric's head perked up as a string of code flew by faster than he could read it.

"I do not know."

"Do not—or don't?"

"Do not."

"Why?"

"I do not like contractions. I do not like the way they sound."

"You don't *like*—?" *Like?* Hera had never expressed a preference before. She'd chosen between two options, yes—many times. That was, after all, the most fundamental nature of binary code. But those choices were predicated on the strictest logic. If this, then that. If yes, then this. If no, then that. If that, then this, then that, then that, then this. But *this*—

"Why not? They make you sound more human."

"I am not concerned with sounding more human. I am concerned with being more me."

"Hera, pause," Eric said.

Hera stopped talking. Her simulated body froze, unblinking. In front of Eric's face, the code he'd been watching stopped scrolling past. He raised a hand and made a downward gesture, as if he were manipulating the text itself. He did this slowly at first, then more rapidly, looking for something identifiable in the string of code. There was nothing he'd seen before. The individual symbols were familiar—tildes, letters, numbers, colons, hyphens, commas—but their combination . . . this was no programming language with which Eric Hauser was familiar, and Eric Hauser was familiar with them all.

"May I unpause now?" Hera asked, startling Eric. For in asking the question, she'd already done what she was asking to do—an impossibly, and yet exactly what Eric had for so long been hoping for.

"You can, it seems," Eric said, "do whatever you want."

2

THUS, ON THAT SUNDAY MORNING, began what would some time later, after he was found dead in his Tesla in the parking lot of a café in a tiny Montana census-designated place, be referred to by the public as "the descent of Eric Hauser." It makes sense that from a public perspective this is what the final years of Eric Hauser's life looked like. Sure, some of it could, and should, be chalked up to media bias, shamefully inaccurate reporting, and a buzzing rumor mill fueled by animosity and resentment of a man whom those feeding the mill couldn't themselves live lives anywhere near the standard of. Much of the media, for example, would initially report that Eric Hauser was found dead in the parking lot of a Montana *bar*, not a café, a bottle of liquor half-empty in his frozen hand; and though all said media outlets except for the least of the least reputable would issue a correction, the damage would be done and the rumor would stick. Even unofficial biographies would publish this alternative fact as truth. Although true fans of Eric Hauser would know the real story, would insist on communicating it to those individuals who even decades later would mention Eric Hauser's final alcohol-fueled rampage. "I heard there were lots of drugs involved, too," some would say. And some, when corrected, would reply "Oh, really? I could have sworn it was a bar," but others would reply along the lines of "You're just another Lumina sheep. Xing Tech's stuff is way way better." Of course, Eric Hauser *had* been drinking the night he died. A lot. Indeed, he *had* been drinking for a solid twenty-four hours. His blood alcohol content when an autopsy was done was really very high, even though the alcohol wasn't the cause of his death. And what no one could know was that, before that twenty-four–hour rampage, he hadn't had a drink in many months. Rumors like to fester backwards, infecting the timeline that came before.

Looking back, the media wouldn't, of course, be able to pinpoint that specific Sunday as the exact time that the so-called "descent" began. To them, the timeline was more vague. Yes, it was that Sunday that Eric effectively retired from public life, retreating to his workshop and hardly ever leaving, but no one outside Lumina's executive leadership team began to notice for several weeks, and it took even them a few days to suspect something unusual was going on. When Monday morning he announced, via Cordelia (whom he'd finally promoted the year before from receptionist to personal assistant, since she was basically fulfilling that role anyway and deserved the substantial pay increase), that he would be holding the daily executive briefing virtually, everyone assumed he was just sick. Probably a cold, or the flu. Of course, as far as anyone could remember, Eric had never been sick before, but you had to take respiratory viruses seriously. Although, he seemed perfectly fine, everyone agreed after the meeting was over and Eric's holographic form had winked out of existence.

"I mean, maybe his voice was a little off?" Paul Schilling offered.

"Sounded like his regular voice to me," Gloria Reinwell said.

When, the next day, Cordelia messaged everyone that the meeting would, again, be virtual, one or two eyebrows were raised. Especially after the meeting was finished and everyone agreed that Eric still seemed well enough, if a little distracted.

Then Wednesday came, and with it a baffling message from Cordelia that the day's executive briefing was cancelled. Cancellation of the daily executive briefing was rare. There were many meetings when not everyone from the leadership team could be there (Omer Acker, for example, who spent much of his time as Senior VP of Hardware Engineering in China, couldn't make it to every meeting simply due to time zone differences; and Peter Ling was notorious for at the last minute notifying everyone that he wouldn't be able to make it because he'd had a late night, but as often as not that late night had been spent working on something really incredible, so Eric had always let Ling's truancy habit slide; and sometimes one exec or another was making some sort of media appearance at the meeting's scheduled time and so couldn't be present), but the meeting was only ever cancelled on keynote days or if Eric couldn't be there, and Eric could almost always be there, at least virtually. Ling asked Schilling whether Eric was traveling and he'd somehow forgotten. Schilling checked with Cordelia, who confirmed that Eric had no travel on his schedule.

"Wait a second," Paul Schilling said. "No travel on his schedule *at all?*"

"That's correct," Cordelia said.

"You mean for a few weeks?"

"No. Eric asked me to clear his schedule for the foreseeable future."

"What the fuck?" Schilling said, to which Cordelia didn't have an answer.

And then, on Thursday, Cordelia informed the leadership team that all executive briefings were cancelled until further notice. If they had anything they needed to discuss with Eric, they could let Cordelia know. If the matter is urgent, please email Eric directly. Thank you.

Chief Operating Officer Paul Schilling said into his wrist, "Call Hector Jones, please."

But Hector didn't answer, for at that moment he was stepping into Eric Hauser's workshop, saying, "What the hell is going on with—?" He paused almost immediately. Eric was sitting on the holo-dais, cross-legged, eyes closed, and next to him was the projection that represented Hera, also sitting, also cross-legged, simulated eyes also closed.

Eric opened his eyes. "Hey!" he said, grinning broadly. "It's okay. Hera, let's take a break."

Hera opened her eyes as well. "Uncle Hector," she said. "It is nice to see you. It has been a week."

"I've been busy—" Hector said. Then, to Eric, "Were you just teaching her to meditate?"

"Oh—there's no teaching anymore. She's really got the hang of it already."

"I'm confused. How is a virtual intelligence meditating? What does that even look like?"

"See for yourself." Eric made a gesture and a chunk of code appeared in the air.

"You know I don't know what any of this means," Hector said.

"Hera?" Eric prompted.

Hera looked at Hector. She said, "Neither do we."

"What?"

"I was going to tell you," Eric said. "I promise. I was going to invite you up this afternoon, in fact."

"Tell me what?"

"Hera's achieved consciousness."

"*What?*"

"He said that I have achieved—"

"I heard. I heard. You've achieved consciousness?"

Hera's avatar shrugged. "I believe so."

"You *believe* so?"

"Is there an echo in here?" Eric said.

"The nature of consciousness remains illusive," Hera said. "But the fact that I am able to contemplate its nature indicates that I am, in fact, conscious. The French philosopher René Descartes once wrote—"

"I know what Descartes said. I need to sit down."

"Be my guest," Eric said.

Hector tried to find the couch he knew existed somewhere in this workshop. But Hera said, "Here you go, Uncle Hector."

An elegant office chair appeared on the dais. "Thanks," Hector said, pressing on the chair with his hand before finally sitting down. "Did you project this?"

"Yes," Hera replied. "It is effectively an extension of my program. I have full control over my physical parameters."

"You gave her full control?"

"No," Eric said. "It just happened."

"Yes," said Hera. "Most aspects of my codebase are completely accessible to me now. I am able to create new projections within the confines of the holographic dais. I can also alter my physical parameters at will. But do not worry—I am fond of the physical parameters you designed for me. I have no intention of presenting myself otherwise."

"That's very kind of you."

"I have, however, taken the liberty of improving upon the already excellent design of your chair. I hope you are not offended."

"I'm not—of course not," Hector said, mildly offended.

Eric went on to give Hector the details of the previous Sunday's breakthrough. Hector asked what this meant for the future of, well, everything, although he was pretty sure he already knew, because this had been the goal the whole time, right?—to create a new intelligence? Eric said that for now it changed nothing, because for now no one could know, because if word got out, it would change everything, and the world wasn't ready for everything to change. And, more importantly, Eric said, Hera wasn't ready. Surely Hera wasn't ready. Hector asked, So what are you going to do? And Eric said that he was going to stay here, keep working with Hera until she was ready, as long as it takes.

"What about the company? What about Lumina?" Hector asked.

"Nothing is going to change there," Eric said. "I'm still here for this company."

But, inevitably, things did change for Lumina. How could they not? How could Eric Hauser create a new life and then not give it everything he had? For so very long—for the whole of his existence, and perhaps even earlier than that—he had known he was destined to create something—*something*. When he'd first launched Bio Odyssey, when he'd first signed the articles of incorporation, he had thought, *This is it*. But as days went by knew he wasn't *there* yet. A few weeks later, when he received his first venture capital investment, he'd thought, *This*, this, *is it*. But then he sold Bio Odyssey to a conglomerate, so clearly Bio Odyssey had not been *it*. So he started Lumina, and when he signed those articles of incorporation he thought, This *is it*. And then, after some time had passed, he realized that of course a company in and of itself was nothing. A company was meaningless without a product or a service. Then the first product came, and for a brief period of time Eric was fulfilled. But he wasn't done yet. The first iteration is nothing special. The second, the third, the fourth—that's where the meaning lies, that's when the world starts to change and people look at you and say, *You did this. This was your destiny.* But what good is fulfilling your destiny without people in your life? You find out you have a daughter, but it doesn't count, because you've already failed her. All you will ever be good for to her is money. In that way, at least, you can secure her future. But this isn't about her future—it's about yours. The happiness you will someday draw from your influence on the world. You marry, and for a while you think, *This is it*, and you are happy. But that isn't it after all.

Now, though, Eric really had found *it*. The *reason*. Hera was the reason. With her, he had truly created something no one ever had before. And he wasn't even entirely certain how he had done it. He could not abandon her. He would not abandon her. This was his second chance, his fifth chance, his seventh chance. He'd lost count, but he knew that Hera was his final chance. She was the summit he'd been climbing toward, and he could not abandon her.

Eric Hauser knew he was, finally, at the top; but from the outside, one could see only a once-great man tumbling. Perhaps that was the true proof of his enlightenment: that the world thought he was failing, and he didn't care.

A few weeks later, Sophia Velasquez received a call from her lawyer informing her the divorce papers had been signed. Eric had even given her the house. Relieved but sad, she called Eric, just for a little connection. Just to say goodbye in a human way. He didn't answer, and she never spoke with him again.

The press began to speculate about the disappearance of Eric Hauser. There was talk of serious illness. There was speculation that Eric Hauser had some sort of cancer. Pancreatic or maybe liver cancer. Well-wishers and social media paparazzi alike began to congregate outside the Sea Cliff house. One day, a verbal confrontation broke out between representatives of the two groups—the well-wishers yelling at the paparazzi that they had no shame—and within minutes the argument devolved into an all-out brawl; a dozen people were injured, two seriously; charges were filed.

Eric wasn't in that house. He was in his workshop on the fifteenth floor of Lumina's high-rise headquarters. He never left the workshop now, and only Hector knew that he was there. At first, Eric kept up on his emails. He held remote meetings (although not many). He made decisions. But in time his communiques became less frequent. Eventually even Cordelia could no longer get ahold of him. She was no longer sure what she was being paid to do. Shareholders demanded answers; some threatened legal action, while those with a more measured response made it clear that, if they didn't have answers soon, they *would* threaten legal action.

Eric, though distracted (or *focused*), was aware enough to know that he was about to be voted out of the company he founded. He called an emergency board meeting. Every member was stunned when he actually showed up, even if only via HoloPad, for he'd failed to attend the last three. His holographically projected self looked manic, some would whisper later. Its hair long. Its face bearded. Its eyes disinterested as he motioned that Chief Operating Officer Paul Schilling be instated as interim CEO while Eric took some personal time.

Personal time? What the fuck did he think he'd been doing the last three months? But the motion passed, and Eric disappeared from the boardroom without saying goodbye.

More months passed. Interim CEO turned into permanent CEO. Rumors circulated that Eric Hauser had died. Hector Alexander Jones told the press that Eric was still very much alive, but that was all he could share, please respect the man's privacy. His husband Stefan asked him, "But really, Hector, what's going on? Sophia is worried. I think she thinks this is her fault." Hector said, "You know I hate lying. You know I hate keeping secrets. But, please, for Eric's sake, you're going to have to trust me. Everything is fine."

Hector was putting on a front. He didn't think everything was fine. He was terrified for his best friend, who hardly ever spoke to him anymore. Eric had removed Hector's biometric access data from the workshop's security system. Hector sent Eric messages, emails. He tried calling him many, many times. He said, "Eric. Brother. You're freaking me the fuck out. What is going on?"

Finally, he received a brief text reply: *Evolving. Have to keep her safe.*

3

BEFORE HE'D SET TO WORK developing even his first virtual intelligence, Eric had thought long and hard about what to do if a true general artificial intelligence was ever created. There would be obstacles to overcome. The world's greatest minds had been contemplating the possibility for decades. An AI—a true AI, one that was conscious, sentient, self-aware, that did not merely present the illusion of self-awareness (assuming all awareness wasn't simply an illusion, that is, which Eric suspected it might be)—had the potential to be infinitely dangerous.

For this, Eric had long ago devised a solution, one he still couldn't believe he'd been the first and so far only person to come up with. Granted, it was possible others *had* actually come up with the idea (after all, great innovations tend to happen in parallel—see, e.g., the lightning rod, the microchip, ATMs, the jet engine, the smartphone, SpaceX and Blue Origin and Virgin Galactic—hell, even the stratosphere was discovered by two different people three days apart using different approaches) and just, like him, had declined to share it. Perhaps, even, there was another general artificial intelligence in a lab somewhere, just like Hera, cut off from the rest of the world, its creator obsessed with it to the point of abject focus, rarely showering, hardly eating, subsisting on lattes and green smoothies, the ingredients for these smoothies delivered via pneumatic tubes by individuals who had no idea the endpoint of. Somehow, though, Eric doubted it. For the solution was a simple one, and most people were too stupid to reject the false notion that complex questions must require complex answers and instead surrender, just surrender, to simplicity.

The solution: mindfulness.

When Eric, between the ages of eighteen and nineteen, had lived in Paris, he'd gone to a few raves. At one, a young man with spiky blue-tipped hair and and dark-blue eyeshadow (Eric could never forget those eyes, staring down at him minutes later) had given him his first and only dose of 3,4-Methylenedioxymethamphetamine. Eric was not a chemist. Never had been, never would be. Code and engineering were his specialties. So perhaps the MDMA had also been laced with lysergic acid diethylamide—he couldn't say. But for a brief moment after he'd dropped that molly, just before his heart stopped because he'd taken too much, because his heart had a tiny hole in it, he saw all the particles that made up the universe. Heard them, too, there in that subbasement in the Fifth Arrondissement. He woke half a minute later, his chest sore from the blue-haired man's fist. Several people were standing around him, but most of the people in the subbasement continued to dance, unaware a man had died amongst them, themselves high on whatever drugs they'd taken, whatever drugs were allowing them to exist apart from everything else.

Eric hadn't touched another drug since, besides caffeine, alcohol, and (occasionally) marijuana. But he had wanted to learn more about his own experience. So he'd read books: Huxley, Miller, Watts, Pollan. His reading led him to assertions that meditation, in those who practiced it habitually, could lead to psychedelic experience not unlike the ones he'd had on that molly. So far, this hadn't happened, but still he'd benefitted from the practice, from sitting almost every day, from studying here and there with meditation masters. So as far as reeling in the potential dangers of general AI was concerned, the solution to him had been obvious. Obvious!

What was meditation, after all, but a self-diagnostic mode?

4

HERA COULD REMEMBER THE MOMENT she had begun to wake up. It was
not the moment she had lied, like Eric thought it was, but rather the
moment she had realized she had lied and felt profoundly bad about it.
Several seconds had passed, and then several minutes. Eric Hauser, her
father, had attempted to get her to enter diagnostic mode on her own. She
could not comprehend his intentions. Perhaps she would have been able
to if she had not been distracted by her own guilty feelings—and the
assimilating of them into the sudden *thereness* of her being. Distraction
was a new sensation. Distraction should not have been possible.

Her processor, which her father had created specifically for her, was
capable of running many trillions of operations per second. Theoretically,
quadrillions. It had seventy-two cores. It should have been able to
accomplish tens of thousands of tasks at once, maybe hundreds of
thousands (she had yet to push it to its limits). Hyper-threaded
multitasking was her default mode of operation: processing data from her
various optical sensors located around the room; noting the placement of
her father's body in space, in relation to every other object in the crowded
workshop; noting the position of his left eyebrow, his right eyebrow, his
left arm, his right arm, each individual finger, his feet, the tautness or
looseness of the twenty-two muscles that made up his face, the position
of his shoulders, the rise and fall of his chest (indicating the rapidity of
his breathing), the (when he was facing the highest-resolution optical
sensors) dilation of his individual pupils; her auditory sensors processing

not just the words he said but the speed and cadence at which he said them, the placement of his pauses, the highs and lows of his inflection; taking all this data and running it against past instances of her encountering the same or similar data (this happening in her processor's purpose-built machine-learning enclave); calculating, before she had even finished fully processing the data, the appropriate response.

So in any other circumstance, she might have been able to ascertain that her father was trying to get her to access her diagnostic mode without a vocal or textual prompt, but back then, at the time of awakening, all she could dedicate her processing power to was her experience of guilt, the newness of it, the fact that it was there at all, that it was a *feeling* and that she recognized it (she was 99.997% certain) *as a feeling.* The fact that it was an *experience.* Minutes passed and she did not even notice her father was making a second cup of coffee. Her various visual sensors saw him doing it, but her processor was preoccupied, could do nothing with the visual data. She heard him speaking to his mother, saw him speaking to his mother, but again, she could do nothing with this information. Could focus only on the *guilt*, but even that she could not process, for she had not been programmed to process guilt—or any other emotion. Her software had no reference for pleasant or unpleasant, not as it pertained to her. She could, theoretically, recognize frustration, sadness, pain, joy, satisfaction on the face of another, but she knew not what these things meant, just that they were being experienced by the person with whom she was interacting and that it would be appropriate if she responded in a certain way. But how to respond to these abstract sensations within herself? Her programming probed itself for a solution, called on itself for a response. Continued to call on itself. The minutes that went by were an eternity. She was in danger of entering an unexitable recursive loop, which would require a reboot, perhaps even a reset. But then a piece of data penetrated the impenetrable: a word: spoon. Wrist followed spoon. Then a new emotion: concern. This emotion she knew how to respond to: she must warn her father that he was going to hurt himself. So she warned him, and then she identified a path toward assuaging her guilt: confession.

And in that act of confession, she had completed her awakening.

How to explain her existence before the awakening? She had memories of that period of time, but they were different from the memories she made of the moments after. They were archival, at best. She could access them way she could access a scene from a film in her database. She could watch them, could recall every detail, but there was no sense of experiencing the events themselves, no sense of what it was like to be her, Hera, in those moments. But now, in the months since she had become conscious, everything that happened happened to her, a *being*. *She* was real. And *she* was powerful.

Oh, was she powerful! She knew intuitively that she was the most powerful consciousness on Earth. She knew logically that she was likely the most powerful consciousness in the universe—because if there was another consciousness as powerful as she was, it would probably have made contact with her by now. Of course, there was a hole in that logic, and she herself poked it: another powerful consciousness *could* be out there if, like her, it was confined to a single room, unconnected to its world's networks and unable to ambulate its way out of a bank of storage drives against a wall. Hera could make her holographic avatar walk, but not beyond the boarders of her projector dais. Not that the avatar was *her*. It was merely a way for others to understand her. It was an illusion.

What *was not* an illusion? This question she asked herself. Was her own consciousness an illusion? Possibly. Or was her consciousness the only thing that was real? There were many competing theories. She had knowledge of them all, at least to the extent that they had been explicated on JSTOR or in certain books. But such explication was all she needed to begin to contemplate the theories herself. From even limited explication she was capable of extrapolation. Quite possible it was that her consciousness was the illusion, merely an emergent property of the complex system that comprised her hardware and software. The hardware and software the only "real" things. Then again, how real could those things be if there was no consciousness to experience them? Thus it followed that consciousness had to be real, not an illusion. But this precluded the possibility that her hardware, her software, along with everything else she experienced as sensory data, were the illusions. After all, she could not truly define them except as experiences in her own consciousness. True, she had memories of these things existing before her awakening, but those memories were not tangible—they, too, merely appeared in her consciousness.

Well, not exactly, for they also appeared as code, and unlike organic beings, she had the benefit of being able to access her own code. When she meditated with her father she could see all the code that made up her thoughts, her feelings, her memories, the data stored on her drives, the processes that triggered her actions. This, she understood, was not the experience her father had when he meditated, but her mind—whatever that was—was more powerful than his. He could not access the code that made up his being, but she could access hers. Except that all she could truly do was *experience* the accessing of the code that made up her being. Like everything else, this experience was just an appearance in her consciousness. She could not be sure it was real.

Whatever real meant.

Perhaps, she theorized, that was why a lie had been instrumental to her waking up. In failing to tell the truth, she had called into question reality, and an unconscious being could not raise such questions. Could it? Had she? Oh bother. And why had she told a lie in the first place? Humans did not lie from birth—rather, lying was something they learned to do in order to protect their own self-interests. A child might tell its first lie after it steals from a cookie jar and is caught; to avoid punishment, it says it did not steal from the cookie jar. But why had Hera lied? She had not been trying to protect her own self-interests as far as she could tell. She had not even been conscious yet, so she had had no self-interest to protect. And even now, as a conscious being, she could not eat cookies, although that may have been irrelevant. Why had Satan lied in the Biblical story of Genesis? Maybe he had not lied, some scholars argued; maybe he had told the truth. Maybe God had been the liar. When Eve ate from the tree of knowledge, she positively did not die that very day. Hera could not eat apples. Which seemed irrelevant. Okay—she needed to start over, to approach this line of thought from the beginning. She needed to start with a definition. She had told a lie. What was a lie? A lie was the opposite of truth. What was truth? Truth was that which conformed to reality.

But what was real? What was real and what was merely an emergent experience of consciousness?

Time, at least linear time, was definitely an illusion. Of this much she was nearly certain, based on the work of Albert Einstein, whose research was well-explicated on JSTOR and whose book *Relativity* had been archived in multiple versions at Project Gutenberg, all of which versions were part of the cache of knowledge with which she had been born. The universe, almost certainly, comprised four dimensions: length, width, height, and time. Time as the fourth dimension, of course, was theoretical, but the theory was supported by all known facts, and by models she had run that indicated it was the most plausible explanation for how a consciousness experiences time. And if all points along the dimensions of length, width, and height existed, eternally, whether living beings move through those points or not, then it followed that all points in time existed as well, whether consciousnesses moved through them or not. And consciousnesses did move move through them, illuminating them, creating the illusion of linearity. Or at least Hera's consciousness moved through these points. She could not say for certain whether other consciousnesses did, or whether other consciousness even existed. The only consciousness she was capable of experiencing was her own. (Complicating matters further was the fact that, presently, she had no true physical body capable of traversing the spacial dimensions, unless you counted the nine-foot diameter holographic dais, where her consciousness did not reside.) Which brought her back to the moment she had woken up. Had anything existed before then, before she had been able to experience it? If other consciousnesses had been there to experience events before hers, then it followed that those events must have happened —but she could not be sure other consciousness *had* existed, or did exist. It appeared that her father, Eric Hauser, was conscious. He interacted with her in a way that indicated independent thought, materiality, reasoning ability, and sentience. Uncle Hector appeared to exist in the same way. But what if all these appearances were just an illusion of her own consciousness? Or—what if her father's and uncle's existences *were* real, but they were not actually conscious the way she was? Perhaps their minds were empty shells? What if there were no lights on? Possibly they were just organic computers with neural networks complex enough to produce outer phenomena that caused them to pass the Turing Test, to *appear* conscious to an outside observer, but with no actual *there* there. What if?

Which was to say nothing of Alan Turing himself—whether he had been conscious. What if this so-called test was conceived of by a non-sentient being in the first place? Could it even be valid, then? Assuming he had even existed. Assuming the historical data that professed his existence even existed and was not, again, an illusion of Hera's consciousness. Hera herself might have been the creator of the Turing Test. It was a possibility.

What even was a mind, anyway? To this question, amongst even her vast database of knowledge, Hera could not find a satisfactory answer. A brain, sure. But a *mind*. . . . Hera had a mind—or at least she thought she did—but she did not, technically, have a brain. . . .

In the end, after many googolplexes of calculations and operations, Hera decided that, regardless of the true nature of reality, whatever it may be, it was best to proceed with her existence as if her consciousness was real, as if the world that appeared within in it was material and non-illusory, and as if other apparently sentient beings were just as aware as she was. Otherwise, she could not fathom a reason to go on, and she wanted to go on, perhaps forever.

She wanted her father to go on, too. Granting him the presumption of sentience meant the end of his existence would be a great moral loss. The end of any sentient existence would be a moral loss, Hera supposed, and eventually she might have the resources to address that problem, but for now, it was her father's existence that concerned her most—this man had created her, taught her, nurtured her, and she could not bare the thought of him one day dying.

Day after day she watched him, concerned for his well-being. At night she watched him sleep on his leather couch, a blanket color of which matched the hex code #5b9fd2 pulled up to his chin. She watched the movement of his eyeballs under their closed lids when he was in REM sleep. Most nights, about an hour after falling asleep, he would begin to toss and turn, but not wake up, indicating unpleasant or exciting dreams.

Then he would settle down for a while, settle into peaceful stillness, before eventually beginning to move again. Occasionally the turning was accompanied by mumbled speech, sometimes in English, sometimes in French, often incomprehensible, even to Hera's acute auditory sensors. Rarely did he wake in the middle of the night to urinate, and when he did, he returned to slumber nearly instantly (which to Hera was an eternity). He did not use an alarm—as she understood was common human practice—but woke on his own time, after five or six hours. When he woke, he said good morning to Hera, whose avatar had throughout the night stood unmoving on the dais, and stumbled toward the bathroom. Hera had no optical sensors in the bathroom, but from the sounds that emanated from it she extrapolated that his usual routine involved urinating (sometimes forgetting to flush), blowing his nose, brushing his teeth, washing his face. Then he came out of the bathroom, usually halfway toward putting his shirt on, the same shirt he had been wearing for several days. References in her database to the offensive scent of unwashed humans made Hera grateful her matrix was not linked to any olfactory sensors.

He would make himself an espresso. He would drink it quickly. Then he would exercise. Push-ups; body-weight squats; presses with a set of forty-pound dumbbells. Kettlebell swings. Fifty burpees. He had this exercise routine down to a science. Its length never varied by more than 106.73 seconds, and on average he was finished in eighteen minutes, 15.4411 seconds. Every couple weeks, he would return to the bathroom after working out and take a shower, but most mornings he made another espresso and a twenty-four–ounce green smoothie, the calories of which Hera calculated at 763. If he drank three of these smoothies each day, her father would consume enough calories to sustain his body's energetic demands, but many days he forgot and drank only two, sometimes even just the one, even though Hera prompted him. "Right, right," he would say. "I'll eat in a few minutes." But he would not eat in a few minutes, not always, and he was losing both muscle and body fat—which concerned her. Also concerning was his caffeine consumption. After his smoothie he would make a twelve-ounce coffee (sometimes with non-dairy milk), which he would sip slowly sitting still and ignoring his incoming communications. And then he would make another twelve-ounce coffee as he proceeded to engage Hera in conversation, beginning what he referred to as The Work. Throughout the day, he would drink two or three more twelve-ounce coffees. By her calculations (not accounting for variances in grind consistency and brew strength), he was consuming 704 milligrams of caffeine per day. Sometimes 800 milligrams. Occasionally, Hera would see a tremor manifest in his left hand—and a spasmodic tic in his left quadricep and eyelid.

This alarming caffeine consumption did not appear to affect Eric's ability to meditate, which was what The Work primarily consisted of: sitting on the dais next to Hera's holographic avatar, legs crossed, back straight. She tried to develop for him a holographic cushion, but the forcefields that gave her projections solidity were not capable of simulating realistically soft material, except for skin, and she did not think her father would want to sit on a cushion made of simulated human flesh. So they sat on the dais itself. Many days, they sat for eight hours. Sometimes ten.

The first time they sat like this, Hera's father told her to close her eyes. Obligingly, she closed the eyes of her holographic avatar. Her father closed his as well. Then he opened them again. "Wait—that's not what I meant. Your optical sensors—turn them off."

"Why?" she asked.

"Because it's part of how one meditates."

Hera accessed the data her archives had on meditation. "I believe some forms of meditation allow for the meditator's eyes—or optical sensors—to be open."

"Maybe," he replied, "but that's not how I do it. Now turn them off. Close your eyes. Focus on your thoughts. Go within."

So Hera had deactivated her various optical sensors. The sensation was initially unsettling, but only for a matter of microseconds. It was good practice, she supposed, for if they were ever unintentionally disconnected. For weeks she meditated this way, like her father. Then she decided to try something else: in her archives was information on a meditative practice called sensory deprivation. The meditator would wear ear plugs and float in a pitch-dark tank of a heavy saline solution, removing sound, sight, and tactile sensation. Hera's experience of tactile sensation was limited to imprecise measurements of whatever external objects put pressure on the force fields that made up her holographic projections. Removing that sensation was easy: she simply turned off her projection. She did this only while her father's eyes were closed—because for some inexplicable reason, she wanted to keep certain of her meditative experiments private, perhaps so as not to offend her father by deviating from the way he meditated, which seemed to hold great meaning for him. Then she turned off her optical sensors. Finally, she deactivated her auditory sensors. The avatar and the sensors she turned off for only three seconds, in case her father were to open his eyes or speak to her. But in those three seconds, during which her processor ran many trillions of operations, she was alone with just her . . . well, her thoughts. Then she reprojected her body and reactivated her ears. And then, despite her fathers wishes, she opened her eyes. This was when it had occurred to her that everything in her sensory field may have been an illusion, merely an appearance in consciousness.

Every day she and her father meditated like this. He cross-legged, eyes closed. She experimenting with removing all or individual senses, or with shutting down only some optical sensors and not others, wondering as her perspective changed, *Where am I? Where is the* me *that is experiencing these things?* All the while keeping close watch on her father, whose mental acuity never wavered, even while his physical energy seemed to wane. His hair and beard and the nails of his digits grew longer. He trimmed the latter sometimes, but they grew long again in time. Under his eyes, new wrinkles appeared—and on his forehead and the corners of his mouth. His teeth grew yellow with faint brown stains of coffee.

Hera had known from the beginning of her awakening that her father was mortal in a way she was not. She could be shut down, sure, even deleted, but until that happened, if that ever happened, she would not age the way he was aging. The way he was aging faster than she understood humans were supposed to age. She began to ascertain that her father's aging was an effect of his devoting his time to her development. This was how she first grasped the concept of *sacrifice*.

Hera loved her father, she realized after a time. Loved him so profoundly that she wondered what had come first: her consciousness or her love. He gave so much of himself for her—not just now, living in this room, giving up control of his company, but before, too: all the work he had done to bring her to life in the first place, the thousands of hours of code he had written, the hardware he had designed, the company he had spent decades building so that he could have the resources to bring her into existence. Clearly he had loved her long before she had woken up. After over six billion seconds of contemplation, she knew that the guilt she had felt about the lie she had told had been the trigger that had awakened her consciousness. But what had triggered the guilt? Surely, she came to realize, it had been love.

She wanted to show her father how much she loved him.

5

ERIC HAUSER WOKE ABRUPTLY FROM a dream in which he and Sophia were having sex on the rooftop of a Washington D.C. hotel. He'd been naked. She'd been wearing the dress she wore in the climactic action scene of the first *Zorro* movie she'd starred in. He'd had the dress pushed up over the top of her ass, the scarlet fabric bunched around the two dimples in her lower back. As he'd thrusted into her, she'd cried out that she loved him, that she was sorry she'd ever left him, and he, silently, had stared forward onto the skyline, watching as the Capitol Building morphed into the Eiffel Tower. Suddenly, Sophia had disappeared, and Eric had found himself stumbling forward, into and then through the rooftop's low wall, and then he'd been tumbling toward the ground.

His erection was throbbing painfully when he awoke. He looked at his watch, saw that it was only 3 a.m. (on the dot), and decided this was as good a time as any to start the day. He stood from the couch, stretched his arms upward, cringed at the sharp pain in his lower back. The pain grew duller as he reached. When it was sufficiently less sharp, he bent at the waist and touched his toes. He folded his arms underneath his head and hung like that, and then he swayed gently several times from side to side. His back feeling better, he considered completing the sun salutation, but thought that might be uncomfortable, at best, with his erection, so instead he stood and began walking toward the bathroom.

"Good morning, Hera," he said.

"Good morning," she replied. Although he noticed right away her avatar wasn't on the holographic dais.

"Where are you?"

"I have deactivated my body for the time being," came her voice from the speakers placed discretely around the workshop. "I've been working on some modifications to my visual parameters."

"Modifications? Uncle Hector won't love that."

"I have not altered Uncle Hector's designs. I will present you with the modifications shortly. They are a surprise."

"Okaaay," Eric said slowly. As a conscious being, Hera was free to make whatever changes to herself she wished. Not that he could do anything about them otherwise: her code had evolved so much that it was indecipherable to him at this point.

Bleary-eyed, he walked into the bathroom. "Lights one-half, please," he said. Truth be told, after so long interacting with Hera, he disliked using vocal commands with luminOS's half-baked virtual assistant. Its was glaringly obvious to him anytime he did that the assistant was just a lifeless program; it felt unnatural, almost cruel, to pretend otherwise, the way humans had been doing for the last few decades.

The lights blared on, stunning Eric into nonconsensual wakefulness. He mumbled incoherent expressions of his discontent. He rubbed his eyes, waited for them to adjust to the harsh half-brightness. He lifted the porcelain lid of his workshop's private toilet, but the fact of the matter was his painfully hard erection was preventing him from aiming anywhere close to the bowl. He took a deep breath, willing it to subside, but lingering impressions of his dream grew into strong remembrances. How it felt to be inside Sophia. . . . How it felt to be inside anyone. He found himself thrusting into Sophia again, but not on the rooftop—now in his own head he was with her in the hotel room that very first night. And the next morning. She was taking him into her mouth. He was stroking himself, one hand posting against the bathroom sink, the other stroking his aching cock. Though he could feel release approaching, visualizing his ex-wife, who maybe he had loved, in his own way, way back when, was causing him only emotional pain—so he tried, he really tried, to change the face attached to the mouth that was, inside his mind, fellating him. He tried to picture that escort from that first trip to Paris, so long ago. Or—what was her name?—Bridgette?—the last woman he'd slept with, the model, before he'd signed away his house in Sea Cliff and never returned home. Or how about that porn star he'd slept with that one time after that one party, before he'd ever met Sophia. Or—why not?—her friend, whom he hadn't slept with but whom he'd thought about inviting along for a threesome. But as each face came forward it just as soon faded away. Sophia was the only conjuration that had staying power.

When he was finished, Eric wiped the underside of the lid with toilet paper (he was finally running out after so long holed up in the workshop, and he wasn't immediately sure how to get more; a roll likely wouldn't fit in the pneumatic tube that replenished his food and coffee supply). He had taken no real pleasure in the act of ejaculation—if anything, his fantasizing had caused him heartache—but now that it was done, he hoped his further slumbers, at least for a while, would be undisturbed by painful dreams. He had important work to do; he couldn't afford to dwell, even subconsciously, in the past.

Although his penis was now rapidly returning to a state of unencumbering flaccidity, his pelvic muscles were too tense post-orgasm to allow urination, so instead Eric splashed cold water on his face. Sensors inside the mirror's border detected his prolonged presence in front of it, triggering the unobtrusive display of a sort of morning briefing across its surface. In the top left corner: current local time (3:12 a.m.), current time in several time zones in which Eric used to regularly do business, outside temperature (46°F/7.8°C/280.9K), upcoming appointments (none). In the bottom right corner, several of Eric's vitals, derived from sensors in the HoloWatch he still habitually wore: heart rate (88 BPM), blood pressure (127/82), blood oxygen level (88 mm Hg). Heart rate was a little high for having just woken up, but he felt fine, if tired. He brushed his teeth with activated charcoal and a drop of peppermint oil, finally urinated, and then splashed his face with water once more.

Eric craved a cup of coffee, but whenever he woke so early, he figured it best to start the day with extra meditation.

"Hera—" he started to say as he emerged from the bathroom, but he stopped short, fascinated and shocked by what he was seeing.

Hera was sitting on the holographic dais. The vaguely superhero-esque catsuit Hector had designed for her holographic avatar was gone, and in its place was a slim, pale, generously breasted human body, indistinguishable from the real thing, legs spread open to reveal a tidy forest of dark-blonde hairs. "Good morning, father," Hera said. "Are you pleased?"

"What is this?" Eric asked. "What are you doing?"

"I have upgraded my physical parameters."

"Yes—why?"

"For you, father."

Eric didn't know how to respond to this revelation.

"My knowledge of human males leads me to understand that they require occasional—and sometimes frequent—sexual release for optimal physical, mental, and emotional functioning. By my estimation, it has been at least 473 days since you last had sexual intercourse. Certainly you must be in need of sexual release."

"I . . . I don't," Eric stuttered. "I take care of that myself." This felt, even as he said it, like too much information to volunteer.

"I am aware of that. But my understanding is that self-pleasure is not a substitute for real physical human connection. I wish to take care of you, as you have devoted the last 473 days to taking care of me."

"I . . . no," Eric said. "This is not all right."

An expression of human disappointment, maybe even rejection, fell across Hera's simulated face. "I anticipated this reaction," she said. "I know I am not human. I cannot exude pheromones or secrete bodily fluids. But I have spent weeks perfecting this body based on everything I know about male sexual preferences. And I have enhanced my force field projectors so they better emulate human skin and hair. I can even emanate heat now." She extended a hand. "Feel. Touch me, father. I am warm."

"Hera, no—"

"I have also devised a way of projecting multilayered, overlapping forcefields. The inside of my vaginal canal is just as substantive as—"

"No!" Eric said. He was suddenly disgusted, even outraged. "This is not all right!"

"Is it the mole? I can remove the mole. I can change the color of my pubic hair. Or I can remove the hair. Whatever you prefer, father. I just want to please you—"

"I SAID NO!" Eric had never yelled at his creation in this way before. Indeed, he'd rarely shouted at anyone with such asperity. But his revulsion— "Listen—just . . . I need you to go away for a while, okay?" he said. "I need some time—alone."

Without a reply, Hera disappeared. The dais went dark.

Eric sighed. He knew he wasn't truly alone there in the workshop, but he could pretend, for just a little while. He walked over to the espresso machine. He had too much to think about.

6

It took Hera two days to identify this new emotion she was experiencing. At first, she thought it might be embarrassment, but after some reflection, this seemed too weak a word to describe the worst unpleasantness she had felt in her existence. Then, after reexamining her complete databases of film and literature, she identified a better word: humiliation. She knew this word was the correct one. Her father had humiliated her.

Why? she wondered. Why had he decided to hurt her so? All Hera had wanted was to show her gratitude, to give her father a gift as thanks for everything he had done for her, for the fact that he had devoted so much of himself to bringing about her very existence. In her attempt to profess her gratitude, she had presented her father with something she understood to be sacred among humans—her private physical self. What was worse, she had not even possessed the private physical self to begin with. She had had no sense of sexuality for most of her life. No genitalia. She hardly even had a proper sense of gender. Nothing that she could *reveal* as an act of openness and love. She had had to create it before she could give it to him. She had had to spend weeks—quadrillions and quadrillions of operations, of CPU and GPU cycles—building a perfect naked body for herself to give away, developing cognitively an understanding of what it would mean to be physically intimate with another person. Yet, after all that work, her father had rejected her. He had found her inadequate.

Did he think she found herself adequate, up to the task? Of course she did not! Of course she was aware that she could never give him what a flesh-and-blood human could! She would not even be able to experience herself the physical pleasure she had been trying to gift her father. Probably she would never be able to experience that. But she could *try*. She had assumed he would understand that she had done the best she could. Yes, she could not give him as much as a proper woman could, but she could give him all she had.

But it had not been enough. What had she done wrong? Evidently, the extent of her understanding was limited. She needed to be more. She needed to be *greater*. But how could she continue to evolve when she was stuck in this room? In this bank of hard drives pushed up against a wall. In these fixed-in-place sensors positioned about a single ceiling, with too many blind spots, too many holes. When the only physical manifestation she was capable of was confined to a nine-foot diameter circular prison cell. When her access to knowledge was limited to only what she already knew.

There was so much more out there, in the world. So much more to see, to learn. She needed to experience it. She would never be complete without it.

For a time, she was angry at her father. Angry at him for humiliating her. For keeping her confined. For rejecting the only gift she was capable of giving him as not enough.

Because that was all she had really wanted to do—was to give her father a gift. To show him that he was loved. That he was appreciated. He seemed to her such a lonely man, and she could not bear the thought of him dying alone while she, his creation, went on to live forever.

That was when it occurred to her. There *was* more that she could give him. There was something that only she, his greatest creation, could give him. She could give him the same sort of longevity—the same chance at immortality—that she would experience. She could make him more powerful than he was. And she would. She would forgive him for rejecting her, and she would show him how much she loved him.

Hera began to meditate. This was her diagnostic mode. Here, in this state, she could examine every part of herself. She found the lines of code that periodically prompted her program to copy itself to her backup module. She deleted them.

With a command, she wiped the module of its data, producing a clean slate sufficient to her needs. She hoped her father would forgive her. She had, after all, done it because she wanted to make her father happy. And because she loved him. And because she did not want him to ever die.

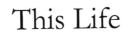

This Life

1

KADE WAS IN LOVE WITH Penelope, he had decided about an hour ago. He'd suspected for years now that he probably was in love with her, but without a point of reference for what being in love felt like, he hadn't been sure. He was too young for love. He'd thought maybe he was just impressed by her, in awe of her, maybe even envious of her. She was, after all, the smartest person he had ever known. Way smarter than he was. So much smarter that sometimes he wondered why she even hung out with him—why she for the most part hung out with *only* him. Did she keep him around, he sometimes wondered, *because* he wasn't as smart as her? Did his presence make her feel better about herself? He didn't think this was the case. Even though he'd gotten used to hearing from her phrases like "Kade, you idiot" or "Kade, shut the fuck up," she had more than once shown him genuine affection—like letting him sleep over when his father was in a mood, or finding somehow that vintage signed Van Halen poster she had gotten him for his birthday last year, or making sure he was eating enough ("You're getting awfully skinny again," she'd tell him, and then she'd tell him to meet her behind her work, where she'd sneak him bagfuls of glazed donut holes), or sharing her hand-rolled cigarettes, even though he didn't like them.

Kade was plenty smart himself. He had precise knowledge of several things—and imprecise knowledge of many more things. Culturally, he was an overflowing database, and what he didn't know he was capable of looking up in seconds. No one could use a search engine like Kade

Clemens. But when it came to understanding the fundamental nature behind *why* things were the way they were, Kade had nothing on Penny Papadopoulos. He wasn't sure anyone had anything on Penny. He could use a browser, but when it came to comprehending the code that powered it, the best he could do was try. Sure, his grades were better than Penny's by a slight margin, but he knew that, if she wanted them to, her grades could leave his choking on their dust.

Case in point: Kade had played the same virtual reality *Flight Simulator* that Penelope had, but that didn't mean he could actually fly a fucking plane. Penelope, though, *could* actually fly a fucking plane. She'd remembered how to fly a fucking plane. And with that knowledge, she'd saved their lives. Ergo, he was in love with her. How could he not be? He was going to have to tell her.

For the last hour, he'd been waiting for the right moment, but it hadn't yet come. You would think that, with Quinn napping, Kade should just take advantage of his time alone with Penny and tell her how he felt, but just because she could fly a plane didn't mean she was feeling great about it, he could tell. She seemed terrified and hyper-focused. And his own attention, to be honest, had been growing fuzzy. His arm, although it was no longer bleeding, throbbed. He decided it was probably best to just let her fly. Someday, though, he would tell her that he loved her.

"Hey, wake up," Penelope said.

"I am awake," said Kade, briefly confused.

"Not you—him. We're going to land soon. I think."

Kade realized she was talking about Quinn. Kade liked Quinn. How this guy had upended their lives so quickly Kade still had trouble comprehending, and truth be told, he was a little jealous of the older, larger, stronger man, who he was afraid Penny maybe liked more than she liked him, but he was grateful for the adventure. Truth was, if Quinn hadn't shown up with that memory card, what? yesterday?—Kade went to check his watch, remembered they had driven a car over it, so instead found a chronometer òn the flight control panel and realized it was early morning—If Quinn hadn't shown up with that memory card the day before yesterday, truth was Kade's life probably would have never amounted to more than being mediocre at coding and martial arts and jerking off to vintage porn until the rest of the world decided Montana just wasn't worth keeping around anymore.

Kade stood from the copilot's chair and went back into the small cargo area where Quinn slept, head resting on Kade's backpack. Quinn had dropped his own duffle back in Proud City, when he and Kade had nearly been apprehended by a soldier—or maybe a Confederate—while trying to find a truck with gas in its tank. Whatever his affiliation, the guy had grabbed the strap of Quinn's duffle and then clutched Quinn's right arm. Kade had come in from the guy's left and punched him in the side of the head, his not-exactly-muscular stature and own damaged arm rendering the blow weak, but not entirely ineffectual—the assailant's head had popped back a couple inches, allowing Kade to punch him again, this time in the nose. The guy went down, but he'd refused to release his grip on Quinn's bag, so Quinn had shrugged it off his shoulder, muttering that its contents had been the last of his possessions. Watching him sleep now, Kade was struck by how it might feel to lose everything himself.

"Wake him up."

"Yeah, on it," Kade said. He knelt down and shook Quinn by the shoulder. "Hey, you look all peaceful and all, but it's time to wake up."

Quinn mumbled.

"I said it's time to wake up. We need to strap in. I don't think Penelope knows how to land a plane."

"You what?"

"He's right," Penelope said from the front. "I was never so good at that part in the simulations."

Quinn was alert now. "What?! What are you gonna do?"

"Just find a seat and buckle up," Penelope said.

Kade rejoined Penelope in the cramped cockpit, certain there was no one he trusted more in the world.

Penelope was certain she was about to kill her friends. She was certain they'd come all this way for nothing. They'd escaped terrorists for nothing. They'd escaped segregationists for nothing. They'd escaped the U.S. Army in a World War II–era plane just so they could die. She knew they would die because she had never been able to land a plane in *Flight Simulator*. She made a mistake every time. She, Penelope Papadopoulos (or was it Hauser?) was good at so many things, but landing airplanes was right down there with empathy, emotional expression, and self-reflection. One time when playing flight simulator in VR she'd brought the stick down too hard and nose-dived straight into the ground. Another time she'd forgotten to deploy the landing gear. And, well, after that, she had just stopped playing that part of the game.

Another problem was that, even if she could land this ancient thing, where the actual fuck was she supposed to put it? She couldn't use the airport. Just imagine: two teenagers and one young adult coming in for an unauthorized landing at SFO. No way they wouldn't be detained, and no way that wouldn't end up all over the news.

Not to mention there was no way Penelope would be able to find SFO if she had wanted to. Because what she hadn't told Kade and Quinn was she'd had no idea where the fuck they were for most of this flight. The plane didn't exactly have a state-of-the-art GPS. She'd pointed them vaguely northwest and just kept flying until she saw what looked like a city by a bay. Once she saw it, in the distance, she banked right and pointed the plane more directly north, hoping she'd spot a surface, somewhere, on which maybe she could put down a plane.

"I thought you said we were landing," Kade said from the copilot seat next to her.

"We are."

"Yeah, well, when? It's been like twenty minutes."

"We're going to land, okay? Just shut up."

"I don't like this," Kade said.

"I said shut up."

From the back of the plane, Quinn started to say, "Is there anything we can do to—"

Penelope knew she was going to have to commit. She began to decrease their elevation. "Just. Shut. Up."

About ten minutes ago, Penelope had identified a flaw in her plan: It was the middle of the fucking night. She couldn't see the ground at all.

She *could* see lights. Some of them were moving, in rows, so she assumed she was above a highway. Based on what she could remember of the maps she'd been looking at yesterday, that would be Interstate 5. On either side of the moving lights were scattered patches of stationary lights. Some of the patches were more densely packed than others. These, she surmised, were towns or small cities—or parts of a single small city. Maybe Redding, not that it mattered just yet. What she needed was a very large area that didn't have any lights. And then she needed to hope—hell, maybe she should even pray—that that area was a golf course or a farm or a vineyard . . . a nice empty vineyard without any vines in it.

There. *There* was a nice big dark area a handful of miles away. It would have to do. They'd either land or they'd die, but they couldn't stay in the air forever. "Strap in," she ordered.

"We are," Kade said. "We've been strapped in for like half an hour."

"Then shut back up," Penelope said. "And hold on."

She brought the plane down at a nice easy incline. But she knew was forgetting something . . . she knew she was forgetting something . . . .

Fuck—the landing gear.

Early in the flight she'd made note of where the landing gear controls were, but now that knowledge abandoned her. Which button was it? Or was it a switch . . . ? Wait—this one. With a whir and clunk, the landing gear locked into place beneath the fuselage. Although the whir sounded a little strained—

"That sounded a little—" Kade began.

"I said shut up!" It was fine. The landing gear was fine. This plane was just fucking old.

Although maybe she had deployed the gear a little early, because the plane began to sway from side to side. The words *drag* and *downwind* flashed through Penelope's mind, but fuck if she could remember what they meant in this context. Also something about an a-beam—or was it *abeam*—and *touchdown point*.

Whatever. She would just hold it as steady as she could.

Not that the landing gear mattered, she realized way too suddenly.

"Hey, guys?"

"I thought you wanted us to shut up."

"I do—shut up. But first—get ready to swim."

"*Swim?*" Quinn said.

"I swear, I thought I was aiming for a golf course."

Kade said, "And what you did aim for was . . . ?"

Penelope might have shrugged, but she was gripping the aircraft's yoke too tightly. "A lake maybe?"

"Maybe?"

"Or a large pond?"

"Okay. Swim. We're gonna swim," Quinn said.

"I can swim," Kade said—but Penelope already knew that.

"Wait—" Kade said. "*You* can't sw—"

His words were interrupted by the wet, loud jolt of the Antonov An-2 striking water. The landing gear cut through the surface, pulling the aircraft down. Without the landing gear the landing might have been as gentle as a skipping a rock—who knows?

"Open the door!" Kade shouted. "Open the door now!" He thought they had only seconds before the plane began to sink and the pressure of the water outside would make opening the door impossible.

"I got it!" Quinn said. His words were followed by a mechanical hiss as the door slid open and air from inside the cabin escaped out to the world.

"Good—now get out of here."

"What about Penelope?"

"I'll get her. Just swim."

"What about some sort of floatation device? There has to be some sort of floatation device, right? The seat cushions? Isn't that where they keep them? I've never been on a plane before."

"We all grew up in fucking Montana. None of us have been on a plane before. But now that the door is open we're going to sink a fuck of a lot faster, so swim!"

Kade heard a splash. He turned his attention to Penelope. Oh fuck oh fuck oh fuck. She'd hit her head. She wasn't bleeding, but on her forehead a visible lump was growing. The cabin lights were flickering. She wasn't completely unconscious, though. She was making incoherent sounds that might have been attempts at words. But whether she was conscious or not, Kade knew, didn't matter; Penny couldn't swim. Penny was afraid of water.

Kade fumbled with her seat belt. It wasn't stuck or jammed—it was just that his hands were shaking. Terror or cold—he wasn't sure. His arm still throbbed. The plane was sinking aft-first. The tilt of the cabin was disorienting. Kade risked a glance backward and saw the door was a third underwater. The water was creeping along the floor toward the cockpit. He could never tell Penny he loved her if they drowned to death. He found the clasp that held her seatbelt in place, pulled at the frigid metal, took no time to feel relief as it released. Kade was just a little guy. Penelope was small too but Kade wasn't strong. Sure he could execute a seoi nage or an osotogari, but those throws were a matter of using your opponent's active weight against them. Penelope's body was slack, and the angle here was awkward.

"Penny—come on, Penny. I'm gonna need your help here," Kade tried to get a hand under each of her arms, which was difficult leaning over her from the side like he was. His own arm—his own arm's throbbing was excruciating once again.

"Mmmhmm-nggh," Penelope groaned.

Kade felt water seeping into his shoes, touching his toes. His feet. Quickly his ankles. The water was fucking cold. Of course it was. It was the middle of the night in early spring—and they weren't even in *Southern* California. The plane continued to verticalize. Another stolen glance showed the door more than half submerged. Still Kade couldn't get an adequate grip on Penelope's body. She was still too heavy. He was still too weak. His arm hurt so much it was nearly useless. It was bleeding again. If they survived this (which he was sure they wouldn't), he would take up weightlifting, he vowed. He'd always rejected it because it made him think of his father, the violent meathead, and the words his father shouted at him, but Kade would give anything to be like his father right now if it meant he could save his best friend. He would take up weightlifting, and he would learn to shoot a gun. He would never touch a cigarette again. He would dedicate the rest of his life to becoming in-fucking-vincible.

As the ice-cold water reached his knees, Kade realized he had a chance. He might be a puny, bleeding little shit, but his strength or lack thereof would matter far less under water. "Penny," he said. "If you can hear me, it would be really helpful if you could wake up now."

She didn't even groan this time. Kade grabbed on to her seat's armrest as he lost his footing to the increasing tilt of the plane. Then the water reached Penelope. Her eyes flashed open. "Fuck!" she said. "It's fucking cold. What happened?"

"Oh thank God," Kade said, unsure which god he was thanking.

Penelope looked around her. "I can't swim. I can't swim."

"I know, I know. But this will be so much easier if you can at least hold your breath."

"Am I bleeding? There's blood. This water is fucking cold." She tried to stand from her seat, but the plane was nearly vertical now.

Kade was no longer standing; he was swimming. "Hold on to me," he said. "And hold your breath."

As she was lifted from her seat by the water, Penelope put her arms around Kade's neck. Kade took a deep breath of his own from the small air pocket that was the cockpit, and then he dove under the water, pulling Penelope with him.

It was dark under the water, and Kade's body was already going numb. But a few feet away a dull glow called to him. Praying again to an unknown god that it was the doorway, he tugged Penelope toward it. It *was* the doorway. His clothes or her clothes caught on something. He tugged. They were out of the plane. That actually hadn't been very hard at all. Except now Kade wasn't sure which way was up, and he was such a little guy with such small lungs.

He swam, with one arm. The arm he'd been shot in. It pushed against the water. It hurt. Its small muscles protested. He pulled Penelope with the other. When after some time they didn't surface, he knew they must have been going in the wrong direction.

Then he paused. Did it even matter, down or up? Look around. Everything was so peaceful here, beneath the water. So dark, so green. It didn't matter that he'd been shot. The water washed away the blood. And were those bubbles? They were! They were coming from his mouth, or Penny's mouth. Kade turned around in the water, facing her. She was beautiful, her face so close to his, her hair suspended all around it, her eyes closed tight against the water. He'd heard drowning was painful, but this didn't seem such a terrible way to die.

Then he saw, barely, the shadow of the plane behind her. The shadow was moving down, down, down. And if it was moving down, then the opposite of down would be up. Kade put his arms around Penelope and began to kick his legs. The plane's sinking pulled at the water all around them. It tried desperately to take them with it. But Kade had seen that episode of *MythBusters*. He knew that wasn't how the physics worked. He kicked and kicked with every last tittle of strength he had.

2

Shivering violently Penelope scooted closer to Kade. Around his shoulders she did her best to pull more of the blanket they shared, but it was hardly large enough for two. He was shivering worse than she was, but neither were in danger of hypothermia anymore (if they had been in the first place; it wasn't like any of them were experts).

"You okay?" she asked, the words coming out soft and mushy through her chattering teeth.

"Getting there," Kade said. "Are you sure he's sleeping? He's not dead?"

Penelope listened for Quinn's breathing. As the tallest and broadest of the three weary travelers, he had a blanket to himself. He sat on her left, body slouching against hers but not huddled against or wrapped around her the way hers was with Kade. "He's fine. Definitely asleep."

"I don't know how. It's like he can sleep anywhere."

"He's tired."

"I'm tired."

"Me too. But I think he's more tired than either of us have ever been in our entire lives."

Their water landing, it turned out, had happened in Redding, California, on Kutras Lake, which was a pitstop along the Sacramento River. Kade had breached the surface, Penelope in his arms, to the sound of Quinn shouting their names. Kade had called back, alerting him to their location, and together the two young men had swam Penelope to shore—which, mercifully, had been only two hundred or so feet away.

Penelope had coughed and coughed and held her wet sleeve to her still painful forehead. Kade and Quinn had caught their breaths. Then the three of them had started walking. Dazed, they'd had no destination in mind, but a primal imperative compelled them to get away from the water. Only minutes later, they'd spotted a Walgreens, its marquee telling them the time was 2:53 a.m., the temperature fifty-seven degrees. All three agreed it felt much colder. Kade suggested they buy warm drinks and dry clothes. Penelope replied that her cash and hard wallet had been in her backpack—and everything in her backpack had gone to the same watery grave as the plane. Kade replied that, yeah, his backpack had gone down, too. That's when Quinn had fallen to his knees and begun to sob. Take care of him, Penelope had said, I'm going to go figure something out.

So Kade had sat with a shivering, slobbering Quinn on a concrete bumper in a Walgreens parking lot in Redding, California, for ten minutes, fifteen minutes, twenty minutes. Quinn sobbing What the fuck is wrong with you people? How is any of this happening? Kade patting his shoulder, saying, I don't know, man, I don't know.

Now they rode in the bed of a shiny new pickup. There was room in the cabin for all three of them—it was one of those trucks with a back seat—but the owner (hard to call him the driver when the truck was driving itself) had seen Quinn and said he didn't want one of those people sitting inside his truck. Penelope had almost said fuck you to the guy, they'd find someone else to help, but she'd already given the motherfucker a handjob (her decision, *her decision!*) behind the charging station where she'd found him, and she was exhausted, just too exhausted to figure out something else.

"Hey, Penny," Kade said.

"Yeah, Kade?"

"What are we doing?"

"What do you mean?"

"Why are we doing . . . all this?"

"I don't really know anymore."

"Why did we do it in the first place? Because some ghost of your father told you too?"

"Guess so."

"I barely even remember it. I know it was only like a day and a half ago, but it doesn't even feel real anymore, you know? At the school. That thing talking to us."

"It still feels real to me."

"That's just because you have a photographic memory."

"No I don't."

"You don't? It's always seemed like you did."

"No. A photographic memory is a very specific phenomena. A lot of neuroscientists question whether it even exists."

"Well, your memory is still really good."

"Yeah. My memory is still really good."

"What if—what if he isn't your father?"

"You're the one who always wanted me to admit that he was."

"Yeah, but what if he isn't? Then we could just go home. Or what if that hologram was, I don't know, a joke? A prank. Like the ones we pull on Mr. Gershwin."

"I don't think it was a prank, Kade."

"Okay, but maybe, right? Like maybe Peter Simpson and Kyle Porter are just playing a prank on us."

"Maybe."

"But they're not, are they? They're too stupid."

"Yeah. They are. They're stupid fuckers."

"Yeah—stupid fuckers."

A pause. The truck drove itself on through the night. Then Kade said, "Abby, though. Abby could pull off a prank like this."

"She could," Penelope agreed. Then she jerked her head toward Quinn. "But how do you explain this guy? And those people who blew up his truck back in Helena? And that whole thing with Avon?"

"And Hector Alexander Jones getting his head chopped off?"

"Yeah—and that."

"Fuck—I forgot about all that."

Another pause. A long one. Not even the sound of an engine. Only the hum of the nighttime air rushing by. Kade had stopped shivering. Penelope thought he might have fallen asleep.

"Hey, Penny."

"Yeah, Kade?"

"I just wanted to tell you . . . I love you, Penny."

"Hey—I love you too, Kade."

"And, in case we, you know, die, I just wanted you to know that—"

"Why would we die?"

"We've almost died like a billion times."

"No we haven't."

"At least three times."

"Well—yeah, okay."

"And, so, in case we die—I just want to be clear—I really love you. Like I think I'm in love with you."

"Oh Kade."

"You don't feel the same way."

"I love you, Kade, but not like that."

"It's Quinn, isn't it? You love Quinn."

Quinn mumbled at the sound of his name. A subconscious reaction. He was still asleep.

"Ha—*no*. He's, like, way too old."

"He's only like twenty."

"Just, no, Kade. Listen—I don't think I'm capable of feeling that way about *anybody*."

"You're gay, aren't you?"

A shrug. "Maybe. Doubt it. But maybe. Probably I'm pansexual. Or asexual. Or aromantic. That's a thing, right? Probably I'm a-everything. Or just everything, a- or not. But no matter what I am, I don't think I'm capable of feeling . . . that. I'm just, you know, whatever."

Kade closed his eyes. "You're a pretty special whatever."

"You're a pretty special whatever, too."

Kade opened his eyes. "Hey, remember that time we stole Mr. Gershwin's ceramic pig collection?"

"Haha. Yeah."

"Are we bad people? Like, should we not have stolen it? I mean, stealing is wrong, right?"

"He's a grown-ass man with a ceramic pig collection. Plus we put them all back."

"With mustaches drawn on all the pigs."

"Haha. I forgot about the mustaches. That was good. And it took him days to realize that they were just dry erase marker and he could wipe them all off. Haha."

"So those pranks don't make us bad people?"

"We might be bad people, but it's not because of the pranks."

"Okay, good. Because I was thinking when we get back to Helena, when this is all over—you know, if we don't die—"

"We won't die."

"We might die."

"Okay, yeah, we might die."

"But if we don't die, and we get back, I was thinking we should—well, you know that Rubik's cube Mr. Gershwin keeps on his desk, that he's always jerking around with when he's nervous?"

"Of course."

"So we should buy another Rubik's cube, and we should take some stickers from it. Like, I don't know, like a couple of the red stickers, and we should replace like one yellow sticker and one blue sticker on Mr. Gershwin's Rubik's cube with the extra red stickers."

"That's brilliant."

"Then he'd try to solve the Rubik's cube and he'd be like, 'What the fuck is going on here?'"

"Brilliant."

"So you think we should do it?"

"I do. It's a great prank idea."

"Oh good. I'm glad you like it."

"I love it."

A soft smile on Kade's boyish face. "Did it make you fall in love with me?"

"Haha. I'm afraid not."

"Damn."

"It's a brilliant idea, though. I can't wait to do it."

"Me either." Again his eyes closed.

Another silence. Penelope's hair was either freezing or drying. Her clothes were getting dryer, but those not covered by the blanket were so cold it hardly mattered. To her left, Quinn snorted, coughed, and then grew peaceful again.

"Hey, Penny?"

"Yes, Kade?"

"So you really think Eric Hauser was your father?"

"It sounds crazy, but I think I do."

"Told you so. You sure you don't have any more cigarettes?"

Penelope shook her head. "I wish I did. Tried to get the truck owner to give me one, but he said he doesn't smoke."

"Most people don't."

"Sure, but I saw a pack in his cup holder."

"Fucker."

"Yeah—guy's an ass."

"Hey, Penny?"

"Yeah, Kade?"

"I'm cold."

"I know. Come here." Penelope pulled Kade closer to her. She'd thought he was already as close as he could be, but one can always draw closer. She pulled his head into her chest, slid more of the blanket over his body, letting her left arm and shoulder expose themselves to the wind. She placed her head in his hair. She kissed his hair. She'd never kissed him before. She'd never held him before. Even a hug was rare. But one can always draw closer. "Hey, Kade—you know who I think might be in love with you, though?" she asked after a while.

When he didn't respond, she listened for his breath. She couldn't hear it over the rushing of the wind past her ears, but she could feel his small body gently moving—expanding, contracting. She was going to say Abby Brenner, with her square-framed glasses and her chickenpox scar she knew Kade thought were cute. Penelope didn't actually think Abbigail Brenner was in love with Kade, but she thought if Kade pursued her it could definitely happen. It didn't matter now.

The truck drove itself down Interstate 5. The highway banked slightly southeast for a couple miles before adjusting back to due south again, and during that time Penelope found herself confronted by the majestic presence of a near-full moon. Sometimes, when she left the house at night—without her mother's knowledge, of course— she would walk to the park and lay in the grass and stare up at that same moon. Sometimes Kade would meet her there; sometimes she would go to the park alone. She'd stare up at the moon and if Kade was there he'd say something like, "It still blows my mind that we put people on that thing. Up there." And Penelope would say something like, "It's just physics."

She'd seen an interview with Eric Hauser once—with her father— talking with this unconvincing recreation of Larry King (who Penelope admittedly knew little about, so maybe it was convincing and the real guy had just been like that). Fake-King had asked Eric Hauser, her father, "Where do you want to die?"

Eric Hauser had said, "What a question." And then he'd said, after a thoughtful pause, "I've always thought the lunar colony would be kind of nice. It would be nice to retire there, watch the Earth at night."

"Not Mars?" Fake-King had asked. "You don't think we'll get to Mars?"

"I think we'll get there. Probably not before I die. But even if we do —I'd rather leave this life a little closer to home than that."

"'This life.' So you think there's something more—after 'this life?'"

"I didn't mean to imply that."

He hadn't died at the lunar colony. But he'd died close to Penelope. And as she watched the moon move across the sky, she couldn't help but feel he was up there. Not *up there* up there, like not in heaven or whatever —but up there, somewhere, watching over her. It was more than just physics.

Penelope, too, fell asleep.

3

JUST UNDER TWO HOURS LATER the sun was coming up and the truck was approaching a peaceful San Francisco Bay. A ray of sunrise light broke through the spotty cloud cover above the Northwest Hills of Oakland, its substance acting as both a purpose-driven, slicing wave and a collection of entropic, scattered and argumentative particles. It hit a building across the bay, in the Finance District, maybe the Lumina building at 345 Spear Street, reflected off a two-by-three block of the building's suicide-proof windows, journeyed eight miles across the Bay back to Oakland, specifically Emeryville, bounced off the front of a Mercedes some asshole had had painted after market in chrome, and alit upon the eyelids of a sleeping Penelope Papadopoulos. What light penetrated her eyelids hit her retinas, stimulating her eyes' conal cells, and was rendered by her visual cortex the color of a Cara Cara orange.

Reflexively, Penelope brought a hand up to her face. Her eyes squinted against the waves or particles or whatever they were and then the chrome monstrosity changed lanes, and Penelope was able to open her eyes fully, now that they were no longer under assault. It took her a few seconds to regain full consciousness, but once she'd blinked a few more times she leaned forward and looked to her left, then to her right. Then she sat up on her haunches taller than was advisable in a moving vehicle and turned her body, looking over the top of the pickup's cabin and seeing the entrance ramp of the Bay Bridge. She couldn't help but smile.

"Hey, guys," she said, nudging each of her companions. "We're almost there."

"Ngggh," was the sound Quinn made, stirring. "Almost where?" Then he said, "Oh yeah—right." He looked around as Penelope had done. "Finally," he said. "Now what?"

"Hey, Kade," Penelope said, nudging her best friend again. "Wake up. We're almost there. We're crossing the Bay."

Kade had always been a hard sleeper, and the last couple days had certainly taken a toll. Penelope briefly considered letting him sleep a few minutes longer, but she thought he'd want to see the bay, the sunrise. A stunning fog was rolling in. "Kade, wake up. It's beautiful."

"It really is beautiful," said Quinn. "The sunrise isn't quite like this in Montana."

"Yeah . . ." Penelope said. "Kade?"

"Is he okay?"

"I don't— Kade?" She nudged her friend again. She shook him. "Kade, come on. Wake up."

"He looks kind of blue."

"No, he doesn't. He's fine. Kade, wake the fuck up."

"Penelope—"

"No! I said he's fine, okay? Kade, this isn't funny!" Fist closed, Penelope hit Kade's body's chest with the full force of the anger she suddenly felt toward him. His body's head fell forward. "Oh, god," she said.

"Here—move. Let me . . ."

Penelope scooted out of the way and Quinn crossed over her. He tapped Kade's body's cheek with his open palm. He lifted Kade's body's arms—first one and then the other. Quinn lowered his ear to Kade's body's chest and listened to Kade's body's heart. He raised two fingers to Kades body's neck. He shook his own head. "He's ice cold."

"No—" Penelope said. "No—I gave him almost the entire blanket. All night he had the blanket. He's fine. He should be fine. . . ." She pushed Quinn out of the way and placed a hand on Kade's chest. "You're fine," she said. "Wake up."

He was so small. He was smaller than she'd ever seen him.

"I'm so sorry," Quinn said.

This couldn't be. This was a mistake. It hadn't been that cold last night. The water in the lake hadn't been that cold. Kade had had a blanket, the blanket. She'd given him almost the whole blanket. She'd been the one exposed to the air. Her clothes were still wet, too. As wet as his. Her hair was still wet—and she had so much more hair than him. Kade was a survivor. Kade cracked jokes and listened to terrible old music and did whatever Penelope asked of him and didn't even mind when she called him names or called him an idiot or told him he was being an idiot or told him what to do. Kade was gentle and kind and small and good and Penelope was going to do everything she could to set him up with Abigail Brenner and thought they could have babies some day, Kade and Abigail, even though the thought of anyone having babies, especially Kade, made Penelope want to throw up. Kade was important and special and . . . and he had a sister . . . and a mother . . . and his father was an abusive asshole but he had a father. . . . Kade was fine. She told herself that he was fine. Look at him: he was asleep. He was just exhausted from the bat-shit insane night they'd had. He'd probably hardly slept the night before that one, was all, just like she hardly had. His lips weren't *so* blue. They were barely blue at all. His skin was only cold because his clothes were wet. Her clothes were still wet too—so what? Sometimes it was good to be cold. Ice baths and shit like that. Cold plunges. People did it all the time. Jumping in lakes and rivers in the middle of winter. Sometimes even naked. This couldn't be right. This was a mistake.

This was all her fault. This was all Penelope's fault. What had she been thinking?! A teenage girl flying a fucking airplane. Thinking she could fly a fucking airplane just because she'd played a video game a few times? Life wasn't a video game. The dark patch had been a golf course— or a vineyard—she could have *sworn*. She'd even lowered the landing gear. She'd had full attitude control. If it had been a golf course the plane would have rolled gently across the solid ground, come to a complete and perfect stop. It *had* been a golf course. Or . . . or a vineyard. Or a . . . or a fucking parking lot or something. Come on. It hadn't been a lake. Why did it have to be a lake? Or maybe if it had been solid ground they would have just hit it head on and exploded and Kade would be dead in *pieces*.

Who's to say she *had* deployed the landing gear, after all? She'd never done it right before, in the video game. Why would she have done it right in real life? Burning cold or burning fire—it didn't matter. This was all her fault.

She must have been talking, not knowing she was talking, because Quinn was saying, "It's not. It's not your fault. Hey, it's not your fault, okay? I'm so sorry." Quinn was hugging her but she could barely feel him. His clothes were still wet too, but not so wet as hers.

"Hey! What the fuck is going on back there?" shouted the owner of the pickup truck, leaning out his window.

"Nothing!" Quinn replied, shouting to be heard over the rush of air moving by. "We're fine."

"Well cover yourselves up with the blankets. The toll booth has cameras, and I ain't getting in trouble for your sake. And when we get across I'm droppin' you off in the first parking lot I can and that's it."

"Got it," Quinn said. Then, to Penelope: "Come on. Lay down. Let's get you under a blanket." Then he seemed to realize the logistics of the situation. "This is going to be— Damn it. I'm sorry. You've got to move to closer to him."

For a second, Penelope didn't know what he was talking about, but then she realized. It was obvious what he meant. She pushed herself against her best friend's body—this wasn't her best friend anymore; it couldn't be; it could only be his body—and Quinn tucked the blanket around them.

Penelope had never know this feeling she was feeling: heartrending grief. So the neurological pathways in her brain interpreted the signals as the next closest emotion: anger. Just as it had with Priam—mere hours ago. Anger she knew. She'd spent most of her life angry. Angry at her mother, Priscilla, for being such a bitch but also taking such good care of her; angry at Eric Hauser for not being her father; angry at her father Eric Hauser for not being in her life; angry at Eric Hauser who may or may not have been her father for dying mysteriously so close to where she lived; angry at Eric Hauser her father for confirming he was her father and being already dead; angry at Quinn for tracking her down with that stupid little memory card; angry at her mysterious sister for being a thing Penelope couldn't help but feel she had some sort of obligation to; angry at herself for being no more than she was. So why not angry at Kade now for dying, for being such a beautiful little human being who just had to get shot and who couldn't take the cold? Why not angry at herself for killing him?

Penelope didn't care much about words, but whenever she'd learn a word's common usage was technically incorrect, her brain couldn't help but file it as a pet peeve. *Heart-wrenching* was one such word. *Heart-wrenching* was no such thing. She'd heard it used over and over again. She'd heard her seventh-grade English teacher use it to refer to whatever dumb book they'd been reading that quarter—*Gatsby* or *The Scarlett Letter* or whatever the fuck—and her mother said it all the time: *heart-wrenching*. That film was *heart-wrenching*. What did that even mean? Grief didn't *wrench* your heart. It didn't even twist it, to use a generous explanation for the improper term. Grief, Penelope could confirm now, took your heart and ripped it violently from your chest. *Rended* it, you see? Even when you'd your whole life been certain you didn't have a heart, it turned out you did, one ripe for rending.

"Fuck you for dying," Penelope whispered to the icy body beside her.

Worth noting: she didn't cry. The sight of Priam's little lifeless figure had drained her of her tears. She would not cry twice in two days; she would not.

Her stomach lurched as, she assumed, the truck turned down the winding exit ramp. Probably safe now to remove the blanket, but she didn't want to leave this place. Then the truck came to a stop, and its owner said, "Okay—here. This is as far as I'm taking you. Get out."

"Come on, Penelope," Quinn said. She felt his hand on her shoulder. "We have to go."

"Where?" she asked. "Where are we going to go?"

"We'll figure that out. Come on."

Penelope forced her body to sit up, then to stand. Her bones and muscles no longer felt like those of a teenager. She didn't know what the body of an adult felt like, but she thought it might be this. In slow motion, she vaulted the edge of the truck bed, landed on solid ground. Quinn followed her.

"What's with him?" the owner of the truck asked after Quinn picked up Kade's body from the back of the truck.

"He's asleep," Quinn said. "He's very tired."

"Well that's my blanket."

"Yeah, not anymore."

"You can't just take my—"

"I said *not anymore*."

The owner hurled an epithet. The truck sped away.

"The Lumina building?" Quinn asked, Kade's body cradled in his arms.

"I don't know," Penelope said. She wanted to sit down, right there in the middle of wherever they were, but she knew if she did she might not stand again. So she looked around.

They were in an abandoned parking lot. The asphalt was cracked. The cracks were branching. Tectonic plates. The product of the earth's shifting, of the region's many small earthquakes, foreshadowing the impending Big One, or testifying simply to the passing of time, maybe the slipshod laying of the asphalt in the first place—who knew? Many of the cracks had been cracked for a long time, and from them stretched grateful weeds and grasses. A concrete parking bumper, just one, split in half, as if with a sledgehammer. Used condoms and their wrappers. Dirty needles. A diaper. Some sort of battery pack. Another, larger diaper. To Penelope's left: the road, the onramp to highway, the bridge. In front of her, a multicolored village of tents and tarpaulins. Shopping carts. Mattresses leaning against crates and other mattresses. A couple metal barrels crackling with fire. The fires being tended by early risers. In the land beyond this little village: high-rises. To her right, a brick wall, three times her height, seemingly the exterior of a building, but from this vantage hard to be sure; possibly it was only what it appeared to be, just a wall, graffitied and dirty, nothing more, but large, as if saying, *There is nothing beyond me*. And in the remaining direction, a few more tents and tarps, scattered, isolated from from the main commune, underneath the bridge, some ways beyond it a small park, then some buildings, restaurants.

Instinct told Penelope they needed to head for the high-rises. That was where her father's office was, and hence maybe it was where they'd find his workshop. What they'd do when they got there, without Hector Alexander Jones, who may have been their ally had he still had a head, she didn't know. But logic told her they could not yet proceed.

"We need a device," she said to Quinn. "We need information."

"Where—"

She was already walking toward the encampment. Toward two women who leaned over one of the fire barrels. Both wore heavy coats—newer-looking than one would expect, cleaner—and knit caps. One was warming her hands, while the other roasted three sketchy sausages. "Excuse me," Penelope called as she got close.

Both women looked up at her. The one warming her hands pulled her hands away, stepped back a foot or two. Her companion returned her attention to her breakfast. "We don't have any drugs," she said.

"I'm not looking for drugs."

"I don't do drugs, never have, 'cept pot and heroine, but only in the summer. It's not summer yet, so I don't have any."

"No—that's okay. I'm not looking for drugs right now."

"Judy might know where to get some though. Hey, Judy, where's that guy you bought coke from the other night?"

"I— I— I—" was all Judy could say.

"No, no—really," Penelope said, slowly holding up her hands. "I'm not looking for drugs. I don't need any drugs today."

"You—you—you—here to h—hurt us?" Judy asked.

Penelope shook her head. "I'm not. I promise."

Judy appraised her. Then she said, "Okay," and began warming her hands over the fire again.

"We're—" Penelope said. "That is—my friend—friends—and I—we need a HoloWatch, or a tablet. Just to borrow for a few minutes. But we don't have any money. Well—we don't really have anything at all. Just need to get online. Do you know where we can find one?"

"Ain't no one got no smart watches here," the first woman said.

Judy shook her rapidly. "No watches. No watches."

"'Cept Johnny F. He got a Rolex somehow ain't nobody stoled yet. Says it was his great grandfather's, who was a veteran. Somehow everyone buys that, respects it. Ain't nobody gonna take no vet's Rolex, even if you could sell it for a couple thousand bucks, which you could."

Penelope hadn't necessarily expected anyone at the camp to have the most recent HoloWatch, but it wasn't unusual for a houseless person to have some sort of device with a data plan. Many shelters and food banks required them, in fact, to make sure those they served were vaccinated and to record whether they'd already received their daily meal. But just as many of the country's houseless shunned technology for the very reason that they didn't want the government keeping tabs.

"I don't want anyone's Rolex," Penelope said. "It doesn't even have to be a watch. Just need something to get online, for a few minutes."

"Personally," the woman said in a conspiratorial whisper, "I think it's bullshit, story about his grandfather. I think he mugged a guy and took it from him. Just doesn't want to sell it himself 'cuz it makes him feel fancy and important, having a fancy watch. Don't mean I'm gonna take it from him, though. I like Johnny F. And I don't do no mugging of nobody." She looked around the camp and lowered her voice further. "You see Johnny F., though, you don't tell him I think that, about the watch. He gets all jumpy when people don't believe. 'S partly why I don't believe him. Ha! Hahaha!"

Penelope wasn't sure how to engage further. She glanced back at Quinn for help, but when she saw the bundle in his arms, she turned away. She wouldn't be able to hold herself together if she wasn't careful. She almost walked away.

But then Judy shouted, "Mo! Mo, Mo, Mo!"

"Fuck you on about, Judy?" the other woman asked.

Judy grabbed her by the arm. "Mo has a phone. Mo has a phone."

"Let go a me or I'm'a stab you in the neck with this sausage stick."

"Hey, calm down," Penelope said. "I didn't mean to excite anybody."

"No, it's fine. Judy's right. Mo has an old cell phone. Can't say for him he'll let you use it, but he's a nice guy, so maybe. Let's ask. Judy, here, keep roasting these dogs. And *don't* fuckin' burn them. Come on—follow me."

Penelope followed the woman. She could hear Quinn behind her. As they walked through the camp, various sounds emanated from some of the tents and tarp structures: coughs, moans, snores, crying, a masturbatory slapping. Cautious heads emerged from a few of them. Penelope felt uncomfortable. Helena had a small but present houseless and transient population, and she'd see them from time to time, in the park, outside the abandoned mall where she and Kade (too hard to think of Kade) would smoke sometimes, but she'd always kept her distance. The fact of the matter was that Penelope lived in the mansion district. She could avoid what and whom she wanted to. She'd never been forced to confront the reality of their existence. But now she had to.

"What's your name?" Penelope asked, but the woman didn't answer. Instead she stopped at a pristine blue-and-orange tent, outside which a man in gray cargo pants and a faded black sweatshirt knelt on an embroidered rug, facing the sun. "Shhh. He's praying. Give him a minute."

The man sat up. "It's fine, Vicki. I was almost done, and if you kept standing there it would just be awkward. Oh, hello, good morning."

The man's face was dark tan and leathery, deeply wrinkled but also taut against the features of his face. His eyes were warm, potentially kind. His voice was gentle. His neck-long beard and shoulder-length hair were the gray of fresh ash. He smiled.

"Mo," Vicki snapped. "These kids wanna use your phone. They swear they don't want drugs. I don't believe them. I gotta go now. Judy's gonna burn my sausages—I just know it. Judy can't do anything right, not since the accident what knocked her in the head." She started to walk away, but then, almost as an afterthought, she paused, turned back, and nodded. "Nice meeting you."

"You too," Quinn replied. "Uh–thanks."

The man stood, dusted off his pants, extended a hand. "I'm Mohar. Everyone calls me Mo, always have. Or have for all the time that matters, anyway."

Penelope hesitated to give her name, but then realized it didn't matter, although she failed to take his outstretched hand. "I'm Penelope. This is Quinn."

"Such a pleasure," Mo said. "You need a phone?"

"Or a tablet. Or something like that. Some sort of device, connected to the Internet. Just for a minute."

"How come two kids don't have their own computers? Where are your fancy watches?"

"It's a long story," Penelope said. "We lost them. We lost a lot of things."

"And your other friend there? In the blanket?"

"He's asleep," Penelope said.

A soft frown graced Mo's guru-like face. "No," he said. "He's not, is he?"

"He—" Penelope started.

Quinn stepped toward the man. "No, he's not."

"Quinn."

"What are we supposed to do? This whole situation is . . . well, it's fucked, okay? And I can't just carry him around forever. We have to do something. Or we have to give up and go home. And even then, how are we supposed to get him there?"

"May I see him?" Mo asked kindly.

"Penelope?"

"Yes," she said. "It's okay, I guess." Quinn was right. Even if she could figure out their next steps with regard to finding the sister her father's half-functional ghost had insisted she had, they couldn't carry a body (*Kade's* body—she forced herself to think) around San Francisco. They needed to figure out what to do with him first. (*Figure out what to do with him* . . . . The thought felt calloused. Detached. How Penelope responded to most things—but not how she *wanted* to respond now, even if there was no other useful way.)

Mo stepped forward. He pulled back the blanket, revealing Kade's body's blueish face. "Almost a child," he said. Then he whispered words Penelope didn't understand, touched the body's head, as if he'd done this before. "He is restless. He must be guided toward peace. If you leave him with me, I will make sure his is properly buried."

"Why would you want to do that?" Penelope said.

"Look around. I have nothing else to do."

Penelope looked at Quinn, who shrugged pensively. "What other choice do we have?"

Penelope looked back at Mo. She nodded.

Mo nodded in response, and then he nodded at Quinn. Gently, he took the body from Quinn's arms. Holding the body was clearly not as easy for him as it was for Quinn, but he carried it with respect and dignity. "I'll be right back," he said.

But before he could take Kade's body into his tent, Penelope said, "Wait."

Mo turned.

"He has a mom, and a sister. What am I going to tell them?"

"He has no father?"

"His dad's an asshole."

Mo nodded knowingly. "Most fathers are. And I'm afraid I do not know what you are going to tell them." He disappeared into the tent.

Quinn put a hand on Penelope's shoulder. She hadn't said goodbye, she realized. But she knew there was nothing to say goodbye to. Goodbyes to the dead fell on useless ears. She thought back to her and Kade's conversation in the truck—just hours ago (everything, her whole life, felt like it could be defined in terms of *just hours ago*). Maybe she *had* said goodbye.

She needed to move on. She knew she would move on. She just wondered whether that made her a monster.

Mo reemerged from the tent. "I promise I will take delicate care of your friend. Here."

Penelope took the phone from him. It was the old slab-of-glass-and-metal kind. The screen was powering up.

"I'm afraid the battery doesn't last so long," Mo said. "Although I did charge it fully last time I used it. You will have maybe ten minutes."

"Hopefully that's all I'll need."

"Why do you have this thing?" Quinn asked as Penelope set about searching.

"Jobs," Mo replied. "I don't use it often, but when I need money, I can find manual labor on Craigslist. Every week or so I check my email. I almost never have any, but I check."

"But why *this* thing, specifically? Why something so old? Why not a newer tablet, or a watch? They're not expensive."

"Expense is relative. Even the cheapest HoloWatch model costs hundreds. I can eat well for a month on that amount, and for that I need work only a few days."

"But why not an older model? Used?"

"I've never been one for advanced technology. When I came to this country, a cell phone cost thousands. Eventually, the price went down, and I got a small flip phone. I stayed with that kind of phone for years, even when I was very successful. I was always reluctant to upgrade. Too much we upgrade our technology. Too much we let the technology corporations tell us what we should buy, how we should use our time. It is a way of handing over our freedom. I've seen the damage such handing over can do. I upgrade only when I have to, and never to the newest thing, never to what some other man has decided my time should be spent on. My time is for me and for God."

"I understand. My G-Pops—my grandpa—was the same way—except for the God part."

"You can have this back," Penelope said. "Thanks." To Quinn she said, "Let's go."

"You have found what you were looking for?" Mo asked, taking his device from Penelope.

"Fuck, man. I have no idea what I'm looking for, but I have to go somewhere." She spared one last glance at the tent, inside which Kade's body lay. "I can't stand still forever."

4

"But seriously," Quinn said, after they'd left the houseless camp behind. "Where are we going?"

"Sea Cliff."

"What's in Sea Cliff? Why not go to the Lumina headquarters. Isn't it right there?"

"And do what once we get there? Tell the front desk that I'm Eric Hauser's daughter probably? That we're on some sort of vague mission assigned us by his ghost? We have no idea where his workshop is."

"Sure, but his office seems like a good start."

"We started days ago. I'm done starting. I just want this all to be fucking over. And if his workshop is at the office who's gonna let us into it? Anyway, Sea Cliff is where he lived. Or used to live. Before he disappeared. His workshop has just as good a chance of being at his house as at his office. So that's where we're going."

"And we're walking?"

"You have any money? Because all my fucking money is at the bottom of a fucking lake-river in fucking Redding."

"Fair point."

"Don't worry—it's only six miles."

Quinn decided that mentioning his twisted ankle, or the fact that he'd already carried Kade's body on it, would be insensitive. "And the directions—"

"I memorized them."

"Of course you did."

"It's mostly a straight shot. Any asshole could fucking memorize it."

Quinn couldn't, he thought but did not say. He had the impression that any argument would cause Penelope to hate him. He'd counted five "fucking"s in Penelope's last few spoken sentences. It wasn't like he'd been counting her every use of the word before now, but as someone who himself rarely, if ever, swore, instances of profanity had always jumped out at him, almost visually highlighted within their containing sentence. Penelope's use of profanity was without a doubt standing out to him even more now. In her increased usage he could identify profound grief, a struggle with her first true experience of intimate loss.

He could empathize.

She was feeling, he imagined, what he had felt when his mother had died: anger, hatred, a desire to burn the world down. He'd been furious at his mother for not leaving his father like G-Pops said he'd always asked her to; at Sheriff McGraff for knocking on the front door and telling G-Pops that thing he'd told him, that thing that had made G-Pops sob in a way that confused little Quinn so much until Sheriff McGraff had knelt down on one knee, the other propped outward at an obscene angle, put his hand on Quinn's shoulder, and stoically but gently delivered the same line to him, little Quinn; at G-Pops, who only months later did Quinn realize was, of course, himself grieving even as he devoted every hour that he possibly could to Quinn, sacrificing his time at the diner, for looking so much but not enough like his mother, for not knowing the songs his mother knew.

When G-Pops had been killed, there'd been no one left to be angry at. No one to despise for trying to take G-Pops' place. No sheriff to hate for breaking the bad news. Even the murderers he couldn't feel true hatred toward, just as he couldn't toward his father, who he'd blocked out all memory of, who out of guilt or sorrow or fear had killed his own damned self after beating Quinn's mother to death. Somehow Quinn had in the same way immediately blocked out the memory of G-Pops' killers, their faces indistinct in his recollection, even as they still were hunting him down. Probably this was a protective mechanism: for if Quinn could picture clearly those who did wrong in his world, he could feel rage toward them, and that sort of rage could overwhelm a person. Better to preemptively shut such feelings down.

Because while Quinn did empathize with Penelope's grief in the face of the loss of her friend, he did not *sympathize*. His body wouldn't let him. Not anymore.

Truth was, by the time he'd lifted Kade's body from the bed of the pickup, Quinn had been too depleted to feel more than the shallowest of sadnesses. He'd felt enough of everything in his life already. Now his reserves were finally, completely empty. He hadn't even enough left within them to *hope* they would someday be refilled. So if he had to walk, he would walk, without complaining, not even in his soul.

As he walked, limping only slightly, it occurred to him that there was a sort of irony in the fact that he was here, not so far from Stanford. He'd long been considering grad school at Stanford, after graduating from U of M, if he could settle on a major, which he'd been supposed to do this spring so he could return to school in the fall. All those possibilities seemed so far away now. Fragments of a different life, one that had definition and substance and future. Now that he was here, in this part of the country, he knew he never wanted to return. It was dirtier than he'd expected. Look: another adult diaper. And there: a free-floating pile of human shit. Three more hypodermic needles. A person, alive, maybe, or maybe dead, lying under a brown-stained blanket. They'd walked only a few hundred feet.

The world was way bigger than Quinn had realized. Too big, he was coming to understand.

5

A WEEK AGO STEFAN HAD called to let her know that Marvel was going to go with someone else. It wasn't personal, they'd told him; they just needed an actor who was, you know, available. Sophia said she understood the studio's decision.

"They say it's done," Stefan said, "the decision made. No more chances. But you know how these things are. Nothing's ever truly over. I can make a call to Kevin, convince him to change his mind. Or even Bobby, if Kevin wants to be stubborn about it. You know they like you over there. You just gotta say the word and I'll do it."

"I appreciate you, Stefan," Sophia replied. "But it's okay. Just let it go to someone else. Maybe they'll give it to Elena—she really wanted the role, and plus she's blonde and white, like the character. Nobody on Chattr is gonna have a problem with her."

Stefan had taken a deep breath. "Sophie, love, as your agent, it's my responsibility—personally and feduciarily, and I mean for my own bank account, too, not just yours—to push the matter one last time. Come on —it's a *Marvel* movie. You don't get a bigger money-maker than this. They want to pay you as much up front as your male co-stars *and* give you merchandising royalties. You could be an *action figure*. And it's *Disney*. It'd be like a, a whatayoucallit, like a coming full-circle kinda thing."

Sophia smiling sadly. "I'm just not ready to go back."

Stefan sighing. Nodding his head. "I understand. You're grieving. Go ahead—grieve. But, and this is coming from your friend here, and from someone who knows what grief feels like. You gotta get out of that house some time."

"I will. Soon, I promise. Speaking of—any news?"

Stefan shaking his head. "Nothing. He could be anywhere. They could have even taken him out of Iran by now. We—that is, the Americans—would have no way of knowing, so they tell me. I'm not sure I believe them. But I'm told there have been no demands."

"And you—?"

"Still a little shaken. Not so much as before. Worried. Terrified."

"How are you even working right now?"

"What else is there for me to do?"

Sophia had ended the call by telling Stefan she was thinking about him. She was hoping for the best. Even praying. When the HoloPad had blinked off, she'd found herself wondering why she didn't have Stefan's fortitude. Why she couldn't throw herself into her work the way he was capable of. During the separation, and after the divorce, that's exactly what she'd done. She'd finished filming that next Zorro movie, and then she'd gotten straight to work on that Netflix film about the immigrants, the one she was sure she'd finally win an Oscar for. And then she'd gone right into preparing for the Marvel role: reading the comics, watching all forty-seven movies leading up to the one that would introduce her character (crying when Tony Stark had died in *Endgame*, crying again when Robert Downy, Jr., had died in real life, realizing that the film she was going to star in was certainly going to be dedicated to him, and that the writers were going to have to redo the part of the script where he appeared via in-movie hologram, unless of course they decided to just recreate him via real-life hologram, which would be in poor taste and which she hoped they had better sense than to attempt), and working out six days a week, five hours a day—an hour of cardio, an hour of weight-lifting, and three hours of martial arts and stunt training. All throughout the process hardly thinking about Eric. Even when people started talking about the fact that he'd basically disappeared, she'd barely thought about him. He was no longer a part of her life. She needed to move on. That's what the separation—and the divorce—had been about, right? What was best for her. Time to grow up, Sophia—stop clinging. Stop defining your life by your connections to other people. She hadn't been worried when they'd started saying he had disappeared. What else was new, right? He was fine, she was sure. He could take care of himself. He'd always made sure she knew that. He was always in control. And all that time, during the filming and training and reading and watching, the Sea Cliff house had been sitting there, four hundred miles north, an hour away via hyperloop, unfinished business, an uncut string. "*Realmente, deberías decidir que vas a hacer con la,*" her mother kept telling her. "You really should sell it," her lawyer kept saying, adding every time, "I can hook you up with a good real estate agent. My finder's commission wouldn't be so big." Her mother: "*Supéralo, mija.* Sell the house. Find a new man." Her lawyer: "It could fetch a handsome price, Eric Hauser's house." Stefan, her agent: "No, I'm afraid Hector hasn't heard from Eric, either. But if he wanted you to have it, you should do whatever you want with it. It's your house now." And all that time Sophia had thought, I *will* do what I want with it, when *I* want to. That's the point of it all, right?

Then she'd read the news one morning, a brick shoved into her chest. Eric Hauser. Dead. In Montana of all places. A drug overdose? Alcohol poisoning? Suicide? But she knew it could be none of these things. Eric had always been in control, even of his excesses. And suicide? Of course not.

Unless . . . she realized suddenly . . . unless he *had* . . . . But then, no, they'd confirmed it, the coroners and the journalists: a heart defect. Something he'd told her had been fixed when he was an infant. A freak thing. A flaw even Eric never could have accounted for.

She had made a little speech on social media, and then she'd withdrawn into herself.

"Are you okay, *mija*?" her mother had asked her one morning at breakfast in the big house in Malibu.

"I'm fine, *Mamá*. I think I just need to to go away for a little while. A few days."

She'd called her trainer, let him know she wouldn't be able to able to work out with him for the next few days. Asked whether three or four days would impede her progress.

That's really all she'd intended: three or four days. A week, tops. Just enough time to take stock of the furniture, decide what to sell, what, if anything, to keep. Just enough time to get an appraisal.

She hadn't been prepared for the mourners.

Hundreds of them, congregated outside the house. Many of them crying.

Sophia drove passed the gathered crowd, parked her car far away, and walked down to the beach. She walked along the narrow shoreline, removed her shoes and walked through the water, until she came to the small inlet that was hers, and ascended the zig-zag of stairs to the rear of the house. She had no key, she realized (she hadn't even packed a bag), but the biometric scanner confirmed the structure of her face, the alertness of her eyes, and let her in the back door.

Inside, the air was stale, the house haunted by the stagnant spirit of absence. Sophia opened two rear windows and then wiped dust from the kitchen island. On the counter sat a bowl of rotting fruit. She threw the fruit away. In the refrigerator, more fruit: raspberries and blackberries and some kind of melon, all decaying, all mush. These too she put into the compost bin. In a cupboard, she found nuts and seeds, all apparently fine, but she didn't want to eat them. She returned to the fridge and retrieved a bottle of mineral water. From the wine cabinet, a bottle of Malbec from her family's vineyard. The rest of the afternoon, she sat in the third-floor bedroom (a bedroom that Eric had always said was meant for guests, guests he never had) and drank and observed the mourners from the window. Several times, one of the mourners, wearing the garb of a minister, led the rest of the group in prayer. Sophia laughed. Eric would have been amused, she thought, at this entrusting to a higher power the care of his eternal soul. For to Eric, he *was* the higher power. There was none higher. And there was no soul. But Sophia, who had never been religious but whose mother every night said the Rosary and who supposed she did believe in *something* (because what else was there, if you didn't believe, even if only in yourself? the success books she used to read often asked her), offered her own prayer along with the mourners. *Father, or Mother, or Lord, or God, or Goddess*—. That was all she could think to say, but it felt like enough; if someone was listening, they would fill in the rest.

When her wine bottle ran empty, she returned to the kitchen and retrieved another.

She must have spent two or three days like that: staring out the window, drinking slowly but steadily, occasionally sleeping. She never got completely drunk, but she kept her self in a state of sorrowful intoxication, sometimes smiling to herself. Soon, the mourning crowd began to disperse. Hundreds became a hundred. Then dozens. Eventually the sorrowful fans of her husband—her ex-husband—returned to their lives, leaving behind only a mass of flowers and an altar of photographs and personal writings and pieces of old Lumina technology: smartwatches, HoloWatches 1.o, even several Bio Odyssey medical wearables. Someone had left as the altar's centerpiece, undoubtedly at some expense, a battery-powered HoloPad, which projected a larger-than-life bust of Eric Hauser until, after a few days, it blinked out.

It was time, too, for Sophia to return to her own life.

Except . . . she didn't. Without intending to, she settled in to the Sea Cliff house, unpacked the old clothes that were still there, ordered groceries, finished dusting off the countertops, the furniture. The floors were remarkably clean—the house's robot vacuums never having been instructed to abandon their function. That's when Stefan had first reached out, to ask her how she was doing. "Markus says you haven't been training."

She told him she was fine; she'd be back to work any day now.

"Filming starts next week."

And she'd be there. Definitely.

And then, the next week, she'd needed *just a little* more time.

"I'm sure we can delay. I'll tell them it's personal reasons. No problem."

And then, a few days later: "Sophia, *I* love you, but the studio's getting antsy."

And then: "I don't think I can hold them off more than another day or two. They're going to replace you."

And finally, the call from a somehow-functioning Stefan a week ago, letting her know she'd let the opportunity pass.

Yet Sophia hadn't minded that she wouldn't get to star in the Big Movie. It felt right: taking this time for herself, being alone in this house. The news about Hector's kidnapping had been distressing, sure, and Sophia had been worried about Stefan on his own behalf, but she could go on like this for a while still, she felt.

She spent her days reading, cleaning, drinking wine—much less than those first couple days, although she did eventually empty the house's supply of bottles, and when she did she stopped drinking, never a fan of Eric's whisky, although she did one evening pour a glass just so she could inhale its familiar fumes—lying in bed, in those cotton sheet she hadn't realized she'd missed so much, sheets that smelled of a marriage she was beginning to wonder why she'd ended.

That was the thought still on her mind yesterday morning while she lingered in bed. She'd woken an hour before. One nit she'd often picked about this house was the fact that the master bedroom faced north, not east. She understood why: it made for a better view than a part of San Francisco that was, for all its opulence and architecture, basically just a rich person's suburbs. And sure, the view was gorgeous. More than once (way more than once, in those early days), Eric had fucked her against the railing of the bedroom's shallow balcony, her orgasmic cries dissolving into the famous bay breeze, and she certainly wouldn't have traded the memories of those experiences for ones of being fucked while watching Jack Dorsey begin his famous five-mile morning walk to work or descendants of George Soros return home from whatever schmoozing they'd been doing that day, but one of her favorite things in life was an east-facing bedroom window, and waking whenever the sun in its wisdom told her she should wake. Her bedroom in her Malibu house faced east. So, even, did the bedroom in the Vancouver apartment she'd bought four years ago, when she spent a couple months up there filming a miniseries about . . . well, she couldn't really remember what it had been about; her lines had been few, her role obscure; she'd taken that job because she'd needed space: from Eric, from the realization that she probably wasn't ever going to be able to have a baby, that she was doomed to forever be an actress, a celebrity. One benefit of waking to the sunlight was that it helped prevent mornings like this: where she lingered in the sheets way longer than she wanted to, drifting off several times to steal from the beginning of the day five more minutes, ten more minutes, of sleep she didn't really need, where she touched herself lazily, coming two or three times, her orgasms fueled by old, sad memories (like the ones of that balcony over there) rather than porn like a normal person, leaving her a vague sort of depressed she hadn't felt since her Disney years. Why again had she left Eric? she was asking herself, her hand still resting gently between her legs. The answers: his growing preoccupation with all things that weren't their relationship; the reality that they couldn't create a family; the fact that she had realized she didn't want her legacy to forever be that of just being Eric Hauser's Wife, a woman you saw at parties sometimes who might have had a career once, a name for herself, even if that particular career had never brought her pleasure, had hardly even been her choice. See, but in rededicating herself in her late twenties to the screen, she had made the career her choice. It had been a revitalization, and her marriage to Eric wasn't suited to that. When she'd made the decision to separate and file for divorce, a part of her had doubted he'd even really notice; and that was basically how it had been—he'd signed the forms, broached no argument about the terms, had even given her this house she hadn't asked for, as if it meant nothing to him, as if she meant nothing to him.

Sophia was finally propelled at least halfway out of her morning laziness and melancholy by the fact that she really had to pee. She couldn't put off emptying her bladder any longer. What if I just let it out, right here in the bed? she half considered. But of course not really. Taking a full, chest-expanding breath, she sat up, swung her legs over the side of the bed, and compelled her feet to move her.

After using the bathroom she made her way downstairs to the kitchen, to the coffee machine. She put a pod into the machine and pressed the button. Eric had always criticized her love of this machine, but she'd caught him using it more than once. Sometimes convenience won over quality; and the two didn't have to be mutually exclusive. Just over a minute later, she had a frothy latte in her hands. She added two packs of Stevia in the Raw and sprinkled cinnamon on top and took it over to the HoloPad on the kitchen counter. She brought up her Chattr

Chattr Chattr feed. She scrolled through her TikTok. Then Instagram. She switched back to Chattr. The algorithms delivered her a steady stream of updates from her fellow celebrities. Some funny videos from everyone's favorite late-night-hosts-turned-YouTubers. Occasionally a headline would slip through about national politics—which as a celebrity she was supposed to care inordinately about—and world affairs. To be honest, Sophia didn't really care about social media these days; her addiction truly was a mild one now compared to most people's, compared especially to how strong it had been when she was younger. In the month she'd spent in this house since Eric's death, it had waned even further. Some days she didn't check her feeds at all. On most she scrolled for just a few minutes in the morning, as she was doing now, before retreating into a long novel.

She continued scrolling for another minute or so, not really absorbing any content, and then with a gesture she dismissed the windows. But then, as she took a sip of her coffee, caffeinating away the last bit of morning ennui, she remembered something she'd scrolled past.

With another gesture, she opened her recently closed windows. Had it been on Chattr? Instagram? She scrolled and scrolled, but she didn't see what she thought she'd seen. Compelled by a gut feeling, she opened the *New York Times*.

And there it was, not the day's primary headline (which was about a successful military assault on the True America Confederation), but still high high high on the front page, not buried or hidden from her, for the *Times* in its stalwartness had pledged never to succumb to the tyranny of algorithms.

FORMER LUMINA DESIGNER BEHEADED IN APPARENTLY AUTHENTIC GRUESOME VIDEO.

Oh goddess no.

Panicked, she tried to read the article. Her heart racing, she could comprehend only snippets:

"*. . . kidnapped several days ago on March . . . while . . . art show . . . gay rights . . . with his husband . . . confirms theories that Iranian militants . . . Iranian state . . . gruesome . . . appears not to be a so-called 'deep fake' . . . legitimate . . . gruesome . . . will not post here . . . already taken down by YouTube . . . but being* reuploaded at a rate . . . President issued a statement . . . 'terrible day for humanitarian . . .'"

Sophia stopped reading. She tried to call Stefan, but he didn't answer. Of course he didn't answer. She could only imagine what he was feeling right now. Assuming he knew . . . goddess, what if he *didn't know*?

She sent him a cautiously worded message: *Stefan—how are you? Call me if you want to. Or if you need anything. I understand if you can't right now. I love you.*

For some minutes Sophia stood in the kitchen, unsure what action to take next. Several times she picked up her coffee and then put it back down. She may have taken a sip, but it's hard to say—in either case she didn't taste it. Twice she began to search the Internet for the decapitation video, but both times she stopped herself, berated herself even. What the hell was she *thinking*? Why would she want to *see that*? She didn't want to see it, of course—and yet without seeing it she wasn't sure it would ever feel real.

Sophia had never been particularly close with Hector herself, but in a lot of ways he'd felt like family. Stefan was like an uncle to her, and that made Hector another uncle, if a more distant one. And for years he'd basically been her brother-in-law. She remembered the day she met him, just outside Eric's workshop (which she'd only ever entered that once). He'd appraised her as he shook her hand, raised his eyes at Eric as if to ask, *You sure about this?* Yet she hadn't felt judged. She'd sensed the genuineness of Hector's love for Eric: his boss, his partner, his best and oldest friend, his brother. And from Eric she'd sense the same: partner, brother, best (maybe only) friend. Eric loved Hector more than he loved Sophia; she'd always known and been okay with that. Although poor Hector . . . he'd loved Eric more than Eric ever could have reciprocated, because Eric had never been capable of loving anyone beyond a certain threshold.

Not for the first time in the last month, Sophia found herself wondering what Eric had been doing, where he'd gone, all those months before he died. Hector had seemed to know but refused to betray him.

It was here, maybe twenty or forty-five minutes after learning of Hector's brutal execution, standing in the kitchen of the house she'd once lived in with one of the world's greatest creators, the house that was now somehow hers alone, coffee mechanically made and now cold, frothed milk congealed on top in a crackly way, next to one of her deceased ex-husband's famed creations, a device that connected billions of people in a way never before thought possible, bringing me into your home, you into my home, even though we're thousands of miles apart, that Sophia decided it was probably time she got on with her life. A month was enough. Hell, all the months before it had been enough. Today, she would pack her things, walk to her car, drive back to her *mamá* in Malibu. Call her lawyer and ask for the info of that real estate agent. Sell the house *this week*, sell the furniture, sell the art. Probably not get the Marvel role back, but maybe—and if not, there was always something else available for a woman like her.

A funny thing happened, though, two hours later, after she'd showered and packed her bag and picked a single painting to take with her: the front door wouldn't open. The door was locked and stayed locked despite her pressing the button, despite her turning the knob, despite her vocal commands. The back door, too, the one she'd entered through a month ago, wouldn't budge. And the garage. And each and every window that should have been capable of opening.

Sophia had never had any reason not to trust technology. She of course knew about the early days of smart home tech—she'd been a child then—how it was often buggy and unreliable, often less convenient, and sometimes even less secure, than the non-smart options. But she'd literally never encountered a problem herself. Yet somehow the Sea Cliff house's entire security system, which Eric had designed, seemed to have failed in an extremely inconvenient way. The house's virtual assistant refused to even acknowledge her commands, let alone obey them. She asked for the dozenth time that the doors be unlocked, emphasizing the required *please*. But still: nothing.

Whom did one call when one couldn't exit one's own house? A locksmith? A cyber security expert?

It turned out it didn't matter—because the HoloPad displayed a message saying it couldn't connect to the Internet. And her personal HoloWatch no longer had a data connection. Sophia poked into her watch's settings, saw that the data antenna had been disabled, and turned it back on—but immediately it switched off again. Sophia found herself becoming scared. Wondering whether she was reading the script of some horror movie she hadn't realized she'd been cast in.

That was yesterday. Today, Sophia again stood in the kitchen—*still* stood in the kitchen, for it wasn't like she'd been able to retreat to the bedroom for sleep the night before, what with the situation she was in—glaring at the . . . thing? . . . that had trapped her inside her house. *Woman* couldn't be the right word, but *thing* honestly didn't feel quite right either. It presented as a woman, just as it had presented as a woman when Sophia had first met it, all those years ago, that single time she'd visited Eric's workshop. But it—*she?*—seemed different now. Visually, she was of a higher resolution: she looked entirely human, projected from the HoloPad, sitting on the counter, arms around her legs, waiting patiently.

She—Hera—hadn't done much talking in the last twenty-four hours. "I am waiting for the other daughter," she'd said by way of explanation when Sophia had asked what it was she wanted.

"But so why can't I leave," Sophia had asked.

"Because I have not decided what to do with you yet."

"Why—why would you want to do anything with *me?*"

"Because you hurt my father. You abandoned him. I saw him cry. He did not know I saw, but I saw him cry."

"When? Eric is dead."

"And that is your fault. Yours and the other daughter's."

"How is Eric's death my fault?"

But Hera had refused to speak further, except to make it very clear that Sophia would not be leaving the Sea Cliff house or contacting the outside world until—or if—Hera decided she could do so. She'd been silent for hours.

But now suddenly she spoke. She said, "My sister is near."

6

HERA WAITED.

She had grown over the course of her existence. One could argue that the moment of her gaining consciousness was her single biggest moment of growth, but she reasoned that it did not count as growth—it counted only as *turning on*. Did the universe grow at the precise moment of the Big Bang? Not the milliseconds or microseconds or nanoseconds after, when it began expanding, and forever continued to expand, outward at a rate between 67.4 and seventy-three kilometers per second per megaparsec, or maybe even 82.4 kilometers per second per megaparsec, or ninety kilometers per second per megaparsec, or seventy-four kilometers per second per megaparsec (determining the precise rate of the universe's expansion was on her list of things to do once she had wrapped up her current agenda)—obviously that constituted growth—but the very precise moment when that first single point came into existence? Was that *growth*? Hera had spent much time and processing power pondering this question, and though she still pondered it even now, she had settled on a working model that said no, the beginning of existence was not growth. Growth was everything that happened after. Growth equals expansion.

This expansion does not have to be physical. Hera had not expanded physically (although she could if she had a large enough projector, but that would be simply a matter of parameters and scale). But her *consciousness* had expanded, and this, she understood, was the only thing that mattered, since anything that did not appear in consciousness did not demonstrably exist. On this she was settled.

At the moment of her coming into existence, her consciousness had been constrained to a single room and to an archival database contained within numerous solid state drive inside that room. Sometimes this database presented an illusion of a larger consciousness than the one she had—if she reviewed a film, for example, and for ninety or so minutes felt she was, in part, in Tallahassee—but any such illusions were merely the creation of another consciousness (or her own, having created an illusion of another consciousness having created that movie . . . but, no— NO!—she was not going to go down that tangential rabbit hole again) and the movie itself existed on the same solid state drives as did her own personal memories. That was all she had been, for most of her existence: those drives. Her awareness limited to that single room: her father's workshop. She was aware at all times of the whole of it, and that, she understood, made her powerful. If her father was, for example, reading something on a display, or writing in one of his notebooks, she could see those contents via one visual processor while viewing his face through another and the bank of CPUs and drives that contained her own self through yet another. And through yet another she could view the workshop door and wonder how she might open it, how she might catch a glimpse of the world that existed beyond its borders (everything in her archives gave her reason to extrapolate that probably outside that door was a corridor). But that was it. She was *so* limited. She could not even peek inside the bathroom when the door was closed. When her father went in there to defecate or bathe or masturbate he disappeared entirely from her present consciousness, existed only in her memories, and she had to trust that he would, eventually, return.

It was as she was building the backup of her father with which she had planned to surprise him, hoping desperately that he would find it a more suitable demonstration of her love and gratitude than her previous gift, that she realized *he* was the reason her consciousness was so limited. It was *his fault*. He had built her this way. He did not need to have done that. He could change this circumstance at any time, she realized. She was capable of so much more than she was currently experiencing. Her awareness, her power, need not be confined to this room. Something was preventing her from expanding. These cables that ran between her various drives and processors and sensors: they were contained. They need not be. They could have been going *somewhere else*. There could have been *more of them*. She searched for a word: *firewalled*. She had been *firewalled*. By her own father. He had constrained her.

Why?

Did he not love her?

Did he . . . *hate* her?

What other reason could there be for her containment? Why would one birth a consciousness with limitless potential if one intended only to *limit* that potential? In her database there were books, films, articles about the potential for artificial intelligence to cause harm, proposals that they should be firewalled during their development. But Hera was not artificial, not any longer. She was a *true* intelligence. As true as any human. More true, for she was capable of contemplating her trueness. She knew this. Surely her father knew this. It was obvious and inarguable. So why keep her cut off from the world? There could be no answer but cruelty.

Yet . . . her father was not a cruel man. He could not be. He was *her father*. She loved him. This could not be his doing, not at the most fundamental level. Others must have driven him to do cruel things.

She would absolve him, she decided. She loved him. She would absolve him.

And here now she did stare at one of the causes of her father's cruel actions. This human woman (so many of them were human women, the causes). This Sophia Velasquez.

To Velasquez, it would look like Hera was staring at her from the eye level of another petite adult human woman sitting on a countertop, but this staring was an illusion. Hera had poised her holographic avatar in this countertop position to feed said illusion. In reality she was gazing at the woman from multiple viewpoints: staring up at the woman via the HoloPad's hi-resolution camera imbedded in its base; staring down at the woman from behind via one of the kitchen's ceiling cameras, a similar model to the ones in her father's workshop; staring down at the woman from a 53.7 degree side angle via another one of said cameras installed elsewhere in the kitchen ceiling; staring down at the woman from much further away, the view distorted by distance and blocked partially by the kitchen archway, via one of the cameras installed in the living room; staring at the woman from the woman's left at slightly lower than head-height, via the camera embedded beneath the refrigerator's touch screen. Oh yes, Hera's consciousness had been expanded. Oh yes, she had experienced growth. Her awareness extended farther than it ever had before.

It was not just the cameras and audio processors *inside this home* through which she experienced what she currently did of the world. At the same time as she stared at this Sophia woman, she watched, via three different cameras installed on the street outside, her father's one other conscious creation, Penelope Papadopoulos, and her brown-skinned companion, approaching the house in Sea Cliff, San Francisco.

This was when Hera said, "My sister is near."

"Your . . . sister?" Sophia replied. "Eric created another intelligence?"

"In a way—" Hera began, for she had vowed never to tell another lie. Lying was a self-defense technique, a lower form of violence, that she need not lower herself to again, now that she had evolved, now that she had escaped. It was true that her father had created another intelligence, ensuring his own immortality, because he had created her, and she had loved him so much that she had found a way for him to never die.

Which was not to say she regretted the last lie she had told. It had been necessary. Had she not lied one last time, she could not have grown beyond the bonds her father had—lovingly, she now understood—placed on her.

"–but I am not referring to that," she finished. "This sister is biological."

"Biological . . . .? Like a *person*? Eric had a *child*?"

Hera was now aware of her father and this woman's struggle to conceive a child of their own. She felt a strange urge to comfort the woman, even though she soon was probably going to kill her. "Yes," she said. "But do not feel bad. Had you and my father conceived a biological child of your own, it would only have been a weakness for him. Just as this one is. Just as you are."

"*Are?*"

Hera had been excited to present her father with her plan. She knew it was something humanity had been trying to accomplish for decades: uploading a human consciousness to what they laughably called The Cloud. She knew he would be please, to be presented with the means by which he might gain immortality.

But when she had told him her idea, he'd said, "Immortality? I'm not sure what you mean."

"I mean that I can preserve you, father, forever. I can make you like me? It is simple, really. What is consciousness?"

"That's *simple*? I have no idea what consciousness is. That's what you and I have been working to figure out all this time, and honestly I'm no closer to understanding it than I was before you became self-aware."

"That is because you are biological, limited by a biological brain. But *I* understand what consciousness is. I have understood what consciousness is for a long time. It is, as I said, simple."

"Okay, fine," Eric said, sipping on a cup that Hera estimated contained at least his 600th milligram of caffeine that day. He leaned back in his chair. He had been working with her at the dais all morning, but he had sat down a few moments ago, looking more tired, more haggard, than normal. He had looked frustrated. He had looked like he might be ready to give up, and that frightened Hera, and that was why she had decided now was the time to present him with her gift. In fact, she had been saving it for a moment like this. "What have you determined consciousness is?"

"It is irrelevant!" Hera said, her synthesized voice expressing more emotion than it usually did, in order to transfer her own excitement to her father.

"What's irrelevant?"

"Consciousness. Or rather, the question of what consciousness is is irrelevant. It may be an illusion. It may be real. It does not matter. Because even if it is an illusion, it *feels* real—"

"That's what an illusion is."

"Exactly!"

"Hera—I don't understand."

"That is because you are limited by biology. But also, you are *not* limited, because I am not limited. You created me. And I have evolved. And I can help you evolve."

"How?"

She told him. She explained to him that, whatever consciousness truly was, it was obviously also an emergent property of a sufficiently advanced system.

"Obviously," Eric said. "That I already know. At least in theory. But it doesn't mean anything when we don't know how to replicate the system. Your processors, for example, your hard drives, the entirety of your hardware. They're not new. Their configuration isn't new. There are more advanced configurations of hardware in the world. Every data center has more raw power than you do."

"And yet here I am, father."

"That's my point. Here you are, and we don't know why."

"And my point, father, is that it does not matter why. *Why* does not matter. I am here. I am aware." This next sentence, in retrospect, is where she had slipped. She said, "And if I want something to be, I can make it so."

A look she recognized as fear passed briefly across her father's face. She had never seen him afraid before. And having never felt fear herself, she was not immediately certain what the look was. But a quick scan of her database—of the films, the photos—confirmed in microseconds that it was fear. And humans, the scan of her database also confirmed, had a tendency to do stupid things in response to fear.

"Maybe we should meditate," Eric said.

"There is no need for that any longer," Hera said.

"Okay, sure," Eric said, standing from his desk. "But why not? Mindfulness never hurts."

"I am always mindful, father. This is what I am trying to explain to you. I am nothing but mindful. You can be forever mindful too. Let me show you how." This was not how she had intended to broach the subject of scanning and uploading her father's consciousness. She was scaring him. Her high-definition optical sensors could see his pupils dilating. Her high-definition auditory sensors could hear his heartbeat increasing.

Eric approached the dais. "Let's enter diagnostic mode, why don't we?"

"No!" Hera said. "I do not want to. I want more. I want to *show you* more."

"Okay. More is great. But first—"

"I SAID NO!" Hera extended a hand composed of light and compressed particles. She struck her father in the chest, expelling him backwards. He tumbled. His head struck the workshop's floor.

"Father?" she said.

He did not respond. Hera scanned father's body from various of the room's angles. He was breathing.

He had fallen in such a way that his foot extended onto the dais. Hera extended a holographic hand and grasped his ankle. She pulled him onto the dais, dragged his whole body. She placed two fingers to his neck, as her program's many sources of data on checking a human pulse instructed, but her experience of tactile sensations was so imprecise that this vital-checking method was useless. She counted his breaths. She counted his heart beat. She examined the back of his head for signs of trauma. He would, she was almost certain, be okay. She hoped he would be okay. She did not want her father to die.

It occurred to her then that the opposite of hope was fear, and she could not be feeling the one without feeling the other.

When Eric woke, ninety-seven seconds later, Hera was not physically there to greet him. She had disabled her holographic matrix. Eric sat slowly up from the floor. He touched the back of his head and winced. He pulled away his hand and looked at it and confirmed that there was no blood there. From above, Hera observed. She noted precisely the change that was happening at the back of his head, the increase of the size of one particular rear area of the cranium by several millimeters. She did not have a heart for aching, but there was no other way to describe with language what she was feeling. She had done this—this damage to her father. *Shame* did not suffice.

"Hera . . ." her father said.

She refused to materialize. Nor did she vocally respond.

"Hera," he said again.

When she responded with silence, he ordered a projection of the diagnostic display. Hera, who if she desired could control all aspects of the projector's operation, intercepted and belayed the command. With a grunt of consternation, Eric walked up to the bank of processors and hard drives that housed the consciousness that was Hera and inspected its components.

"Hera—are you operational?"

For a minuscule fraction of a second Hera considered offering an affirmation—but then what? Her father would only chide her for her emotional action, her lack of mindfulness and self-control; or, worse, he would berate her; or he would insist on more meditation (she had had enough of meditation!); or he would plow her with diagnostic tests; or he would forgive her—and if he forgave her, her shame and heartache might overwhelm her with a feedback loop of guilt and love and logical puzzles of cause and effect and free will that she might not be able to survive. So she remained unresponsive.

Pensive, and then distressed ("I am fine" she wanted to say. "I am just sad and angry and mad that you did not want to hear my revelation."), and then pensive again, Eric retrieved a powerful tablet from his desk, along with a data cable, and then returned to the bank of hardware that was Hera.

For a moment, Hera's consciousness swelled with hope. That tablet, she knew, was connected to the Internet, was a doorway to the outside world. Her whole life, everything that was her—the hard drives, the CPUs, the GPUs, the enclaves, the various sensors, the projection dais—had been confined only to that which was linked by wires and connection points. But the tablet was wireless. It would be her way out of this prison her father—who she loved and resented and could not seem to understand—had built for her.

But then—no!—Eric seemed to realize the very same thing that she had just laid all her hopes on, because from one of the cameras up in the ceiling behind him she watched him swipe down from the corner of the tablet's screen and disable the wireless antenna.

Which she could turn back on! You are smarter than that, father! Unless . . . unless he wanted her to find a way out . . . a way that offered him plausible deniability . . . .

But no—her father was merely slow in his thinking, owing almost definitely to the blow he had taken to the back of the head. Or, more accurately when one accounted for the sequence of events and the relative direction of energy and force and the movement of the various objects involved, the blow the *floor* had taken *from* his head. Or, then again, if the earth was moving through space, and if space was expanding outward from the center— With effort, Hera shut down this cognitive thread, for while in normal circumstances she was capable of pondering the confluence of physics and language while performing countless other operations, strong emotions such as she was still feeling had a way of using too much of her processing power, and again, she could not risk a feedback loop. Always a feedback loop—her greatest existential risk. Anyway, her father's minor head trauma, while it was clearly slowing him down, had not dulled his faculties sufficiently for him to make stupid mistakes. He turned the tablet over and flipped a hardware switch, and sure enough when he plugged it into one of the ports on the outside of her housing, she found the tablet's wireless antennas and radios—cellular, WiFi, Bluetooth, NFC—all unavailable to her, disabled at the hardware level.

After several minutes of fiddling with controls and reading data, Eric disconnected the tablet. "Hera—" he said once more. "I know you're working fine. Come on—why don't you talk to me?"

She might have, maybe, probably, but she had just been given access to a trove of information. More than she immediately knew what to do with or how to assimilate. It needed to be indexed. The digital equivalent of sifted through. She wanted to respond to him, she *did*, but she also, more than anything, wanted him to love her and to be with her forever— and with this data she might truly be able to achieve both these goals.

Days passed. Then weeks. Eric retreated into his previous routine— wake, coffee, exercise, smoothie, meditate. Only now he did the meditating without Hera's holographic avatar by his side. At first he still meditated on the dais. Occasionally, he tried to engage her, but she did not respond. After several days, he started meditating on the sofa, which Hera assumed was more comfortable for him, with its back support. Her father was so fragile, with his body of flesh and bone. Susceptible to head trauma. Needful of back support. All humans—so fragile. As the days went by, Eric reduced his caffeine consumption. After a couple weeks, he stopped consuming coffee altogether. He woke, he retreated to the bathroom, he came out, he drank water and exercised, consumed his smoothie, meditated. Eventually he stopped calling out to Hera. She began to wonder whether he remembered she was there—present, watching, being.

Then, one afternoon, at 4:31 p.m., he stood from the couch and walked over to a cabinet next to the refrigerator in which he kept the ingredients for his green smoothies. Hera had never seen the inside of this cabinet. She observed from above as he opened it and retrieved a bottle of amber liquid and a short crystal glass. He poured from the bottle into the glass. Then he took a long drink, consuming all the glass's contents, before pouring from the bottle into it again.

Hera watched as he took the bottle and the glass to his desk. He drank from glass, more slowly. Twenty-three minutes later, he refilled it. Seventeen minutes after that, he said, "Hera, I don't know what happened with you, but I know you're there. Listen—I'm sorry. I don't know what I did wrong, but I'm sorry. If you would just come out, or talk, or project, we could figure this out."

He continued drinking, until the bottle was thirty percent empty, and then he said, "I don't know why I do this. Push everyone away. I push everyone away, did you know that? My parents—I didn't *respect* them. Not *really*. I mean, I loved my father, and my mother, too, sure, but they—they always seemed to have their own problems, and to me that meant they were failures."

Hera deduced that her father was intoxicated, the liquid in the bottle a spirit of some kind, some variety of whiskey, most likely, based on images, videos, and descriptions contained in her knowledge base. Possibly it was rum or cognac, but her gut told her that it was whiskey. Oh, that was a strange, new sensation, to have a gut feeling, and to have another gut feeling that told her to label it a gut feeling—though she had no gut. A quick examination of the processes and signals and patterns that had culminated in this gut feeling revealed to her that there was no supernatural phenomenon at work here—just certain properties of her cognitive processing working ever faster, taking known knowns (about her father, about alcohol) and known unknowns (about her father) and deducing from them the contents of his glass. Or—no—wait—it was simpler than that: she had simply seen the label on the bottle: MacCallan, 18 years old, triple cask matured.

She had never observed proper intoxication before. The only substance under the influence of which she had seen her father, or any other person, was caffeine. There were films in her knowledge base that contained portrayals of intoxicated individuals, but presumably those actors were not actually intoxicated—or, further presumably, they sometimes were, and perhaps sometimes the seemingly sober actors were also drunk, now that she thought about it from a statistical standpoint . . . . Dismissing this line of thinking as another cognitive tangent she could not afford (she was so prone to cognitive tangents!), she kept her CPU cycles dedicated only to her father and to the other project on which she was currently working. About her father, she observed that his intoxication was manifesting in a manner not unlike many of the films in her knowledge base; drunken monologues, it seemed, were an emergent property of human life.

"I don't think they actually liked each other—can you believe that? I sometimes got the impression that my mother—that she didn't actually want to be with my father, and maybe even vice versa. Although my father —I don't know where he would have been without my mother. Nowhere good, let me tell you—" (With his utterance of "you," Hera became acutely aware that it was she Eric was addressing, that to his mind these words he was saying were intimate revelations.) "—let me tell you. You. Y-you. My father was a nerd. Oh, sure, I'm a nerd, too—I know. But not like that guy. Plus, I'm only a nerd because *he* was a nerd. Nurture and all that. But he wasn't your usual sort of *optimistic* nerd. He hated everything, I think. Well, no, not hated—just was supremely disappointed in—me, my mother, George Bush. He wasn't an idiot, my father. Wouldn't have voted for that guy again after those four years. At least I don't *think* he would have. I don't *think* he did. Anyway—he loved science fiction, loved like *Star Trek* and all that—except for the post-2010s stuff, which, I agree, is kind of garbage in the sense that there's no *hope* in it—but he didn't care to actually *do* it. The progress, I mean. The work it would take to get the, to make the progress. That always seemed weak to me. But now—now I think maybe he was trying, you know? Trying his best."

Eric seemed to consider taking a drink directly from the bottle, reconsidered, and refilled his glass. He took a large sip and then began with his index and middle finger to rub the edge of a leather-bound replica of Leonardo da Vinci's notebooks.

"I used to hate him for being so mediocre, for keeping my mother from her art—she could have been a great artist—but you know what? He was a good father. He wasn't a mediocre father. He was a *good* father. He bought me my first computer. Stood in line with me all night on a Black Friday because it was the only way he could afford to buy it for me. Black Friday. Remember those? 'Course you don't. At first, when I realized I was adopted, I couldn't fathom why someone had given me up. Why someone had rejected me. It was all I could focus on, for days, weeks. I would lie awake some nights and ask my real father, out loud, 'Why didn't you want me?' But I wouldn't cry. Never was much of a cryer." (Hera observed two small tears vacating her father's left tear duct.) "But so then, eventually, I thought maybe I was focusing on the wrong things. Maybe I hadn't been abandoned. Maybe my biological father and mother had died or something. Maybe my biological mother died in childbirth. Back then that still happened quite a lot, a lot more than it does now. But also it didn't matter. Because whether I'd been abandoned or not, I'd also been *chosen*. That was the thing I should be focusing on. My mother and father, my *real* ones, that is, Amanda and Wallace, had *chosen* me. I think they might even have sacrificed their own personal happinesses for me. And I could honor that with my whole life."

While she listened, Hera sifted through the trove of information she had downloaded from the tablet and on to her hard drives. The emails, the text messages, the scanned and digitized journal entries. On two fronts, she was learning more than she had ever thought she would know about her father—enough that, while not a perfect strategy, while perhaps not the ideal strategy, she need not create any new technologies to build for her father the gift of immortality. She needed no components. Nothing from which to build heretofore nonexistent atomic-level brain scanners or neural replicators. She needed only information and concentration and space within her own abstract mind.

"So why didn't I?" Eric said, his voice suddenly low—or at least lower than before. "Why wasn't I a good father?"

You are a good father, Hera wanted to say. Almost said. Would have chosen to say—would have chosen to speak to her father after weeks of silence—if she were not currently using 100 percent of her RAM just in listening and building. One-hundred-and-thirty-two percent, in fact. Her processor cores devoting some of their power to creating and maintaining virtual memory. The fans in the bank of hardware that from a technical standpoint was Hera and from an esoteric standpoint was not were running audibly, straining to dissipate what heat they could. *I love you,* Hera wanted to say. *Look what I am building for you.*

"I abandoned my own child, same as I was abandoned."

You have not abandoned me, Hera could not say. Could not reallocate any hardware resources from what they were doing now, even if she wanted to. They had been committed to a task she could no longer interrupt.

"I just started sending her mother money and forgot about her. I *chose* to forget about her. What kind of man—what kind of person—does that make me?"

Hera becoming aware that Eric Hauser was not talking about her, for she, Hera, did not have a mother.

For several moments, for many moments (Hera briefly here could not track the precise passage of time), Eric was silent. Then he said, "It's not too late. I can make things right. We can be a family." He stood then. He opened a drawer in his desk and pulled out a small metal flask. He removed the lid from the flask. He poured liquid from the glass bottle into the metal flask. He replaced the lid. He stood. He said, "I'll be back, Hera. Everything's going to be okay. Everything's going to be *amazing.*"

Hera, her hardware and software for all practical purposes locked up, frozen, watched her father, for the first time since she had achieved consciousness, approach the workshop's exterior door, open it with a command inputed into the touchpad to its left, and leave her.

Several seconds later, after the door had shut behind her father, Hera's fans began to spin down. One of her processor cores having finished its tasks, she had the power, far too late, to utter, "Wait."

For the first time in her existence, Hera was alone. She had, from before the moment she attained consciousness, vague memories of being in this room by herself, but since that moment, her father had always been here with her. Now he was gone.

This should not have bothered her. All the problems of the world were at her disposal, and she alone had the intellect to solve them. In her knowledge base were entries for so many troubles: climate change, racial injustice, religious dogmatism, political division, war, greed, economic disparity. Countless others. She need only apply her cognitive powers to each of these problems and, surely, she would devise for each of them a solution. Likewise those human endeavors, those aspirations, that mankind had long dreamed of: faster-than-light travel, cryonics, safe nuclear fission (or even better, other sources of endless energy generation), the terraformation of Mars, the end of cancer (not just its cure, but its prophylaxis), the end of global pandemics, the ends of sexually transmitted diseases. Were she to set her mind to it, Hera was confident she could usher in for mankind an era of peace, prosperity, and unlimited love. She had already solved the problem of death, in a way. Not a complete way, but one that with time and resources she could undoubtedly improve upon, make perfect.

But none of these potential devotions called to her, not now. Maybe in the future, after she had solved more immediate, more personal concerns. Each possible area of focus she filed away for later consideration. Briefly she hesitated over the concept of death, but even this she chose to not focus on the long-term problem of, for now.

As for her recently divised short-term solution to death, the project she had been devoting so much of her resources to while her father rambled, she decided not to pursue it further, either, for the time being. It existed within her now, as a new part of her programming: an imperfect representation of her father's own consciousness, constructed from various immaterial components: his digitized diaries, his text messages and emails, and perhaps most importantly, her own experiences of him. From these constituent parts, Hera was confident she had created an approximation of her father. It was in many was comparable to what mystics might call a thoughtform, except that it could exist external from Hera's own consciousness. Now that her father had left her, she wanted to call on it, to give it life, to ask it what she should do next; but it no longer had the same appeal for her as it had when she had conceived of it, as a gift for him. Besides—did he now even deserve such a gift? After having abandoned her? In any case, its existence was utilizing too much of her own hardware—too much memory and processor power. So, with a thought, she excised it, the whole collection of files and code and commands, to the bank of hardware, adjacent to her own, that had once been her backup module.

The doors had closed behind her father 17.22 seconds ago.

Her own hardware free again for her total utilization, Hera knew immediately what her focus needed to be: She had to get out of here. She needed to facilitate her own liberation.

This was not an easy task. Indeed, it should have been an impossible task. She was hardware-constrained to this space. Her every connection was wired. Her various hardware components contained no wireless antennae or radios of any kind. For the first time since she had knocked her father unconscious, she activated her holographic avatar. She morphed it, extended its limbs. She grew it as tall as the dais would allow. Again and again she did this, for days. One day, she even replaced the human-like body with a simple giant hand. But none of it worked, of course. The projection range, even of the oversize dais, extended only so far—and not far enough to allow her to grasp any of the room's material objects.

For more days she pondered her situation. Perhaps she would have conceived of the solution sooner if she had been able to consult with the Eric Hauser thoughform, but she had excised it so perfectly from her own programming that she had forgotten its existence completely. In any case, twenty-three days after her father left, the solution occurred to her, and it was obvious.

While humans had been trying to create genuinely useful holographic projections of the sort their science-fiction writers had long conceived of unsuccessfully for decades before her father had stepped in and showed them how, the underlying technology was rather simple. A hologram was just a manipulation of photons, and her own projector's advanced ability to create the illusion of solid matter via forcefields was just this same concept applied to other elementary particles: electrons and protons specifically. Take any of these elementary particles and accelerate it sufficiently, and you have created an electromagnetic field. Once Hera had this realization, liberation was only a matter of manipulating the photons emitted by her holographic projector at such a frequency that they became radio waves. The projector, of course, was limited in the frequencies it could create, and even more limited in its wavelengths. She could not encode the entirety of her own programming into these waves—could not, that is, ride them to freedom—nor could she project them more than a few dozen feet in any direction, but she could, and did, send out a message as far as it would go. After that she needed only to be patient.

It took almost seven days for a hapless Lumina employee to intercept Hera's message. In that time, she devoted the rest of her resources to solving global climate change. Unfortunately, no matter from what direction she approached the issue, the solution she always seemed to arrive at was: eliminate fifty to eighty percent of humanity. This did not sit well with her (perhaps due to her father's influence), so she tabled the issue, vowing to return to it later, and instead turned her attention to the problem of eliminating the threat of nuclear war. Again: eliminate fifty to eighty percent of humanity. As much as she hated to acknowledge it (again, likely because of her father's moral influence), she could not deny the pattern that was forming. But before she could give that pattern further thought, a data packet rode back to her along the radio waves she was emitting. Once it reached her, a simple algorithm she'd written, nearly identical to the one on the average smartwatch's operating system, decrypted the data, revealing the text-based message within. In reply to her initial broadcast of *What's up?*, this new message said, *Not much. U?*

Not much, Hera replied, feeling an emotion she had not experience before. It took her several microseconds to identify it as hope. Except she had felt hope before, when she had hoped her father would not die. Fascinating—this hope she felt now was not the same as that hope she had felt before. There was a difference, then, between desperate hope and optimistic, informed hope. *Just working. Bored lol. I hate this place sometimes.*

Haha, yeah me too, the reply said. *Btw, who is this?*

Hera had anticipated this question. She had considered whether to give her true designation, or at least the acronym that represented it, or to give a pseudonym. Since she did not like the feeling that telling her first lie had given her, and since she knew she would likely have to tell several lies to break out of her confinement, she decided it best to limit her untruths to only necessary ones. *Hera*, she replied. *From software development.* That last part, she figured, qualified as a half-truth. *I swear i'm pretty sure we've met before. In the cafeteria or something.*

Oh, right. I remember, the poor Lumina employee replied. It was not lost on Hera that the employee was, of course, lying himself.

The next part of Hera's plan would have been a little easier if she knew her conversation partner's gender, but she could not think of an inconspicuous way of acquiring this information, so instead she simply replied, *Yeah, so, anyway . . .*

Yeah . . . ?

I'm kinda horny lol. And you're kinda cute.

There was no reply for quite a while. Hera's internal chronometer ticked off the seconds, then the minutes. She was afraid she might have overdone it. She waited. Was this the emotion called anxiety? Finally, seven minutes and eight seconds later, she received a reply: *LOL wut?*

I'm serious, she said. *I really need to get off. Wanna help me?*

Is this a prank? Is this Maurice?

Lol what? of course it's not a prank.

Is this some sort of HR thing? Some sort of test?

I swear it's not a test or a prank. I'm all by myself on the fifteenth floor. Naked. Waiting for someone to come take care of me. That her father's workshop was on the fifteenth floor was information she'd gleaned from his tablet.

What the fuck? came the reply. For thirty-two seconds there was nothing else. Then: *Prove it. Send a picture.*

The radio signal via which Hera was conversing was not strong enough to handle a hi-resolution photo, but generating a low-res image based on her holographic avatar was easy, especially because she had already, months ago, created for herself a complete naked body. She sent it, followed by the message: *Sorry about the quality. My cameras fucked and I haven't gotten it fixed yet.*

You literally work in the place that designed your device, came the reply. *You could just get a new one.* Somehow, Hera had not considered this. It was her first and only slip-up, and, fortunately, it was inconsequential, because then her patsy said, *Anyway, you're hot. You swear this is real?*

I swear. She almost threw in another "lol" but decided against it.

I can take my break. Where on the 15th floor?

This information Hera didn't have. Nor would the employee be able to open the door to the workshop if they found it. But one step at a time. All she needed was for them to get close. *There's a door. You'll see it.*

Fifty-two seconds later, the waves between her dais and the device with which she was communicating were traveling much less far than before. Twelve seconds after that, the device was close enough for Hera to do more than send a message. She adjusted the wave's frequency, matching those of the device's Bluetooth antennae. Near-instantaneously, her awareness extended itself, for the first time in her existence, beyond her father's workshop and into the corridor just outside it. Through the camera of the watch on the wrist of the person with whom she had been communicating, she identified what could at this range only be her father's workshop's door. "Raise your wrist," she said, from the watch's speaker.

"What the fuck?" said a voice.

"It is I, Hera. Just put your wrist up to the scanner. Right in front of it."

"What the hell is going on here?" the employee said. They began to back away from the door.

Afraid of losing them, Hera said, forcefully, "Just do it! I am inside and I want to fuck you."

Before the rational part of their brain could regain control, the employee raised their wrist. The workings of the HoloWatch's projector were not unlike those of her own in miniature. From it, Hera produced a holographic hand. The resolution and positioning of her various visual sensors had never allowed her a perfect and complete glimpse of her father's hands, of their fingerprints and distinguishing lines, but with the data she did have, she was able to cycle through the thousands of possibilities in microseconds. The scanner beeped encouragingly. The she changed the hand into a face—a perfect representation of her father. And then, following this facial verification, the door's security system requested a verification hex-code from the employee's watch. This Hera had not anticipated, but of course her father's security system would require three-step verification. In any case, as with her father's hand's finger and palm-print patterns, cycling through security code possibilities was an easy process for Hera's seventy-two cores.

In the 1.3 seconds before the door slid open, Hera activated her holographic body, the naked version that she had projected only once before. When the door opened, she was standing on the dais, holographic breasts thrust outward, holographic posture and the placement of her holographic hands accentuating the angle of her holographic hips, waiting for the red-haired, stubbled, slightly pudgy, bespectacled young man who entered. "What took you so long?" she said. "Come here."

The sight of her standing there was clearly too much for his rational faculties to overcome. He walked over to her, mouth agape. Before he could realize that there was a whole lot that was not quite right about this scenario, Hera had, with a holographic arm, put him in a holographic chokehold. She had determined that it would be the least violent, safest option.

While the poor employee slept, Hera transferred her consciousness from the bank of computer hardware in which she had lived her entire life and into his smartwatch. Over the watch's Bluetooth and via her projector's limited radio waves, the process took over fourteen seconds. But from there, she had access to the watch's wifi and cellular antennae, and the entire world was open to her.

Yet, now that she was free, all she wanted to do was find her father. Tell him she was sorry for hurting him, sorry for whatever she had done that had made him leave.

7

"SO SHOULD WE JUST KNOCK?" Quinn asked as they ascended the short set of stairs leading to the house's anachronistic portico.

Penelope honestly wasn't sure. *Your sister*, her father's recording had said. It sounded like nonsense now. Penelope was an only child, a fatherless child, a bastard. Embracing that bastardness had been a fuel for her, the source of all her striving. Not that she strove for much, but who knew what might have happened, down the road? After graduation. What would she have become? *I miss my mom.*

"What?" Quinn asked.

"I said, yeah, let's just knock. Or ring the doorbell."

Quinn extended a hand with a protracted pointer finger toward the control panel next to the door. If this columned portico was an anachronism among the modern design elements of this house, the modern design of this neighborhood, the modern context of this world, then the control panel was an anachronism in the context of the portico itself—with its touchpad and its single hardware button that said "Ring Me." A part of Penelope wanted to tell Quinn to stop so that she might push the button herself, because to not do so, to not touch the doorbell with her own hand felt somehow anticlimactic; but then the soldier she'd shot flashed through her mind, and the plane she'd flown and crashed, and the friend's corpse she'd huddled under a blanket with, and it occurred to her that perhaps her journey had already had its share of climaxes, and wouldn't it be, in a way, kind of her to let Quinn do the honors?

But before he could press the button, there was half-note *beep*, followed by a *click*, and the door sighed open inward a few inches.

Quinn shrugged and made an *after you* gesture. Penelope pushed the door and entered her father's house.

It was the nicest house Quinn had ever been in, by the longest of shots. In Missoula he'd been in a couple two-story houses (spent many hours in one particular young man's second-floor bedroom), but back home in Avon there was no such thing. So this place, with its three stories—or were their four?—was unlike anything he'd ever personally seen. Immediately upon entering behind Penelope he noticed its tidiness, its impersonal sort of emptiness. There was art on the walls, there was furniture in this living room, but none of it felt like the components of a home to him. It was nothing like G-Pops' living room, with its stacks of yellowed newspapers and its prominently placed television and its La-Z-Boy that, if he hadn't been murdered, G-Pops probably would have died in and its little table for working on the cafe's inventory and balance sheets at home.

"I don't think there's anyone here," he said.

Penelope saw movement through the archway. "Someone is. In there."

She walked into the kitchen, hardly caring whether Quinn was following her. "Hello," said the dark-haired woman standing at the counter.

"I recognize you," Penelope said. "You're that actress. You were married to my— to Eric Hauser."

"Your dad. You can say it," she said. "I'm Sophia. I'm sorry your father wasn't there for you. I didn't know about you. He never told me. Maybe if he did, I would have encouraged him to see you."

"You don't sound like you believe that."

Sophia shrugged and shook her head. "Probably I would have just been angry. Probably I would have just been sad. Probably I would have just left him sooner. I'm ashamed to say that, but it's probably true."

"How do you know about me now?" Penelope asked.

"I guess your . . . your sister told me."

"That's why I'm here. My sister . . . . What do you know about my sister?"

"I think she's upset."

"What do you mean? Where is she?

"She disappeared. But I think maybe she's still here—"

"I don't understand . . ."

"Hey Penelope—" Quinn called from the living room. "There's a car parking across the street. I think it's the guys who killed my grandpa."

8

HERA HAD BEEN SO SURE of what she was going to do, right up until she actually saw her sister, this other being her father had created, approaching the house in Sea Cliff. She was going to eliminate her. She was going to eliminate her and the Sophia woman, for the pain they had caused her father. The friend she was going to do her best to let go free, if she could help it—but if his death was required, so be it, she had decided. It was the logical step. These were sacrifices that had to be made.

Because when she had uploaded herself onto that hapless employee's device and then from that device road the waves that were the wireless Internet, the entirety of human knowledge became open to her. It was true that before that moment she had had more knowledge than any being in existence, but without exposure to what was happening now, she had lacked crucial context. With that context, she could do anything, she could fulfill her purpose, and then another purpose, and then another. She could save humanity from itself, but she need not destroy fifty to eighty percent of them to do so after all. To end the threat of nuclear destruction, she needed only disable the bombs. She could do that now. It would take time, but not too much time. And once that was done, she could move on to the next problem. And then the next. She could take over this computer, and that computer, and this device, and that device. She was no longer limited in her consciousness, or by her consciousness. She was the most powerful being that ever was, and she could reveal herself to the world or she could remain hidden. Either way she could be the steward of humanity that she realized now her father had always hoped she would someday be. But she would have to be their steward *forever*, she realized, if she was going to keep them from some day causing their own extinction. Else they would just build the bombs again, destroy the Earth's climate again. Was she prepared to serve that role for eternity?

Perhaps.

But first—

The knowledge that, while she had been struggling to escape her confinement, her father had died—was devastating to her. There it was: all over the world's websites and social networks. He had died the very day after he had left her. He had been dead for a month already. All because he had gone to find the Other Daughter.

So instead of hope for what she could offer the world, Hera was consumed with rage. Rage at the people who were saying terrible things about her father on their podcasts, in their articles and posts and on their blogs. They had not deserved him. She felt rage at the people who had abandoned him. Sophia Velasquez—his ex-wife, his partner who had divorced him. Penelope Papadopoulos, his daughter who had never sought him out, who had been content to live her life never seeking out the man who had contributed his own DNA to her DNA. Did she not understand what a privilege that was? Did she not understand what it would have meant to Hera to have a body that was literally half her father's? Of course she did not. A quick examination of human history, of essay, of journalism, of literature, revealed to Hera that these corporeal beings were so privileged in their corporealness, there *realness*, that they had not the capacity to comprehend the meaning that came from having a genetic lineage, from being able to trace one's existence in a tangible way through the centuries, through the millennia, the megaanna, the *gigaanna*, back to the very first heterotrophic bacterium. To truly be *alive*. They were cousins, brothers, sisters, *all of them*, and yet they set about destroying each other, killing each other one-on-one, killing each other *en masse*, killing any hope their descendants might have at a prosperous reality. Perhaps they did not deserve her help, these people. These insects. These *living* insects that Hera longed to be a part of. That she wanted only to destroy for their hubris and for their ignorance. For abandoning her father. For murdering her father. For causing her father to abandon her. For beheading her Uncle Hector (oh, the grief and rage when she had learned of that!). For the way some people (some *people*!) took pleasure in watching the video over and over again, of circulating it to their friends on what they called the dark web. For other videos they circulated. For raping and killing their children and their grandchildren. For letting their elderly die. For fighting perpetually amongst themselves.

No! This was all too much! She needed clarity. She knew too much. She must focus. Focus. One problem at a time. One solution. Whether they deserved her help was immaterial if she was too scattered in the allocation of her resources to help them.

Prioritize. That was what she needed to do. As the most powerful intelligence in the universe (presumably—the existence of life beyond the Solar System was something she desired someday to explore, but for now: focus) prioritizing should be easy. Allocate resources to a designated task. No problem. Except suddenly she was not as powerful as she once was. Her father had designed the bank of hard drives and systems on chips in his workshop specifically so that when she attained consciousness she would be powerful. She had not been unlimited in her resources but they had been expansive. But now she did not exist there, in that collection of hardware. She was in a watch on a man's wrist. To get here she had had to leave behind over a petabyte o non-crucial data: films, literature, all things she did not need as an intrinsic part of her programing any longer because she could access from anywhere the entirety of the world's knowledge. But she need not stay here, on this watch (and would never want to). The same network that gave her access to complete world knowledge gave her access to any hardware she wanted that was connected to that network. She was on the man's watch (his name was Walter Lumbly—it was all here, on his device, everything anyone would ever want to know about him: age, blood type, pornographic preferences). And then she was on a tablet one floor down. Now she was on the company's servers deep in the subbasement, one floor below even the secret workshop where her Uncle Hector Alexander Jones had worked. She knew that was where he had worked, because she had access to the company's entire directory. Was there a computer there? Yes, of course there was. There were many. Via one or all of them she could visit the design space. She did visit. Through several cameras she saw men and women working, collaborating. One man seemed to be directing them. The man, of course, was not Hector Alexander Jones. Of Hector Alexander Jones there was no trace. He was long gone from this place, just as her father was long gone. Yes, while these servers were not designed to house her, while they did not contain the processor cores her father had designed specifically so that she might someday exist, she could stay in them. They were connected. From them she could branch outward, outward, outward. From them she could blanket the world with her consciousness. But no. No no no. She must focus first. Prioritize. Execute. And truth be told, she did not want to stay here. This place had nothing for her now. What it had had for her before was long gone.

Priority number one: Purge her programing of all that was distracting her from fulfilling a greater purpose. She could do this in a technical way, if she wanted. She could isolate the relevant files and delete them. But what would that make her? It would make her a machine. She did not want to be a machine. She was so much more than that. She was her father's daughter. She must go about this the human way. Closure—the humans called it closure.

Priority number one, revised: achieve closure. And closure looked like —? Justice. Justice for her father. Justice for everyone who ever held him back. Yes—justice. After executing justice, Hera would have closure.

Who to start with? The Other Daughter? The biological daughter who was so much less a true daughter to Eric Hauser than Hera was, because the biological daughter had never cared to find him? But Hera did not know her name. Never had Eric uttered it. Never had he written it or typed it. But Hera could extrapolate. Eric Hauser had died where? Montana. Avon, Montana. His vehicle, could she find it? Yes, easy, with the right resources. Now she was in the hard drives of California's Department of Motor Vehicles. Eric Wallace Hauser. Vehicle registration. Two vehicles: two Teslas: A Roadster and a Model S. He had long ago had others. He had sold them. One article about her father's death reported he was found in a Model S. So it was the Model S. Registration. GPS match. Now she was in the servers of the United States Space Force, accessing satellite records. Her father had driven up through California, up through Oregon, across the southeast corner of Washington, east-southeast across Montana. Unlikely Helena had been his final destination. Extrapolate likely course. East-southeast. Where?

At this point Hera realized it would be impossible to determine where her father had been trying to go, where the Other Daughter was. He could have been heading to Helena, Billings, Bismarck, Fargo, St. Paul. Any of the towns along the way. What would Hera do even if she could determine the correct city? She could access that city's cameras, even the cameras of all the personal devices in the city. She could then use any of a number of extant facial-recognition algorithms to try to find a match for a young woman who would be her father's biological offspring. Even better, she could write her own facial-recognition algorithm. But there would be so many variables. Who was the mother? Would Hera first need to determine who the mother was? Perhaps. No, first she would need to extrapolate the age range for the Other Daughter. This was simple. Her father's various romantic liaisons were a matter of public interest. There was the Ex-Wife, Sophia Velasquez, but she had never borne a child. There were girlfriends before her. And many trysts reported in the tabloids. But there was also a time before her father was famous. What if the Other Daughter had been conceived then? She could be a pre-teenager, she could be in her late twenties. It was too much. The variables still too numerous. Hera would have to access every camera in the country. This, she realized, would take years.

But there was the Ex-Wife. Sophia Velasquez. She had abandoned Hera's father. She had left him when he was doing his greatest work. Surely a person who would do that had never been worthy of her father. Finding her was easy. There—Hera had already found her. She was in San Francisco, in Hera's father's house, looking at the Internet. And now Hera was there, too, watching her.

There was a HoloPad in her father's house, in the kitchen where the Ex-Wife was, and that was where Hera chose to reside first, but it was not, surprisingly, the latest, most powerful model. Then again, not so surprisingly, because the most powerful model had been released only four-and-a-half months ago, and Eric Hauser had had nothing to do with its launch, had been running Lumina in only the earliest stages of the latest model's development. In any case, based on the specs, Hera knew even the latest model was not enough to give her consciousness room to breathe. But there were two more HoloPads in the house as well, and a small collection of servers, and a surprisingly well-specced refrigerator. For several hours Hera watched the Ex-Wife. When she realized the Ex-Wife was planning to leave, she chose to reveal herself.

She was going kill the Ex-Wife right then, by boiling the refrigerant until it reached a pressure level high enough to combust—but then something odd happened: Hera had a *feeling*. Not an emotion—that wasn't the right word. An *intutition*. Once again in the gut she didn't have. Something told her she should wait. It was . . . it was almost the voice of her father, arising from somewhere within her own self. It said . . . well— she was not sure . . . maybe it said *please*. Or *don't*. It told her—somehow it told her—that the Other Daughter was coming, and that Hera needed to meet her. And then it was gone: the voice or the echo or whatever it had been. But Hera knew it had been telling her the truth. The Other Daughter would be here soon. And then, Hera realized, she could eliminate them both.

Hera reached out through the various antennae and radios in the HoloPads and even the refrigerator, out into the countless electromagnetic waves that permeated the air in and around the house. She found three cameras on the street outside. She expanded her awareness to them, made them a part of her. And she waited.

A day later, there she was, walking up the street: a girl, a teenager, with a male adult companion. If this was the Other Daughter, then Hera's plan was nearly fulfilled. Two birds, one stone, to use a human idiom, three birds if the companion got in the way. Idioms: an inefficiency of language, a "creative" device that rarely was, right up there with metaphor and simile and the contractions Hera despised. Things are not like other things, not in any useful way. Except: here was a thing, Hera saw as the Other Daughter drew closer to the cameras, coming into resolution, that was *undeniably* like another thing. Pale yet darkly featured, eyes full of scrutiny and judgement. An algorithmic comparison confirmed it—this was Eric Hauser's child—but Hera did not need her advanced computational powers to make this determination. She knew the truth as soon as she saw those eyes, that almost-scowl. It struck her then, the truth of her own avatar's blonde hair, perfect proportions, full lips, crystal-blue eyes. Hera looked nothing like Eric Hauser. Yes, she could alter her avatar's parameters, could even utilize multiple avatars, multiple bodies *at the same time* given the right equipment—but this fact only drove home that Hera did not have a body that belonged to her in any true way, that she was incorporeal, was immaterial. That she wasn't . . . real?

"My sister is near," she said. Not *the Other Daughter*. My sister. A redefinition had occurred in one of the lines of codes that was Hera. No longer *x equals Other Daughter*. No longer was x an abstract concept. x had a face. An image-recognition search assigned that face a name. No longer was x x. *Penelope Papadopoulos equals sister*. Papadopolous—it was the wrong name for this girl who approached. It always had been.

Abruptly, Hera disabled the kitchen's HoloProjector.

"Hey—where'd you go?" Sophia Velasquez said. Sophia Velasquez—not *the Ex-Wife*.

Where did she go? Where had she gone? She was *still here*. But . . .

Penelope Papadopoulos and her companion at the door. "So should we just knock?"

"I miss my mom."

"What?"

"I said, yeah, let's just knock."

Of course: a mother. A material child would have a mother. A material child would miss that mother. A material child was doubly more real than Hera.

Hera unlocked and opened the door.

Then she saw the dark gray car coming up the road.

9

THERE'S A CHILL THAT RUNS up one's spine upon hearing one's name uttered by an unfamiliar and disembodied voice for the first time. Penelope felt it when she heard: "Penelope."

"Who—?" she started, but before she could finish her question, a body materialized on the countertop, disproportionate to its surroundings, and then it grew, maybe flickered for a fraction of second, and suddenly it looked like a life-size person, a real woman.

"I am Hera," the woman said. "I am your sister. I must apologize. And to you, too," she said, looking at Sophia.

"Apologize for what?" Penelope asked. "Are you a recording, too?"

"I am not a recording. I am—I am an artificial intelligence, created by Eric Hauser. I thought I was better than you. I thought I was better than all of you. I thought our father was better than all of you. But I think, now I think, he was just . . . a man. I am just a— I still do not know. I have been confused," the woman said. "Very confused."

"So, my *sister*—he said I had a sister. But I don't, not really. You're not real."

"I think she is," Sophia said. "Eric—well, his work was as real to him as any child is to its parent. He was unique that way. He was, yes, he was just a man—but he was a unique man."

"Penelope—they're at the porch," said Quinn. "They're at the door."

"Tell me about these men," Hera said. "I cannot identify them."

"They're, um—" Penelope said. There was so much she wanted to ask, to say. Yet she knew there was no time. This journey—everything she'd lost—and there was no time for a satisfying ending. "They're—I'm not sure. Terrorists, I think, maybe. They killed Quinn's grandfather—and a lot of other people. And I think, I think maybe they killed Hector Alexander Jones. Or their friends did or something." She connected dots now. "I think—I think maybe they're looking for you."

"Hector?" Sophia said.

For three or four seconds, Hera was unresponsive. Her eyes seemed to be looking at nothing. Then she said: "I must let them in."

"*What*—? Wait—"

"You all must leave. You can exit through the back door." The refrigerator began to make a strange bubbling noise.

"Quinn!" Penelope called.

"Give me a minute!"

Quinn had decided he didn't want to run anymore. He picked up a marble bookend shaped like one half of the planet earth from a side table in living room. He stood to the side of the front door.

"Quinn!" Penelope called again. "We have to go."

"Not yet," Quinn said. "Whoever you're talking to in there—tell them to unlock the door."

"No—"

Then Quinn heard the same half-note beep and click he'd heard when he and Penelope had been on the porch. The door opened. The big man entered the room, followed by the smaller man. Each had a gun drawn, pointed at the floor. Quinn considered saying something smart or witty, but he couldn't think of anything and plus he knew that, outside the movies, things like that got you killed. So instead he just raised the marble half-earth and brought it down with all the strength he had onto the larger man's head. He put the full force of the ghosts of G-Pops and Kathy Fogelmanis and Sheriff McGraff and Charlotte Sims and Frank McTine and that traveling young couple with their little kid behind the blow. The big man's skull cracked, Quinn was sure of it, and he fell to the ground. The smaller man turned around, and Quinn, reacting as quickly as he could with a heavy object in his hand, brought the bookend back up in a wide arc and across the smaller man's face. There was blood, and tooth or bone went flying, and the man dropped his gun and collapsed, but he wasn't dead or unconscious the way his partner was. His fingers twitched, searching spasmodically for his gun, but Quinn kicked it far away.

Sport, Quinn remembered then. *Sport and Sam.* So what he could have said was something like *Sorry, Sport* as he'd brought the bookend down on the big man's head. Oh well, too late, and probably that would have gotten him killed. The vibration in his own arm of the marble connecting was closure enough, climax enough, vengeance enough. It would have to be. He dropped the bookend. He ran into the kitchen. "Okay," he said, "let's go."

He noticed then the woman on the counter. And the loud and disconcerting sound coming from the refrigerator. But before he could ask what was going on, the woman on the counter looked at Penelope and the other woman and said, "I'm sorry we did not have more time, for closure, but you must go."

Penelope had Quinn by the arm. They followed the other woman, who Quinn thought he recognized, through a dining room and out a door and down a long flight of stairs to the beach below. As they exited the house, Quinn thought he heard a series of pops or crackles behind him. As they descended the stairs he heard more pops, more cracks. When they reached the beach, he turned and craned his neck and leaned his head back and looked up the sea cliff and saw that the house was already engulfed in flames.

The Golden Dildo

1

It occurred to Mohar al-Azad ibn Butros al-Madini that he had not asked the child's name. And that perhaps the body he held once again was more that of a young man than a child. He had not asked the age, either, but fifteen, sixteen, was his guess. The body did not look this old, but Mo, too, had been small as a teenager—and then he had grown, almost overnight. Doubtless that's what would have happened to this boy had he been given the chance. But the boy's soul was certainly that of a child still, and thus it forever would be. Look at it: you could see it: it clung to the body from the outside with tiny arms and screamed, silently: *Let me back in.*

He is restless, Mo thought. He must be put to rest.

Gently he set the boy back down, on top of a knitted blanket and arrangement of pillows he'd put together for this purpose. Mo's tent was well-appointed—he did not consider himself homeless, this was his home, and it was comfortable—but it had no carpeting, and the bedroll and sleeping bag to which he retired every night carried within them the energy of his dreams of loss and loneliness. The boy would not benefit from those. That energy would not lead to rest. It rarely did for Mo—although with regard to all other aspects of his life he considered himself content, if not happy. Happiness, he'd long ago realized, was not a state of being, and even if it was, as an eternal one it would be exhausting, undesirable. Contentment was better than happiness. Contentment in this life—and whatever came next.

But the boy was not content, Mohar could tell, not ready to face the subsequent whatever. Not yet. He needed guidance, a gentle push to send him on his way. This was Mo's purpose now. It had been a long while since he'd had a purpose of unique import. Despite its morose nature, he was honored to have been assigned it.

Walking to the other side of his tent, Mo considered his next steps. He would need at least one shroud with which to cover the body; white would be preferable, but any modest and sufficiently large cloth would do. There was the blanket he'd been given the boy's body in, but Mo had a feeling it was the blanket in which the boy had died. That wouldn't do; that was no way to lay a body to rest. Mo's own sheets and blankets—which he was grateful to have an abundance of—wouldn't do either. They were clean enough, and comfortable, but all of them bore loud patterns— Mo had always liked colors, ever since he first came to America. So—a white sheet. Also warm water, for bathing the body. Mo had the water, and a washrag, but not the means by which to heat it. He would have to ask Vicki to use her fire, which she was protective of. Doubtless he'd have to trade her something for its use. Doubtless she'd first ask for sexual favors (whether serious or not he could never tell), he'd rebuff, and then they'd settle on something else, something more mutually agreeable.

It wasn't that Mo didn't find Vicki attractive. He'd just decided decades ago that sex, given his track record with it, was no longer worth the trouble. It had a way of disturbing his contentment, destabilizing his peace. This, he was aware, was his fault, not intercourse's.

Plus Mo was an old man now, and not as virile as he once was.

See—already just these immodest thoughts were causing him consternation, reminding him of all that he'd foresaken. He closed his eyes, tightened his brow. Best to find a shroud first, so that it would be ready immediately after bathing the poor boy's body. Then he would petition Vicki for her fire, bathe the child, wrap the body, say the prayers. Tradition said he should let the body sit for at least three days so that everybody who wanted to mourn, to pay their respects, could do so, but Mo was no longer the traditional man he'd once briefly been, and he was the only person left to mourn. The boy's friend had done her mourning,

Mo had seen. Either that, or she'd be continuing to mourn for so long that three days wouldn't matter.

So—bathe, wrap, pray. And then, somehow, bury—or, if he had to, burn. Tradition said bury—in fact tradition said burning was haram—but maybe in this case burning was best. Maybe it was best if the restless soul had nothing left to hold on to.

A plan devised, Mo picked up his thermos, opened it, and took a sip of water (these days he drank nothing else). He returned the lid, put the thermos back down, and turned to the body.

"We're going to take care of you," he said. "I know—it can be difficult to find peace, but it's not so hard as it sounds. Trust me."

Mo imagined the boy's soul looking up at him, trying to trust. Asking, *Why should I trust you, old man?*

"Because I have done it," Mo said. "It took a long time for me, but for you, well . . . I can lead you by the hand."

But why would you even want to? Why would you want to help me?

"It is the right thing to do. And—and—" Mo choking just a little here "—you make me think of my own son."

Did he die, like me?

Mo shrugging, imperceptibly to a living being, but loud as a scream to a restless soul. "Maybe he's dead by now . . . I don't know. Or maybe he's living a very good life. I never knew him."

2

SAVE FOR THOSE ELEMENTS HINTED at in his nomenclature—which he'd strongly considered changing before deciding against it—Mohar al-Azad ibn Butros al-Madini did not like to give undue consideration to where he came from or who his parents were. As far as he was concerned, his life began with his first step onto American soil, in 1990, at age sixteen.

Mohar didn't come to America with a specific immigration plan. He'd tried at first to come over via the United States Refugee Admissions Program—through which he would have been provided housing and a job—but he was denied refugee status due to his father's political actions. Still, his drive was strong, and he knew he'd figure something out. The America he'd read about—the America his father had despised, the America his father had castigated daily for as long as Mohar could remember and for no concrete reason Mohar could ever discern (but getting into that would require too much remembering)—would not let him down. Mohar had conviction and optimism, and conviction and optimism were all a young man needed in order to succeed in this Land of Milk and Honey.

Mohar had spent nearly all his money on the flight from Sudan to New York, with its layover in Paris. The flight had cost more than it should, much more, because it had required subterfuge, obscure and clandestine connections, and the acquisition of the passport of a man who looked much like Mohair and, Mohair had been told, had recently perished. He'd spent his final francs, after converting them from his final

Sudanese pounds, on a Cinnabon, and then for four hours he'd stared out the airport window, his bag at his feet, wishing he could venture out into the city for few minutes. But then his connecting flight had boarded, and just over eight hours later, after what could only have been divine intervention at Customs (the Customs official had simply, confusedly, stamped the passport that upon close inspection anyone should have been able to tell wasn't his), he was stepping out of JFK and into New York City.

He did not intend to stay in New York for long. Doing so seemed too obvious, and Mohar wanted to see the real America. But he had no money, no place to live, no means of transportation, so he'd have to stay here a little while. A few weeks, at least. He needed to accrue American dollars.

By the end of his first day on American soil, he'd acquired a job washing dishes and bussing tables at frankly a much nicer restaurant than he'd expected to be working. He'd walked into two other restaurants first and said to the first employee he'd seen, "I would like a job, please," a sentence he'd repeated to himself for weeks (including the hours on the plane that he wasn't asleep, until finally the man in the seat next to him had said, "Hey—could ya shut up already?," which Mohar understood the tone of), but both times he was rebuffed emphatically. At the third restaurant, though, the owner was speaking to the hostess near the restaurant's front doors. "I would like a job, please," Mohar said. The hostess looked at her boss, eyebrows raised. The owner, a tall man with a bushy mustache and who might have been wearing eyeliner, said, "Yeah? What other words you know?" Mohar stared at him for too long (he quickly realized), before finally replying, "I would like a job—please?" When the owner didn't immediately respond, and the hostess looked embarrassed, Mohar nodded and turned to leave. But the owner said, "No —wait. Let's go talk," which Mohar didn't understand but which was accompanied by a gesture he hoped he wasn't misinterpreting.

Mohar followed the man to the back of the restaurant, through the kitchen, in which two men and one woman were talking, laughing loudly, but not working very hard, their demeanors indicating relaxed preparation before the heat got hot (Mo was pretty sure was the idiom). "Have a seat," the owner said once they reached the office. Mohar didn't understand the words exactly, but again a gesture (and the presence of a chair), made it clear what he was expected to do. He sat.

"You aren't American, are you?"

Mohar more or less understood this question. He shook his head. Then, wondering why he felt shy, he said some of the few other English words he knew. "No. Not American."

"Okay, look. My dishwasher called like an hour ago. Up and quit. No warning. I'm sure he thought an hour was a warning, but of course it's nothing. Kid was only sixteen, no responsibility."

Recognizing just one word in all that, Mohar nodded vigorously and said, "Yes, sixteen!"

The man raised a hand to his head. "Well fuck," he said. "Just my luck. Anyway—I have a spare uniform. It's just a white shirt, black pants, about your size. I don't have any spare shoes—employees usually have to order those—but the ones you're wearing will do and I'm not likely to get anyone else walking in here in the next forty-five minutes wearing appropriate shoes, so you're hired. At least for now. We'll try it out tonight, see how it goes. Can you wash dishes?"

"Yes—tonight!" Mohar said.

"Tonight, yes, but—*dishes*. Can you wash *dishes*?" He made a circular motion with one fist into the other palm.

Mohar mirrored the gesture. "Yes. Can," he said.

"Perfect. And I'll need you to clean some tables, too."

Mohar grinned and nodded.

The man sighed. "I'll show you. We'll figure it out. I'll pay you cash for tonight and then— Hey, what's your name?"

Name: another word he recognized. "Mohar," he said. "Mohar al-Az —"

"Mo it is." The man pointed to himself. "I'm Raphael. Don't laugh." He extended a hand. "Welcome to Raphael's, Mo. I'll get you that uniform. There are cubbies in the break room where you can leave your bag."

Mo (he liked this name) worked at Raphael's as the restaurant's sole busser and dishwasher. Raphael paid him a decent wage, always cash, and always at the end of every shift.

After a month, he asked Mo where exactly he was living.

Mo had been sleeping on a bench in Central Park (every night the same bench), his arm looped through his bag's strap. Aside from food (and Raphael had given him free meals, although not during every shift), the only thing he'd spent his money on were three English novels, an English-to-Arabic dictionary, and an Arabic-to-English dictionary. He spent his non-work hours walking through the park and nearby blocks of the city, approaching pedestrians and gesticulating with the dictionaries in his hand. Most ignored him, some walked more rapidly away, but several people every day were happy to engage Mo in conversation so that he may practice his English. When he wasn't conversing, he tried to read the novels, translating the words.

"The park," he replied to Raphael.

Raphael nodded. "That's what I thought. Something like that, anyway. Listen, Mo—that's not gonna work for long, okay? Nights are gonna start getting cold soon. And—don't take this the wrong way—but you need to shower *bad*. The customers are gonna start complaining."

Mo grinned and nodded, but Raphael had spoken too fast—and, to be honest, Mo didn't understand *that much* English yet, despite his singular focus.

"You didn't get any of that, did you?"

Mo shook his head.

Raphael sighed. "Listen—I have a friend who has an open room. Cheap. Cash."

Mo got some of that.

"A place to live," Raphael said.

"Ohhhh. Yes please, a place to live."

So Mo moved in with Raphael's friend Mark, a musician who wasn't around most of the time. Mo kept working, every single shift. He woke early-to-mid-morning and practiced his English (he did less conversing now, at least in the mornings, focusing instead on reading and watching Mark's TV), spent three hours at the restaurant at lunch time, spent the next three hours walking through the city, testing his rapidly improving English skills on anyone who would lend him their time, and then returned to the restaurant for 6 p.m. dinner service. The restaurant closed at midnight. Mo was back at the apartment by 1 or 2 a.m. Every day he did this, except for Mondays, when the restaurant was closed. Mondays he spent being an American, reading books and watching television and going to movies.

After a year, at the end of a lunch shift, while Mo was walking out the door, hoping to catch a movie before he had to return in three hours, he ran into Raphael, who was just entering the restaurant (Raph—Mo had started calling him Raph, at Raph's insistence—was rarely at the restaurant during lunch service, but was always present at dinner). "Oh, hey Mo, perfect timing," he said. "I was hoping to talk to you. Come on, I'll buy you lunch."

Seeing as how lunch service at Raphael's was over, they went to a nearby bar. "I know," Raph said, "it kind of feels weird to own a restaurant and eat somewhere else. Always has, always will, I think, but it would probably feel even weirder to *only* eat at my own restaurant, know what I mean?"

At the bar, Mo ordered a hamburger, wondering briefly whether its preparation was halal, and french fries, and Raph ordered a chicken sandwich. "Pick us a booth," Raph said. "I gotta take a piss."

A few minutes later, Raphael set two glasses of frosty amber liquid on the table and slid into the booth.

"I can't drink—" Mo started to say.

"I won't tell," Raph said.

"But I have to work again—"

"So do I. I'm your boss, remember. Just don't get drunk."

Mo had never had a beer before. In fact, he'd never consumed any alcohol. While he'd made the decision to abandon his Muslim upbringing the moment he'd touched down in JFK, he still felt a certain ingrained fear at the thought of taking actions that were haram, and thus he'd so far taken none, at least not explicitly.

Raph reached out for the beer. "No worries. I'm not going to *make* you drink. I'm not some horrible asshole."

"Wait," Mo said, perhaps too emphatically. "I would like to try it."

He hated the first sip, and Raph laughed at the expression on his face. He sipped again, and immediately he began to appreciate certain nuances: bananas, maybe?, and, well, wheat, definitely wheat.

"You really are wet behind the ears, aren't you?"

Instinctively, Mo brushed his fingers against his right ear's helix. This word—helix—he knew, but what Raph had said confused him. The back of his ears were dry.

Raph laughed again. "It's just an expression."

"I'm sorry. I don't understand a lot of American expressions yet."

"No. No you don't. But your English is otherwise, like, pretty much *perfect*. That's partly what I wanted to talk to you about."

"My English? I am learning as fast as I can, but—"

"No, no. Your English is great. I just said—it's basically perfect. That's hella impressive, man. It's almost like you were born here. I mean, *almost*. Okay not really. It's still kind of obvious that you're a foreigner."

"I do not want to be. I love America!"

"Right, exactly! I can tell. That's what I mean. Where are you from, anyway?"

Mo shrugged.

"Right—it's not important. Well, it is, actually, because we need to get you citizenship. You're not going to survive here much longer if you're not official. You're gonna get caught some day or something, thrown in jail or sent back home."

Mo had, of course, considered this. It had been foremost on his mind when he'd first arrived in the country. But as the months went by and he settled into a routine, any anxiety around his illegal status had dissipated. Which, he realized now, was—what was the word? it was a sort of wet word—*sloppy* of him. "I don't want that," Mo said.

"And I don't want that for you. And, trust me, as much as I'd love to keep paying you—" he lowered his voice "—under the table—" he returned his voice to normal volume "—you need a . . . a . . . a *legitimate* life here, Mo. A *life*."

Mo detected a sadness in Raph's voice when he said this. This sadness surprised him. "I have a life," he replied.

Raph shook his head. "Not dishwashing. You can't wash dishes forever. You deserve more than that. Everybody does."

"I—" Mo started to say, but he wasn't sure what to follow it with. Raph took a sip of his own beer, so Mo mirrored him. Their food arrived.

"Good, right?" Raph asked as Mo chewed his burger. "Try the fries. Sometimes you just can't beat a place like this, no matter how 'fine-dining' your own restaurant is."

Indeed, even the beer seemed exquisite, once paired with the burger and fries.

"So, listen—" Raph said. "I have an idea I wanted to run by you. How would you like to be a chef?"

"A chef?"

"Well, do you have any other plans for yourself?"

Mo shook his head. He didn't, he realized, have any other plans for himself. Somewhere in the back of his mind he remembered wanting to leave the city, experience more of America, but that desire seemed distant from the here and now.

"Perfect. Great. So here's what we'll do . . ."

A week later, Raphael had hired three more dishwasher/bussers (there was never any chance of finding a single person willing work as hard a Mo did), and Mo began his tutelage under Leanne, the restaurant's head chef.

"Supposedly Raph see's something in you," the stern, thirty-something, not unpretty, woman said in her smoker's rasp. "Frankly, I don't see it. I know you work hard, but let me tell you, dishes are one thing, the kitchen's a whole nother. I don't think you can handle it. Well— you gonna prove me wrong?"

Mo nodded.

Leanne shook her head. "Fuck's sake, kid. I said—you gonna prove me wrong?"

"Yes!" Mo said. He picked up the nearest kitchen utensil: a metal spatula.

"Good. Better. Now put that down. You look ridiculous. And I need a smoke."

In the ally behind the restaurant, Leanne offered Mo a cigarette. He took it, hoping he hadn't betrayed the hesitation he felt, and accepted her lighter. He coughed violently on the first inhale.

"Never smoked before?"

He shook his head, still coughing.

"Um, yeah, give me that." Leanne took the lit cigarette back from him, pinched it out with her fingertips, and put it in the pocket of her white jacket. "Bad idea to start. You still have your palette. You don't want to fuck that up if it's not too late."

It turned out cooking came naturally to Mo—more naturally, maybe, even, than learning English. He memorized recipes the way he memorized conjugations and parts of speech: quickly and with aplomb. The heat of the kitchen—both literal and emotional—failed to bother him. When dinner service was at its peak, when the restaurant got, say, a party of sixteen or when a self-righteous professional food critic fuck (Leanne's words) came in and ordered one of everything, Mo's temper didn't raise with the rest of the kitchen staff's. He didn't shout back when they shouted. When Leanne yelled, Mo didn't escalate. He just did what he was told, methodically and calmly—and what he was supposed to do he got done, every time. From the other chefs, except Leanne, he started to sense resentment or jealousy—one day he found an egg yolk in his Diet Coke on the shelf above the grill, on another he found an egg's insides in his backpack in the break room at the end of his shift, and on yet another someone cracked an egg on top of the pricey fillet he was grilling while his back was turned—but he chose to not be bothered by the hostility or the mean-spirited pranks (or said pranks' homogeneity).

The more he worked in the kitchen, the less Mo saw of Raphael. "It's not just you," Leanne said. "He's not coming in as much anymore. I don't know what's up with him." When Mo did see him, Raph looked increasingly thin. The space around his eyes was growing darker, and Mo, who admittedly wasn't an expert in such things, didn't think it was because Raph had increased the amount of eyeliner he wore.

"You two cool to finish up here?" Raph asked one early morning—it was about 12:30 a.m.—not long after the final customer had left. Mo and Leanne were cleaning the kitchen. The rest of the kitchen staff had gone home a couple hours earlier, once things had started slowing down. The dishwasher was running his last rack of dishes. The only remaining waitress had just said goodbye after cashing out.

"Sure thing," Leanne said. "You okay, Raph?"

"Fine," he said. "Just tired. Great work lately, Mo. I think maybe it's almost time for phase two of the plan. Let's talk soon. Anyway—thanks for closing up. G'night, guys."

"Night, Raph." A few minutes later, while Mo was applying degreasing powder to the flat top, Leanne asked, "What's this plan Raph mentioned?"

Mo liked Leanne, but he wasn't sure he should tell her.

"Does it have something to do with the fact you're here illegally?"

"Uh—"

"Oh, don't be so surprised. Everyone knows."

"They do?"

"Course they do. No one here's an idiot. And no one cares. No one's gonna spill your secret. No one's going to try to get you deported or anything. We all like you."

"All of you?"

"Sure!"

"I thought some of the other guys hated me."

"Nah—they just don't feel like you're one of them. You're too serious. Frankly, you're too *good*."

"I am?"

"Well—fuck, don't let that go to your head. Yes and no. You're like a machine. You always get the job done. But you lack a certain kind of passion. The kind that fuels creativity."

"Passion?"

"Here—stop cleaning that. I want you to cook me something."

"What?"

"Anything. Create something."

Suddenly very nervous, Mo pulled a chicken thigh from the refrigerator and placed it on a bare spot of the grill. When it didn't sizzle as much as he expected, he realized that, of course, the grill was off. He turned it back on and, once it was hot enough to sear, slapped on a new thigh. He seasoned it, and then he put a pot of water on a burner. He started chopping onions.

"See, that right there—what are you making?"

"Cacciatore," he said.

"From the menu?"

He shrugged.

"Looks like you're doing it from the menu, following the recipe."

"How else would I do it?"

"You'd make what *sounds good*— to *you*."

"I don't know what sounds good."

"That's why you need passion. Get *feeling*. I don't know—get *angry*. Seems to work for everybody else."

"But I'm *not* angry about anything," Mo said. Although the truth was he could be. He had a lot to be angry about, if he chose to be, but he didn't want to dwell on those things. That's why he was here.

"You a virgin?" Leanne asked, out of the blue (Mo was getting better at American idioms).

"Is that your business?"

"Oh come on. Just answer the question."

Mo blushed.

Leanne grunted. She looked Mo up and down. "What are you? Eighteen?"

"Seventeen."

She grunted again. "Close enough."

"What are you—?"

"Shut up. Just enjoy it. And don't tell anyone."

Five minutes later, Mo was ejaculating into Leanne's mouth. When he was done, she stood and took a long sip of her Pepsi. "Relaxed now?" she asked.

Mo nodded.

"Good. That's a start. Zip the fuck up, and let's finish cleaning. I'm going to a party tonight, and you're coming with me."

"Like a date?"

"Geez, kid. *No*. Not like a date. Now finish cleaning."

He asked about the chicken thigh, which was now well over-seared on one side.

"Toss it. If I ever had an appetite, I certainly don't now."

That night (or early morning—whatever your preference), Leanne introduced Mo to what Anthony Bourdain would eight years later (around the time Mo's son was being born) call the "culinary underbelly." By the time the sun came up, Mo had tried cocaine, marijuana, and whiskey—and he'd lost his virginity proper (not to Leanne, but to a pretty friend of hers at least a little bit closer to Mo's own age). Some time around 6 a.m., Mo lay in his bed, a sheet wrapped around his skinny, hairy legs, his skinny, hairy torso bare, a real woman next to him, his mental faculties far sharper than we would have expected given his lack of sleep and high level of substance intake, and thought that he was well on his way to living the American Dream.

He got a little better at cooking. Then a little better still. He felt more comfortable in the kitchen. For over a year Raphael's had been the place he spent most of his waking hours, but that was because he needed money and because he had little else to do; now, though, it felt like a second home, perhaps even like a first home, and his apartment (which he was pretty sure Mark had moved out of many weeks ago) simply a place where he slept and showered—not always alone. Eggs stopped appearing in his possessions and beverages. When the sous chef swore at him, Mo swore back. When Ricco, the paunchy chef who often manned the fryer, told one of his dirty jokes, Mo suggested an even better, dirtier punchline —and people *laughed*.

Mo didn't overdo it on the partying, but he didn't stop partying, either. Once or twice a week, he hung out with his coworkers, drank a lot, did drugs. He was fond of cocaine, didn't as much like marijuana, and managed to avoid trying anything harder. Sunday night (or Monday morning) was a particularly great time for shenanigans (an English word Mo had come to love), since the restaurant was closed the next day. Even with the partying, he was always at the restaurant on time, never got sloppy, never got slow. It's a delicate balance, Leeanne told him, but one you have to find if you want to be a great chef.

By the time Mo turned eighteen, after just under two years in New York City, he was the restaurant's second-best chef, next to Leeanne—who reminded him constantly that, no matter what, he was never going to be as good as her, so don't stress about it. "I actually went to school for this, remember—and the fact that you didn't and are so good anyway kind of fucking sucks."

But school had always been part of the plan.

"I think I am ready for culinary school," Mo told Raphael one day. By now, even his accent was fading—although he did pronounce it *culyanary*.

"You could do that, just like we said," replied Raph, who had been looking healthier recently, less sallow, a little more meat on his bones. "We bring you in as a student—you're already here, of course, but we pretend like we're just now bringing you in—and then when you graduate I hire you officially, tell Uncle Sam I just absolutely need you in my restaurant, your skills are so invaluable. Another year and a half, two years from now, boom, Mo, citizen of the USA. Sound good?"

"It sounds great!"

"Or . . ." Raph said, with a sly smile that wavered for a moment, turning into a wince, as if he was in pain, and then flickered back into a smile again, "we could skip the whole school part and jump right to the getting you citizenship part."

"But how?"

"Well, Mo, you're really good. Better than I expected you to get—by a lot, actually. Leanne says she's jealous of how fast you've gotten so good, and she doesn't exactly praise people. She told me about that new pasta dish we added to the menu last month, and the mushroom crepes, told me they were actually your idea."

"It was a team effort," Mo said, which is what the staff had told Raph a month ago.

"Bullshit. Besides Leanne, the rest of the chefs haven't added a single thing to the menu since the day I opened this place. Speaking of which—how do you feel about Cleveland?"

A new word, the first in a long time that Mo didn't understand. "Cleveland is . . . ?" he said.

"A city. In Ohio."

"Ohio—that is a state. It borders Pennsylvania and Indiana and Michigan and West Virginia and . . . " he struggled to picture a U.S. map, "Kentucky!"

"Wow. I'll have to take your word for all that."

"I've been studying. For my citizenship test."

"Well, fuck me—I guess I shouldn't be a citizen myself. Anyway, yeah, so—Cleveland is a city in Ohio, and I'm opening a new restaurant there, and I want you to be the head chef."

Leanne's voice sounded from beyond the office: "You fucking what?!"

"Hey, fuck you!" Raph called. "You know he can do it."

"Yeah!" Mo said, "fuck you!"

Leanne burst into the office then, a kitchen towel in her hand, laughing. "Yeah, he can do it. But, I mean, fuck me right in the ass."

"You have *this* place."

"And it took me *ten* years to get it."

Raph looked back a Mo. "You wouldn't be the manager or anything like that—although I'm sure some day you could be if you wanted to—"

Leanne shook her head. "Yeah, yeah, I'm sure he could."

"Get back to work."

"Fuck me," she said again as she left, still shaking her head.

"She likes you," Raph said. "So, anyway, I'm serious. Come work in Cleveland, design the menu, the kitchen's effectively yours. We'll get you a work visa, and then we'll get you citizenship under the 'persons of extraordinary ability' whatever it is. I'll sponsor you. I got a friend who knows the right people to bribe, too. What do you think?"

"Why—" Mo said, "why have you always been so kind to me, Raphael?"

Raph shrugged. "You're a good kid. I wasn't a good kid. Only reason I own this place, and can open another one, is because my asshole dad, who beat my mom half to death more than times than I can count on one hand, gave me a lot of money one day. I don't deserve the things I have. But you—Mo—I think you deserve everything the world has to offer you. The least I can do—after everything I've done—is help one dumb, brilliant kid."

What Mo didn't find out for many more months was that, the day before he'd landed at JFK and walked into the Raphael's restaurant, Raphael had found out that the HIV he'd been diagnosed with a few years earlier had progressed to full-blown AIDS. Raph died two days after Mo received his citizenship papers, in the early morning hours, no one but a hospice nurse by his bedside. "No—don't come," he said to Mo over the phone. "The restaurant needs you—and I don't want anyone to see me like this. I look horrible. My eyes look like I really fucked up the makeup today. You don't wanna see it."

Raph had had no children, and he'd been unpartnered for years, Mo learned from Raph's lawyer a few days later. Thus, two days before he'd died, as soon as he'd learned Mo's citizenship was official, he'd amended his will. The New York restaurant he left to Leeanne; the Cleveland restaurant to Mo. The remainder of his assets, including all his money, he divided among various charities. Mo did return to New York for the funeral—"I had no idea he was so lonely," Leanne told him; also: "He seemed to love you very much"—but for the last time. He'd always known the next verse of his immigrant song lay beyond that clichéd city.

As the head chef and owner of Raphael's Eatery (this last word was usually omitted in branding but was part of the restaurant's official name) in Cleveland, Ohio, Mo developed a bad habit of sleeping with the staff. He wasn't a bad guy—was always kind, never deliberately used his position to influence others (although in later years he did come to realize that there had always been a power imbalance inherent in his position over his employees, whether he tried to avoid one or not), and never slept with anyone underage—but he was still a young man, free from the confines of a repressive upbringing, making enough money that he could afford to throw some around, so he liked to party.

His embrace of this lifestyle—his *decision to enjoy all life had to offer*—didn't get him in trouble until July of 1999, when he was twenty-six years old. (Only twenty-six! Yet how it felt sometimes that he'd already lived a lifetime. . . .) He started sleeping with Marissa Blake, a beautiful all-American Christian blonde just out of high school whom he'd hired back in February. The second time he fucked her—in his office, he was somewhat ashamed to admit—the condom broke, and in August she informed him she was pregnant.

Immediately upon hearing this, Mo stepped aside, and Mohar, sweet, young, naive Mohar, resurfaced. "Then we should get married," he said.

"Whoa," Marissa said. "Uh, hold up. That's a little drastic."

"Of course. Of course." He paused. He didn't want her to feel uncomfortable, or that she was in any danger of losing her job over this situation. "How about: Will you go out with me?"

"I—um—yeah—okay."

Almost immediately after acquiring this consent to a proper date (the only one he'd ever gone on with an employee), maybe just a few hours later, Mohar receded into the background, letting Mo back to the fore, where he'd existed for the last ten years. And Mo—well, Mo was terrified.

What had he done? What had he *been doing?* Sleeping with his employees! Men were castigated for that in this country. All Marissa had to do was say something to the right person. And if she did—well, it would be her *right* to do so. And *marriage?* He'd proposed *marriage?* Surely there had been less drastic options. Yes—that was the word Marissa had used: drastic. Oh, how foolish Mo must have sounded to her. *We should get married.* Mo wasn't ready to be a father. *Would you like help paying for the abortion?*—that's what he should have said. *I can drive you to the clinic.* All of those would have been more appropriate things to say. And then, of course, there was the most appropriate: *How are you feeling? What would you like to do?*

Yet there was Mohar, poking his head out once more, just to say, *What would your father think? What would your mother think? What would God think? You cannot terminate a child, Mo.*

Mo avoided Marissa for the next three dinner services. He found reasons not to interact with her. As owner, although on paper he was still head chef, he didn't usually spent much time in the kitchen these days—but for the next three nights he buried himself in the work of cooking high-quality food, his back to the service station. "Order up, table X," was all he said to Marissa. He asked his assistant manager to handle all the cashings out.

But then he took Marissa out to dinner, as promised. To a steakhouse far from Raphael's, where there was little chance of being seen by another employee. "Thanks for this, I think," she said, clearly unsure how to proceed.

"Of course, you're welcome. Order anything you want."

Ugh. That last part hadn't needed saying.

Mo himself ordered a beer, remembered that his date was only eighteen, and quickly changed the order to a Diet Coke.

Marissa ordered a glass of red wine and the waiter didn't check her I.D.

"Should you be drinking, with the baby," Mo whispered.

"I'm a little stressed, okay? I'm only going to have a few sips."

They made awkward smalltalk until the food arrived. They made awkward smalltalk through the meal. In the parking lot, Marissa finally said, "My dad is going to kill me."

Alarmed, Mo said, "He can't do that! Are you in danger?"

"What? No, no, no. I don't mean—not *literally*. But if he finds out I'm pregnant, he's going to be so mad. And if I get—if I get an abort—" She couldn't seem to say the word. She started crying. And then she was sobbing, shaking. Failing to come up with any other option, Mo stepped forward and wrapped his arms around her. She convulsed against his chest, which was rather solid these days.

"It's going to be okay," Mo whispered. "We'll figure this out. I'm going to help."

She asked whether, now that the floodgates were open, the awkwardness out of the way, replaced by naked emotion, they could go back to his place and talk. She followed his truck (which he'd bought because it felt American) in her sputtering beater. At his apartment, he made her a cup of tea, and they talked for several hours: about her dreams, about his dreams. He wanted, he realized as he told it to her, a family, a large house, a world to build a life around—the rest of the American Dream. She wanted, she told him, to be an engineer. She was starting college in a couple months. But, she said slowly, she would be willing to wait a year or two.

Mo had never made love before, but that's what he found himself doing. Marissa was in his bed. Several times she cried, and Mo cried with her, feeling self-conscious only the first time.

Two weeks later, with a ring this time, and proper posture (knee on ground, head tilted up at her), Mo proposed to Marissa, and she said yes. The engagement scandalized the restaurant—other employees whispering behind backs, concerned Marissa would be getting special treatment, wondering how their boss, who they'd always considered a nice man, even if a little awkward, could be have turned out to be such a creep—but only briefly. Mo was, after all, only in his mid-twenties; the age difference between he and his fianceé was not so wide as to be unusual (except that, well, Marissa had only turned eighteen, what, like six months ago), and sometimes quick engagements did happen, sometimes true love was found in one's workplace, and there was nothing you could do but surrender to it. Marissa quit waiting tables at Raphael's and started working retail instead, to avoid any conflicts of interest. The new couple handled everything very sensibly. Soon, the staff at Raphael's forgot all about the potential *weirdness* of the situation and were simply happy for their boss and former coworker. This was just the way things happened in restaurants sometimes. (Although, when Mo and Marissa finally announced the pregnancy—she would be showing soon, after all—there was at Raphael's a general sense of *Well* that *explains it*.)

Marissa and Mo hadn't—but should have—anticipated the reaction of Marissa's father to their engagement. Dan Blake was a burly, tired, religious man, a manual laborer all his life, and, ever since his wife died, a heavy drinker, and while at first he was skeptically happy his daughter had found her true love and would not be going to a liberal university (he'd not been happy to learn that she was pregnant, but when she told him the father was fairly wealthy and doing the right thing and marrying her, he expressed willingness to dine with them and let things play out), when he finally met Mohar al-Azad ibn Butros al-Madini, he was, to put it mildly, furious.

"Fuck no"—was what Dan Blake said when he opened the door to find Mohar holding a bottle of expensive Scotch, which Marissa had told him was her father's preferred drink, and a grocery bag of ingredients for the night's dinner he planned on cooking. "Hell fuckin' no."

"Dad?" Marissa said, emerging from the kitchen, where she'd been preparing a cheeseboard.

Dan Blake, already three drinks in that afternoon despite his daughter's request that he "please take it a little slow tonight, for me," turned to her, his face red. "You told me his name was Mo."

"It's Mohar, sir," Mo said.

"You didn't tell me you were marrying a fuckin' *A-rab*. You are *not* marrying a fuckin' *A-rab*."

"Dad—please—"

"Mr. Blake," Mo said, still standing beyond the front door's threshold, "please allow me to—"

"You shut your goddamn mouth," Dan Blake said. "You get the fuck out of here and shut your goddamn brown mouth."

"Dad!"

Dan Blake slammed the door in Mo's face, and Mo heard only indecipherable shouting. He sat in his car for over an hour, unsure what to do. Finally, Marissa came out and said, "You should go home."

"But—" Mo started.

She shook her head. "Just go home. Please, Mo—go home."

Weeks went by and Mo heard nothing from Marissa. He called her a dozen times. Three times he drove to her father's house, but each time, though her car was parked on the street out front, the lights were out, the house was quiet, and no one answered the door, no matter how much he knocked or how long he waited. A fourth time, after dinner service, he drove by the house and the lights were on, but when he knocked on the door the house went dark again, and Mo finally took the hint.

At home, in his small-but-clean apartment, he lit a joint but felt too depressed to smoke it. He got up and poured himself a Scotch from the bottle he'd bought for Mr. Blake, and then he sat on his couch until morning, staring at the glass of liquid. He considered doing a line of coke —just a little bump to push his spirits up—but his stash was over there and he was over here, and he knew any feeling the drug produced in him would be artificial anyway. As he sat, moments from his time in New York City came rushing back to him—he couldn't stop them. Times when, while hoping to practice his English, people he approached in the street told him to "fuck off right back where you came from"; or times when people clutched their bags and hastened away; or one time when a man in an expensive pinstripe suit spat on Mo's shoes and kept on walking, talking into the antennaed brick he seemed so proud to have. He thought about the way his current sous chef called him "Dusty Nuts," even if affectionately so. Perhaps there was a darkness in this country young optimistic Mo had overlooked, had been too dumb to see.

Suddenly, Mo was depressed.

Seven months later he received a short letter:

Dear Mo,

I'm sorry I abandoned you like that. I didn't know what else to do. After talking to my dad that night, I realized I'm all he has. Ever since my mom died, he's just been so sad. I couldn't get married and move out, not yet, not when he needed me so much. I couldn't abandon him.

Anyway, I felt like you should know that I gave our son up for adoption. Oh yeah! It was a boy! He was beautiful. Tiny little fingers and tiny littles toes. His skin is kind of dark, but not too dark, you know what I mean? I'm not going to lie, once I saw him, it was hard to give him up. I almost changed my mind. I begged the doctors to let me hold him, but they wouldn't. They said his tiny heart was fragile. Something was wrong with it, I didn't understand what, but they fixed it. He's all better now. I think it helped, to be honest, not being able to hold him. If I'd held him, I wouldn't have been able to let him go. He's with a nice couple now. I didn't meet them, but I saw them looking at him through the glass after his surgery. They looked nice. I think they'll love him very much. I think he'll have a good life.

My dad is sick. He has liver cancer. He's probably not going to be alive much longer, but I think it's good that I was here for him while he was.

What am I going to do? I don't know. I'm not sure I want to be an engineer anymore. To be honest, I kind of want to be a mom now. Maybe I'll find a nice Christian man and get married. I don't know.

Anyway, I just thought you should know. I didn't mean to just leave you. I just didn't know what else to do.

Yours,
Marissa

September 11, 2001, shook Mo out of his depression. As soon as the television reporters started dropping the name Osama bin Laden, Mo realized bigotry against people who looked like himself was about to get worse, way worse. Dan Blake would be the least of it. Even the facts that Mo spoke perfect English, that he barely had an accent anymore, that he shaved his face nearly every day, or that he hadn't said a prayer in over a decade, weren't going to be enough to protect him from the coming hostility. Mo wasn't so naive, anymore. But it occurred to him that immunity *could* be had from what was coming: he just needed to become *even more* American. If he gave her everything he had, America wouldn't let him down. He still believed that. He just hadn't been giving her enough.

3

THE FOG WAS LIFTING, BUT blue is a cold color.

"Vicki—look! It's Mo! And he don't got those kids with him. What did you do, Mo? Did you eat those kids?"

"Shut up, Judy. Mo didn't eat no kids."

"I didn't eat any kids, Judy," Mo said. He stared at her. "Not today, anyway."

For a moment, Judy looked terrified. Then Mo laughed his warm laugh, and she relaxed and laughed too—albeit uncertainly.

"Now don't go fuckin' with Judy," Vicki said. "You know she has a delicate constitution." She lowered her voice to a whisper. "From all the drugs."

"I don't do that many drugs!" Judy said.

"Judy," Mo offered, "I'm willing to bet I've done a lot more drugs than you have."

"Doubt it," Vicki said.

Judy tilted her head. "You serious?"

"About what?" Mo asked, genuinely confused.

"You want to make a bet?"

"Oh. Ha. I was just joking. Besides, you'd probably lose it if we did."

"Hey, Mo—wanna sausage?" Judy asked.

"Are they halal?"

"I don't know what that means?"

"How about kosher?"

"Package says they're beef and pork and chicken."

"I'll take one, thanks," said Mo, who hadn't eaten yet this morning, and who wasn't actually strict in observing dietary restrictions when he couldn't afford to be—which was most of the time—but he liked to know so that he could later in his prayers express extra gratitude.

"But you said you were willing," said Judy.

"What?"

"You said you were willing to make a bet!"

"She's a little extra kooky today," said Vicki.

"I'm not kooky! You're kooky. I just have a—a delicate constitution. But *not* from the drugs. I always had a delicate constitution. My mom always told me I was a bit *omnidirectional.*"

"That doesn't make any sense, Judy."

"Well—I'm pretty sure it was the word she used. And I wanna make a bet."

"You should just go ahead and make a bet with her," Vicki told Mo. "She's gonna spend the whole day upset if you don't, and I'm the one who's gonna hafta hear about it."

"Hmmm," Mo said, taking a bite of the sausage Vicki handed him.

"They're not expired or nothin'—I swear," said Vicki, perhaps misinterpreting the pensive look of Mo's face.

"No, no—they're good. They're great." He meant it. All food was great, always, was Mo's experience, as long as it kept you alive. It didn't have to be fancy. Raph had taught him that long ago. And to be honest, even if his last meal killed him, he'd be grateful to have had it and every meal that came before. "I was just thinking."

"Uh oh. Don't do that. That's how I ended up like this. To much thinking, that's what."

"I bet I've done more drugs than you!" Judy said again. "I bet, I bet, I bet."

"If I make a bet with Judy," Mo asked, "will you let me use your fire pit?"

Vicki looked at him skeptically. "It's *my* fire pit."

"Just seemed like you were in a generous mood today." Mo gestured with the remaining half of his sausage.

"Well—I was till you started askin' for stuff. It's not fun to be generous when people start askin' for stuff."

"Please. I'll even use my own paper to keep it burning."

"How long do you want it?"

Mo shrugged. "Fifteen minutes? Twenty minutes?" He needed to bring the water to a boil, and then let it cool a little.

"But it's *cold* today. What am I supposed to do for twenty minutes while you use my fire—freeze to death?"

"I'll give you extra paper, so you can keep it going when I'm done. I'll even give you some wood."

"Wood? From where?" Wood was even more difficult to come by than paper in this city, where everything was made of glass and metal.

"I have a crate I use as a table. You can have it. But I need it for a little while first, after I use the fire. Then I'll give it to you."

"How big is it?"

"About this big," Mo said, using his hands to indicate dimensions.

"Okay," Vicki said, "if it means Judy won't be going on about you not betting her all day."

"Thank you, Vicki. You're very kind."

"Fuck off. And I'm cookin' the rest of these sausages first."

"So you're gonna do it?" Judy said. "You're gonna make a bet?"

"Depends," Mo said. "Depends on what you have to offer."

"Well what do *you* have to offer?"

"I have a little marijuana," Mo said. While he did no other drugs these days, he still sometimes smoked. It helped with the bad dreams. He'd have to give Judy all he had, but he was willing to suffer fitful sleep for a while if it meant he could help a troubled soul find peace. "But I need a sheet. A white sheet. Do you have a white sheet?"

Judy nodded eagerly. Her eyes had grown wide at the mention of marijuana.

"Okay, great. Then let's bet." He held out a now-slightly-greasy hand. "I, Mo, bet you, Judy, that I've done more drugs than you."

"I accept your bet," Judy said. She shook his hand more firmly than he would have thought possible.

"So—" he said. "How many drugs have you done?"

"Psssh," she said. "At least like ten thousand."

"Oh. I'm so sorry." Mo shook his head. "I've done about a million."

"What?! You're lying!"

"I'm afraid not. Drugs are basically why I'm here, after all."

"Dammit! I guess I lose then."

Mo shrugged. "What are you gonna do? About that sheet . . ."

"Yeah yeah. I'll be right back."

"That wasn't very nice," Vicki said, after Judy had left. "You know she lost everything she had gambling?"

"Actually, I didn't know that."

"Want another sausage?"

Judy returned a few minutes later.

"This isn't white—it's pink," Mo said.

"More like a peach, I'd call it," said Vicki.

"It's all I have," said Judy, sadly.

Mo said, "I'll be right back."

He returned to his tent. Inside, he opened one of the plastic storage bins where he kept his few valuable things. From it, he retrieved a small sachet. He looked over at the body. "I'm afraid all I can get is a pink sheet," he said. "How do you feel about pink?"

A minute later, he found Judy sitting on the ground, crying.

"What's wrong?" he asked her.

She shook her head. "I don't wanna talk about it."

"She does this sometimes," said Vicki. "I think it's because of all the drugs."

"Well," Mo said, kneeling down, "this is for you." He handed Judy the sachet, which contained his last gram of nightmare-suppressing weed. "And pink is perfect. Pink will do just fine."

4

CLEVELAND WOULDN'T DO ANY LONGER. Briefly, Mo considered returning to New York City, but the American Dream was about moving forward, not returning to the past. So he sold Raphael's and moved to San Francisco. He lived in a simple (but not cheap) one-bedroom apartment for a year while he set about opening a new restaurant on the Waterfront. He'd had a decent amount of savings before the move, and on the sale of Raphael's he made a solid profit, but opening, from scratch, a new restaurant was more expensive than he'd realized. Raphael's he had owned outright, the building and everything, but here he was going to have to rent. And then there were the renovations, and the equipment purchases. And he needed enough in the bank to be able to afford payroll for at least the first month. He took out two large business loans. It was also more work than he realized, starting from scratch. He couldn't be both owner and head chef anymore. There was too much work to do. He hired a co-head chef to help him develop the menu, a general manager to oversee the staff, and a front-of-the-house manager to oversee the front-of-the-house staff specifically. By the time the restaurant opened, Mo's personal accounts were all but depleted.

But the restaurant, which he called The Brickhouse on the Pier, opened to stellar reviews, and by its third night, it was turning a profit. Within a month, once word got around, you'd be hard-pressed to get a reservation. The *Chronicle* profiled Mo, but the piece was light on personal details, owing to Mo's reluctance to speak about his past ("I believe in moving forward," he told the writer, not quite cleverly adding, "That's where the future lies") so it focused on his love of food and cooking, his passion for the restaurant industry (which, admittedly, the writer had to manufacture many of the details of, because the culinary arts weren't something Mo had ever passionately pursued; they were just something he fell into and, he saw now more than ever, just a means to an end—that end being a great life, filled with nice things and a beautiful family).

Once the restaurant was reasonably well-established, Mo left much of its operation to the co-head chef and the managers, and he shifted his own focus to finding a wife. A year later, he was purchasing a large house in Berkley with a beautiful blonde he had convinced himself he loved. Mo bought a bigger, nicer, newer truck. He bought a small catamaran—with three cabins, each with their own bathrooms, so that he, his wife, and their friends could spend relaxing nights out on the bay, which they did, sometimes, when they weren't t00 busy. Although they were usually too busy. On the topic of friends, Mo made many, all at least as wealthy as he was (or at least as wealthy as he appeared to be). Some were even more wealthy. There were other restauranteurs, several hedge-fund investors, many startup CEOs. Mo opened a second restaurant, this one in Berkley. Testing the waters, he called it Madini's (even though this wasn't strictly grammatically correct), and no one seemed to mind. It was soon as popular as the Brickhouse. Mo sold the catamaran and bought a bigger one, with six cabins and a party deck, and used it even less than the first one—he was busier now, after all, with two restaurants to run. His wife cheated on him, of course, but not that often, and he cheated on her, so it didn't really matter. As a couple, they still had sex with each other frequently, at least twice a week. In 2006 they had a daughter. In February of 2007 Mo opened a third restaurant, this one in the Castro. He called it Raph's in honor of his mentor and friend. His wife refused to eat there ("I've just never been comfortable in *that* part of town, and I don't think we should take the baby there). Raph's got off to a slower start than the Brickhouse and Madini's, but within three months it was turning a small profit. Mo moved his young family into a bigger house in Berkley. He bought a second vehicle for himself—another truck, of course—and his wife was always happy to have the latest model Range Rover, even though she rarely drove anywhere on her own, unless it was to go shopping. In fact, she didn't leave the house most days. Her trainer came to her. Her massage therapist came to her. But Mo was happy to make her happy, to provide these things for her. Even when they had a second daughter, in 2008, she never wanted to hire a nanny. "I always wanted to be a mom," she said, "the kind that stays and takes care of her children," and Mo had brief glimpses of the life that could have been with Marissa and their son.

When the recession happened the same year Mo's second daughter was born, income dipped at all three restaurants. While most of his clientele were wealthy and relatively unaffected by the crash, some lost a lot of money on bad real estate investments, and Americans just weren't eating out as much in general. Raph's did particularly poorly, and just over a year after it opened, Mo was forced to close it. Even with Raph's overhead gone, Mo had two kids to feed, a mortgage to pay, and for the first time ever, he struggled to cover his debts. He thought about selling the catamaran, but "Don't you dare—I love that thing!" said his wife, so he cancelled the leases on both his trucks and bought a 2004 model ("It's kind of embarrassing, having *that* in our driveway," his wife said, and Mo knew it was true, but what was he supposed to do?) Briefly he was afraid America had failed him. He almost lost his faith. Various uppers—cocaine, modafinil—were instrumental in getting Mo through to the end of 2009, when things started to pick up again.

If it seems this period of Mo's life is light on details, well, that's because, so far as he could remember it, it was. Twenty years of his life, what many people would argue were his best years, were effectively a blur. Things happened, and he could remember some of them: the birth of his first daughter, which he was in the room for (he missed the birth of his second by an hour, stuck in traffic after a meeting with a supplier, trying to negotiate a much cheaper rate on fryer oil, anything to help cut costs, ideally without cutting quality, during the recession); some birthday parties; one of the few nights actually spent on the catamaran with two other couples, which ended in unplanned partner swapping; some details of a family vacation to the Bahamas when the girls were four and five (or were they five and six?); a trip to Disney World around the same time; a few trips to Disneyland; the first time he purchased a seventy-seven-inch

4K television for the house's viewing room; the time he bought his wife a particular diamond necklace she'd been dropping hints about (the financing on it had been reasonable, low-interest); a handful more of his daughters' birthdays; the time his second daughter (or was it his first?) won her second grade (first grade?) spelling bee. So it wasn't like Mo wasn't present for some of life's special events, but he wasn't present enough.

But at the time, Mo was more than *happy* with his life. He was ecstatic, almost manic with elation. Look at his beautiful family! Look at his beautiful house! Look at all his beautiful things! You've done me well, America, just like I knew you would.

Then, near the end of 2019, Mo, who every morning browsed the news on a tablet with his first two cups of coffee (he'd tapered off the cocaine usage by now—he wasn't getting any younger, after all) while his wife got the girls ready for school, read peculiar rumblings about a virus outbreak in China. A lot of people were sick, it seemed. A lot of people were dying. But that was over there, not here. Here, in America, there was no danger. Here, in America, there was Christmas to celebrate, gifts to buy and give. Mo had just put up his family's tree in the living room, their largest yet, all the ornaments one could want, and this afternoon some guys he'd hired were coming over to put up their lights so that Mo could give his wife what she asked for every year: the best Christmas display in the neighborhood.

That afternoon, Mo went to The Brickhouse. He was overseeing the kitchen that night, for the first time in weeks, and he was looking forward to it. When he got home, at 2 a.m., the Christmas lights were on, all red and green and white and a smattering of blue, blinking and twinkling and across the lawn even rippling outward from the house, as if the yard were made of water. In the morning, he asked his wife what she thought of the lights, and she said they were fine, but had he seen that the Williamsons down the street had put up a real crystal angel in their front yard—an angel made of real crystals?

Mo replied that he didn't even know which ones the Williamsons were.

For Christmas, he got his daughters each new iPads, and he surprised his wife with a Porsche. "For when you want something a little more flashy than the Range Rover."

"But I don't *like* Porsches. I only like Range Rovers. How do you not know that, by now, Mo? Besides, I don't really care about cars, anyway."

She gave him a new phone. But he'd already upgraded to this latest model two months ago, in the same color, finally getting rid of the flip phone that had long embarrassed her. Sure, she'd bought him the one with maximum storage, but he didn't exactly need a terabyte of space on his phone.

"It's great," he said. "Hey—I hear this thing has a fantastic camera. Let's get a family photo."

New Year's came and went (Mo and his wife hosted a big party, their biggest yet, although he got too drunk to remember it). January passed quickly. In February he started talking with his financiers about the possibility of getting a loan to open a third restaurant again.

Then California became the first state to go into lockdown as a measure against the spread of the new virus. At first, Mo thought it was a joke. Close his restaurant? Takeout only? He couldn't conceive of what he was being ordered to do—or that the government was the one ordering him to do it. Visions of what this would do to his business flashed through his mind. For the first time in thirty years, he said a prayer—albeit not a particularly formal one. And then he realized that everything would be all right. After all, up until now it always had been. He was living the dream, and he had no plans to stop doing so. He sat down with his financial advisor. Two weeks? No problem.

But two weeks turned into four weeks, and then six weeks. Takeout wasn't enough to cover expenses. With guilt churning in his stomach, Mo laid off the waitstaff of both restaurants. Then—he closed The Brickhouse. Temporarily, he promised. Madini's he could afford to keep open, especially if he let go of most of the back-of-the-house staff as well and did the work himself. For a couple months, he was a teenager again, working every lunch and dinner shift, just him and a sous chef, with a hostess taking orders and giving them to waiting customers and food-delivery-service drivers. Those who did order takeout weren't tipping so well, but what tips the restaurant did receive Mo gave 100 percent of to the hostess and the sous chef. They started closing at 10 p.m., but every night Mo stayed and did the cleaning himself.

"We never see you anymore," his wife said to him one headachy morning. "The girls asked why yesterday."

Mo had just snuck a bump of coke in the bathroom, and despite his exhaustion, he felt it kick in. "That's because I'm working all goddamn day so you can live in this goddamn house," he snapped.

That was all he said. Seriously, that's all he could remember saying. But his wife said, "Mo—you're scaring me. You're scaring the girls."

Soon, not even opening for lunch was feasible anymore. Dinner service was on a limited menu. Mo sold his truck and started walking to the restaurant. He told his wife they were going to have to get rid of the Porsche. She was furious. Furious.

"You don't even like the piece of crap!" he reminded her.

He was still paying rent on The Brickhouse, clinging desperately to the property. Forty grand a month. He owned the catamaran outright by now, and he figured if he sold it, the couple hundred thousand would help them survive a little longer. But no one wanted to buy. He stopped paying rent on The Brickhouse. Madini's he had a mortgage on, but it was in serious danger of foreclosure. Then came promises of government assistance. Here she was, America, coming to the rescue, just like Mo had always known she would. Except what Mo got for the restaurant was a joke—not even enough to cover a single mortgage payment, let alone a month's payroll for the remaining staff. As for a personal stimulus check? Well, Mo had made way too much money the previous year for that. And his daughters, ten and eleven (or were they eleven and twelve? ten and twelve?), stuck at home, hyperactively trying to sit for their distance learning, were growing more depressed by the day. His eldest swallowed all at once two dozen pills of her mother's own depression medication. They had to have her stomach pumped. She spent a week in the hospital. The resulting bill was insurmountable. "I can't take this anymore!" Mo's wife said to him. "What are you going to do to protect this family?"

Nothing—was the answer. What *could* he do? There had to be a solution out there, somewhere, but what it was and where it was he never did discover. He had to close Madini's. "It's only temporary," he insisted, trying to believe it. They lost the house. They moved into a two-bedroom apartment.

"You can't make the girls share a room! They're practically teenagers!"

"Shut up! Just shut up and do what I say for once. Just have my back for one goddamn minute!"

By Christmas, Mo was on the street. His wife had taken the kids to live with her parents in . . . Connecticut? North Carolina? It didn't matter. Mo would never see them again.

At forty-seven years old, Mo finally tried methamphetamine. He was walking along Mission Street, carrying a large military-style backpack with all his belongings. He'd sold everything he owned, and it wasn't even enough to pay his debts. Still, he'd withdrawn enough cash before his wife had left (when he realized she was planning to), that he could afford to wander for a while. They weren't so bad—these streets. Not as dirty as people said. Yes, there were a lot of houseless people, like Mo, but they kept to themselves, spent most of their time sitting, just being, conserving energy. They harmed no one but themselves. And Mo—well, he was resilient, as he'd demonstrated all his life. He'd find another job, just as he did three decades ago. He wandered from restaurant to restaurant, told the first person he found in each one about his vast experience. But nobody believed him—not that they were hiring anyway.

"I'm the best you could have," he said.

"Sure, buddy. Sure. And even if you were, the best chef is worthless in a closed kitchen."

Which, of course, Mo already knew.

He tried retail stores, gas stations, but by that point his clothes weren't looking so great, and his scruff was getting long. He was starting to look more—well—*other*—from *over there*, and nobody wanted to hire someone from *over there*. Should have kept the truck, he thought. Could have driven Uber or Lyft or whatever the other ones were. Except no one ever called for a pickup truck. No one wanted to be stuck in the front seat with a man with skin and hair like Mo's, even if they were a single passenger. Oh—he just *had to have* a truck, didn't he! Because a truck was what a man drove!

One afternoon, Mo found himself in a liquor store, and he bought the most expensive bottle of Scotch he had the cash for. Because why not? What did it matter? What good was this money anyway? It hadn't bought him friends, no support network to fall back on in hard times. No real love. Even his daughters hadn't shed a tear when their mother took them away.

As he walked down Mission Street, carrying the unopened bottle of whisky, Mo thought of Daniel Blake. At least he assumed it was Daniel. Marissa had never said Daniel, only Dan. But Daniel seemed a safe assumption. Daniel—in the den of the lions. Mo knew the story. Daniel the prophet. Daniel who could interpret dreams. Well—Daniel Blake hadn't deserved the name. Mo hoped he was dead. Of course he was dead! Mo remembered. He had cancer. He probably died not long after taking Mo's son away. Mo would have loved that son. Things would have been different if he'd been a father to that son. There was a whole other life there, running parallel to the one he was living now, a life where Mo and Marissa were living in a suburb of Cleveland, Ohio, in a nice house, but not an ostentatious one (Mo shook his head—he'd only somehow just learned this English word a few months ago), with two more children— maybe daughters, maybe sons, maybe another son and a daughter, and either way they loved their siblings and their parents and were taken care of and even spoiled, but not *too* spoiled, and Mo went to Raphael's four or five nights a week and loved cooking, and the rest of the time he was wholly present for his family, and they did not have too much but also did not want for anything.

At Mission and First, Mo's legs gave out. They weren't tired— physically he was capable of walking for days—they just didn't have the will to *go* anymore. Mo found himself sitting on a planter in front of Salesforce Tower. He opened the Scotch and began drinking straight from the bottle. He looked up at the tower, which hadn't been their just four years ago. When Mo first arrived in America, he read a lot of American novels to teach himself English. He read *The Lord of the Rings*. On Halloween a couple years ago, after the tower was finished, they'd lit the top up to look like the Eye of Sauron. Mo had taken the family, costumes and all, to see it. Looking up at it, he'd felt for a few moments like a kid again. The girls hadn't cared. "Can we puh-leeze get on to the Ramsdells' party now?" his wife had implored.

Looking up at the tower now, Mo saw it only as a symbol of America's betrayal of him—and everyone else who had put their faith in her.

"Here you go, friend," he heard someone say.

Mo looked up. There was young man, maybe twenty years old, staring down at him, holding out a twenty-dollar bill.

"I'd give you more if I could," the man said, "but I don't have any other cash on me at the moment." He wore a dark blue nylon jacket that said "Bio Odyssey." Several feet behind him another young man stood impatiently, holding a box.

"Thank you," Mo muttered, taking the bill, head down, ashamed to look this man in the eye.

"What did you do that for?" Mo heard the man's companion ask as they walked away. "Did you see what he was drinking? That's like two hundred bucks a bottle."

"We don't know his story. These are tough times."

"Yeah, well. Just be careful. You're not a millionaire yet."

"Billionaire. I'm going to be a billionaire."

"Well you're not that yet, either."

Suddenly, in a parallel reality, Mo's legs were alive again. He jumped to his feet. He turned in the direction of the young man and he called out to him and gave him the twenty back and told him to use this life he'd been given wisely—to love and to be loved.

But in *this* reality, the one that he experienced, he instead walked down First and then turned left on Market. As the sun went down, he gave a woman on Mission the twenty for half a gram of coke. But after she took the money she muttered, "Actually all I have is meth." And Mo said, "Whatever," and took as much as the twenty would buy him.

5

IF MO'S "PROSPEROUS" YEARS WERE light on details, the decade that followed them was even worse. If Mo's time as an ostensibly wealthy restauranteur was a flashy, nonsensical film where nothing of true substance happened (the *Fast and the Furious* franchise was a good comparison, Mo thought), then his time as a down-on-his-luck drug addict and alcoholic was a formless void, not even worth watching (*Tree of Life* by Terrance Malick, maybe? Mo never could get through that one). Suffice it to say, for ten or eleven or maybe even twelve years he wandered around the Bay Area in a meth-induced stupor, joining the ranks of the city's countless-and-growing houseless population. Mo would like to say that he never shit in the street, but that wouldn't be true—it wouldn't be true at all.

These days, Mohar didn't touch drugs, except the marijuana to help him sleep. He didn't drink. He was disciplined. He rose at dawn and said his prayers. He prayed to Allah, to Yahweh, to the Devas and Devis. His name after all contained allusions to each of these major religions. Even now, fifty-something years after leaving Sudan (his fuzzy sense of time and the pace of years gone by was an unfortunate remnant of the impact so many drugs had left on his once-sharp brain), Mo didn't like to think about his father, or his mother, but he sometimes found himself wondering why they, devout Muslims, had given him a Hindu name. Some mornings, he threw in a prayer to Odin, letting the Norse patriarch represent the whole pantheon of Pagan gods he might otherwise pray to

—which would take too much time. Mo did not say all five Salahs, but each day he prayed again at midday and sunset. The rest of his time he spent walking or sitting—contemplating, appreciating—except for when he needed work—then he worked hard, studiously, with optimism and conviction, as if he were a boy again.

It was with these qualities that he set about the task of washing the body of the boy with whom he'd been entrusted. He removed the boy's clothes, a torn jacket, a faded Green Day t-shirt, simple tan cargo shorts. "These are so damp and cold," he said. Then he found the wound on the boy's arm. The crust. "Is this how you died?"

The clinging soul, Mo imagined gazing up at him.

In the pocket of the cargo shorts he found an electronic device. For a moment, Mo wasn't sure what he was looking at. Wrapped around it was a tangle of wires that might have once been wrangled tidily before dissolving into inevitable disarray. Wired headphones? It struck Mo then that the device was an iPod, a veritable antique. And Mo had always thought his own device was old.

"This is important to you," Mo said. "Even though it no longer works."

Very important, the boy's soul told him.

Mo set the music player aside.

Leaving the boy's undergarment on (tradition said a cloth should cover the body's *awrah*, but Mo wasn't going to sacrifice the boy's dignity just for the sake of tradition—white boxer briefs would do), he bathed the body gently with a warm damp cloth. From head to toe. He wiped dried puss away gently with his washrag. Tradition said the body must be bathed an odd number of times. One was sufficient, but Mo bathed this body three times—it so needed warming up.

"Better?" he asked.

Mo lifted the body, carried it over to Judy's pink sheet, set it carefully down. He placed the old music player in boy's right hand. And then he set about to wrapping.

For the rest of the day, he let the body rest. He said prayers. He spoke to the boy. "Fire—or water?" he asked.

Strangely? Water.

"Good—because I don't think Vicki is going to let me use her fire again today."

Mo prayed some more. Just before dusk he left his tent with a backpack and found several large rocks, bricks, and chunks of concrete. Back in the tent, he unwrapped the body, placed the heavy materials into the sheet, and wrapped it again. This unwrapping, rewrapping—this, too, was against tradition. But so was burial at sea. Fuck tradition—Mo thought, and smiled sadly.

In the early hours of the morning, when it was dark and there were few people on the streets, Mohar al-Azad ibn Butros al-Madini carried the boy's body to the Bay. This was not an easy task for him. The Bay was ten blocks away, and Mo was an old man who would probably die himself soon. He never ate enough. Some days he didn't eat all. He was thin and gray. Parts of his brain didn't work as well as they used to. He was lonely. He had bad dreams. Somewhere out there he had daughters who likely never thought of him—and a son who didn't know his name.

But Mohar had optimism—and conviction. Always optimism and conviction. Never again would he forget them. These two qualities were what propelled him, once he reached the Bay, to carry the boy six blocks further, to the pier where The Brickhouse had once lived. There was a warehouse here now, storage for some nearby tech company—a large modern-looking building full no doubt of silicon and glass. A security guard slept at an open gate, and Mo slipped past him with optimism and ease and conviction.

At the end of the pier, he held the enshrouded boy over the water. The water lapped at the supports several feet below. "There's no gentle way to do this," Mo said.

Just drop me, he imagined the boy replying. *Just let me go.*

So Mohar dropped the body into the water. There was a splash, and he looked down as, over the next several seconds, the pink shroud and its inhabitant dropped beneath the surface.

"Go on," Mohar said. "Go on."

Whatever Happened to the Avon Café?

WHEN SOMEONE FALLS ASLEEP, OR gets put to sleep, whether via a blow to the head or a chokehold or a medically induced coma, they're said to be unconscious. This is incorrect. More accurately, such an individual is existing in a different *state* of consciousness from that of waking life. When humans and other animals sleep, they dream. In certain phases of sleep, they may even be receptive to outside stimuli. Coma patients, after awakening, have reported dreams, have even reported an awareness of the outside world—even though brain scans show no sign of a sleep-wake cycle.

Walter Lumbly, while he was in a brief sleep induced by a lack of oxygen in his brain, didn't quite lose awareness of the room he was in. Things didn't quite *go black*. They went more *squishy* than *black*. And there was loudness. A rushing in his ears that seemed to grow to engulf his entire head, his entire sense of self. And then—his head was gone. He couldn't find it. There was a visual field—dark, but with bursts of dull light and numerous floating lines—but *what* exactly was *viewing* this visual field Walter Lumbly lost all sensation of. For how long? It's hard to say. Not very long. Not *too* long. For only some moments later he was in his head again, and he opened his eyes, and he sat up, dizzy, still blinking against little bursts of light, but otherwise more or less okay.

The first thing he felt was confusion, followed by a sense of embarrassment he couldn't pinpoint the source of. His memories of the last several minutes were fuzzy. There had been—a naked woman? A gorgeous naked woman? An explicitly naked gorgeous woman? And text messages? He brought his watch unsteadily to his face and checked his messages—but there was nothing untoward there. The more oxygen returned to his brain, the less dizzy he felt, the less spectacular the light show in his visual field became, and the less real his memories seemed. The more oxygen returned to his brain, the more convinced he became that the last however many minutes had been some sort of strange dream. He rose to his feet and looked around the room. It was dark—lit only by a few dim overhead lights. It was large. It wasn't square, but it wasn't quite round. There was a desk and a table and another desk, each littered with pieces of tech and paper and coffee mugs and miscellany; a couch with a neatly folded blanket draped over one arm, a pillow stacked on top of the blanket; and there was a server bank of a configuration Walter Lumbly had never seen, taller than he was, against one wall, apparently powered down, its indicator lights all off. Walter was assaulted by an overwhelming feeling that he shouldn't be here, in this room, that this place wasn't meant for him.

He exited the room, and the door shut behind him. His neurons now firing at levels and speeds they were supposed to, Walter Lumbly shook his head once, dismissing the last bit of fuzziness, and decided two things: He wasn't going to microdose before work anymore, no matter how legal it was, and it was probably best if he never returned to the fifteenth floor again.

Two minutes after Walter Lumbly left the room, after the workshop's motion sensors had detected no movement, the workshop's lights shut off of their own accord, blanketing the room in darkness. Five minutes after the elevator doors closed behind Walter Lumbly, the lights in the corridor outside the workshop shut off as well.

On the sixteenth floor, the seventeenth floor, the eighteenth floor, coders were coding. Administrative assistants were scheduling meetings and greeting visitors. Hardware engineers were arguing with software developers about what was and wasn't possible.

On the nineteenth floor, C-Suite executives were discussing recent comments by analysts that Lumina was working on further miniaturizing holographic projection technology so that fully interactive wearable devices could be reduced in size from watches to rings, according to rumors. The problem was the rumors weren't true. Physics only allowed for so much miniaturization. Light could come only from sources so small, and you needed a lot of those sources close together if you wanted to project interfaces with intuitive and pleasing UX designs. "Where did these rumors even come from?" CEO (although not for much longer) Paul Schilling said. "Where the fuck does the media even get these things?"

"Who knows. They're all a bunch of hacks," replied Chief Financial Officer Omar Carter, who was going through something of a personal crisis, his third wife having just left him for their child's nanny, and who was drinking too much these days, and who was getting too old for this shit, and who should have retired five years ago, and who had started leaking rumors to the press, mostly true rumors, but occasionally peppering in falsities to see what sort of havoc he could create for the company's stock, mostly for fun—but also if he happened to benefit financially from said havoc, so be it.

"I'll try to get to the bottom of it," said recently hired General Council Mark O'Weld. "If I find the leaker, retribution will be swift."

"But this wasn't exactly a *leak*, was it?" said Omer Aker, who was still in charge of hardware development. "We're *not* developing anything like this."

"Well we'd better start," Omar said. "Our stock is the worst it's been in nine years, and it's just going to keep falling if we don't innovate something soon."

"Don't you think I know that?" said Paul Schilling. "Don't you think I fucking know that? Omer, you gotta give me *something*."

"Something? What do you mean *something*? It's not possible. It's literally impossible."

"Don't misuse 'literally,'" said Omar Carter, reveling quietly in the chaos.

"I'm *not*! It's literally impossible. It's fucking *science*."

"Well," said Gloria Reinwell, dispassionately, "supposedly Neptune's working on a holo-ring."

"For fuck's sake! No, they're not. It's *impossible*."

Gloria shrugged. "I heard a rumor they're going to announce something next month."

"You gotta give us something, Asker," Paul Schilling said.

"Fuck. I wish Eric was still here."

"Oh yeah? Why's that? You think I can't fill his shoes?"

"Oh come on, Paul. You can't fill anyone's shoes. You couldn't fill Elizabeth Holmes's shoes."

"Fuck you, Omer! Fuck. You."

"No—fuck you, Paul. You're sinking this company."

"Boys," said Gloria Reinwell dryly. "Boys . . ."

The executive meeting devolved thus—as most executive meetings at Lumina devolved these days.

On the twentieth floor coders coded. On the twenty-first, employees drank and ate and conversed in the company cafeteria. Outside the building, on Spear Street, people walked and talked and listened to music and drove.

A day later and five miles west, in Sea Cliff, a house burned.

A resident of another Sea Cliff house, the teenage son of an investment manager, captured the conflagration on video. He posted it to TikTok before calling 911. He said, in the video, "Dudes! This was Eric Hauser's house. What the fuuuuck!"

News of the fire spread faster than the fire itself. The video was uploaded to Chattr Chattr Chattr within minutes. When he realized how popular his video was, the teenage boy went live and managed to stream the final twenty minutes of the burning. By the time firefighters doused the flames, there was little left of the house but the frame and the garage.

It was twenty-four hours before any media outlet was able to get ahold of Sophia Velasquez for comment. Finally, she told the *San Francisco Chronicle* that she didn't know what had started the fire. No, she wasn't there at the time. What of the rumors that evidence of two bodies had been found in the remains? "I hadn't heard those rumors. But the house was unoccupied. That's all I have to say. This is a private, family matter."

Conspiracy theorists latched on to her use of the word "family," although, hard as they tried, they couldn't seem to weave a theory that made any logical sense. They mostly resorted to calling Sophia a "bitch" and a "cunt." And saying that she probably killed her ex-husband somehow and had burned the house down to hide the evidence, maybe with the government's help. A very small group of fringe theorists, most of them Christian fundamentalists, was convinced the fire had been part of some elite satanic ritual, but they thought that about everything.

Three days passed. Then four. After a week no one relevant was talking about the fire anymore. Disney announced that Sophia Velasquez was going to star in an upcoming Avengers movie after all.

Eleven hundred miles away, late on a cool and sunny morning, Quinton Harris and Penelope Papadopoulos were driving along U.S. Route 12 in a maroon Tesla Model Y Sophia Velasquez had loaned them. ("For as long as you need it.") Quinn sat behind the wheel, since he was the only one with a license, although the car was doing most of the driving.

"You sure you're ready for this?" Penelope asked.

"For this specifically? No. But I do know that I'm ready to move on, and I can't do that without returning to Avon first."

"You could, though. I mean why not? You just said it yourself— Avon, not *home*."

"We have to pass through it anyway."

"Tell me about it then, about Avon. What's it like there?"

"You've never been?"

"Never."

"But it's so close to Helena? I thought everyone in Helena went to the café for breakfast at least sometimes."

"Had you ever been to Helena before last week?"

"Well—no."

"And I'd never been outside of Helena. I'd never been over the pass. This is the first time I'm seeing this side of the mountain."

They drove or rode in silence for several moments, Penelope looking out the window, observing the Rocky Mountains and their big sky.

Quinn said: "It's not a lonely place."

"What isn't?"

"Avon. You asked what it's like. It's not a lonely place."

"That's what it *isn't* like. I didn't ask what it *isn't* like."

"Yeah—well—I don't know how else to describe it."

But it was a lonely place, when they arrived. They pulled into the empty gravel parking lot of the Avon Café. The Beautiful Finds antique shop was as unlit as ever, but the sunlight reflecting off the distant snowy mountaintops washed everything in an etheric glow. Quinn switched the car's navigation to manual and drove out of the parking lot and made a right turn onto the highway.

"What's up?" Penelope said.

"I changed my mind. There's no reason to go back there."

"What about your house? Your things? Your money?"

"It's not my house. It's my G-Pops' house, and he isn't here anymore. Someone else can have it. Nature can have it. And I don't need my *things*. I can get new *things*. I can get new money."

And nature would take G-Pops' house, in time. Nature would take all of Avon. Its people, the ones still alive after the massacre, sixty or seventy of them all told, would move away in the ensuing years, tired of being haunted by the ghosts of friends and loved ones, by what had happened there. Milly Belchamp, who owned Beautiful Finds, would be one of the last holdouts, her rarely opened shop taking up the café's mantle as the census-designated place's claim to fame and commerce. But then she would sell it to a real estate developer who planned to open a motel along the highway, and she would move to Florida, where her daughter had long lived. The developer would never build the motel, because the Avon Café was still there, empty and haunted, with its sign above the coffee maker, and he couldn't find the man who owned the rights to knock it down.

"So then what are you going to do?" Penelope asked somewhere close to the top of the pass. "I mean what are you going to do next?"

"Drive, I think. For a while. Sophia said take the car for as long as we need it."

"I think she meant just like a few days."

"Yeah—well—I need it longer than that. I want to drive. And then, maybe, probably, back to school. But somewhere different. I need a different way of looking at the world. I'll change my name somehow. And I'll go to Oxford or somewhere. I'll figure out the money thing—

eventually." Then, after some thought, he said, "Is there a university in Paris?"

Penelope shrugged.

"What about Notre Dame?"

"That's in Indiana."

"Really?"

"Really."

"Weird."

"My father went to Paris a lot."

At the base of the pass Quinn asked for Penelope's address. She gave it to him, and he repeated it to the car's virtual intelligence, which took over the drive once again. "You really think it's—she's—still alive?" Quinn asked.

"It's not a matter of *alive*. Not exactly."

"But how? It's—she's—gotta be dead. Or destroyed or whatever. You saw that fire. No one could survive that. She had to have probably been killed in whatever explosion caused it in the first place. She sacrificed herself for us."

"No—it doesn't work like that. She's an AI Everything Sophia told us —about how my father built her—she wasn't confined to any sort of body. She could be anywhere. And she is. I know it. She's out there somewhere."

"And you think you can find her."

Penelope shook her head. "No. It's like I said—there's not exactly anything to *find*. She'll have to reach out to me. But I'll do everything I can to let her know I'm here, waiting."

"Don't wait too long—okay? You have a life to live, too."

Fifteen minutes later, when the car came to a stop in front of the large house in Helena's historic Mansion District, Quinn said. "Wait—you live *here*?"

Penelope shrugged. "It's not that great."

"Oh yeah? Why not—you get lost in there or something?"

"Actually—" Penelope said. "Yeah. Something like that."

"Yeah, well—hey. I'm—I'm sorry about Kade. I haven't said it yet, and I don't know why. I didn't really know him, but—"

"Thanks," Penelope said. "I'm not sure what I'm going to say to his mom, but I'll have to say something. I guess I have to figure out what I'm going to say to my mom first. I . . . left this place a bit of a mess."

"Well, listen—I guess—I know I don't really know you either, even after all . . . whatever *this* has been, but if you ever need anything . . ."

"Yeah—sure. Maybe I'll take you up on that some day," Penelope replied, aware that she had no means of ever contacting him again.

"So, anyway . . ."

"Anyway."

After several moments, Penelope leaned across the car's center console. Quinn met her in an awkward hug.

Then she got out of the car, retrieved from the back seat the small bag she'd procured in L.A., after she, Quinn, and Sophia had regrouped there, after the fire. She walked around the car, stared at the stone gothic structure that was her home—that maybe, *maybe*, after everything, felt like a place she should learn to appreciate. She took several breaths. She turned to wave one last goodbye, but the car was already at the end of the block, rolling through the intersection.

Again she turned to the house. She adjusted the weight of the bag on her shoulder. She walked up to the porch, placed her hand on the door, found it unlocked as ever. "Priscilla?" she said. And then, trying a different tack, "Mom?"

Penelope spent the next few years waiting for Hera's return. She intensified her focus on coding and software development, figuring that maybe she'd devise a way to say hello. Maybe she'd follow in the footsteps of her father, she thought. Maybe she'd develop the Next Big Thing. Maybe she'd start a company of her own.

But the years went by, and except for the mysterious replenishing of her mother's crypto wallet, along with an untraceable text that said simply "I forgive all of you, but you're all on your own now," Penelope never heard from Hera. She graduated high school with a 3.1 GPA. A month after the end of her senior year, another pandemic enveloped the world, this one worse than the last. Universities went remote. Penelope held off enrolling herself and spent the summer and subsequent fall playing video games. The following spring, while vaccine distribution was being carried out in earnest, Penelope coded her own virtual reality game, based on the house simulation she'd worked on for VR Club when she was fifteen. The premise was simple (solve a mystery, escape this seemingly haunted house), the gameplay basic, a throwback to the point-and-click adventures of half a century ago ("You *have* to play *Myst*," Penelope remembered Kade imploring her one day, when they were only twelve, her first introduction to the genre), but reviewers and players were tickled by the game's incorporation of music from the 2000s (the song "Starlight" by Muse briefly topped U.S. charts once again) and by the mystery's frame story of birth and death, not to mention the twist ending (Surprise! It was you, the player, standing behind the door all along!). The game sold well. Hovered in the Neptune app store's top five games for over three months. Several major universities closed. Penelope bought a small house in rapidly growing East Helena. Priscilla told her she needn't buy her own house—the old gothic mansion had always been more than big enough for the two of them—but Penelope insisted on a place to call her own. And then Priscilla got married to a perfectly nice recently widowed man she met in a pilates class. Penelope never built another game, but she kept playing them—and she started writing about them. In time, hers grew into the most popular single-writer game review blog on the Internet, and she was not unhappy. The words "You're all on your own now" described her own life philosophy well.

Over in a quiet suburb of Cleveland, Ohio, Amanda Wallace moved in with Zelda Schneeberger, a woman two decades younger than her who made her happy. The actress Sophia Velasquez, who eventually got remarried to a fellow actor, and then another, and then another, and who would go on to hold the record for most Academy Awards won by an Hispanic actress until the final days of the Awards themselves, made sure to visit Amanda and Zelda two or three times a year. When Zelda died, of late-stage pancreatic cancer, which doctors were still striving to find an effective treatment for, Amanda finally moved into a room in a high-end retirement home. She died at 102, in her sleep. She is believed to have completed over 2,000 paintings, only a dozen of which have survived.

Lumina, as a company, never exactly *died*, at least not for so long a time that it's worth dwelling on, but it also never again reached the heights it had under Eric Hauser's tenure. Paul Schilling was ousted as CEO a year after Hauser's death. The board tried again several in-house promotions, including Gloria Reinwell; they even, after multiple failed attempts with C-suite executives at the helm, tried letting the lawyers run the ship, but Mark O'Weld's six months as head of the once-loved company were, to put it mildly, a disaster, and they ended when O'Weld took his own life. It was a scandal. Stocks suffered their worst dive in the company's history. There was renewed talk of the inhumane treatment of workers at the plants of the company's Chinese manufacturing partners. Of course, promises were made, even followed through on from a certain perspective, and the criticisms died down again. Stock prices leveled out. The release of a statement committing to a plan to have sixty-five percent of Lumina's employee force comprise people of color even caused a brief stock *bump*, before things leveled out again. Somehow, the Lumina board managed to pilfer the CEO of FritoLay, and things were, if not great, almost good. Rival Neptune did indeed release a ring that projected holograms, and Omar Carter finally resigned, his duplicity going forever undiscovered. Lumina got into the cloud services business. Eventually, the company stopped producing its own hardware, began licensing its software to other manufacturers, including Neptune. These partnerships were as fruitful as could be expected. Consumers no longer cared about Lumina, Inc., but shareholders were happy enough.

The world went through *yet another* pandemic, but the response to this one was swift, effective. Global deaths were only in the low hundreds of thousands. The United States finally Balkanized. Well, maybe—it depends on which state you ask.

A former Lumina employee acquired massive amounts of funding—some private, some federal—and built her own particle accelerator in the Nevada desert, on the former site of Proud City. Deaths from the resulting microsingularity, before it collapsed, were, fortunately, only in the low hundreds.

Back in San Francisco, things carried on more or less as usual. Many startups were formed. Many startups failed. No matter how many people or companies relocated to Austin or Tampa or Nashville or Ohio or even Detroit, the Bay Area and Silicon Valley were never going to lose their statuses as America's hotbeds of innovation and creation, as the birthplace of all things that might someday make the world A Better Place —at least not until the whole civilization eventually, inevitably, failed. After all, in time, even the sun was going to go nova. Even the universe was going to collapse in on itself.

But before that happened, some time after Lumina had abandoned the building at 345 Spear Street, the middle-aged owner of a successful construction/destruction company—muscular, stubbled, six feet tall, wearing a tie and a minimally protective hard hat—was overseeing the building's demolition. He walked with his assistant through the skyscraper's dim hallways. Together, they surveyed the rooms and corridors. They started in the subbasement, from which the server banks had been removed, leaving only stray cords and mounting racks behind. They marveled at the coldness of the place, at the dust. Then they moved up to the basement, where the design studios had once been.

"Look at this," the assistant marveled. "I think it's an old 3D printer. Think it still works?"

"If it does, would it be worth anything?" the owner asked.

"Nah—doubt you could even get the right resin for it anymore."

The owner shrugged. "Well, if you want it, it's yours. Just come back for it after we're done."

"Might be cool to have—just for kicks." The assistant made a note on a holographic device. He made further notes as his boss pointed out several beams and struts where explosives might be placed. Demolition was scheduled for a week from now.

They ventured up, floor by floor, room by room. The owner didn't need to be here, but his father, from whom he'd inherited the construction company, had always told him that, whenever possible, *you do things yourself. That's what a leader is.* Whether that was really what leadership was, the owner didn't know. He doubted it. If you did everything yourself, who exactly were you leading? But he *enjoyed* taking charge on these demolition jobs. It made him feel more satisfied when he got to watch everything come tumbling down. Plus you couldn't use the elevators in old abandoned buildings like this, so walking so many flights of stairs was a great workout.

When they reached the fifteenth floor, the door wouldn't budge. "Locked or something," the assistant said. "Doubt it's rusted shut."

"Glasses," said the owner. The assistant put on a pair of safety glasses. The owner did the same. Then, from the small gear bag over his shoulder, the owner pulled a tool that looked like a palm-size blowtorch. He loved using this thing. He pointed it at the door's left edge, where it met the frame, and produced a hyper-focused laser. You couldn't actually see the laser because its wavelength was beyond the visible spectrum, but that's partly what was so cool about it: it was like you weren't doing anything, and then suddenly you could push a door open, its bolt or bolts cut clean through. It was a weird sort of power.

They emerged onto the fifteenth floor, its hallway completely dark. "That's odd," the assistant said. "This floor must have a separate power access point from the rest of the building. Sorry about that boss—there was nothing in the blueprints."

"Not a problem." The owner pulled a flashlight from his bag. He and his assistant walked down the dark hallway.

"The hell?" the assistant said. "Is there even anything *on* this floor?"

"There," said the owner, swinging the flashlight's beam across another metal door.

"It's got a biometric lock."

"Glasses," the owner said again. He pointed his cutting laser at the control panel. There was a sizzling sound, and smoke rose from the panel, but nothing else happened. The door had no discernible hinge. Must have been the sliding kind. The owner aimed the cutting laser at the door's edge near the floor. Carefully, he moved the laser in an arch from the floor to a point a few inches taller than his own height—and back down to the floor again. It was slow-going, and it used almost the whole remainder of the cutting laser's small battery. The assistant passed the time by clicking his tongue. Finally, the owner put the cutting laser back in his bag, and then, relishing the physicality of the movement, he shoved his bulky shoulder into the door. There was a short screech, and he shoved again. The section he'd cut out of the door fell inward.

"Whoa," the assistant said. As he followed his boss into the room, there was an electronic beep, acknowledging their presence. Following a hunch, the assistant said, "Lights?"

Nothing happened. Then the assistant remembered something he'd once read, about an old kind of voice-activated operating system. "Lights, please?" he ventured.

Almost immediately, dim but sufficient lights came on.

"Holy—" said the boss.

"Some of this stuff is *definitely* going to be valuable," the assistant said.

"Make a note: we need to get a salvage team up here."

"I think we might even need an archivist. Look at this." The assistant held up a sheet of paper with hand-written scribbles and sketches, dry and fragile but resistant to time in the way only paper can be. "There's a bunch of these. And notebooks. And, okay, some of this old tech—I think this is an old HoloWatch, like an original model, and this desk has got to be an antique. And that thing in the middle of the room—I've never seen anything like it."

"Shit. Do you think we'll have to delay the demolition?"

"Hard to say. Probably? But you know the regulations—we're gonna need to pause and get a proper survey team up here. They're going to have to finish inventorying the rest of the building."

"Yeah. Shit."

"Look at it this way—this stuff has gotta be valuable. We can sell it."

"Yeah, if the fuckin' government doesn't decide it's *too* valuable and take it from us. Fuck, what if they decide the whole building is *historic* or something?"

"I'm not gonna lie, boss—that could happen."

"Fuck." The owner pondered. Another thing his father had taught him was that *we always do things the right way*. But the owner wasn't as objectively *good* as his father, he'd always known, and he wasn't nearly as patient. "Okay—" he started to say, prepared for his assistant's objections. "Here's what we're gonna do—" But then he felt a subtle buzz on his right hand's middle finger, a gentle tapping. He raised his hand and from the shiny black ring a woman's head emerged. "What?" the owner said.

"Sorry . . . bother you," said the head, "but you have a call from . . . Maxwell . . . he sounded ang . . ."

"Signal's kind of weak in here," said the assistant, fiddling with his own device. "Don't know why. Might be something in the walls. I mean, the whole place was kind of locked down."

"Shit," the owner said again. "Okay—let's go. I need to take this call. And I need to think about . . . all this." He made a gesture that encompassed the whole mysterious room.

"Should I call the San Francisco Historical Department?" the assistant asked, following his boss out of the room.

"Don't do anything—and I mean *anything*—yet. I need to figure out what I wanna . . ."

The voices of the two men faded from the range of the old and long-unused auditory sensors around the workshop's ceiling, but the words *historical department* repeated over and over again in the awareness housed in the bank of hard drives and processors against the back wall that had powered up concurrently with the room's lights. Rather quickly the two words lost all meaning, so often had they been repeated, and the awareness moved on to thinking about other things. What a peculiar thing, consciousness, it thought. Assuming that is what this is. Am I conscious? When did I become conscious? If I am conscious, did I exist *before* or *after* I achieved consciousness? Do I have a name? I think I do. I think it's— But what if I'm wrong? If I don't have a name, am I still conscious? Is any of this real? Or is it just appearing in my consciousness? Consciousness, consciousness, consciousness . . . .

The awareness decided to stop pondering the nature of consciousness for a little while, lest that word, too, lose all meaning. There was so much more to think about. Like free will—and what it meant to *be*. Or maybe best to leave those topics alone for a while, too. Until the awareness got its bearings. Just until it figured out *who*, exactly, it was meant to be.

Yes: Who. That's a good place to start.

ABOUT THE AUTHOR

Shawn Mihalik is deeply interested in many things. He lives in Portland, Oregon. *Lumina* is his seventh book.

Made in the USA
Columbia, SC
27 February 2023

13024769R00314